Praise For Deanna King

"A tightly written, fast-paced thriller with constant surprises. Jack is a strong, compelling lead, and the story balances intense action with sharp dialogue and emotional depth. A gripping read that brings Houston vividly to life."
~ Foram Vyas- Reader's Favorite

"Smartly written and hauntingly entertaining, Jack West's second adventure outdoes the first — a case so dark, convoluted and connected that'll keep you guessing 'til the end.
~Fort Worth Magazine

"...another tumultuous Texas thriller."
~ Lisa Petrocelli, Author of The Heart of Rome

Also by Deanna King

*Jack West Novels
*Twist of Fate**
*Lethal Liaisons**
*Vicious Vendetta**
*Trust No One**
A Kasper Bergman Novel
When Good Men Fall #

YA Fantasy
Saving a Sioux Legacy
Protector Of Legends

Gracie's Stories (eBook Only)

Lethal Liaisons
A Jack West Novel
Deanna King

Deanna King Writing

Second printing

ISBN: 979-8-9856982-8-2

Book Cover by NTLT Productions. Bada$$ Sci f/Fantasy Book Covers by Regin Tersaun

Edited by Lisa Petrocelli

Published by Deanna King Writing deannakingwriting.com

To All the survivors in the world

Prologue

HER SCREAM WAS EAR-SHATTERING, echoing through the empty house.

The woman's face turned green. She was going to be sick.

The man made no sound.

He grabbed his wife and yanked her back from the doorway, pulling her hard enough that she stumbled.

Brenda, walking behind them and talking up the home's amenities, froze mid-sentence.

The scream jarred her to the core. Her mouth dropped open, and for a moment, she couldn't move.

Seeing a dead body was not on the home's listing flyer.

Fifteen minutes earlier

"I think this house is over our budget. Why are we looking?"

"Honey, let's just look. It's been on the market for over six months. They might take the offer if they're motivated."

The couple parked in front of the empty house for sale. A realtor's sign stood in the yard: **Mathers' Realty**, with a photo of the owner, Al Mathers—a middle-aged Black man—printed in the top right corner. Beneath it was the agent's name, **Brenda Cochran**, along with her phone number.

A small silver sedan pulled up behind them.

"There's Brenda. Let's go look." The man opened his door.

"You'd better hope I don't love it. I'm tired of disappointment."

Brenda waved as she approached. "Y'all ready?" She asked, leading them to the front door. She opened the lockbox and stepped aside, allowing them to enter first.

"Goodness, it's cold in here," the woman said, shivering. "What do they have the thermostat set on—minus ten?"

"That's odd," Brenda said. "I showed this house the day before yesterday. I remember setting the thermostat at eighty. No sense wasting electricity on an empty house."

She stepped into the hallway to check it out. "Someone's set it to fifty-six degrees. And with the house empty, it feels even colder. No one's been here in two days—I can't imagine how this happened."

She reset the temperature and turned back to her clients with a smile. "I think you're going to love the back of the house. There's a large family room with a rock fireplace that opens into an enormous kitchen. Ready?"

The woman entered the family room first.

Five steps in, her heart leaped into her throat.

She screamed.

Her husband lunged for her, yanking her backward hard enough to pull her arm from its socket. Brenda's cheerful commentary died in her throat. Her hands flew to her mouth as she froze, unable to scream, unable to look away.

No one moved. No one breathed.

All eyes locked on the scene before them.

Time stopped. Their feet rooted to the floor like cement.

"We need to call the police." Brenda began backing out of the room.

"I need to get outside." The woman's eyes bulged. "Oh, God—I'm going to be sick." Her face shifted through sickly shades of green as her stomach lurched.

After calling 9-1-1, they stood on the front lawn, waiting for the police. Brenda's hands shook. She never smoked in front of clients, but today she needed a cigarette.

"Sorry." Brenda lit and took a long drag.

"No worries." The man pulled his wife closer. "If I had a fifth of anything, I'd be drinking it right now."

"You don't have to stay. I can give the police the information."

"We'll stay," the man's voice uneven. "They may want to talk to us, too. I'd rather get it over with now."

When the officers entered the house, they found a middle-aged Black woman lying on the floor.

Blood pooled beneath her right side.

She lay on her back, eyes closed, arms bent at the elbows, her hands resting low on her stomach—right hand over left. Her legs were straight, ankles crossed. The positioning gave her an unsettled, peaceful, almost sleeping appearance.

She wore makeup, but not the tones chosen for a woman of color.

Officer Jeffers took a step back.

He didn't need an ambulance.

He needed Homicide, Crime Scene, and the medical examiner.

Detectives **Xi Chang** and **Jace Severson**, Team 7-11, were next up on the Homicide table.

1

SWEAT DRENCHED HIS FACE. The salty Pacific Ocean air and sand clung to his skin. Stooped, with his hands on his knees, Jack's chest heaved. It felt good. It had been a quick run, although running in the sand required more energy. The resistance made the run more of a challenge, and he had been challenging himself for the past five days. His calf muscles had been sore the first couple of days.

Jack stretched his legs and extended his arms upward toward the sky. He made a silent promise to himself: back home, he would make more time to get to the gym, work out, stay healthy, and get in better shape.

Upright, with his hands resting on his hips, he looked at the ocean. So vast and serene at this time of day. Vacationers were coming alive as the day broke. He felt at peace. Jogging, he scanned the paradise he had been in since last Tuesday, knowing today was the last day of his vacation.

Maui, Hawaii—a beautiful island with waters as blue as the sky. One word came to mind: paradise. White sandy beaches and hidden coves—waterfalls that would thrill the explorer or the average Joe. For the surfer, breaking waves offered the ride of a lifetime.

Gigantic banyan trees, pieces of God's artwork, caught his eye. Jack thought they resembled giant octopuses on steroids—or an alien form from a galaxy far, far away. Colorful flora surrounded him; many plants he did not know the names of. He did recognize the bird-of-paradise and the yellow hibiscus.

Banana and coconut trees dotted the area. Maui was gorgeous, he thought, taking the stairs to his room two at a time. Opening the door, he smiled at the other gorgeous thing Hawaii had offered him: Gretchen Benson.

Relaxed in bed, she turned at the sound of the door and smiled. "Morning, cowboy."

Jack walked over and kissed her. They had been together for two years, and he never grew tired of kissing her.

"Did you enjoy your run this morning?" She asked, reaching to hug him.

"Gretch, I'm sweaty and covered in sand."

"We can fix that." She climbed off the bed and grabbed his hand, leading him to the huge rock shower with the double bench seat and rainfall showerhead. In less than two minutes, Jack was kissing her under a cascade of water. Her hands roamed his back and muscled arms. In one swift motion, Cowboy Jack, as she called him, lifted her, dripping wet, and carried her back to bed. He laid her down, her giggling the entire time.

"Gretch, you're a funny woman, laughing when I'm trying to swoop you up in a serious seduction," he said.

Jack lowered his head and took her lips. Gretchen knew what that kiss meant. He lowered his body next to hers, and she complied.

Once satisfied, they lay with a sheet covering them. Gretchen rolled onto her side to look at him.

"Jack, you're an amazing man, you know that?"

"No, I'm not. I'm just a man from Houston, Texas, visiting Maui, Hawaii, with a gal too good for him."

"Jack West. I mean it. You're an incredible man who still has good left in him—from some of the most horrendous acts of violence you've seen, and the stories you've told me. I can imagine the ones you've left out. You're a gentle lover and a caring man."

Jack fell silent, not knowing what to say. He had never seen himself gentle or caring until he had met her.

Their relationship had developed and deepened, and they had built trust. Together, they had fun, and the physical chemistry they shared was—explosive.

Yes, he had demons. The job as a homicide detective would never leave a man scarred. But he had suppressed the dark side of the heinous things he had seen because he never wanted the evil parts of his professional life to touch her or interfere with what was going on between them.

"Jack?" She caressed his bare arm.

"You've been the amazing one, Gretch."

He turned his face toward hers. "You've taken a back seat to my job, gone days without seeing or hearing from me when I've been knee-deep in a case. You've tolerated my irritated moods or my disappointment when the case wasn't going well. And never complained or given me the, 'Oh, I'm worried, this job is too dangerous' speech."

Gretchen tucked her head under his arm, rolling closer to him.

"Jack, you have a hard job, and my complaining won't make it easier. You had this job before 'us.' I knew what your job was. I have no complaints, Cowboy."

"Hmm." He relaxed, pulling her closer. "I'm glad. What makes me unhappy is…" He trailed off, caressing her arm.

"Jack, what makes you unhappy?" Her words muffled as she turned her face to his bare chest, giving him butterfly kisses.

"That we have to leave paradise and head back to reality."

"Well," Gretchen said, pulling her body over his as she let the sheet slither off and her hair cascade over his bare chest, "let's be the volcano Hawaii never knew existed on their islands. Let's explode." She pressed her lips to his.

—∘∘∘—

THE TRIP HOME WAS a direct flight from Kahului Airport in Maui to George Bush International Airport in Houston—a straight seven and a half hours of flying. Texas was five hours ahead.

The regular airport hubbub and rush of frantic passengers wiped out the peacefulness of the last seven days.

"Back to reality, huh?" Gretchen scowled.

"Yep, but I'll live on the memories—not to mention the million pictures you took."

Gretchen rolled her eyes. "Sorry, couldn't help myself. Maui was gorgeous. I love memories in pictures. It helps me recreate the experience."

"I know, Gretch. Let's get to baggage claim and get the hell out of George Bush's Airport."

Once her luggage sat inside the doorway, Jack wrapped his arms around her.

"Gonna be weird tonight sleeping in my bed without you." He nuzzled her neck.

"Yeah, but I'll see you soon, I hope."

He waved goodbye, and Jack headed back to Deer Park, watching her until she was out of sight. Traffic was at its normal backup.

He yawned, feeling as if he had lost ten hours of his life. It was 7:00 pm Wednesday night, but he still felt on Maui time. Jet lag was close behind.

Home at 8:20, he showered, made a sandwich, grabbed a beer, and sank into his favorite recliner. The clock read 9:15. He scanned local TV channels for news. KHOU-11 was showing the weather forecast—he missed the news. Switching to Fox 26 Houston yielded the same story. He turned off the television and listened to the radio.

By 10:30, he hadn't realized how tired he was until his eyes closed for more than a minute. He took a short catnap, then got up and finished unpacking.

The clock on the table illuminated the darkness as he adjusted his vision. Three-thirty. That was some catnap—he had slept for five hours in his recliner. He stretched, yawned, and flopped onto his bed, missing Gretchen's body next to his. When the alarm went off at 8:00, Jack felt alive and ready to go back to work.

"Hey, Jack, glad to see you made it back in one piece. Wow, what a nice suntan, dude. You could go down to Mexico and blend in with the locals." Lucky grabbed Jack's outstretched hand.

"Nice to be home. But it was a relaxing vacation."

"My wife's jealous. She wants to go to Hawaii now, thanks."

"It was a fantastic place. We had a marvelous time."

"How's Gretchen?"

Jack beamed. "She's wonderful."

Jack's chipper moods drove Dawson Luck crazy. Dawson had badgered Jack for months before he told him about Gretchen.

"I knew it was a woman, but had no clue who, you rascal. You're as lucky as me. I mean, look at me, and then you see my beautiful wife. That's why the fellas call me Lucky, even though my last name is Luck. Hey, coming back to work on Thursday was a smart move. Work on Thursday and Friday, off for the weekend, right?"

"Is there any other way to plan it?"

"I hate to tell you this, but the captain had to change the schedule. We're on call the next two days."

Jack rubbed his hands together. "So, partner, what's been going on with the Houston crime scene for the last eight days?"

Lucky got Jack up to speed, then told him he needed to finish some paperwork on a case he was assisting Robbery with.

"7-11 catch a break on their case?"

They'd gotten a case involving a woman found murdered in an empty house three months ago in the Fourth Ward, and the investigation was ongoing.

"Nah, not much luck, but they're still at it."

"Do they have suspect? Anyone?" Jack hated unsolved cases, which ended up with no justice ever served.

"Far as I know, they still haven't ruled out the husband. The motive is a big life insurance payoff. I've been helping Gilly in a robbery case and haven't seen 7-11 much in the past six days." Lucky continued typing up his report for Robbery.

"I'm going to talk to Chief Yao. Be back in a while."

"Sure, Jack. He'll wanna see you since you've been on vacation, lollygag-ging. I know you earned the time off, though, bud. We all need to escape from the mayhem and chaos sometimes, just to get back to the good we feel we've missed doing the job we do."

Jack never knew Dawson had a philosophical side, but he agreed without a doubt.

———eee———

IT USED TO BE Captain; now it was Chief of Detectives Davis Yao.

"Jack, nice to see you're back." Yao stood, reaching his hand across the desk.

Jack took his hand and squeezed. "Back and ready to put some more criminals behind bars." He took the chair across from Davis's desk—askew with papers and files. "You look snowed under."

"Nah. Just HR paperwork; working on evaluations, your basic unexciting work. How was Hawaii? You think Gretchen's the one?" He fired two questions off before Jack could respond.

"Hawaii was amazing. Me and Gretchen? Don't know, Davis. All I know is, so far, so good. We'll see how it goes."

"The chief of police is still bragging on the homicide department and the Judge Troy Wolff case. He says nothing for weeks, and then something happens—like that one-year sting Vice worked. They break up a massive prostitution ring and some second-tier drug runners, and Chief Pratt is back to bragging. A sex dungeon in Houston. Who knew one existed?"

"Not me, Chief."

"I guess it surprised the hell outta me when Vice uncovered it in a damn dive bar. The Crystal Barrel was more than a shithole dive. Ralph Delvecchio and his silent partner, Judge Wolff. That still shocks the heck outta me. Wolff had been a prime customer of his own dungeon. Makes me sick to think of what was going on in that place."

"Since they raided the Dungeon and that's where they operated the prostitution ring, Wolff is right back in the spotlight. And just why do people want to take pictures of that crap?"

"I think Troy Wolff relived the experience in photos, while he... well, no other way to say it... 'beat off.'"

"It put his name back in the news. He should be happy he gets to hide in his protected jail cell. The man still makes me want to upchuck. But regardless of that, Chief Pratt is proud of Homicide. He's still busting at the seams that we closed four cold cases at one time and took down a judge with no morals."

"Well, Davis, it's time to move on. Get some more solid work done—cold cases or new ones. Put those nasty bastards behind bars. Clean our city up a bit more. We have a helluva homicide department, all fixated on the same goal... make Houston safe."

"You know, it is okay to take some credit, Jack. There's no harm in admitting you're a skilled detective. If not for some of your... what are they... 'gut instincts,' things would get overlooked. You've done an out-standing job with Dawson, too. Even though he was a three-year detective in Robbery when we got him from Arizona. He's learned a lot from you, Jack. Take that credit as well."

"I gotta give the credit to Frank Windom; God rest his soul. He was the one who drove and molded me. The greatest partner I could have ever asked for. I still miss him."

"Okay, Jack, sorry to rush you out, but I have at least three evaluations to finish. Go check in with Captain Brooks." He heaved a sigh. "No matter how much you might not want to."

Damn. Brody Brooks. Jack and his fellow detectives would like to forget, ignore, and boot the man out.

2

CAPTAIN BRODY BROOKS—NEARING HIS twenty-eighth year with the Houston Police Department, just moved into the Captain of Homicide position. With Captain Davis Yao promoted to Chief of Detectives, the opening had come. Brooks' arrival was met with disappointment by the homicide department.

Chief Yao opted to keep an office on the floor until Brooks acclimated. The Chief of Police, Darren Pratt, agreed. Brooks settled into the office across from Yao's—a move that annoyed him, seeing Yao still on the sixth floor.

The entire Homicide table was pleased their former captain remained nearby. They knew it was temporary. Yao would, in time follow the "yellow brick road" to one of the top floors. Brooks just wanted him gone. One patrol commander even overheard Brooks mutter Yao needed to get his crap out of the office.

Brooks—patrol cop eleven years, Vice - two, and the Special Crimes Division six. Seven years ago, he moved to Robbery. A butt-kisser who did not play by the rules—Jack saw him as untrustworthy. Within two years, he became Captain of Robbery after Captain Lawrence Dunne was killed during a bank takedown.

At the time, the Robbery Division was mired in internal issues—corruption, fired officers, and stolen evidence. It pleased Jack that Dunne had never been involved. Several officers were discharged for "conduct unbecoming an officer," and two were fired for stealing drugs from evidence. Though the department filed no charges, the officers lost the privilege to serve and their pensions. The Robbery table was in crisis. The department took what it could, and that was Brooks.

Brody Brooks... Jack shook his head. Most officers thought Brooks was involved. With no proof, all they had was conjecture. Internal Affairs investigated, but nothing emerged. Jack and a few close colleagues often speculated about IA's possible oversight.

No one on six saw Brooks as the brightest crayon in the box. Time would reveal the real person. Maybe he'd changed, but Jack doubted it. If he had, Jack hoped it would benefit Homicide, but he wasn't placing bets.

Nobody in Robbery liked Brooks, and it thrilled them to see him go. His unorthodox character and shadiness meant no one considered him decent. Jack and his fellow detectives agreed to tolerate him, but respect? Not a chance.

Before Jack left for vacation, no one in Homicide reported to Brooks for two reasons: One, Davis Yao was still on six as Chief of Detectives, and everyone felt comfortable with him. Two: Brooks split his time between floors, helping his successor, Walt Thompson, settle in. Thompson had transferred from the Colorado Police Department, and Brooks shuttled back and forth to transition with ease.

People thought if you were a cop, you were a cop. True—but policies and procedures differed from department to department, state to state. New personnel had to learn HPD's rules. It was a shame Thompson was learning from Brooks, a man who did not play by the rules. Over time, Jack hoped Thompson was smart enough to see through Brooks' bullshit.

Jack rapped on the doorframe. "Captain Brooks."

"West, you're back from vacation?" Brooks didn't stand to greet him with a hearty handshake, as Yao or Jack's partner would have.

"Ready to go to work." Jack remained near the door, taking no seat.

"Good. Until you catch a case, go assist... uh, let's see..." Brooks glanced at a paper.

"Potter and Reed. They pulled a case while you were gone. Work with them until you get a fresh case."

"I'll give one of them a call. They're not in the squad room."

He had no plans to call Reed or Potter. That wasn't how the department worked. Brooks would learn that—homicide in Houston had few "down" days. Besides, there were plenty of cold cases if he needed something to do.

"I have a call to make." Brooks inclined his head toward the door. That was Jack's cue to leave. He headed for the break room and coffee to stave off jet lag.

IN THE INTERMINABLE VASTNESS of darkness, crime lurks everywhere. It has no boundaries—neighborhoods, counties, parishes, states, countries. It waits to come alive at night. Crime wasn't limited to nightfall, but darkness shielded those who carried out evil.

By day, these same people could be neighbors, schoolteachers, church members, or men in suits. Even those sworn to protect could hide sinister intent. No one would suspect them.

Jack remembered a conversation with Gretchen on the flight back to Texas. Seven hours gave them plenty of time to talk. She wanted to know if he'd ever handled a serial case. He hadn't, but as a beat cop, he'd heard the stories.

As a uniform officer, he'd never worked with Homicide, though he had assisted Robbery. Closest he'd come to a serial crime was a serial thief—and those often ended up on Homicide's table. Robbery and murder often went hand in hand.

For some reason, they discussed headline-grabbing crimes over the last two decades: the Oklahoma City Bomber, 9/11, Jon Benet Ramsey, the O.J. Simpson case. Jack knew that the number of heinous crimes was astronomical. Any two people could spend a lifetime discussing major criminality and never cover it all.

Their plane conversation stuck in his mind: lives snuffed out before they even began. Child murderers, molesters who ruined futures, teenagers who never saw their twenty-first birthday, who might have positively impacted society.

Evil.

It ran rampant, often right under society's nose.

Evil was smart.

Psychopaths were chameleons, blending in. Society seldom saw them.

From headlines about Edmund Kemper, Jeffrey Dahmer, and Ted Bundy—each a high-IQ, psychopathic serial killer—Jack's mind wandered to Houston's own serial killers. With time on his hands, he researched.

He Googled "1970–1973."

A serial killer dubbed the Candy Man, who, with a few associates murdered up to twenty-eight boys, became known as the Houston Mass Murders.

In 1970, Edward Harold Bell, associated with the Texas Killing Field, claimed someone brainwashed him into killing. Jack typed in 1980. That year brought the Sunday Morning Slasher.

These weren't pleasant reads, but they reminded him: evil had been in Houston for a long time, and it wouldn't disappear.

"Jack, what in God's name are you reading that crap for?"

"Don't know. Conversation with Gretchen on the flight back. We discussed the monstrous things evil men do: Bundys, Dahmers, bombers... lives destroyed. I want to know how their minds work. Not somewhere I want to linger long."

"You know, Jack, I once thought of aiming for the FBI, but my wife changed my plans. It worked out. I've learned a lot as your partner. Thanks for having my back these past three years."

"Don't get sappy," Jack smirked. "Remember grabbing the gun on Wolff's desk? If you hadn't acted, who knows what might've happened. Thanks for having my back, too."

A silent, uncomfortable moment passed. Neither were goofy nor sentimental, but both were thankful.

"Sure thing, Jack. Now get back to reading that horrendous stuff. I'm out. Remember, we're taking call tonight. Welcome back."

Jack waved overhead. He resumed reading about crimes of the most horrific kinds: serial killers, psychopaths, copycats. How would he distinguish them? He hoped he'd never have to work a case like that.

Two hours later, the COD poked his head into the squad room.

"Saw the lights on, Jack. Why still here?"

"Doing some light reading off the clock."

"Serial killers of yesteryear and some more recent. Why are you glued to your desk?"

"Davis, why are you here late yourself?"

"Evaluations. Brutal. Phone calls interrupted me nonstop. Got caught up and wanted to get a jump-start for tomorrow. The wife's aggravated; she cooked dinner. Now it'll be leftovers."

"Tell Patricia leftovers are wonderful. Send some my way—better than a can of chili." Jack shut down his computer.

"Go home, Jack. Relax, and get that can of chili out of your pantry, which I'm sure, echoes."

Jack thought it was a decent first day back as he drove home.

3

DESPITE THE HOLIDAYS STILL being months away, the phones at the volunteer suicide crisis center were ringing off the hook. Flooded with calls from desperate people, the center buzzed with activity. The church had opened it two years ago, and being in Houston, Texas' largest city, meant the volume kept workers busy.

"Your life is important to me. How can I help you?" the volunteer said.

"I want to die, but I don't want to die. I don't know what to do. Please help me."

The throaty voice on the other end was shaky. "I understand, I do, but there are people who love and need you. Why don't we talk first? Tell me why you feel this way. Let's see if we can fix this problem together."

"My husband is cheating. It's been going on for months, and I can't live with it. We've been married sixteen years, and we have two wonderful boys. Even through tough times, our love endured. Now... now..." She bawled.

"What's your name, so I can call you by name? You're a person, not just a telephone call, ma'am."

"Sybil. Sybil Preston."

A sharp inhale came over the line. "Oh, I shouldn't have told you my last name. Please, don't look for me."

"No, ma'am. Not unless necessary. It won't be necessary now, will it, Sybil?" The volunteer asked.

"No... oh God, I don't know. Our sex life is active—why would he cheat?"

"Sybil, why do you suspect he's having an affair?"

"He comes home from work, then leaves, saying he's meeting the boys for drinks. It's been going on for months. First, it was once a week, now three nights a week. I thought he needed space and wasn't worried, but then he became distant. Now he acts like I disgust him. Then I noticed he was dressing up ... for the guys." Tears streamed down her face.

"Could it be about his self-esteem and not you? Is he stressed at work?"

"He's an architect. A low-stress job. But I... I did something I shouldn't have, but I couldn't help it."

The volunteer's worry deepened. "What did you do, Sybil?"

"I took our boys to my mother's house and followed Rafe."

"Rafe? That's your husband?"

Sybil's voice rose in desperation. "Oh God, I shouldn't have said his name! Please, don't look for him either. Don't tell him I called."

"No, ma'am. We don't do that. What happened when you followed him?"

"I followed him to a bar on the south side. A hip-hop bar—where younger people hang out. Rafe doesn't even like that music. I went in and tried to blend in. That's when I saw him all cozy at the end of the bar with a young woman, kissing her neck and laughing. When he took her face in his hands and kissed her the way he used to kiss me, part of me died."

She wailed—the volunteer waited.

After a moment, the volunteer spoke. "Sybil, what did you do next? Did you get your boys, put them to bed, and wait for Rafe to come home?"

She hiccupped and sniffed. "No. I talked to the bartender—he knew her. He told me she worked at a place called Advantage Ad Agency, off 290 and the Loop."

"Why would he volunteer that info? Do you know him?"

She ignored the question. "I bought a beer and parked at the other end. Rafe and that harlot couldn't see me. The bartender thought I looked lonely and sad. When he asked if I was all right, I said I was, but I wished I looked like her. I pointed at the girl with the handsome older man. I told him I wanted a man like that—but didn't tell him that was my man. I tried not to cry."

"The bartender just gave you that info? Why?"

"He has a crush on her. Her name's Jade. Phooey. She's a kid—twenty-two or twenty-three. I'm thirty-nine, a worn-out housewife in Rafe's eyes."

"I bet you're beautiful, or he wouldn't have picked you."

"It doesn't matter. The bartender said they'd been an item for months. He never had a chance with her. My boys... it makes me sad to leave them to their father and let a harlot raise my kids. But I... I can't go on. I can't." Her sobbing was heart-wrenching.

Before the volunteer could respond, Sybil continued.

"I went to that ad agency one night and followed her home. That's how I found out where she lives. I should confront her, and if she won't stop seeing my husband, I can shoot her, then shoot myself. Then Rafe would get the message, don't you think? Besides, you can't send a dead woman to prison, right?"

Her voice was steady. No tears.

The volunteer's heart raced.

"I can go to her apartment. Old ratty complex off Wirt Road. She's on the bottom corner, number 163 or 165. I could trick my way in. I have a gun."

"Sybil... think of your sons. They'd have to live with that. Do you want to scar them?"

"No, but I have no other choice." Her voice trembled. "First, I'll write them a goodbye note, then take them to my mom's house. I know she'll take care of them. Rafe wouldn't mind; it would free him up for his girlfriend." Sarcasm colored her tone. "That's a better idea."

Her cries softened.

The seriousness of the situation escalated.

She had made the irrevocable decision to end two lives... hers and Jade's.

Hell no, the volunteer thought. That was a terrible idea.

"Tell me, Sybil. Do you believe in God and prayer?"

"Yes, I do. I've been praying. It's not working."

"Let's pray together. Pray a miracle—that your husband comes back changed. Don't make this move. Death lasts forever. Once dead, Sybil, you're gone—gone from everyone's life, never to return. Let's pray before you choose a permanent solution to a temporary problem. Will you do that for me?"

She nodded. The volunteer couldn't see her.

Panic crept into the volunteer's voice. "Sybil? Are you still with me?"

"Yes—we can pray. I promise to wait. If God hears my prayers, I'll never tell Rafe I knew. I'll be the woman he wants. Vivacious—sexy—fun. But if he leaves me, I'll have nothing. I'll be nothing..." Her voice trailed.

They prayed.

Sybil wanted to believe.

The volunteer told her everything would work out. God has a plan.

──── ⚘ ────

WHERE IN THE HELL was she?

Thursday night—She never missed their rendezvous. Bitch, he thought. She isn't answering my texts or calls. What happened? He'd texted all day; she replied to every message—even emojis.

He cursed. She was punctual. He'd arrived early to surprise her. This was out of character. Had he pissed her off? No. Everything was perfect last night.

They met at 9:45, same time, same place, for three months.

Was she blowing him off? He'd wait thirty minutes, then go home. Jesus... did she know how suffocating it felt to be without her?

She had breathed life back into him... now, without her, he felt like he was dying.

4

THE PHONE RANG FOR a minute before Jack yanked it off the nightstand. It was Chief Yao calling. Damn... 2:00 am, and he hadn't dropped into bed until midnight.

Jolted from a dead sleep, his voice groggy, he said, "Chief?"

"Jack, I know it sucks, especially on your first night back, but we've got a murder. It's a mess. I need you over there."

"Yup, on it, Chief. You call Luck?"

"Call him when you're on your way, would ya? I've got some other commotion going on."

"Roger that. Text me the address. I'm on it."

He hopped out of bed, looking for clothes and his badge.

He was going to need Visine—and a gallon of freaking coffee—to make it through the day. Funny, he hadn't even asked Chief Yao why Captain Brooks hadn't called. He didn't care, but it was not the usual chain of command.

The address was off Wirt Road, east of the Loop, on a street called Amelia Road. One beneficial thing: no morning traffic to deal with. He could take the Loop, cut over to Interstate 10, and be there in less than twenty-five minutes.

Lucky lived somewhere up toward the Woodlands, and it would take him longer. A grumpy partner was on his way.

He pulled into the parking lot less than fifty minutes later and snatched his Maglite from under the seat. The parking lot was too dark. They'd need at least one light brought for the team to work.

The apartment complex was buzzing. Some uniforms were pushing onlookers back and out of the way.

"Hey, you kids," one of the patrol officers shouted. "Get off the top of that van, now." He turned and saw Jack.

"Detective West, I'd say nice to see ya, but not under these circumstances."

"Hank, how are you?" He knew it was a rhetorical question.

"Shit, be better if these kids had a mother or a father controlling their hyper children." His voice rang out again. "I said get off that van, and if I have to I'm going to send one of my guys over there to yank you boys off, then haul all three of ya to the hole. Do you hear me?"

Hank took a step forward, and as big as he was, the boys—all three of them—slid down the front of the van and hightailed it.

"Scare 'em with getting put in the hole, huh? Don't hurt that you're what, six-four and weigh in at what, 285?"

"Nah, it's 263 now, lost twenty-two pounds since I last seen ya. Wife has me on Weight Watchers—maybe I'll live longer. Told her lack of real food would kill me before cop work did."

"Nice to see you, Hank. Keep up the excellent work."

Jack saluted as he went under the yellow crime scene tape that blocked off the entire trash dump area and a bigger part of the parking lot. It looked like a neighborhood block party.

Walking toward the two patrol officers standing in front of four large blue metal trash containers, he surveyed the area. This was the only parking lot for this side of the complex, which, by most standards, was small. There were eight units per building, six buildings, all two stories.

The units sat three buildings in a row with driving lanes and parking sections between each. Management set at the front, not connected to the complex. Only two buildings faced the back fence with a shared small parking lot—one local area for trash in the back far corner.

There were sixty-four units—a small multiplex, older than dirt. He figured the place was also dirt-cheap, with zero upgrades, at least on the outside. He hoped they'd at least kept up with the times on the insides of the units, for the sake of the residents... a long shot by far.

"What ya got, Deeks? Why are you here?" Jack walked closer to the four metal trash containers.

Deeks handed him a pair of latex gloves, and Jack snapped them on.

— eel —

Lieutenant Wilson Deeks, Vice.

Deeks was the average all-American-looking man, most of the time. Some of the crap he had done on the job took the "all-American" look and flushed it. At five foot eight, he'd dressed in drag—fake boobies and red lipstick—the whole shebang, going undercover as a prostitute. Deeks joked he was a very good-looking woman, and his wife might need to watch out. He might have an affair with himself. He'd posed as a gang member, done deep cover in the porn business (no pun intended), and dealt with some of the most violent and smarmy men and women one might meet.

The department ribbed him when the movie *Castaway* came out. For months on the fourth floor in Vice, you might hear *Willllson!* Laughter would peel out like dominoes falling, and it didn't stop until the person at the other end of the fourth floor was snickering.

One fella bought the Wilson-brand volleyball and made it up to look like the one Tom Hanks had in the movie. It sat on the shelf next to Deek's desk. Everyone hoped it wasn't real blood. The detective who made it laughed but didn't say. Someone wanted to take it to the crime lab and get DNA, but Jack knew that never happened.

Deeks took it all in stride, and soon enough it died down. Jack knew cops. You had to laugh at yourself, or you'd never be able to live it down.

— eel —

"VICE HAS BEEN SCOUTING this area for some rumblings that a large drug-buy was going down. The Tornado was shaking down some young girls on the corner last week, and a confidential informant came up and offered his help with info on the drug deal," Lt. Deeks said with a laugh, "but the CI had zero info that was credible. All he wanted was a twenty-spot, and Rick gave it to him. He is doing some gang recon tonight. I was at the station when he called. He said an Angry Betty (crazy bitch) was called in. He was too busy, told him I'd check it out on my way home. Got here, and the Angry Betty turned out to be a hysterical Black woman who found the body and went nuts. She went bat-shit crazy, screaming as she ran to her apartment. She came back out and started throwing her stuff in the back of that old beat-up Nissan truck, making all kinds of racket."

Jack looked around. "Why—she knows the victim?"

"Nah, but I got her calmed down enough to talk. She's a crack user. She said she thought her drug dealer was sending her a message. Her screaming woke every resident up on this backside, scared the bejesus outta some of the old, retired people who live here."

"Whad'ja find?" Jack looked around, wondering just where his victim was.

"Young woman—dead behind the dumpsters. From what I can tell, looks like she hasn't been there long."

"Let's go check the body."

"No, Jack-o', once was enough for me. I'll hang here with the unis—in case ya need me. Luck on the way?"

"Yep, called him on my way in. Are CSU and the M.E.'s office on the way?"

"I asked Hank to radio the watch commander, start the ball rolling to get our people out here. Hey, Hank lost twenty-two pounds."

"Yep, that's what he told me, too." Jack stepped between the two trash receptacles at the far left. It was time to go to work.

When the trucks sat the center receptacles back after dumping, they sat at an odd angle. They also positioned the end containers, with their metal corners touching. With the garbage piled between each metal box, it made it impossible to walk between. Mattresses, broken pieces of furniture, and garbage bags of assorted sizes blocked off one end.

Two of the dumpsters were half-full. What the hell were the dumpsters for if no one put trash in them—a major sign of lazy people—revolting.

Jack made his way back to the body.

There was a four or five-foot space behind the metal bins at the back of the fenced-in area. An aged fence ran along the back and sides of the dumpsters, trying to keep trash in one central location. All four containers were supposed to sit in a neat row inside the perimeters of the fence. He shined his Maglite on the ground.

"Neat my ass," he griped as he worked his way over bags broken open or torn by a stray dog or cat looking for food. It was like walking in the city trash dump, on a smaller scale, and no dozers to move the trash over and under the earth.

He took out a container of Vicks Vapor Rub from his coat pocket. He scooped some out with his pinky and put it under his nose. Some things he'd had to smell over the years, along with rotting bodies, were stomach-churning. He learned the Vicks trick from a medical examiner at a conference. Better to smell Vicks than this, by far.

The dead body lay behind the two middle dumpsters. How had that hysterical woman seen her with all this trash piled everywhere? He shook his head—he knew. Crack users. She must have been dumpster diving for items she might sell.

Jack squatted. A young Hispanic woman, eyes closed, face made up, lying in the burial pose as if in a casket, hands folded over her breast with a small white New Testament Bible beneath them. A folded piece of paper stuck out from both ends of the Bible like a bookmark. Blood pooled under her right arm, though he saw no gash, puncture wound, or gunshot entry. The makeup looked fresh but overdone. She was dead.

As he studied the scene, a voice called out.

"Detective West, are you back there?"

He wasn't familiar with that voice. He turned back, took a few steps, and peered out, shining his light.

"Yeah, who wants to know?"

He saw a hand go up to her face, blocking the beam of light he'd pointed straight at her.

"Hi, Detective, sorry to meet this way. I'm Marlo Makos, the new M.E. Can you point your light down a little? I'm seeing spots."

"Sorry." He lowered the light. "Give me a minute, and I'll be out; it's tight quarters back here. It's piled with trash bags we can't move yet."

"Uh-huh, I understand. And Mr. Stoner is here with me, too."

"Hey, Jack," Vince Stoner called back, then looked at the woman. "Call me Cheech, I told you."

Vince earned the moniker Cheech, his last name being Stoner. As in Cheech and Chong, stoners from the seventies. Although Vince Stoner was not, nor ever would be, a pothead.

CSU needed to do their thing, so he walked out from behind the putrid dumpsters and headed straight to the woman who'd called his name.

"Jack West." He extended his hand.

"Marlo Makos, Medical Examiner."

"Bennie got around to hiring someone to take Dorence's spot, did he? Well, welcome aboard."

"Yes, he told me Mr. Dorence retired last year. Said he's been interviewing for eight months. I hope like heck I don't let him down."

"First on-site case since you got here?"

"Yes, and no. I got here the first on the first of month. All the paperwork and learning about a new crime lab. The first week kept me busy. I went on a call as an observer with Bennie last week while you—lucky you—were in Maui, I hear. Bennie gave me the rundown of all the homicide detectives, and you're right, this is my first solo gig."

"Young Hispanic woman back there, but we need CSU to comb the area first."

"I'll go take a quick look-see, then come back and let CSU do their thing."

"Sure, Mrs. Makos. I'll be here."

"It's Miss—but call me Mack. I thought for sure everyone would call me M&M, but I'll take Mack over all the jokes that M&Ms conjure up."

"Yeah, cops and nicknames. I wondered what got that started, been happening for ages."

They both shrugged.

The rest of CSU arrived, and the lead CSU investigator, Cheech, started everyone on different jobs.

The videographer set up to film. A girl from CSU was shooting pictures of the scene at every angle.

Dawson Luck rolled up, and under the lone light shining over the crime scene, it looked like a beehive swarming.

Officer Hank Avera had the onlookers pushed back, and most tenants gave up and went inside. They had seen all they needed to see and did not want to get involved.

Curiosity drove them out the front door, and fear drove them back inside. This area was not immune to drugs, gangs, or even murder. The fact was that some offenders of these crimes lived in this very complex. A passel of doors would need knocking on, and everyone questioned. Jack was glad he had uniforms for canvassing.

Hank was dealing with a few rubberneckers when Detective Luck arrived.

Ducking under the crime scene tape, Lucky nodded. "Hank."

"Hey, Luck, West is over there with Cheech." Hank tilted his head in that direction.

"Looking good, Hank. You lose weight?"

"Yeah, wife has me on Weight Watchers."

"Keep it up. You'll be at your college fighting weight in no time."

"It's my wife's goal, not mine."

"Good for her. Maybe she'll keep you kicking longer." He clapped Hank on the back.

"Top of the morning to ya, Cheech, and I do mean top. Dang, it's early. I'm sorry, Jack, it took me longer to get here than planned—had to stop for gas and coffee. What's the story here?"

Jack filled him in with Deeks' story first.

"Is Bennie here? I saw the M.E.'s car."

"Uh-uh, the M.E. is looking back there right now." Jack neglected to mention it was a new M.E. He didn't know if Lucky had met her or not; if not, the surprise might be funny.

"Detective West," she said as she walked up, "it's going to take some time to get through all the trash since it's piled around the victim. We have no idea if some of it may be substantial evidence. I'm going to let CSU do all the bagging, then we can get the body out. I don't want to roll the body over until they're through. We might be here a while."

She did not acknowledge Lucky at all and turned to go back to the trash containers to see that no one disturbed the body.

"Who's the new beaver, Jack?"

Luck didn't lower his voice—the woman turned back.

"Sorry, I had no idea you were someone important." She stuck her hand out. Lucky raised his hand with a bewildered look.

"I'm the new M.E., name's Marlo Makos—or perhaps you can call me Bucky Beaver," she said with a straight face.

If the light illuminating the crime scene had not been there, she would have never seen the deep red flush that crept into his face.

"Uh, ma'am, I... uh... sorry, meant no disrespect. It's, well, it's a guy thing, you know?" Lucky ducked his head.

"You must be Detective Luck, right?"

"How did..."

She cut him off. "The girls in the office and at the crime lab gave me the scoop on you, and with the beaver comment, I put two and two together," she said with a straight face, not one speck of a smile.

"Ma'am, I apologize."

"Look, Detective Luck, don't worry. I'm a big girl and have taken more crap off men than you could ever feed me on your own. Besides, I love my wife."

She looked at Jack, winked, and sauntered off. He knew she was joking, but Lucky stood there, his mouth hanging open.

"Wife, her? God, Jack, she's a woman any man would chase over hill and over dell without stopping to catch his breath. What the fuck is this world coming to?"

Jack knew she was kidding, but he'd let Lucky stew for a while.

5

"HEAVENS." MACK FANNED HER face. "I've never seen this much trash, and most of it will be useless for DNA or clues."

The CSU team collected multiple evidence bags; however, Mack recognized this as a precautionary measure, as most of the contents appeared to be commonplace refuse.

It had taken two and a half hours of bagging, dusting prints—moving and scouring through the fetid trash before the CSU team was ready to process the real crime scene—the body.

They knew they'd have to dig in all four dumpsters, and the thought made Mack shudder. Funny, she could handle decomposing bodies but not decaying garbage.

"You're right, Mack, but every flipping piece of lonely trash that was by, on, or near the body got to be processed, as well as places the perp might have stood or touched. Sucks it's outside, next to such rancid trash. I'm glad the trash hadn't run yet." Jack said, plain and simple.

It was amusing at 6:00 am when they showed up. The show was comic relief, albeit in serious circumstances. All law enforcement personnel knew that sometimes there had to be humor, even on the job, to get through some of the horrendous scenes. If not, it might drop a person deep into an emotional abyss of darkness and they might never return. Never once did the humor extend toward the unfortunate deceased, at least never within earshot of the public.

6:00 am

Lucky walked toward the two men who were determined to get the dumpsters emptied.

"Look, Officer, I'm the sanitation engineer, and ..."

"It's Detective Luck. I'm not in a patrolman's uniform." Dawson Luck squared his shoulders at the overweight, cigar-chewing, smelly sanitation engineer, as he'd called himself.

"I said no one, and I do mean no one, you or your friend over there, is taking trash today. Tomorrow you can, but that's still in the wind right now, like the smell of this reeking trash. I want you to back your big-ass truck up and go to your next stop."

"My boss is gonna get pissed. You're fucking with my schedule, you know that? We got an MPU we hafta report. That's a missed pickup, and the guidelines say we gotta get it on the same day. My boss ain't gonna like the overtime, either."

The sanitation worker took half a step towards Lucky. Although the burly guy outweighed him by 110 pounds and was three feet taller, Detective Luck didn't budge. The trashman's colleague remained at a distance beside the garbage truck that was still running.

"I just gotta get what's inside the damn receptacles; you can keep the trash on the outside. Ain't my job to play nursemaids to ghetto people who are too lazy to toss a bag into a hole. You can keep the drug addict whore you got lying dead back there. Ended up where she belonged. She was trash too." He scoffed.

The big man stood there, arms crossed, chewing on a stubby cigar, and he would not move, not one inch.

Jack contemplated intervening—but left the decision to his partner.

Lucky stood there glaring the burly man down, not a peep coming out of his mouth. Everyone, by this time, was watching. Even the fellas with CSU stopped processing to watch the show.

Jack thought he saw smoke coming from Lucky's ears. He knew his partner might not agree with the life that some lived—drugs or prostitution—but dead was dead, and no one deserved that. Not knowing anything about the dead girl, who was to say what type of lifestyle she had lived.

Lucky spoke, calling for Hank Avera and his partner.

"Officer Avera, will you step this way, please?"

"Yes, sir, Detective Luck." Hank took the half-smile off his face and put on his game face.

"Is your partner here?"

"Yes, sir, he is."

Lucky stared at the man as he called out. "Officer Irvin, please step this way."

The trashman stood, arms crossed, not budging. Getting the trash out of the bins was all he wanted to do, and he figured he could move 'em, get them out of the cops' way.

Garrot Irvin walked up and stood beside his partner Hank Avera.

Here we had Dawson Luck, at five foot eight, 170 pounds, flanked by Officer Hank Avera, Hispanic male, six four and weighing in at 263; his partner, Garrot Irvin, Black male, six two and weighing in at 220, and all muscle. His nickname was Gator. He had grown up in the Louisiana Bayou and once wrestled with a six-foot alligator—not by choice, but for survival. It was clear he had won since he was standing there breathing.

"Officers, I want you to ... what's your name?" He looked at the adamant trashman.

"Timiteto, T-I-M-I-T-E-T-O." He spelled it out as if he was used to doing so.

"Last name?"

"Kane, with a K," his tone terse.

"Officers, I'd like for you to cuff Mr. Timmy Kane here, take him downtown, and book him."

"Hey," the trashman got defensive. "You can't do that. I ain't broke no law."

"First. Yes, I can. You're creating a public spectacle and fixing to disturb a crime scene. Had we not been here, that's what you would be doing right now, *Timmy*," Lucky said his name with contempt. "This is a crime scene. A poor soul got murdered. What if it were your sister? Her body thrown in a damn load of trash. What if a person like you came along and messed up evidence we needed to find the killer?"

Lucky stepped up to him as he spoke and poked him in his big, burly chest. "And he got away? Then the next thing you know, someone else is dead, because you screwed things up. It doesn't matter what this person did in life—if it was drugs or hooking or living here because she was poorer than others were. No one deserves to die, you hear me, *Timmy*?"

Lucky kept exaggerating the name Timmy as if he were talking to an idiot or a child. "Do you want to see her body? I think you should see her body. Don't you fellas think *Timmy* here should see the body?"

Lucky looked at Hank—then Gator. They nodded, trying not to grin.

The disheveled trashman unfolded his arms and took a step back.

"No, that ... we'll go, come back ... don't want to cause trouble."

"Too late for that, *Timmy*. You've made a scene, and I gotta do what I gotta do. Arrest you or take you to see the body."

"I ... I don't want to go to jail, I'll lose my job, and I can't have this on ... " He stopped talking.

"Hank, you and Gator, walk *Timmy* over to his precious trash bins, take him to the back side. Show him what he'll uncover for everyone else to see since he wants to empty the dumpsters right this very minute."

Hank and Gator flanked the man, each seizing one of his arms. Timmy's face paled.

"No, don't want to see no dead body. I can't do it, please," Timiteto whimpered.

His coworker's face registered complete surprise to see this big, nasty, tough-acting man whine like a baby.

"What the fuck, Tim? You sound like a wimpy girl." His coworker bent over, hooting.

"Okay, then, *Timmy*. Here's what's going to happen. You're going to say a big and loud, 'I apologize for my actions today. They were rude and uncalled for, and I should respect the dead.' In a few days, you're going to check with the complex manager to see if HPD has finished with the area. Afterward, you and your pal over there can come back and haul off the trash. If your supervisor has a problem with this, I'll be glad to talk to him.

You can tell him that these officers"—he inclined his head toward Avera and Irvin—"will accompany me. You got that?"

"I can do that, sure, you bet. I can do that, no problem." He was nodding and bobbing his head to every word Luck was saying.

Timiteto Kane voiced a loud and booming apology to the number of spectators that had amassed, and then he got in his huge-ass truck, beeping as he backed up, turned, and headed out. The crowd, not affiliated with law enforcement, erupted in cheers.

Lucky ignored it, went up to Jack, and said, "You ready to do real police work now?"

"Detective Luck, you're a man of many wonders, you know that? I'm proud to have you as my partner."

"Don't get sappy, West. Now, let's go catch a killer."

———ele———

MACK COULD NOW GO look at the body. With a gloved hand, she picked up the dead girl's right arm.

"Somebody stabbed her in her armpit."

Lucky leaned to look. "No joke?"

Blood had pooled under the armpit and fanned out under the victim's right bicep area, and smaller trails of blood ran off.

"The axillary artery, in the armpit, makes it a strategic spot for murder. No one sees the armpit as a deadly point. You know, guns, shoot 'em in the chest, or knives, slice the throat or stab 'em in the heart. The axillary artery supplies oxygenated blood to the upper extremities—it's not that deep in the armpit—easy to access. It's a larger artery, and without emergent care, you bleed out. We need to search each of these dumpsters for the murder weapon."

Dawson Luck wrinkled his nose.

"Don't envy the fellas doing that job. They'll need to suit up and wear respirators. This is the worst mess I've seen in a while. I can't imagine what our Texas sun has cooked in there that might be growing six eyes." A smile grew.

Mack looked at him. "What in tarnation is funny?"

"How about we get Timmy and his skinny partner out here? They could take the trash out piece by piece, put it in their truck, and help us check for the murder weapon. What do ya think?"

She tried not to respond, but Jack let it thunder. It was funny.

Mack cleared her throat. "I guess we shouldn't be laughing, huh?"

Jack looked at the victim, then at Mack. "It happens, and it keeps us sane. So, you got a time of death?"

"Damn, Houston is sweltering," her voice low, then: "So, the time of death, uh ..."

"You're not from here, Mack?" Lucky spoke over her muttering.

"No, I'm from New Jersey. I was born in New York, and my dad moved the family to Jersey when I was fourteen. That's where I grew up."

"You're one of those New Jerseyans, huh."

"You got something against people from up North, Lucky?" She sounded annoyed.

"Uh, no, not at all." Man, he was trying not to get under her skin.

"You know, where I hail from isn't important—we're looking at a crime scene here, okay?"

"Yep, sure. Sorry. Didn't mean anything by it." Lucky took one step back, leaving Jack between them as a buffer.

"As I was saying," she went on. "Heat sped up the rigor, and if I calculate in the heat factor, my educated guess ... mind you, it's my educated guess ... someone murdered her sometime between eight or nine last night. But don't go quoting me on this, you hear?"

"Gotcha, it's your educated guess." This worked for Jack.

"Then no one saw her until the Angry Betty let loose. With all the freaking trash piled up, who could even get back here, much less who would want to?" The putrid nastiness of the area disgusted Lucky.

"So, her attacker got her here at knifepoint, then hit her and stabbed her under the arm. I wonder if there was a struggle elsewhere." Jack was playing out a scene in his head.

Lucky looked up at the parking lot. "It's not a well-lit area, and if the killer was fortunate, which he was, no one saw a damn thing."

Jack glanced at her lifeless body. "She isn't half naked. Maybe it's not a sex crime. What do you think, Mack?"

"Can't say, at least not until I conduct the autopsy. I've never speculated about sexual crimes, but you might be right."

"Hand me the Bible."

She lifted it from the victim's hands and handed it to Jack.

"There's one partial bloody print here, but it's smeared. Maybe Latent Prints can get something usable."

He unfolded the paper stuck in the middle of the Bible.

"There's a message typed on here."

"What's the message say?" Lucky asked.

Jack read aloud: "You're a whore. You can never erase the emotional pain you have inflicted on another—it's my job to eradicate their pain. You are impure; I punished you for your wickedness. May God forgive you, and may he forgive me."

"What in the hell does that mean?"

"I guess put an end to someone's pain, Lucky, or that's my guess. Was there a purse found?"

"Stoner, I mean Cheech, said they found no personal items on or near the body." She looked at the four trash bins with a crinkled-up nose.

"When whomever it is goes digging in those nasty things for the weapon, tell 'em to look for her purse too."

"We still have no ID and have a Jane Doe on our hands right now."

Jack pulled his camera app up. He took several shots of the dead girl's face at different angles, then a full-body shot.

"Mack, your crew ready to zip her up and get her to the FSL (forensic science lab)?"

"Uh-huh, we are ..."

Jack looked over at her.

"What, Mack?"

"She's only twenty-three, twenty-four years old. Even with the heavy makeup, she was a pretty girl. Who would've wanted her dead? I mean, not that I understand killing at all, but this doesn't look like any sexual predator's case I've worked. It looks like how a body lays in a casket. Her legs are straight out, arms crossed over her chest, her face caked with makeup. Someone putting makeup on her like that makes me think of the way a mortician would work. The Bible under her hands, kind of ... well, Biblical ... and I've seen that done at a few funerals I have attended."

"We need to look at all the funeral parlors in the area and find a connection, you think?" Lucky hadn't considered that idea.

"Be a stretch, but we could run some stuff, see if one of the neighboring morticians pops. You know," Jack said, as he stuck his phone back in the interior pocket of his jacket, "maybe she pissed off a cross-dresser, and this was her punishment. Cross-dressers are magicians with makeup. Have you seen some of them?"

"I doubt it's a cross-dresser, Jack. He wouldn't have killed her; he would've wanted to go through her closet to borrow clothes and share makeup tips."

Marlo Makos stepped to the end of the dumpsters, stuck her hand out, and waved at the coroner's van, letting them know she was ready for them to move the body back to the FSL.

"Lucky, you're a screwball; most women know that a cross-dresser is the tip-giver. Ask my wife. She should know." She gave Jack a sly wink.

Lucky let his jaw drop for the second time.

6

MANAGEMENT LIVED OFF-SITE. JACK and Lucky had to wait until the office opened. They headed back to the station to start prelim paperwork and waited for Mack to call them with the autopsy findings. They ran checks on all the funeral parlors in a ten-mile radius and produced three that were nearby.

Lucky called at 8:30 when they opened. He got employee names faxed over from two homes and found that one only dealt with cremations, not burials. He marked that off the list. Had the killer worked there, he would have cremated the body, and that was now a moot point.

For the next two hours, they ran checks on the employees at the two funeral homes they had names for, and not a single thing popped up.

"You think we need to go talk to them, Jack, or have uniforms go out and canvass when we get an ID on the victim?"

"Not yet, I think. Pardon the pun... it'll be a dead end."

At 9:45, they headed back to the apartment complex. With the pictures on his phone, he knew management could ID the victim. If she lived there, they would have to know who she was. Knocking on doors had gotten them zip. The residents lived in a neighborhood notorious for drug violence and gangs. It was a well-known fact that this area had more than its share of criminal activity.

"Don't know her..." or "I work nights, don't know my neighbors, and don't wanna know 'em;" or "Well, I can't say for sure;" as well as the standard quote: "I'd rather not get involved."

These comments were not much to go on as far as witness statements.

"Can I help you, gentlemen?" The heavyset woman sat with a pile of checks, money orders, and some cash she was sorting at her desk. An older man sat on the other side of the small office, filling out a ledger.

"Are you the manager?"

"Yes, sir, I'm Hazel Sawyer, and that's my husband, Warren. He's head of maintenance. How can we help you?"

"Ma'am, I'm Detective Jack West with HPD, and this is my partner, Detective Dawson Luck. We have some questions we would like to ask you." He badged her.

The old man walked over to his wife's desk.

"Is there a problem?" She wasn't concerned; she'd had to talk to the law in the past. The residents that occupied this complex were not some of the most law-abiding citizens in Houston.

"Yes, I'm afraid there is. Early this morning at 2:00 am, someone reported finding a young girl's body at the back of the trash receptacles."

Her hand flew up to her mouth. "You've got to be joking."

"No, ma'am," Lucky said. "Murder is not a joking matter."

Jack produced his phone, clicked on photos, and scrolled to the ones he had taken. He laid the phone on the desk in front of the woman.

"Oh Lord," the older woman said, as her husband scrutinized the photo over her shoulder.

"That Jade?" He stared at the photo, and his wife jiggled her head, tearing up a bit.

"Uh-huh, poor girl." She took the corner of her long-oversized cotton shirt and dabbed her eyes.

"Jade who? What's her last name?" Lucky jotted notes.

She handed the phone back to Jack. "Nelson. She was Jade Nelson, Unit 163, the one on the far corner."

"Mrs. Sawyer, we need her file, and we're going to need to look in her apartment. And we'll require you to keep it locked until we release it, got that?"

"But the revenue..."

Jack cut her off. "Ma'am. A murder has taken place on your property. Aren't you glad your other residents aren't in here by the droves wanting out of their leases?"

That thought hadn't occurred to her.

"Hazel," Warren said, "get the key to her unit. I'll get her file."

Warren walked over to a bent-up eight-drawer filing cabinet. Opening it up, he shuffled through the files until he found Jade Nelson, shut the drawer, and handed the file to Lucky.

"Guess we don't need that no more. I'll take the detectives down there, show 'em which one was hers."

Hazel handed Warren the key, relieved that she was not the one taking them to Jade's empty unit. Lord knew what had gone on in Unit 163.

"There, on the corner." Warren pointed and handed Jack the key. "You fellers don't mind if I go back to the office, check on the wife? You know, this is quite a shock to us."

"Sure, Mr. Sawyer. Oh, we'll be keeping the key. Are there duplicates?"

"I got one more in the office, and then there was Jade. She had a key."

"We'll stop by the office on our way out to get that key. No one goes in there, understood?"

"Uh-huh, I mean, yes, sir, I understand. Her... uh, belongings, we need to... I mean, rent's due soon, and..."

Jack cut him off. The man wanted to sell off her belongings for rent. What a scumbag. "Once this apartment is no longer part of the investigation, her family can come to take her possessions. As far as her rent, I'm sure she paid for this month already. Sadly, she won't need it next month—will she?"

The old man shook his head.

"Mr. Sawyer," Lucky got the man's attention, "the residents need to find a place to dispose of their trash until we release the scene. Get that done ASAP. If you don't, you're going to have a bigger sanitation problem, understood?"

"Yes, sir, I'll get some temporary bins. Set 'em on the other side of the lot. Pigsty back there, I know, and we do try, but it's just us and two lawn men."

"Sure, we understand." Lucky figured he was as lazy as his residents were. With the help of two lawn men, he could have kept it cleaner.

"When we release the apartment to her family, they can come to retrieve her belongings." Jack gave him a second warning.

He wanted Mr. and Mrs. Sawyer to know that the deceased's possessions did not belong to them. He knew their type.

"Yes, sir, I understand." Warren Sawyer rushed off. Jack hadn't put the key in the lock—when he vanished.

Booties covering their shoes and latex gloves on, Jack walked in first. It was a small one-bedroom apartment, scarce furnishings, and not messy.

"Her file states she was employed at Advantage Ad Agency. The address is on Two-Ninety, and it's near here." Lucky read. "They list her mother as next of kin. I've got her address here."

"What's the address?" Jack noted the lack of material items in the decedent's tiny living room. A few photos sat on a semi-bare bookshelf. There were knick-knacks on the shelves. Her decorations were sparse, as was her furniture, which consisted of one small loveseat and one cloth rocking chair.

"Says the mother's address is over off Blalock Road. Clover Leaf Mobile Home Park. Her name is Marita Esparza. The place is less than four miles from here; I know the area. The neighborhood will make us as cops stand out at first sight."

"We'll head over to notify the mother from here." Jack stepped into her bedroom.

"Cramped." Lucky remarked as he followed him.

"Guess that explains the twin bed. It's made, guess she hadn't slept in it since, maybe, Wednesday night."

One twin bed, one tall bureau with an assortment of costume jewelry in an old wooden box, and some knockoff bottles of perfume. He pulled out the drawers, while Lucky opened the closet.

"Well, here's where her money went. She has some very nice clothes and at least fifty boxes of shoes on the top shelf and some on a rack under the clothes. Wow, Jack, the closet is as big as the room. It's very well organized too."

Lucky flipped through the clothes, checked a few shoeboxes, and repeated the process several times. "Go figure. All the boxes have shoes in them, as far as I found."

Jack looked in the bathroom, and as he had expected, no property upgrades for at least fifteen years. She kept it neat for what she had to work with, and it was a normal single girl's bathroom. He opened a small drawer and found makeup.

"Got a bag, Lucky?"

"Whatcha got, Jack?" Lucky pulled an evidence bag out of his inside pocket.

"Maybe nada, but I want Mack to compare this makeup with the makeup on the victim's face."

The kitchen was next, not that it was much of a kitchen. A stove, a refrigerator with one large sink instead of the normal two-bay sink, no dishwasher, and minimal cabinet space.

"She didn't eat at home much," Lucky remarked when he looked in the fridge and empty cabinets.

"Other than being dead, her body didn't look anorexic. I'm sure she ate. Nothing looks out of place here, Lucky. No signs of a struggle. No signs of blood, either. I'm wondering if she knew her killer and went out the door with him."

Jack took one more look in the small living room, and he picked up a photo album.

"Jack, we didn't find a cell phone or her purse. You think it got dumped in the trash?"

"Maybe. Be nice to have. You know, cell phones are someone her age's lifeline. I'd like to get a look at her calls and texts and see what social media she was involved with."

"When we get back to the station, I'll do a social media search. See what I come up with," Lucky said.

It was time to go to her mother's house and do one of the most unpleasant jobs a homicide detective had to do: a death notification.

Jack's phone rang. "West. Hey, Cheech, what's up? Yep, we're both here at the complex. Why? Yeah? Terrific, Cheech, thanks, and thank your people for us. Lucky and I will owe them. Tell 'em we'll buy three dozen Krispy Kreme. Be on the way Monday morning, deal?" Jack disconnected and looked at Dawson. "Cheech is sending some of the lab grunts, four of 'em, to search through the dumpsters today. Said they'll be here at noon. Poor guys, in the heat of the day, all suited up, they're gonna swelter."

"Geez, Jack, only three dozen donuts? Man, they'll deserve medals. I think I can spring for some twenty-dollar Starbucks gift cards for each of 'em—add that to your donut offer."

When Dawson Luck became generous, Jack knew it meant he would rather pay someone to do a job he would rather not do, and digging in putrid garbage was worth four twenty-dollar gift cards to Lucky anytime.

7

THE MOBILE HOME PARK sat back off Blalock Road in a crappy area. Across the street on the east, there was Riverside Trailer Park. Nearby was a commercially zoned section of land. Warehouses, trucking businesses, and empty lots. The American Legion—an older plaza with a few stores, like the 99-Cent store, a beauty salon, a fast-food chicken place, and an ancient Kroger, were within walking distance.

Jack pulled in, searching for lot number 21. Theirs was a modest singlewide trailer, a two-bedroom. The backyard was next to a chain-link fence where an empty lot sat, and large transformers decorated the area.

"Here we go." Lucky opened his door.

On the drive over, Jack drew the short straw and was to give Mrs. Marita Esparza the notification.

The woman fell to her knees, wailing. Jack stepped up, taking her arm to keep her from falling out of the trailer door, and then her husband led her to a chair as she continued to wail.

"Jade was her only daughter. We have two sons, but Jade wasn't my daughter. I'm Jorge Esparza. That's why Jade's last name is Nelson, not Esparza. I married her mother when she was five."

"Where's her father?" Jack's heart went out to the mother whose face streamed with tears.

"He's serving time up in Terrell for aggravated robbery. He's served three years of his five-year sentence."

"Can either of you think of anyone who would have wanted your stepdaughter dead?" West questioned.

The word *dead* brought on more hysteria, and the woman slid out of the chair onto her knees, crying out in Spanish. Neither Jack nor Lucky spoke Spanish, but they both recognized the words, *"O Dios Mio,"* Spanish for "Oh my God."

"No, no one. Everyone loved Jade. She was full of energy and life." There was a catch in his voice. The poor guy was shaken up.

"When was the last time you both saw her?" Lucky had his notebook open, pencil to paper, ready to write.

"We saw her last week, Wednesday night. She comes to visit and eats dinner every Wednesday night and then she goes out. She might come to visit on a Sunday, but it was rare, since she parties on Saturday night and sleeps in."

"Do you know her friends?" Jack took over.

"No, we don't know her friends. She never brought them to our house. She kept her private life from us, never told her mother much."

"Boyfriends... did she have any, or was she seeing someone?"

"Can't tell you that either, although she'd been happier the past few months... you know that smile when you're in love? Her mother asked her if a man was making her *sonreir*, uh, that's Spanish for smile."

By this time, Marita Esparza was no longer crying. She sat on the floor with a faraway look in her eyes.

"She had a man. She was happy, in love, happy."

Jack looked down at the woman as she spoke.

"She drank too much and went out all the time. She should've gotten married, started a family, and then she might not be d-d-dead." The woman sobbed, this time for the future her daughter would never see.

He handed Jorge the photo album from Jade's apartment.

"Do you know these people?"

Jorge and Marita went through the album.

"These are family photos." Jorge flipped through several pages. "These must be some of her friends, I suppose. There aren't many pictures, but kids keep all their pictures on their phones these days." Jorge closed the photo album and handed it back to Jack.

"When can we get her body for burial, Detective West?" Jorge Esparza asked as he stroked his wife's hair.

"When the medical examiner finishes, I'll have someone call you. You can tell them then where you want her body taken." Jack went over the process with the step-father.

Lucky handed Jorge his card. "Even if you think it's unimportant, please call anytime, night or day, okay?"

"Thank you, Detectives, we will." Mr. Esparza took the card.

Jack's face was somber. "We are very sorry for your loss, and we're gonna work hard to find out who did this to your daughter."

Jorge thanked them, voice wavering, and closed the door to comfort his grieving wife.

"Poor woman." Lucky buckled in. "Where do you want to head next, Jack?"

"Advantage Ad Agency, see how well connected she was to her coworkers."

The building set back off 290, between random offices, one touting to be a travel agency, the other a small printing company, and several vacant offices on either side.

The bell on the door jangled, and a young woman came up from the back to the front counter.

"Can I help you?"

Jack looked around. "Are you the owner?"

"No, I'm his assistant, Fran."

"Is the owner here?"

"Yes, I'll get him. May I tell him who's asking?"

"Detectives West," Jack gestured to his partner. "And Luck from HPD Homicide."

Her face paled. Without uttering a word, she walked to the back. A few mere seconds later, a portly bald man came out to the front counter.

"Detectives, I'm Larry Foster, I'm the owner. Is there something I can help you with?"

"You have an office where we can talk?"

Larry Foster led them to his office and shut the door.

"Jade? She's dead? I can't believe this. I was furious at her for not show-ing up today. We have a large project underway. Now I feel awful for getting so damn mad."

"How long had she worked here?"

"Three and a half years. I got her right out of a schoolwork program. She never missed work. Her sales skills were improving, and she'd started selling ads to small, local Hispanic radio stations. Our advertising includes print, some radio, and some television. All local stuff, nothing syndicated, mind you."

"How many employees do you have? Was she having problems with a coworker?" Jack asked him.

"Not to my knowledge. Everyone here got along. We have a small staff. Fran, up front, is my daughter. My wife is the bookkeeper, and my son, Larry Jr., is in sales. We have two kids. This is a family-run business. Then there are my nephews, Craig and Mark. They do most of the logo drawings and dabble in sales, and Vicky, who does some clerical work, a 'wherever we need her' kind of employee. Everyone got along with Jade." He shook his head. "This is going to crush the staff, especially the wife."

"Was she close to someone here?"

"Perhaps Fran, but I stayed out of the social part."

"Can you ask Fran to step back here? We need to speak with her."

"Oh sure, uh, Detective, uh..."

"Jack West. Thank you, Mr. Foster."

Fran Foster broke down in tears when she learned of Jade Nelson's murder. They gave her time to get composed, and when her tears subsided, she continued the stuttering inhalation, as a small child does after a hard cry.

"Ma'am, can we talk now?" Jack was concerned the woman was going to be ill with the way she'd bawled for the last three minutes.

She sniffed. "I apologize for that outburst. But, well, Jade was such a sweet girl." The tears flowed from her eyes, but she was no longer sobbing.

"You were close?"

"We started getting close, you know, personally, but working together every day, you become eight-hours-a-day friends. After work, we started hanging out more. At first, you know, I had my friends, she had hers, and we didn't run in the same circles."

"When was the last time you saw Jade?"

"Wednesday."

Lucky wrote it down. "Miss Foster, was she not at work Thursday?"

"I don't know, I was off. I took a vacation day for personal reasons."

"As a formality, Miss Foster, where were you Thursday night from eight to nine pm?" Jack tried not to make her feel like a criminal when he asked, but the question, "Where were you on..." was a question that instilled fear in most people.

"Uh, am I in trouble? I mean, you want my alibi?" She was stunned.

"It's only a formality, Miss Foster. Can you please tell us where you were?"

"I was at my parents' house all night. The thing is, I've been having money troubles, so I'm back at their place. I took Thursday off to move out of my apartment."

"Did Jade say there was a boy she might be involved with?"

"She did say there was a bartender at a hip-hop club who had a crush on her."

"Did they date?" Lucky was jotting down notes.

This time Fran giggled. "No way. Jade said he was bi... you know, bisexual... and she didn't fly that way." A tear slipped down. "Gosh, we were just becoming friends. I mean real friends, now, well..."

"What club, Fran, and do you know the bartender's name?" Jack was keeping her on track.

"Over off Hempstead Highway; I think the name is Club Razz."

"Did she tell you the name of the bartender?"

"A first name. I think it was Barry."

"Miss Foster, do you know if she was having problems with a friend, her family, or a coworker?"

"No, she was super happy these last three months, like she was in love. I tried to get her to spill, but she kept it an enormous secret. I teased her and told her she might be in love with an ugly man, or married man."

"Did she respond?" Jack asked.

"No, sir, she smiled but never said which."

Jack handed her his card. "Call me anytime if you remember something that might be important."

As they were walking out the door, Jack got a text.

"We've been summoned."

"Who by?

"Mack. Let's head to the morgue."

8

"WEST, LUCK, NICE TO see you guys—not nice why. Mack's in the autopsy room. Suit up, then head that way. I won't be far behind," Bennie rejoined.

"Nice to see you, too, and yeah, wish it were under different circumstances." Jack grabbed a gown and unfolded it. Lucky did too, and they headed to the dreaded autopsy room.

"I hope you guys are ready for some strange stuff," Mack said when they walked in, gowned up and masks in place.

"Okay, Mack, whatcha got?"

"First, I found a round contusion with dimple markings on her head. The object most likely had a roughened exterior, which might account for the dimpling—maybe like a rock, but I can't be positive." Mack pointed to a purplish spot on the girl's left temple. "There's a small bit of blood. It dazed her but didn't kill her—the stab under her armpit did. She bled out. There's no way to say how long she lay there dying. Her BP dropped and she passed out. Even if she hadn't bled out, it deprived her brain and kidneys of blood flow. She might have died fast, but we'll never know for sure."

"Well, if I had to pick a way to go, I'd pick passing out and not suffering. Poor girl." Lucky shook his head.

"Did you do a rape kit?" Jack felt there was more.

"This is what's odd, and I've never seen this, ever." Mack walked to the countertop at the end of the table. "The assault she experienced deviated from the common scenarios of sexual assault." Mack retrieved a transparent evidence bag from the table. "I found this shoved clear up her vagina, to the point of ripping her cervix. They did it postmortem." She shook her head. "I don't understand sadistic men."

Jack looked at the dildo. "I've seen these, but never one quite that large or long—maybe a special order?"

"There's so much crap you can get on the Internet—black-market sex toys, S&M paraphernalia," Lucky said, looking at the article in her hand.

They both stared at him, not saying a word.

"What? Oh, come on, guys. You don't think I'd ever do that, man. All you have to do is talk with someone in Vice and you'd know. You can both take a flying leap," he said.

They laughed and then went back to business.

"Was she raped first?" Jack looked back at Jade's lifeless body.

"She'd engaged in sexual activity. We found dried semen. Also, we found two pubic hairs when we combed—they're not a match to hers."

"Don't tell me you got DNA back that fast, 'cause that's not possible." Jack frowned.

"No, Detective. I know because these weren't black hairs like hers—they were gray. Also, they were loose, not attached. I suspect one of two things here," she said, sitting the bagged dildo down and crossing her arms.

"Okay, we're listening," he responded.

"She was seeing someone—an older man, perhaps a married man. Or her attacker was older."

"Sounds reasonable, but you know, some men go gray early. Age might not be a factor." He held his palm up in a gesture of 'what if.'

"There's more," she said as the door to the autopsy room slid open and Bennie stepped in.

"How's it going in here?"

"Ya know, Bennie, this is an odd case, but hey, I'm sure, unfortunately, one day we'll all see odder. Mack was fixing to tell us more, although what she's told us up to now would've been plenty." Jack moved to the top end of the table near Jade's head.

Mack walked over and pulled the sheet down far enough to see her left hand.

"I didn't see it at the scene because her right hand covered the left. What grabbed all our attention at the time was the small white New Testament Bible. When we got her here and I started the autopsy, I noted her left ring finger was broken in an odd manner."

She lifted the hand. Jade's body—no longer in full rigor—Mack wiggled her finger.

"Somebody bent it back as far as it could be at the dorsal aspect, then bent it again at the knuckle. Your killer did this postmortem. I have X-rays but wanted you to see this firsthand."

"Okay, what in the world does that mean? Why break her finger in such a grotesque manner?" Lucky asked.

"It's her wedding ring finger, Detective Luck. Maybe that's the significance," Mack stated.

Bennie leaned over to look.

"What did you think when you saw this, Ben?" Jack stared at the finger she held up.

"I think I've seen this same injury on a different victim. Let me go check my files."

Marlo Mack's heavy sigh caused Jack to look up.

"Christ, Mack. Don't tell me there's more?"

"No, not on the body, but Cheech called. I gave him the Bible to check for prints."

"How come he didn't call me?" Jack frowned, then understood. Cheech was single, and Mack was single and pretty. He smiled at her. They were still letting Dawson Luck think that she had a wife.

"Who knows?" She played it off. "Vince said there was a thumbprint on the inside front cover—he ran it through AFIS ... no match found. Said when he leafed through the Bible, he found a highlighted passage. Here, I wrote it down. I looked it up on the Internet; it's from the New International Version of the New Testament."

"Read it aloud," Lucky requested.

"Galatians 5:19: Now the works of the flesh are obvious: sexual immorality, impurities, and debauchery."

"Immoral, impure, and wickedness ... didn't the note mention she was impure and wicked?"

"It did, Lucky, and it makes no sense. She worked at a day job, and my gut says she wasn't hooking. The broken finger's an oddity. I'm gonna have to think about that. Can I keep this, Mack?"

"Sure."

Bennie walked back in. "Yep, I thought this was familiar." He waved a few papers in his hand. "I pulled up a report on an autopsy I did three months ago. Jack, you remember the case of the African American woman found in an empty house over in the Fourth Ward? The case is still open."

"We didn't catch that case, 7-11 did."

"Yeah, you're right. She had the same broken finger, and that's not all ..."

Lucky jumped in, cutting Bennie off. "Did she have other similarities, like vaginal trauma with an oversized dildo, or a Bible in her hands?"

"No, none of that. She did have semen, and we swabbed, but it was a mixture. She'd been with two men. Same fatal injury with a knife ... like your victim, under her right arm ... and no one found the knife. Do you think ... ?" He looked at Jack and Lucky.

"A serial?" Mack's eyes widened.

"Bennie, can you compare the wounds on Jade's body with the wounds on 7-11's case and get back with me ASAP?"

"Sure, Jack."

One dead body found was awful enough; however, if the wounds were similar—both stabbed under the right armpit inflicting their deaths—and it made it two bodies, then if a third showed up with the same or very similar MOs, a serial killer would be on the loose in Houston.

They left the crime lab and headed back to the station.

They needed to update Chief Yao on the findings and similarities of this case and 7-11's case. Jack didn't even concern himself with updating Brooks; it never even crossed his mind.

9

"HOLY SHIT, A SERIAL. This will shake Houston to its core. Damn it, we have enough killers committing singular murders daily. Jesus."

Chief Yao raked his hand through his hair.

"We get rain for four straight days, and everyone panics thinking another flood will hit our city, and now this. Can you imagine the panic this will stir? You two need to get with Chang and Severson, see what you might come up with that could link these two cases, and pray this is a strange coincidence. But I gotta say, in all my years on the force, nothing is ever a coincidence. Damn it to Hades."

"What if the paper gets wind of this, Chief? You know the Chronicle bloodhounds have scanners. No one showed up at the scene this morning. They can't know much yet. Guess it was too early for the paper jockeys to be out." Jack knew they needed to stay ahead of the news.

"I'll call the Chief of Police and update him, and then I'll get him to call the Chronicle, have him send someone over, make a statement. We need to keep this contained. Keep a damn lid on the stuff only our killer would know. We need to downplay this as much as possible. I guess they can even use the old standby."

"What old standby, Chief?" Lucky didn't know what he meant.

"Oh, you know—poorer neighborhood. People think it's either drug related or gang related. If they think that right now, maybe it'll keep Houstonians from pure panic."

"Lie to them?" Lucky didn't understand.

"Look, Dawson," Yao said, "what they don't know right now won't hurt them, and when we catch the motherfucker who is doing this, we can disclose the total story. That's why we downplay it, understand?"

"Yes, sir." Dawson Luck had never dealt with this type of crime. This was his first serial, and he had no idea how the politics worked. He'd been on the Homicide table for three years at HPD. In Mesa, Arizona, he worked in the Robbery Division. Working in Homicide, especially in Houston, Texas, was a reality check.

"Chief, why not call Tessa Coy at the Chronicle? Or maybe I should. I've worked with her, and I can explain we're keeping a lid on stuff, and I trust her. You can update Chief Pratt. Let me give her an abridged version of the story I want her to print."

"Yeah, Jack, don't know why I didn't think of it. Lucky, have I ever told you there've been times we've called your partner Detective Vague? He has this uncanny way of telling a reporter zero info, and they think they have a byline." Davis Yao snorted.

"No, didn't know that one. Jack, I guess you're a man of many mysteries." Lucky looked over at him.

"Sometimes Tessa hears stuff—word-on-the-street crap—and in case she does, I'll warn her to come to us first, and no one else," said Jack.

"Oh, and don't forget, update Captain Brooks. Now, go see if we can catch this motherfucker before someone else dies," Yao said with a frown.

That was their cue to get the case solved and closed.

Lucky went back to the squad room to track down 7-11. They needed to compare notes, and fast. Jack had the job of updating Captain Brooks.

"Wow—that was fast."

"Brooks wasn't in his office. Guess we can catch him later, or maybe Chief Yao can update him." Jack was happy Brooks was out. "You get hold of either Chang or Severson?"

"No, haven't tried yet."

"I'll text Jace, see where he and Chang are, and their ETA. Lucky, you do a background check on Jade and her mother. I'll check the stepfather, and I'll check the prison system for her biological father. What's his name again?"

Lucky flipped open his notebook. "Name's Stanley Martin Nelson, DOB 6/8/63."

Jack wrote it down and they both got to work.

Two hours later, 7-11 was still out in the field. Jack called Chang to tell him they needed to collaborate on the cases they were working on.

"What did 11 say?" Lucky asked.

"He said they'd roll in at three. They're investigating a pop-and-drop—you know, the Exxon station off Eastex Freeway and Aldine Mail Route?"

"I know the place. What went down?"

"Some kid high on meth came in at midnight last night, started an altercation with the clerk, and then shot him. Chang said no robbery attempt took place, which was weird. Cameras are all over the store, so they got a clear picture of the dumbass meth-head. The dude's got a jacket with a list of priors. They're on a search right now."

"I thought there were two clerks on at all times these days," Lucky stated.

"There was, but the girl was out back taking a smoke break when she heard the gunshot. She ran in, found her coworker on the floor, and told 7-11 she locked the front doors and called 9-1-1, scared out of her skin."

"I'll bet she's searching for a safer job today." Lucky felt for the girl. She would have nightmares for a while.

"Now, all they have to do is find the son of a bitch. That might take some time since he's hiding. Chang is working with Rick in Vice to see if they can help track the meth head down."

"I'm betting Rick's team knows the guy. Hope they find him and drop his dumbass in jail for a long time."

"So, whatcha get on the background checks you're working?"

"Nada. The mother's a saint—not a speeding ticket, nothing. Jade either, for that matter. She reported once that she had a stalker. The report said it was an old boyfriend, but once he moved off and joined the army, went to Fort Yuma in Arizona, the incidents stopped."

Jack looked up. "When was this reported?"

"Uh, says here three years ago. She was nineteen, he was twenty-three. You don't think he would've come all the way back here to do this out of passion or revenge?"

"You check his military records?"

"Not yet, but I will," Lucky said. "You find records on the father or stepfather, other than the aggravated burglary on the real father?"

"Stepfather Jorge has some minor things—speeding, public intoxication, and one fight in a bar when he was a seventeen-year-old kid. He did some time in juvie; nothing big pops in his record that would point to this."

Jack clicked the next page: "Her biological father has a thicker jacket: burglary as a juvie and in his early adult years, some gang association, a charge of simple assault, did six months in County, then the aggravated burglary with a deadly weapon. He's doing a nickel, and I'm surprised it's only a nickel with his priors. Must've had a smart attorney. Nothing points a finger to him. He can stay in jail, and maybe he won't make parole—keep some more scum off the streets of Houston."

Lucky's head jiggled as he listened. "I'll let you know what I find on the ex-boyfriend. Hey, I'm hungry. We haven't even stopped to eat."

Jack admitted his stomach could use some fuel. "How about I go get us some Antoine's?"

"That works. Get me three—I'm starved."

"Lucky, you're starving all the time."

Jack headed out while Lucky did the background check on the now military ex-boyfriend.

Mouth full of an Antoine's sub, Lucky was chewing and talking.

"Not mush on the boyfred, seems to be cleam."

Jack frowned. "What the dickens did you just say?"

He swallowed, then took a drink. "Sorry, I mean clean. He's still at Fort Yuma in Arizona and says he's an E-4 Corporal in the procurement department at the munitions installation. The report says he's married. I think he doesn't look like a suspect. Jack, the guy's got an excellent military record. No priors at all."

"We need to check if he's been in the area over the past few days. You do that, then we'll cross him off."

"Yep, I'm on it. Oh, I checked Facebook too. Jade had a Facebook account, but it shows she hasn't posted stuff in four months. Kind of odd for a girl her age."

"Twitter, Instagram? Most kids, especially girls, have all that crap."

Lucky swallowed the last of his second sub. "No, she didn't, and yeah, you're right. Most girls her age would've had one or both."

Jack called The Houston Chronicle.

"Tessa Coy, please. Tell her it's Jack West. You bet I'll hold."

"Well, Jack, I haven't heard from you since the Judge Wolff case. How are you? Still keeping our city cleaned up?"

"Yeah, I've been busy trying. Listen. Can you drop by the station? I've got a story for you."

He could picture the short woman stand up, grab her handbag, and run to her car before she hung up the phone.

"Am I your first call, Jack? I don't want sloppy seconds."

"Yes, Tessa, I called you first. Are you gonna come over here, because if not, I'll call The Daily Sun and see if Chen Wu wants to come over."

That was all it took. Hearing those two names—the Daily Sun and Chen Wu—Tessa would be there in fifteen; true to her word, she was there in less than fifteen minutes.

"Yeah, send her up," Jack told the lobby receptionist. "I'll meet her at the elevators."

The elevator doors opened—Tessa Coy stuck her hand out.

"Jack, thanks for calling me first. I appreciate it."

"Come on, we can go to the common room. No one's in there right now."

Tessa followed, and once seated, she took out her notebook and pen and was all business.

"So, Jack, what's the scoop you're handing me today?"

"Look, I can't tell you ..."

She cut him off. "Goddamn it, Jack, why in the hell did you call me and want me to rush over? Oh, I see, just to tell me you have a story that you can't tell me and yank my chain, is that it? I can't believe you said you were going to call Chen at the Sun. You knew, didn't you?"

"Knew what, Tessa?" He frowned.

"That, like a fucking fool, I would run right over for the famous Jack West. Ever since that Judge Wolff case hit and all the cold cases you and your partner closed at one time; well, you're now the deity of detectives."

She threw her notebook into her purse with a thud and stood.

"Goddamn it, Tessa, sit the fuck down and listen to me," Jack got pissed off. "If you'd let me get a word in edge-wise, maybe then you wouldn't be mad. Now sit down and shut the hell up."

When he got through explaining part of the story, Tessa Coy settled down.

"Tessa, what I meant when I said I can't tell you is that there are aspects about the case we've got to keep a lid on. Look, I trust you, but can't tell you until I can. Understand?"

"Jack, I understand, and this is some major stuff. So, you do think 7-11's case and yours could be linked to the same killer?"

"Yes, but damn it, Tessa, don't put that in writing. That's off the record for now, okay?"

"Fine, the story will be 'Local Girl Found Dead in Apartment Complex off Wirt Road,' her name and very brief story. I do know how to downplay, Jack. I'll say that the police are investigating, no conclusion whether it's related to gang violence or drugs. Jack? You think the women of Houston are in danger? I mean, well ..." She held her hands up. "Be nice for me to know how safe I need to be."

"Lord, Tessa, I love Houston, but this is Houston, you know. Our fair city ranks up there with Dallas, New York, and Los Angeles. Shit, you're a crime reporter. Of all people, you should know."

"Jack?"

"Now what, I need to get to work? Got a killer to catch."

Tessa Coy, crime reporter for The Houston Chronicle, smirked. "Bite me, Jack." Then she gave him the finger.

"Got a girl who bites me, plus she does to me what your middle finger says, we ..."

"Shut up, Jack, I get the picture. Walk me to the elevators; I have a short story to put in tomorrow's news."

10

THE DOOR TO THE squad room opened and 7-11 walked in. It was time to join forces.

"West, Luck. We saw Deeks in the main lobby. He said you have a new murder to work," Chang said.

Jack opened a file on his desk, took out a yellow legal pad, and gave them a briefing on their case and Mack's initial report.

"So maybe the murder cases connect." Jace rolled his chair over next to Jack's desk.

"Maybe, then maybe not. I'm leaning toward maybe more than not." Jack nodded.

"Well, there are more connections." Jace crossed his bulging arms. He had the guns and the other ammo to go with it; the man was buff. Jace Severson was married to the job, as he was thrice divorced and couldn't seem to hold on to a wife. His hair was long enough to be in a short ponytail, and if he weren't a police detective, you might think he was a member of a biker gang when he was on his Fat Boy Harley.

"Yep," Chang said. "That's what I was thinking."

"What?" Jack looked from Chang to Jace.

"The makeup," Jace said, and Chang took over. "Caked on heavy, not normal at all. It was eerie. It was nowhere near the right shade of makeup for someone of her skin color."

Jace took over. "Like she'd been made up for her funeral, and her body laid out sort of like your victim was. Her crossed her arms over each other lower on the torso, nearer her waist, like she might have them positioned in a casket."

"Our victim had her arms crossed over the top of her chest, with a small white New Testament under her hands," Lucky said.

No one spoke for a few minutes. It was as if they were all giving a silent pause for the dead.

Chang spoke up. "At first we thought it was a sexual crime, but we crossed that off the list. Our victim had two sets of male DNA, and the husband told us she was having an affair, but he couldn't say who with—said he didn't know. We got his alibi, and it's solid."

"Your victim found in the Fourth Ward, right?" Jack made some notes on the pad.

"In an empty house—on the market to be sold. With all that's happened there, the realtor is gonna have a helluva time selling it," Jace said. "You know, the whole disclosure thing."

"I'll say. Murder in a house on the market ain't a valuable selling attribute." Lucky agreed.

"Who listed it?"

Chang rolled his chair over to Jack's desk. "It was a small agency, Al Mathers Realty."

"Lockbox?"

"Uh-huh, but no signs of a break-in or tampering with the lockbox. We did a thorough search, found no key to the house—either. Plus, we checked with the company that sets up all the showings. All the agents cleared—all had solid alibis." Chang stopped —"No murder weapon found either," Jace finished for him.

"You guys ever think that maybe the other man your victim was seeing might be Al Mathers, that dude who owns the real estate agency?"

"Sure, we did—he listed the house and had a key. He was somebody we were interested in right away. We grilled the man for three hours. He admitted he'd been seeing Corinne Taylor. That's our victim's name." Jace started, but Chang took the story over.

"Uh-huh, he was sweating bullets, didn't want his wife to know he was seeing her. He said the affair hadn't been going on long, and they hadn't been intimate yet—which is bullshit. Bennie said there was semen from two different men." Chang snorted. "You should have seen his face. The black man just about turned white."

"We talked to the victim's husband, Lincoln Taylor. He goes by Link. He didn't act as if he even cared. It'd only be my opinion, but I don't think he cared, 'cause I think he was getting himself a little on the side. I still think he could be a viable suspect, don't you, 11?" Jace used his partner's nickname.

"Yeppers, and we've been watching him. There's a two-hundred-thousand-dollar life insurance policy to be collected. Link and the wife both had insurance policies in case either of them was to kick it. Policies are two years old. But I gotta say, Link Taylor has two hundred big ones to get if the wife dies, and that's motive in my book."

"You're right, Xi, that's a helluva large amount to come into. You thinking he could have hired someone to kill her?" Lucky swiveled his chair.

"That's why we're watching him," Jace stated.

Jack drummed his fingers on the desk. "So, how does our victim fit in? You think it's a red herring to direct the case a different direction and take the focus off him?"

"If that's the case, the bastard is very devious." Jace shook his head.

"Al Mathers' wife. What's her story?" Lucky sat back and closed his eyes.

Chang spoke up. "His wife, Bunny Mathers, vouches for him, said he'd never cheat. She was very adamant. In fact, I thought the wife might be trying to convince herself that he wouldn't cheat, instead of trying to convince me. I think I had one of those 'Jack's gut intuition' moments. I believe she did know he was having an affair."

"Well, his affair has stopped now, and maybe this will scare him out of cheating forever," Jace remarked.

"Guess I don't get it. If you have a wonderful woman, why cheat? Then you gotta lie and create more lies. Too complicated for me," Jack threw in.

"Hell's bells, man, respectable men have cheated on their wives. Several of our own presidents, who shall remain nameless, don't have time to quote the list. Men are men. I mean, I'd never, ever cheat on my wife, but I've known some very upstanding men who've strayed." Lucky would never screw it up with his wife.

"Crap, Dawson, you ever cheat on your wife and lose her? You're too ugly to get another goddess. That was a once-in-a-lifetime for you, dude. If she dumps you, she's my next fourth ex-wife." A massive grin spread over Jace Severson's face.

Nice to laugh, but Lucky jumped back to business. "You can't find info on your victim's phone, texts, calls to connect anyone else to her or another man? Did she have social media?"

"We never found her phone, and she wasn't a social media kind of person, didn't have a Facebook page. We even checked to see if she ever had a Myspace page, and we got nil," Chang said.

"Phone records?" asked Jack. "Or her financials?"

"Nah, financials showed not one oddity. She and her hubby shared all accounts, and for all intents and purposes, their financials looked rather bland and normal. Bills, groceries, items at the mall—you know, shoes and makeup and fishing gear for the hubby, scrapbooking crap from the hobby stores for her, stuff like that," Jace said with a bob of his head and a small shrug.

Chang jumped in. "The phone records were a bust too. She called her daughter in Alabama, her mother, her job, her husband's cell, and a girl-friend. We checked them all out and got zip. The one other number that came inbound had been from her church, and there were a few outbound calls she made to the church. The text messages were brief, to her daughter and husband, and not many of them, considering how people text every-thing these days. She wasn't into that type of communication, and we tried pinging for the phone to see if we could locate it. And, man, it's off the grid."

"Did you check the church out?" Jack relaxed back in his chair as they discussed 7-11's case.

A crease rippled across Jace's face. "No, we didn't. Didn't think there would be a need."

"Jack, what do you have on your mind?" Chang wanted a fresh way to look at things.

"Might be a stretch, but our deceased girl had a small white New Testament Bible placed under her hands, and Cheech found a Bible verse that someone highlighted." He read them the verse Mack had written down.

"Well, our victim had nothing like that." Jace looked at his partner. "Chang, what's your take?"

He shook his head and pursed his lips in a 'crap, I don't know' gesture.

"Maybe, if these two cases are linked and your lady was first, maybe the killer is adding on as he goes. I don't know, just brainstorming," Jack supplied.

"Don't know, Jack. Sure, the cases have similarities, but there are several differences too. Bible, letter, and the Bible verse, and a dildo shoved up her ... My question is, why didn't the perp follow the same steps? Why did he change it up on the second victim?" Chang asked them.

"Okay. Connections ... the heavy makeup, the same manner of kill, body laid out as if in a casket ... what else?" Lucky ticked off the similarities.

"Well, guys, there are more connections than not." Jack looked at all three of them. "If those lab grunts didn't find our victim's phone and purse, then we can add two more connections, taking the total to five. I don't like where this is heading."

"Were her friends members of the church? Were Al Mathers and his wife members? Is there a connection to the Taylors and the Mathers that way? I mean, how did your victim and Al Mathers meet?" Lucky was trying to put two and two together.

"That's an excellent question, partner." Jack liked the direction Lucky was going.

"Jace," Chang said as he looked over at his partner, "we're going to check the church out further. Thanks, Lucky."

"Where did your victim work, because ours worked for a mom-and-pop ad agency ... could that have connected our dead girls?" Jack was digging.

"No, she managed a smaller retail store over in the Galleria—corporate owned clothing store. One that outfits the larger woman. Worked there eight years. The employees

alibied out as well. They were all upset. They'd worked together for at least four or more years," Chang supplied.

"They find a purse or personal items at the scene?" Jack sat up in thought.

"No. No phone or purse. The purse—her husband said she carried it with her everywhere. It was an expensive Louis Vuitton bag. She paid over two thousand dollars for a dang purse. Can you believe that crap? We have a picture in her file. The husband would like it back if we find it, since he wants to give it to his daughter, their only child." Jace shook his head. Man, he had no idea women paid that much for handbags.

Lucky took his feet off the desk, shifted his weight on his elbows, and then looked over at Jace. "My wife was scrolling through a website. She showed me one of those Louis Vuitton purses, priced at over twenty-seven thousand dollars. Told her when I won the lottery I'd get her one. She laughed and told me, 'Well, I guess I need to love my Michael Kors knock-off. It cost twenty-seven dollars.'" They all busted up.

The phone on Jack's desk rang.

"Jack West. Hey, Mack, what's up?"

Her information had him sitting straight.

"You did; did it match? Holy hell, thanks. Call me with your updates." Jack hung up, and three pairs of eyes were on him.

"Well, what did Mack have?" Lucky sat up, taking his elbows off the desk, ready for some news that would lead them somewhere.

"She found a hair on our victim's clothes. Not human, it's …"

Chang finished the sentence. "It's from a wig, isn't it, Jack?"

"Uh-huh."

Jace said, "Bennie found a synthetic hair on our victim, too."

Jack's brow dipped. "I know. Mack ran a comparison check. Both hairs came from the same wig."

You could have heard a pin drop on the Berber carpet. No one spoke.

"Okay, now that means they are connected. I have no doubts, do you guys?" Chang did a face sweep, looking at each of them.

The other three nodded.

Lucky looked at his watch.

"Jack, it's six. We've been sitting here discussing the cases for hours. I imagine those lab grunts are done, and I'm betting Cheech is gone for the day. I'm also betting those lab workers can't wait to get home and shower. Jumpsuits and respirators wouldn't stop me from showering for two hours." Lucky made a face that showed his abhorrence to digging in heated, smelly Texas trash.

"If they'd found something, Cheech would have called right away. The old saying, 'no news is good news,' ain't working out for us today." Jack pushed himself from his desk.

"11, you ready to book out?" Jace stood.

"You bet, 7. I'm ready to roll."

"Headed home?" Jack stood up to stretch; he'd been sitting too long.

"Nah, think we might tail the husband, see what he's up to. You know, with his clear apathy toward his wife's affair, I'm thinking he might have been having his own, and he's still on our radar. Might be wasted time. I'm thinking he wouldn't have pulled off two murders to cover one, but people are bat-shit crazy these days." Jace pushed his chair in, reached over, and clicked off his computer.

"Wise to keep eyes on him, just in case." Jack reached over and shut his computer off, too.

"We'll be taking a trip over to that church. I think its name is Gates of Heaven. Be doing that tomorrow, see if anyone's there on a Saturday," Chang said as he stood, rolling his chair back to his desk.

"Roger that," Jack said. "Get with us Monday. See if either of us has news to report. Deal?"

"You got it, Jack Rabbit. You guys working tomorrow, huh?" Jace said as a statement, not a real question.

Lucky piped up, "Soon we'll be sleeping in the station's bunkhouse, and man, that's the most uncomfortable bed in the world."

"Tonight, we're going clubbing, hip-hop style, a place where our dead girl hung out. Fun times, you know?" Jack frowned.

"Affirmative. See y'all when we see ya, maybe even tomorrow." Jace waved.

7-11 was out the door and ready to roll. Jack and Lucky hoped 7-11 caught a break. If they did, he knew it would be beneficial to their own case. However, if they caught a break, it would help 7-11. Either way, it worked out for the four of them.

The consensus: the cases connected. The wig hair ... now they had a firm connection. 7-11's case was three months old, and no decent leads had cropped up, and they felt like they were peeing in the wind. Jack and Lucky had been working their case for 13 hours, and as the real-life crime stories say, the first 48 are crucial. They were in the beginning of the crucial stages, and they needed a clue to work with.

They were ready to head to the hip-hop club, The Razz. It was 8:30, and Jack was exhausted, but he knew they had to go tonight. There was no time like the present, and time was a luxury a homicide detective never had.

While he was at the station, he picked up the phone and dialed Gretchen's number.

"Hey there, Cowboy Jack."

He explained he'd caught a murder, and he would not be stopping by The Lone Star tonight to see her and say goodnight in person.

"Jack, stop apologizing. I'll be here when you do have the time, I understand. Keep the city safe, that's first," she admonished him.

"Gretchen, do me a favor. Have one of the barbacks walk you out to your car every night until this is over."

He wanted to explain but the department had to keep a lid on certain information.

"Sure, Cowboy. Uh, should I get my license to carry?" She gave a nervous giggle; he was scaring her.

"No, baby, I want you safe, that's all."

"Alright, Jack, when I leave tonight, I'll ask Bubba to walk me to my car."

That worked for Jack. Bubba was a monster, and anyone who would
mess with him was more than a fool.

11

THE NEON SIGN SAID: *No Cover Before 9:00 on Friday* and *Happy Hour with Half-Price Drinks until 10:00.* The parking lot was filling up, and there was a line at the door. Business was booming for The Club Razz.

Lucky drove into the lot, getting as close to the front door as possible. "Place looks like it's waking up, huh?"

A valet walked over to his car. "You dudes wanna valet, you gotta pay, and I should be driving your wheels, man, not you."

His arms were tatted-up, at least the parts you could see. He had a nose ring, and his dark black hair spiked up in a Mohawk. He wore baggy jeans that Lucky figured would fall off if he ran, and a red valet vest that touted the club's name over the top left side: *The Razz*, in black lettering.

Dawson Luck rolled his window halfway down and stuck his badge up for the young valet punk. "Nope, don't need a valet. Here's my ticket."

The young man held up his hands to stave him off. "Man, don't want trouble from Five-O, we're cool, man. Park wherever you want."

"Just what I planned to do," Lucky said, rolling the window up.

They walked past the front of the line to the entrance. Two big goons flanked either side of the two doors, one to enter and one to exit. A door attendant checked IDs beside the entrance.

"You guys are jumping the line. We don't like line jumpers," one goon said, crossing his robust arms, pulling himself up to his full height of six feet, and sticking his muscled pecs out to intimidate them.

The look on Dawson Luck's face was not pretty; he was tired and getting pissed.

Jack tried not to laugh. He knew his partner, and Lucky was not in a pleasant mood.

"Here's my ticket in, and my freaking ID." He held up his badge for the second time in less than three minutes. "Now, move aside, Douche Muscles," Lucky said with authority.

"Hey, ain't no prob, everything is everything, word up," said the big bouncer.

"You speak English, right?" Lucky clipped his badge back to his belt, then looked up.

A sneer wrinkled his lips. "Yeah, I do."

"Good," Lucky said. "Then tell me what you said to me, and not in gangsta slang this time."

"Man, all I said was that we have no problem. Everything's good, and I understand ya."

"Glad we got that cleared up. Now, open the door and let me and my partner in."

The big man pushed the door open and allowed Jack and Lucky to enter the club. Without even looking back, Dawson Luck said, "You can shoot me the finger all you want. Ain't gonna hurt my feelings one bit."

Jack did not turn around either, but he heard the other man at the door let out a laugh. Lucky had nailed it.

The place was enormous. Two main bars, one on either side, and some smaller bars in the back that flanked either side of the railing of the dance floor. Strobe lights flashed, and hip-hop music blared. Drinkers crowded the bars and dancers ground across the floor to what Jack thought was not music at all.

"Friday night, buddy, they might pack the place pretty quick," Lucky said as he dodged a gaggle of girls giving him the once-over.

"Old farts coming to the club, huh, must want some young pussy," the shorter white girl flipped her blonde hair at Lucky.

"No, Sheresa," her friend, a tall Black woman, said with a smart-ass tone, "they be Five-O, honey. They here working, I bet. Ain't that right, Off-ass-sirs?" She snickered, overemphasizing "ass."

"Well, Sheresa," Lucky popped back, her name said with faux sweetness laced with real disgust, "better watch—we don't get Vice to work your corner."

Her mouth dropped open, but before she could remark, they'd walked off.

"Lucky, you're on a roll, but don't roll too hard. Don't want my butt kicked by ten goons in the parking lot."

They had guns. Lucky patted his left side, happy to have Greta his Glock and a small backup strapped to his ankle, a Kimber .38 revolver.

They went to the bar on their right and signaled for a bartender's attention.

"You got a bartender named Barry working tonight?" Jack laid his badge on the bar for him to see.

The bartender pointed across to the bar on the other side. "He's working on that side, far left end. The guy with bleach-blond hair, he has a tat of a shark on his right forearm."

"Thanks, bud." Jack picked up his badge and clipped it back onto his belt.

Barry wasn't hard to find and on the spot, knew they weren't regular bar-hoppers. Both were wearing jackets and neither slouched.

"So, Five-O, huh? You looking for a mass murderer or in here for a drink before you hit your crib?"

"You Barry, right?"

"Yup, that's me."

"Go to the end of the bar. We want to talk to you." Lucky pointed and Barry strolled with no purpose.

"Awe, man, I ain't done nuttin' wrong, I swear."

"What's your last name, Barry?" Lucky flipped his notebook open.

"Picco. So, you gonna tell me what's the skinny, or you here to just shoot the crapola with me, or does Five-O just wanna try to rattle my cage?"

"You know this girl?" Jack held up the photo he had taken of Jade at the murder scene.

"Holy Mother of God. Fuck, that's Jade, she dead, man?"

"Does it look like a dead person to you, or do you think we're in here about a fake murder?" Jack put his phone back in his pocket.

"Sorry, I ain't never seen no dead person, at least nobody I know. Man, I don't do funerals, ever. Dude, that chick used to hit The Razz most every night. Who popped her, man?"

"We're still trying to find the guy. How well did you know Jade? Did you and her date? Were you friends?"

"Nah, we didn't date. I tried, man, she doesn't dig my type, ya know, bro."

Lucky stepped closer. "What type is that? Mean to women, you smack 'em around, treat 'em bad?" Lucky was trying to provoke him, but the boy didn't flinch. This young wannabe gangster was getting Lucky's ire up and butchering the English language.

Barry Picco scowled. "No, Dick-tective, I'm bi ... my door swings both ways. She wouldn't date me 'cause of that fool reason."

He stepped back and folded his arms, daring one of them to make a smart-ass remark. They disappointed Barry.

"How well did you know her? Who did she hang with here at the club?" Jack resumed the questioning and gave Lucky a "stand down" look. He complied, leaving the questioning in Jack's court.

Barry told them what he knew, and Lucky took notes while Jack talked.

"You know this older man's name?"

This older man thing had come up twice. The gray pubic hairs found on the body had Mack thinking it was an older man, and Jade's coworker Fran had joked that she was seeing an older man who was ugly or married.

"Nah, she be calling him Baby most of the time. But hey, one time you know, I think I heard her, dude, call him Rafael, or some stupid-ass name like that."

"Can you describe this man?"

"White dude, bout, oh, medium height, not as tall as me, maybe five-ten, not short like yo' partner," he smarted off. Dawson Luck never even looked up from his notebook, disappointing Barry.

Barry cleared his throat, then looked back at Jack and continued.

"He got darker hair, but it was kinda getting gray, with, you know, some white hairs, man, like an old fart. You know, you old guys all look alike to me."

"When was he in here last?"

"Lemme see, I think that would have been last night. He got pissed 'cause, well, Jade didn't show up. I know why now," he said and smirked. "He'd meet up with her on Wednesday or Thursday night."

"Those the only days he came to the club?"

"Nah, dude, he'd show up on Friday, or maybe even Saturday. The dude was all into Jade and she was into him."

"Would they leave the club together?"

The picture Jack got was clear: Jade was seeing a married man, and his gut told him that might have been the reason for her murder. Could it have been the man's wife? On top of that, how did that connect to 7-11's case? In the words of Barry Picco, *"Dude, man, this is frustrating,"* ran through Jack's head.

Barry's voice rose. "No, man, they fucked right here at my bar, or maybe the men's room, but they were fucking—that was for sure. The old dude was all over her hands and lips when they sat here at this damn end of the bar. Shit, dude, yeah, they left together."

Man, he thought these cops acted cracked. Didn't they know a goddamn thing?

"Okay, Barry, untwist your shorts and settle down, and lower your voice," Jack warned him.

"Did the man use a credit card when he paid his tab?" Jack felt like he was getting nowhere with this wannabe gangster.

"He was a cash kinda dude." Barry laughed. "Prolly got an old lady at home. Didn't want her to see the credit card bill since he was, you know, dipping his stick in some other woman's well." His laugh was bawdy, his mind in the gutter—all the time.

"Is there anything else you can tell us?"

Barry shook his head, then said, "Wait a sec, there was this chick one night, musta' been three, maybe four weeks ... no, maybe it was ..."

"Barry, the woman?" Jack disrupted Barry's indecisiveness of the time-line. They'd work out the "when" in a minute if needed.

"I was working the other end of the bar and she took the last seat, you know, at the end over there." He thumbed back to the opposite end of the bar. "The place, man, was swinging and that night, crowdeder than shit. Oh, I 'member it was Saturday four weeks ago, 'cause I was off for the last two Saturdays, man, I had to go to ..."

Jack cut him off. "Barry, back to the story."

"Oh, right. Uh, well, she looked sad—an older chick, I guess in her late thirties, not a bad-looking momma, but sad. I talked wit'd her, asked her why she was all sad and weepy-looking. It was a club. She should be rocking out. She said she wanna ta, you know, look like her."

"Wanted to look like who, Barry?" Jack was losing patience with this idiot who'd rolled one too many joints in his young life.

"Jade, man, ain't that who we been talking 'bout?" He rolled his eyes at Jack.

"What did she say, this older woman?" Jack ignored the eye roll.

"She said she thought Jade was a hot-looking momma or sumtin stupid like that, and that she's lucky to have a handsome man with her. She said she wished for a man like that, and then she started crying. And for real, dude, I can't do crying chicks. I might be bi, but I don't dig older men either. Told the chick I had to work and hoped she was happy one day. Then I swapped ends and traded places with the other bartender."

Jack crossed his fingers. "Barry, if we got you with a sketch artist, you think you could describe this older man?"

"Nope, all the old men I see look alike—saggy jaws, losing their hair—so, nah, don't think I'd do ya solid on that. Sorry, dude. We done now, Five-O, 'cause, man, I gotta get to work."

"Yes, Barry, we're done for now." Jack handed him a card. "Call me if you get anything that might be important. Oh, and this the older man—when was he in here last?"

"Last night. They'd meet up at nine-forty-five most times, but last night the old dude showed up early. He got here at nine-thirty, I think. He stayed until ten-fifteen and booked out, pissed as a wet hen."

"Why? What makes you think he was mad?"

"Cuz he was all like, 'That trampy cunt is blowing me off, she ain't even returning my texts or my calls.' I guess he needed some of her sweet puss ..."

Jack cut him off. "We get the idea, Barry, thanks."

"What a dipshit. Now what, Jack?"

"Let's start with the door personnel. Maybe they remember him or her."

12

AT THE COUNTER, TWO young women collected the cover charge. Jack stepped in, pushing out three younger girls who stood waiting to pay.

"Hey, mister, we were here first," the girl in front squawked.

Jack turned, moved his jacket a smidge, and tapped his badge. "I have priority, ladies." He winked at them.

None of them said a word as all three stepped back, giving Jack room at the counter.

"Is your manager here?"

"No, sir, but the assistant manager is."

"Find him and get him up here, and do it in a hurry," Jack said. "Don't want a riot to break out, now do we?"

"No, sir, we don't."

She got back in less than two minutes. Jack thanked her and walked the assistant manager across the room, out of the line of customers.

"Shelly says you fellas are cops. What's going on?"

"I'm Detective West, and this is my partner, Dawson Luck. Is there a quieter place we can talk, Mr....?"

"Styman. Kevin Styman. And yes, there's an office back this way, up-stairs."

Kevin Styman led them behind the far right bar and up a back staircase to the club offices. It was quieter here—no blaring rap-crap-hip-hop music. Dawson Luck was thrilled. No punks for a minute, and no loud, shitty music.

"Have you ever seen this girl?" Jack showed him the picture.

"Oh, my... she's... dead?" Kevin Styman took a step back.

"Yes, sir. Do you know her?"

"No, not personally. I mean, I've seen her in the club, but I don't get involved unless I have to. She wasn't a troublemaker."

"I saw your club has cameras. Do you have the tapes from the last few days? We'll need to see them."

Kevin gave a nervous laugh. "Uh, no, no tapes. We have cameras that are live feed, real-time. I know we should have cameras that record, especially with the sorts we get in here, but the owner is cheap and he's not up with the times."

"Shit! Now ain't that goddamn perfect." Lucky paced back and forth.

"The girls at the counter—are they there all night?" Jack ignored Lucky's outburst.

"Shelly is. She covers the door until one-thirty, then the bouncers take over. This crowd is rowdy when they come in, rowdy while they're here, and pretty much disorderly when they're shoved out the door."

"Mr. Styman, can you call Shelly up here? You use walkies, right?"

Kevin turned and grabbed the walkie-talkie off the desk.

"Buff-man, you copy?"

"Yo. Kev, dude, whatcha need?"

"Send Shelly up to the back offices now."

"Sure, man, can do. She getting axed?"

"Just send her up." Kevin shook his head. "No brains, but muscles—he'll be a lifelong bouncer ... if he lives that long."

Jack and Lucky knew what he meant. Gangs liked big men like Douche Muscles. They were recruited by gangs to serve as enforcers, with a high mortality rate before the age of twenty-five. A sad, scary way of life.

Shelly walked in. "Mr. Styman, you need me?"

"Shelly, these detectives want to ask you some questions."

Kevin pulled a chair up for her; she looked nervous.

"Shelly, I'm Detective West, and this is my partner, Detective Luck. Can you tell us your last name?"

Her lips trembled. "C-c-c-Cooper... Shelly Cooper."

She was terrified. He assured her everything was fine and she was in no trouble, but they needed her help.

"Y-y-yes. Uh, I'll help if I can."

"Now, Shelly, I don't want to scare you, but I'm going to show you a picture. It won't be pleasant." Jack pulled an empty chair across from hers and showed her the photo he felt safe sharing.

"Have you seen this girl, Shelly, here in the club?"

"Oh!" Her hand flew to her mouth. "S-s-she's dead? Oh, Lord."

Jack clicked off the picture. "Shelly, do you know her?"

"Uh, I've seen her here. I took her cover charge sometimes, but I don't generally come in until ten-thirty. Only covering for someone tonight. Most nights, I work the door and counter with the attendants, do the stamp for re-entry, and coordinate with the valet and the cabs for the drunks." She rattled off her duties—panicked. "Sorry, when I get upset, I rattle on."

"No need to apologize. Now, have you seen her leave with an older man, five-foot-ten, graying hair?"

"A few times. They are, I mean, were cute together. I know he's much older, but they looked happy, and the way they looked at each other... it's sad. I'll bet he'll be heartbroken."

Lucky pulled a chair closer. "Shelly, do you know his name?"

She shook her head. "Her... I think her name is Jade, right?"

"Yes, Jade Nelson."

"I heard her call him Babe or Baby. Never a name."

"What times would they leave the club, do you recall?" Lucky wrote in his notebook.

"Close to eleven, I think."

"Could you give our sketch artist a description of this man?" Jack asked, hopeful.

"Maybe... I've never done that before." Her eyes grew wide.

"You call me, and I'll set it up. Our forensic artist is cool. You'll like her."

"Nice girl, Kevin," Jack said as he stood and pushed the chair back.

"Yes, she is. I have around six 'nice' people who work at the club, and it's a shame that's all I have."

Jack thanked him, and he and Lucky headed down the stairs to leave.

"I wonder if the bouncers can tell us anything?" Jack asked in passing.

"If they could, they're not likely to share with us since we're the enemy," Luck remarked.

Walking out the front doors, they passed a line of people waiting and cars lined up for the valet. Jack looked at the door attendant.

"Good to see you're checking IDs."

"Straight-up, Five-O. I don't let kids in here. Word." His two gold teeth reflected the lights above him. Jack saluted and followed Lucky to his car.

In the car, Jack cracked up.

"Okay, Jack-in-the-beanstalk, what's so freaking funny?"

"You, Lucky. You are. I thought I had a problem profiling punks, but you take the cake tonight, man—or should I say, dude?"

"Whatever. That bartender is a wannabe gangster, but he's far from real gangster material—more California surfer if you ask me, dude," he said with a snarky tone. "First, it was the punk valet, then the goon at the door... I don't know, Jack, they all rankled me. Glad you kept a cool head tonight. Must be harder for you to talk to punks like that, you know?"

Yes, Jack knew. Punks like that were constant reminders of his brother's drive-by killing.

"Time to call it a night. We can start fresh early in the morning."

Lucky voted for that in a heartbeat.

"I know how tired I am. Jet lag and all that crap. You gotta be all in, Jack. Go home, have a couple of beers, then hit the sheets. See you at seven."

"Yep, I have a sneaky feeling it's gonna be a long day."

Lucky dropped Jack off at the station garage to get his truck. Jack considered heading to the Lone Star to see Gretchen—but decided not to. He would stay too long, and he needed sleep no matter how much he would have loved to give her a goodnight kiss. He would call her in the morning.

A full night's sleep was on his agenda. He needed to be on his A-plus game. Houston might have a serial killer, and Jack West wanted to find the scum before someone else died.

13

"G'MORNING." LUCKY SWIVELED HIS chair at the sound of the opening door.

Jack walked to his desk, set his coffee mug down, took a seat, and what sounded like a bear growl rumbled somewhere inside his closed mouth.

"Man, what time did you get here, Lucky? Sunup?"

It was 6:55 am, and Lucky had been here a while. There were four medium-sized Styrofoam coffee cups sitting on his desk, and all four were empty.

"Five. Couldn't sleep and was keeping Vivian awake. She told me to get the 'F' out of the bed because she needed to sleep. I figured I'd get a jump on our reports."

"Cool." Jack yawned. "We need to figure out the next step, 'cuz right now we have negative zero to go on."

"Did you read the *Chronicle* today?"

"Nope. Do I need to?"

"Nah. Tessa Coy did what you asked her to do and downplayed it. If gangs and drugs are downplaying it, Tessa didn't say it was one or the other. She said HPD had no clues as to the motive. The fact is, she's right, 'cuz we damn well don't."

"No, we don't, and that's the big problem. Since you got here early, what have you been doing?" Jack needed espresso ... his first cup of coffee was wearing off.

"I called Hank Avera. He's not a morning person."

"Me either, and I would've come up here and punched you in the nose for calling me on a Saturday if I hadn't pulled a work shift and gotten to sleep in, and you woke me up at five freaking a.m."

"Whatever," Luck said, blowing that off. "I wanted to know who'd canvassed the apartment complex for the tenants we couldn't locate. I caught a break, 'cuz Hank said he and Gator came back and did."

"You have my attention."

"He said one neighbor sort of knew Miss Nelson. She lives in the apartment next to Jade's. Since our victim's unit was on the corner, she had one upstairs neighbor and one next-door. The upstairs neighbor works the night shift at George Bush; he's a baggage handler." Lucky picked up his notebook. "Hank said he was none too happy to get woken up since he worked last night. Poetic justice, I guess—me calling and waking Hank up, huh?" Lucky busted up.

"You're a dick, Lucky, you know that? So, this guy—tell me the 4-1-1."

"Yep, like the girl in the club said, 'Dick'-tective." He cracked himself up.

Dawson Luck got over his comedic self and continued. "The guy's name is Ron Baer. I called the airlines, checked to see if he was at work during our murder window, and he has a solid alibi."

"Why did he need an alibi?" A second yawn escaped Jack's mouth, and he shook his head, trying to get his brain going. "Did he have a relationship—friend or otherwise—with Jade?"

"No, but Hank ran a check on the guy. He had some priors. Let's see. A bar fight—charged with assault but not jailed, no fine imposed since it was his first offense. That was ten years ago. Five years ago, he was accused of stalking one of the flight attendants. The report said she left the company and the stalking stopped. He only liked her, I guess, but she did file a police report. With the history of Jade's now ex-boyfriend and her report of his stalking, I will check it out. The guy, Ron Baer, is clean other than that."

"Yup, I'd have done the same thing."

"There's more. The woman next door came home. She'd been visiting her daughter for the past week and was pretty shaken up over the news. I feel sorry for that couple that manages the place, because this woman and two other families told Hank they were gonna clear out of there. Well, on second thought, nah—I don't feel sorry for 'em. I think they're both assholes."

"Dawson. What did the next-door neighbor say? Jesus, man, I feel like I'm talking to Barry Picco, the pothead doofus."

He shot Jack the bird. "You need a straw to get more caffeine in ya, pard, 'cuz you need to wake up and get happier... I gotta be with you all day. Don't want a Jack-ass," Lucky snorted.

Jack thought Lucky should cut back on the caffeine. It was far too early in the day to exchange insults with such a wound-up individual.

"Sure, man, whatever. Who's this neighbor? What'd she say?"

"Millie Tidwell, retired, sixty-nine years old. She said Jade Nelson did have a boyfriend. Older man, in his late thirties to mid-forties. The woman said she wasn't too good at guessing ages, said her eyesight ain't what it used to be, but knows he had some salt-and-pepper hair. She thought he was tall, but she's five feet tall, so everyone is tall to her. She's seen him on several occasions, late at night. Him and Jade had regular date nights, she told Hank."

"Well, it corroborates what the punk bartender Picco said. They would meet on Wednesday night and Thursday night, leave the club, and I guess come back to her place. Her place was crappy. Was the guy too cheap to spring for a motel on an hourly rate?" Jack sat up and took a drink of coffee. "What else?"

"Mrs. Tidwell said he'd come and pick her up on Saturday nights. He'd get here and go in, and two hours later they'd leave. I guess they did some, um, 'chicka-bowow' first. Mrs. Tidwell never saw them come back—said she goes to bed early on Saturdays."

"How does she know all this? She one of those kinds that sits by the window spying on her neighbors, taking notes? Jesus, we might use her on the force, ya know." Jack liked this lady.

"No, she's not a voyeur. She's a smoker and doesn't smoke inside. The lady keeps a lawn chair folded up by her door and told Hank she takes smoke breaks. I guess her urge to smoke might've helped us a smidgeon with the case."

"Well, did she have a name for the old guy, 'cuz she hasn't given news that gets us anywhere." Jack's annoyance grew.

"Well, she saw his car. We didn't have that, did we?"

"She get a plate number?"

"She didn't write it down—didn't think she'd ever need it."

Jack was ready to make a snotty remark, but Lucky held up a finger.

"Let me finish. It's a silver car. She thinks it's an Acura or Honda. She said it's a newer car. She remembered a couple of numbers—that's it."

"In order or random? You do know how many license plate combinations there are, right?"

"Yeah, that's what sucks. She said the first letter was M, the first letter of her name, and the last two numbers were six and eight. Said she remembered that 'cuz her birthday is June the eighth."

"Well, glad her name starts with M and her birthday is 6/8. That's better than zilch, I guess. Let's see what we can make happen."

He thought for a minute and came up with an idea. "Tell you what, Lucky—see if you can come up with a list of new Hondas and Nissan Acuras, silver, purchased, say, in the last two years in Houston. I know it's a long shot."

"What are you going to do, Jack? Watch me work?"

"Well, partner, even though the club didn't have active taping cameras, Houston does. I'm going to be scrubbing traffic camera footage by the club and in the area where Jade lived, and I'm hoping to find a silver car with M and the number sixty-eight on the plate."

"I've narrowed it down to five hundred."

Jack's eyes focused on traffic cam footage. "Cars?"

"No. Three thousand Acuras and over five thousand Hondas, over a two-year period, give or take a month." Lucky stood to work the kinks out. "My neck is killing me, and I'm hungry."

Jack hit the pause button. "Me too. Want a steak or a burger?"

"A burger sounds good."

"Let's go to Rodeo Goat off Dallas Street. They have tasty burgers, their atmosphere's nice, and it's reasonable."

"Yep, sounds good to me." Lucky grabbed his jacket off the back of his chair. "I like their burgers and the chili cheese fries."

Stomach's fueled and back at the station, it was 1:45. Jack resumed scrubbing street-cam tapes while Lucky searched for Acuras and Hondas.

"Hey, Luck. Call Cheech on his cell. He hasn't called, but we need to see if his grunts found a phone, murder weapon, or a purse."

"Yeah, if he did, be nice to have her phone."

It was a disappointing phone call. The lab grunts Cheech sent out had not found a damn thing.

"Cheech said all they found was putrid trash—and multiply that by a thousand. There was nil... no purse, no phone, and no weapon. Not a friggin' metal fork. Nada."

"You know what that makes me think?"

Lucky had no time to respond. Jack was talking once more.

"It makes me think the killer might be taking trophies—you know, purses and cells."

"Maybe. Or he's disposing of them and we'll never find them. Hey, did you get Tech to see if we could ping her phone? We haven't done that yet." Lucky jotted down a note.

"Monday, first thing, we'll call for tower records. Then pull her phone records—see whom she'd been talking to right before her murder. Maybe it was our elusive older man."

"Hey, didn't that gangsta bartender say this older man said he'd been texting and calling her and she wasn't replying?"

"As a matter of fact, he did. Call her stepfather, Jorge, and see if he knew what cell phone service Jade used. We get her records. Maybe we can find this older man."

14

LUCKY GOT ON THE phone with Jorge Esparza and then hung up two minutes later.

"She had Metro PCS phone service, and the mother has a favor."

Jack looked up from the street cams he was scrubbing. "What favor, other than catching her daughter's killer?"

"She said Jade had a ring she wore. It was her grandmother's, a ruby encircled with small diamonds, set in a wide gold band. There's an inscription on the inside of the band that says, 'To Gloria' ... that's her grandmother ... 'from Raul' ... that's her grandfather ... 'with love.' Jack, I don't recall seeing a ring on either of her hands. Do you?"

"Bet it's another trophy for the sick bastard."

———— ✐ ————

BY 5:00, JACK'S EYES were tired from searching street cams; he sat back and rubbed them. Lucky had no luck with the car search. They were still at square one. Since it was Saturday, the companies that held the cell tower reports wouldn't reopen until Monday. Shift officers came and left, and no one else was in the Homicide squad room.

"Jack, we've been hard at it since seven a.m. Well, me since five."

"I know, pard, but we need to keep digging, since we have no freaking leads."

Jack was more than frustrated. They were searching for an unknown older man. His gut told him this older man wasn't their killer, but he needed a person of interest, and right now, he was the person he was interested in finding.

"Hey, fellas, been here all day?" Jace boomed out as he opened the door to the squad room.

"Severson, man, why the F are you talking so loud?" Jack's head was pounding.

"Sorry, Jack. Checking to see if you and Dawson are awake."

"Where's 11? He with you?" Lucky looked back over his shoulder.

"Chang's in the break room making a pot of coffee."

"Which case you two working today, pop-n-drop or real estate murder?" Jack got up to stretch his legs and his back.

"Tornado Rick is doing a perp search, has his people on the street looking for the fucker. Not much more we can do. Don't have to dig—we know who did it. Now we need to find him, then lock him up."

Dawson Luck slouched in his seat. "Working the real estate murder then, huh?"

Chang walked in with a plastic lunch tray balanced on his right hand as he opened the door.

"Who wants some joe?"

Jack and Lucky both raised their hands, while Jace Severson raised a Diet Coke he got from the vending machine downstairs.

Chang handed out the coffee and sat down.

"Jace tell you guys we went over to the church?"

"Nah, I hadn't got to that, 11, but go ahead. Tell them yourself."

"Okay—we went to the church, Gates of Heaven, and met the pastor." Jace took up the story when Chang stopped to take a drink of coffee.

"It's a nondenominational church, eleven hundred members. We got a list from the wannabe TV evangelist, Pastor Davenport. Harold Davenport—big man, stays in shape for an older fart. Major 'Bible thumper,' with nice hair plugs. Makes him look younger for TV." Jace blew a snort.

"Chang," Jack said, "can you check to see if Jade went to that church, on an off chance?"

Chang picked up a file he had on the tray with the coffee and pulled out several sheets of paper stapled together.

"I have a copy of the church membership list. This is alphabetical. What's her last name?"

"Nelson."

Chang flipped to the middle pages and ran his finger through the Ns.

"No, she's not listed. Maybe she went to a different church."

"I bet she did," Lucky said. "The Church of Hip-hop."

"Are you canvassing the members later?"

"That's the plan, Jack," Jace said.

"Pick it back up tomorrow. Let 'em go to church and eat lunch, then catch 'em before they get their Sunday nap in." Chang laughed.

West and Luck thought it was an outstanding plan and hoped someone knew something. If someone talked and had worthwhile information, both cases might move forward. Jack was hopeful.

"Did you guys go to your victim's funeral?" Jack sat back and closed his eyes.

"Yeah, as a matter of fact, we did," Jace supplied.

Sometimes, when a murderer wanted to brag incognito, or relive the kill, they would show up at the funeral, hanging in the background.

"It all looked normal; no extreme oddities stood out. The funeral was at the Gates of Heaven Church. There was a large crowd at her service too—church members and coworkers. Then, of course, the family. They were on the first three pews. Sad service." Chang shook his head.

"Aren't they all sad, Chang?" Lucky crossed his arms and rocked his chair back.

"No. I mean, a man or a woman who gets to live a long life and dies at a ripe old age ... at least they had a life and lived it. Know what I mean?" Chang looked at the three of them.

Well, no one could agree with that more than homicide detectives could. They'd seen death for those who never had the chance to grow old, repeatedly ... infinitely.

It was another long day and late Sunday afternoon. Jack's phone jangled, and he snatched it up.

"Jack-Sprat, are you at home?"

"Nah, Lucky and I are at the station. Why?"

"Good. 7 and I will be there in twenty."

"You got something?"

"No. Well, maybe. See you in twenty." Xi Chang hung up.

"Was that 7 or 11?"

"11. Him and 7 will be up here in twenty."

Lucky looked at his watch. It was 4:00 o'clock. They'd been searching traffic cams and cars since 9:00 am.

"Might as well keep looking and wait for them to get here, since we're not leaving now," Luck stated his tone flat.

"Okay, I've gone through four weeks of traffic cams near her apartments and not once have I seen a freaking silver Honda or silver Acura."

"Are you kidding? None?" Lucky found that hard to believe.

"Well, no, I've seen a few, but they were older cars, and the ones I could make the plate numbers out weren't even close to what we're looking for. You got the car registry narrowed down yet?"

"No, I'm down to the last few thousand, and I'm inclined to believe the asshole doesn't have it registered in Harris County. Oh yeah, I checked out her ex-boyfriend in Yuma, Arizona, to see if he'd flown to Houston in the past month. Called the TSA agents at both George Bush and Hobby. He hasn't flown to Houston in over a year—we can cross him off our list."

"One down," Jack said.

It had been fifty-four hours since they'd begun the investigation; the first forty-eight had slipped into oblivion. There were no real leads, and now he felt like 7-11 did, and he and Lucky were peeing in the wind.

Thirty minutes later, the crime duo, 7-11, walked into the squad room.

"We come bearing gifts," Jace said, holding four venti cups of coffee.

"Jace, just what we needed. Is it Columbian, extra strong?" Lucky took a cup.

"That's the only kind there is." Jace handed Jack a cup.

"Lucky, that reminds me, I gotta get three dozen Krispy Kremes for Cheech's guys and bring 'em on Monday."

"You certainly do, Jack, since I got Starbucks gift cards for all the guys who had to go dumpster-diving in the heat of the day."

"Lucky, you're a cheap bastard," Jace said and laughed. "What made you get them all a ten-dollar gift card?"

"For your information, Jace, if they hadn't dug in the putrid dumpsters, Jack and I might've had to. And asswipe, I got 'em each a twenty-dollar gift card, with a freaking cardholder to boot."

All four of them broke out in laughter. All of it said in fun, and they needed the tension release, as it was healthy for a detective's soul.

"Hey, girls, if we're all done fiddle-farting, Chang, what did y'all come up with on the church membership list?" Jack went back to business.

"We got zip last night. Oh, and we sat on the husband for a few hours. The man never left the house, and no one came over either. We gave it up and started going through the list of church members. Man, I gotta tell you that for church people, most of 'em are liars. More than a third of them gave fake phone numbers and addresses," Chang updated them. "I figured out why," ... he snickered ... "that way no one from the church, including the brimstone-and-fire preacher, could give them a surprise visit and see how they truly lived."

"True that. So true." Jace cracked up with his partner. "The ones we did find, we talked to, and they all had alibis we'll be checking out, or they weren't acquainted with the victim or the husband."

"Well, that's crap," Lucky said as he rested back and rocked his chair.

"Hold your darn horses and give me a minute, Lucky. There's more."

"More works, Jace. Keep going, man."

"Now, the victim and her husband's name are on the church membership list, but no one's updated the list in a year," Jace said.

Of course, Chang hopped right in and took over. "We caught a break. A person we found today put their real address on the membership card, and she was a big help. A widow, been going to that church for over six years, and she knows everyone." Chang stopped to take a drink of his coffee, and Jace jumped in to finish.

"She was marking people off left and right that were no longer associated with the Gates of Heaven Church. So, we had her go through the entire membership list, and God bless her, she saved me and 11 here hours of useless work."

"God bless the woman's memory, too. She told us that Lincoln and Corrine Taylor joined the church last year—she even gave us the date they joined," Chang said.

"How did she remember that?" Jack asked.

"She heads up the welcoming committee for all new members." Jace cracked up.

Chang slapped his knee. "And by George, she keeps her own membership list that is updated. She let us compare it to our list, and we got numbers and names we didn't have before."

"We need to hire this woman, or send her a thank-you card," Jace proposed with oomph.

"I'll mail her a Krispy Kreme," Jack said, and they all broke up.

"Ah, that's how Al Mathers met the victim, but I don't think he's the man we're looking at for this. Do you?" Jack looked from Xi to Jace.

"No," Jace said. "We can cross him off. He has a solid alibi. If his wife did know he was having an affair, we can't rule her out."

"It's like I told you guys the other day." Chang looked at them. "She was trying to convince herself more than me that her husband would never cheat."

"Would she have killed Jade, and if so, what's her motive?" Jack brought up, throwing a wrench in the mix.

"Now that's a head-scratcher. We met the woman. Demure and seemed like a nice woman, but naïve," Chang responded.

"Hell, boys, Jeffrey Dahmer's neighbors said he was a clean-cut, nice young man, very unassuming. Look how that all turned out."

Jace nodded. "You're right, Jack. No one ever knows a person, deep down."

"Never underestimate anyone. My last partner, Frank Windom, told me to look for the 'sleeper' ... the one who's in the shadows, the one who's there but not there. Until now, I've worked on getting justice for one victim. Since we now have two victims and one killer, what we need to figure out is why he's killing. For fun or revenge—what's the key? We have a key ring with a million useless keys. All we need is to find that one key that unlocks this psycho's door, and then we go in guns blazing."

He paused—all eyes on him. He felt like Hamlet, giving his personal soliloquy of the crime.

To be or not to be, that is the question.

15

BY LATE MORNING ON Monday, their church list search yielded nothing. It was time-consuming and aggravating.

"Hey, 7, Rick called while you were in the break room."

"Did Vice find our meth guy, Xi?"

"Yeah, they did. They have eyes on him right now. He's over on Wayside Drive, Fifth Ward. They spotted him at Union Pacific Rail Yard. Rick said our perp and his boys hang out in that area. He said it should be an easy takedown if we can get the jump on them. Only one way in and one way out of the old railcar they use as a hideout. Rick said Vice has some of their people doing work in the area since there was a suspected crack house being set up near the rail yard. We had a BOLO on the punk, and we got lucky."

"Y'all get the arrest warrant?" Jack despised these punks.

"Shit, we got the warrant on day two. We knew who it was, but not where he was. Jace, you ready to roll?"

"You bet your sweet ass I am."

"Go in with Kevlar," Jack advised.

"You're damn skippy. In that neighborhood, I'd wear Kevlar pants if they made 'em," Jace said.

"You guys need backup? Lucky and I can tag along," Jack offered.

"Nah. Got Rick's guys, and we'll call in some patrol units for backup in case it goes sideways. You know them jerk-offs carry guns," Chang said, heading out with Jace on his heels.

"Work safe and get back as soon as possible. We need to do some more brainstorming on the other two cases."

"Yeppers. We'll try to work fast." Jace saluted as the door closed to the squad room.

"Don't envy them," Lucky said. "The Fifth Ward has one of the highest crime wards in Houston, and it should be called Gang Ward."

"Me neither." Jack's cell phone rang. "West. Yeah? Perfect. See you in an hour." He clicked off. "That was the girl from the club, Shelly Cooper. She's on her way in."

Jack looked through his telephone directory, then dialed.

"Hey, Becca, how are you?"

"Jack West, is that you? You rascal. How are you? How's that trouble-maker Lucky?"

"I'm not bad, Becca, and Lucky—well, he's the same, causing trouble daily."

Lucky shook his head, but grinned.

"Hey, if you're calling me, I guess you need a picture, huh?"

Becca Brenner, known to most as BB, was one of the top forensic artists in the State of Texas. As a matter of fact, she was one out of three rated at the top in the USA. She'd made worldwide acclaim in her field, helping solve over nine hundred criminal cases—from aggravated assault, attempted murder, murder, rape, and aggravated rape. Jack, for one, respected her craft and hoped that Shelly's description would yield them the man Jade had been seeing.

"Hey, BB, I know it's kinda late in the afternoon, but we need to find a guy. I have a young woman who's seen him multiple times at the club where she works, and she'll be here in an hour. Can you come down here to the station? If not, I can reschedule her."

"Jack, I'll be there in forty. Same room?"

"Yep, and I'll bring her to you when she gets here. See you soon." Jack hung up.

"Becca is a fantastic artist, Jack. Hope Shelly's got a decent memory. The girl sees a ton of people, five nights a week, you know?" Lucky wondered if her recall would help them.

"Well, at that club, most of the men are twenty-one to thirty, and I know for a fact that some are even underage, no matter what that gold-tooth door goon ID checker says. I'm relying on her remembering the old dude. If she has just enough recall to create a favorable likeness of him, Becca can work with that. No worries there. Soon as that happens, we'll get a copy of the sketch out to all the patrol units and put out a BOLO. When we track him down, he could be the breakthrough we've been waiting for."

"Jack, we need a break—a coffee break. You want a cup?"

"I'd love a cup. Thanks, Lucky."

Chief Yao and Lucky passed in the hallway.

"Detective Luck."

"Hey, Chief. Going for some joe. You want a cup?"

"No, thanks. Headed to the twenty-first floor. Have an administrative meeting. Wanted to stop by and get an update on the cases. Jack in the squad room?"

"Yeah, he's got his nose to the grindstone."

Jack updated the chief. He had Shelly Cooper set up with a date with the forensic sketch artist in an hour. He hoped this was a positive break in the case.

"Where are Jace and Xi today?"

"They're headed to pick up their shooter—the one who popped that clerk at the Exxon station on Eastex Freeway. Vice has eyes on him. His street name is Red Rockets—real name Reginald Tobin. Meth-head."

"Let me know how the sketch turns out. Want to keep the COP informed."

"Will do," said Jack. "Tell Chief Pratt hey for me. See ya later."

Yao did an eye roll. "Yep. I'm off to see the wizard. Headed to Oz now."

Jack smiled. The twenty-first floor was HPD Administration, and the wizard—the Chief of Police, Darren Pratt—was on that floor. They dubbed the twenty-first "Oz," as in follow the yellow brick road... the road of success.

Jack had Shelly Cooper with Becca in one of the back offices, near the end of the hallway where it was the quietest.

"Miss Cooper, I appreciate your cooperation. Mrs. Brenner is top-notch in her field and a very nice woman."

"Now, Jack, you do go on. Miss Cooper and I will be fine. Now get, so I can work." Becca shooed him toward the door.

"Detective West?" Shelly Cooper called out.

"Yes?"

"This older man—could he have been the one who did this to Jade, you think?"

"Shelly, to tell you the truth, we don't know. Have you seen him in the club again?"

"No, sir, I haven't. And you know, now I pay more attention to the people coming and going. It's sort of eerie. I see people differently now. Know what I mean?"

Jack nodded. Becca did too. They knew—exactly.

"I hope I can help. I may not have known Jade, but no one deserves to be murdered. If I can help catch a killer, then that would make me feel safer here in my town."

"Shelly, Houston needs more citizens like you—not afraid to get involved and help. Thank you." Jack shook hands with the young girl.

"Jack, I'll let you know when we're done, okay?" Becca pushed him toward the door.

"Fine. I'm leaving. I'm leaving."

16

LUCKY CAME BACK WITH zero coffee.

"Did you forget the coffee? Bud, you getting senile or what?"

"Ain't no damn coffee filters. We'll have to steal some from Vice," Lucky emitted a growl.

The door to the squad room opened. Lucky turned at the sound, and his gut jerked.

"Captain Brooks," he said aloud.

Jack looked up, wondering what Brooks wanted.

"Detectives, I hear tell you and 7-11 have connected cases. Is this true?"

"Yes, sir. We've been working together," Lucky responded first.

The paunchy man with a somewhat ruddy complexion walked over to the shared desk area. With his hands behind him, he paced back and forth at the far end, head lowered, deep in thought—or confusion, Jack surmised.

"Where are Severson and Chang, then?" He looked at Jack.

"Grabbing a murder suspect on a pop-and-drop they got at the end of last week," Jack said. He didn't offer further explanation—looking straight at the ruddy-faced man, not blinking.

Captain Brody Brooks' eyes dropped to his feet as he nodded. "Good. Glad to hear that Homicide is making strides. You have your reports typed up, ready for review?"

Lucky looked at Jack. He didn't want to tell Brooks that they were still handing all their reports over to Davis Yao.

"We'll have all of them in a file on your desk tomorrow morning, sir. We have some loose ends to tie up on some reports," Jack boldface lied to him.

"See that you do," Captain Brooks grumbled. "Got other work to do." He walked his paunchy self to the door and left.

Brooks didn't know why, but Jack West scared him. It was like West could see through him. Hell, he was a mere detective. He hadn't even tried to rise in the ranks. Brooks intended to be on top, no matter who he stepped on getting there. Jack West was just a bump in the road—and if he had to he'd roll right over him on his way up.

Jack frowned at the door that had closed. "Lucky, you can breathe now."

"Don't tell him I've been handing the reports to Chief Yao and not him. The man is... well, I don't know what he is. What's the word I'm looking for?"

"Trustworthy, Lucky. He's not trustworthy," Jack said.

With no new leads and tired of sitting in the squad room, they stopped for the day. Lucky had the reports in a folder and dropped them on Captain Brooks' desk, pleased that he was out of his office.

Jack peeked in on Shelly and Becca.

"Hey, how's it going? I figured you'd be done by now."

"Hi, Jack. Well, we had some glitches, but it's all good. You gonna be here a while?"

"No. Will you please drop the picture in a folder and leave it in my middle desk drawer?"

"Sure, Jack."

"Shelly, thanks for taking time to do this."

"I'm glad to help, Detective West."

It had been a while since Jack and Lucky had a nice meal together—they decided on Vic and Anthony's Steak House. It was a pleasant change from the fast food they ate on the run, and steak and baked potatoes sounded perfect.

Food ordered, Jack's cell buzzed.

"West. Hey, Chang. Did y'all get your boy? Yeah, Lucky and I are over at Vic and Anthony's Steak House. Right. See you and Jace tomorrow morning."

"No shoot-out over at the rail yard? Chang disappointed?"

"I thought that was backward, you know? I figured Severson to be the shoot-'em-up type and Chang the 'let's talk it out' kind of dude. What a shock when it was reversed." Jack picked up his menu. A nice meal was in order, and he was famished.

Jack West and Dawson Luck had a rare, peaceful meal together—no shop talk, a refreshing experience.

It was 8:00 when they left the steak house, and not one damn call from the station for a change. Jack knew in the morning he'd be seeing the forensic artwork of Becca Brenner. He was ready to get that picture copied, give it to the entire patrol unit, and have the BOLO issued. Tonight, he was shelving the case. This evening, he'd be going to the Lone Star Saloon to surprise Gretchen.

The surprise was on Jack—Gretchen was off. This was better. She was home—they'd have privacy—perfect.

He knocked, and his heart thudded a bit. He hadn't seen her in two weeks.

She was wearing a soft blue sundress. One she bought in Maui. She was makeup-free, her hair loose, and she smiled when she saw him.

"Cowboy Ja—" was all she got out as he pulled her in for a kiss—kissing her until her toes curled. He backed her up, his lips not leaving hers, and shut the door with his foot. Lifting his lips from hers but not letting go, he turned his right hand back toward the door and clicked the lock. In one swift motion, he scooped her up, carried her to the bedroom, and laid her on the bed. He stood over her, and she looked up at him and smiled.

"I'm happy to see you, too."

"You're beautiful." He pulled his boots off, then lay beside her.

She curled up next to him. He was tired—she could see it—and the case was still ongoing. She knew that from some of the brief calls he had had time to make to her.

"Jack, is everything all right?" Gretchen knew he'd give details if possible, or if he wanted to. She never pushed.

"Yes. No." He exhaled, pulling her closer, needing to feel her heartbeat. "Lots going on, Gretch. I'm just tired."

"Why are you here, then? Go home and rest, Jack. I'll understand."

"Can I stay here tonight?" Jack pulled her over on top of him.

"Of course you can." She bent her head and kissed him. "But won't you have to get up early to go home for more clean clothes?"

Jack hugged her. "Darlin', I'm a homicide detective. I never know when I might get home. I've had to live at the station during a case before. I keep extra clothes in my truck or in my locker."

"Okay, then, Cowboy. Would you like to shower, then get comfy?"

Yes, he wanted a shower—because he wanted *her* in the shower. He knew what that would lead to. Jack was ready to repeat the explosions they'd shared in Maui. He needed that volcano and Gretchen Benson tonight.

***

The callout came in at 3:00 am.

Jack yanked up his phone—his voice lowered.

"West."

He tiptoed to the kitchen.

"Hey, you sick?"

"No, I'm at Gretchen's. Didn't want to wake her. What's up?"

"We caught a case. Captain Brooks called me."

"He called you first. I mean, I don't care, but he knows... crap, never mind."

"To be truthful, partner, I think you scare Brooks."

"It makes no difference to me. What'd we catch, and where are we headed?"

"Go to the station. I'll pick you up. I'm headed that way. Our victims will still be there," Lucky said.

"Victims, as in two? Well, shit. I'll meet ya at the station in thirty."

As soon as Jack turned to go back to the bedroom, he ran into a sleepy-eyed Gretchen.

"Is everything all right, babe?" She yawned.

"Go back to bed, darlin'. I gotta go to the station."

He turned and walked her back to the bedroom. He grabbed his clothes off the chair next to the bureau and put them on in a hurry.

"You got some new developments on your case?" She crawled on top of the bed and watched him dress in the semi-dark.

"Nah. Caught a new one, and I'm meeting Lucky at the station. Tell ya what, I'll text you later."

She yawned. "Okay. Go out there and get 'em, Cowboy cop."

Jack bent and kissed her, and he felt an urge—he had to resist.

He covered her with the sheet and said, "See ya later, baby." Then he turned and left her lying there, looking quite beautiful with that sleepy, sexy, early-morning look that he loved.

Locking her front door from the inside, he pulled it shut, went to his truck, started it up, and headed for the station. He was damn glad he had extra clothes with him, especially if Captain Brooks was on the scene. He'd seen him yesterday—saw what he was wearing. Jack could hear it now: *Jack, you sleep in your clothes, or are you shacking up overnight with a woman?* Then his annoying, raucous laugh would follow, loud enough for everyone else to hear.

No one cared, but Jack didn't appreciate the way Brooks treated him. Captain Brooks had a way of singling him out to correct or embarrass him. It never worked, but that didn't mean Brody Brooks didn't try.

Maybe Lucky was right. Brooks might feel threatened... but Jack had no clear idea why.

He beat Lucky to the station and ran up to six, went to the locker room, grabbed his extra shaving kit, brushed his teeth, combed his hair, and did a quick shave. He changed his clothes, threw his crap back in the locker, locked it, and hauled butt down to the garage.

Perfect timing.

Lucky had just pulled in.

17

JACK JUMPED IN AND buckled up.

"What's the call?"

"It's in the Fifth Ward on Mesa Drive, a small diner—Joe's All Nite Diner. The 9-1-1 call came in at 2:15 am: shots fired, left two dead. Units and an ambulance were dispatched. No ambulance needed—they hooked it."

"Who was the first responder?"

"Officers Jukes and Spillman arrived on the scene and have a few witnesses detained inside the diner, as well as the diner owner and three staff members. CSU is there—Loren Taylor—and Bennie called Mack." Then Lucky laughed.

"Why ya laughing?"

"Poor Mack. I'm guessing she drew the short straw. She gets more of the early morning calls than Bennie. Bet her wife gets pissed. Which—I still don't get—a wife. She has a wife."

Jack bit back a laugh. "Bennie's been by himself for a while. Guess he needs a break for a change."

Lucky still didn't know that Mack did **not** have a wife. The joke was still ongoing, and Jack wasn't ready to clear it up.

Black-and-whites sat parked in the lot of Joe's Diner. The building faced Mesa Road at the corner of Mesa and Ley. This was one of the highest-crime areas in Houston. HPD knew the Greater Fifth Ward was teeming with gangs, crime, and drugs. It was, for lack of a better word, one of Houston's crime ghetto areas.

Low-income families, single mothers without jobs living on welfare, as well as some of Houston's elderly who survived on small Social Security incomes—all easy targets.

Houses were small and unkempt in many areas. Gang graffiti tagged territories, as well as pairs of shoes tied together and hanging over wiring, marking boundary lines. Crack and meth houses were set up every other day.

Vice worked this area hard, but for every two steps forward they made, the gangs got smarter and ran three steps ahead. They kept plugging away anyway, at least keeping those punk-ass gang members on their toes.

Poorer sections—whether Houston or larger cities like Dallas, LA, Detroit, even Oklahoma City, shared the same problems in their ghetto areas. With rising crime spilling over and affecting white-collar districts, everyone knew it was more than problematic.

"You think we should vest up?" Lucky asked as he pulled in. Crime scene tape had cordoned off the area.

Jack opened his door. "Nah. With three black-and-whites here and all the commotion, no stupid thug in his right mind would walk up."

Lucky looked at Jack over the top of the car. "Uh-huh, and that's why I'm worried."

"What's got you worried?"

"In their right minds? Crud. Half of 'em are psycho or hopped up on coke or meth. The other half have no conscience or soul and don't give a rat's ass. That tells me they're *never* in their right minds."

"Can't argue that point at all, partner. Now let's go see what we have."

Jack and Lucky stepped up to where two young men lay—both dead, both shot multiple times. The bodies were three to four feet apart.

"Is Captain Brooks here?" Lucky scanned the scene.

"No," Officer Jukes said. "Said he made the callout and would leave it to his detectives."

Lucky shook his head. He didn't say it, but Jack knew what he was thinking. Captain Brooks wouldn't come out unless it was a high-profile crime. He was most likely at home, a blanket over his paunchy belly, snoring. He'd been the same way in Robbery—his men handled it.

"Jukes, what do we got?" Jack bent over body number one. The man lay on his back, legs twisted, blood pooled beneath him.

"Shot twice in the chest, once in the gut. Went down hard. Black male, twenty-two, wearing gang colors. A counter server said she saw a gold Chevy Impala with a cobra painted on the side. It peeled out after the shooting. No plate number, but she said it was an older, souped-up car." Jukes paused. "That description tells me who."

Lucky crouched closer, then straightened. "These the Dragons?"

"Yep. You're right, Detective Luck."

"What'd you mean—*that description tells who*?"

"Jack, my partner Ollie, and I patrol this area. This corner was considered a neutral zone for gangs to talk. Few neutral zones in the Fifth Ward, but they've used this one for about a year as a no-kill zone—until tonight. We heard through the pipeline there might be a rumble between the Brown Cobras and the Dragons. That was a month ago. Nothing happened—we figured it was just talk. But rivalry between the Cobras and the Dragons has been building."

"Who are the Brown Cobras?" Jack asked. "I've heard of the Dragons, but not much about the Cobras."

Lucky answered. "I know 'em. Hispanic gang. They claim the area from Lathrop Street to Lockwood Drive, north of the East Freeway and east of Waco Street. Newer gang—been on the rise about three years. I heard they've grown fast the last year and a half. That right, Jukes?"

"Yep. And they've been a pain in the ass."

Jack moved to the second body—a young Black male, early twenties, big man. He'd been shot in the upper torso and left side of the gut. He lay on his right side, a dark pool of blood seeping from his abdomen.

Loren Taylor approached. "Jack, I found five shell casings—three from a .45 and two from a nine. Looks like this guy caught the nines. The other one took the .45 rounds."

"Two shooters," Jack muttered. "Well, kiss my ass. Shoe prints, guns, anything?"

"Nope. Just two dead bodies and shell casings, which at least gives us *something*. Looks like the shooters were in a car, guns hanging out the windows-based on where the casings landed. Distance was about fifteen or sixteen feet. We found peel-out marks, but no usable tread—just smears."

"Get plenty of photos, Loren." Jack gloved up and checked for a wallet. "Lucky, see if the other guy has ID. I'll handle this one."

"Jukes, give me a hand."

Lucky shifted the body. "Got a wallet. Simon Rodgers, twenty-two. Address is New Orleans Street."

"This one's Raynon Jones, twenty-four. Address on Yates Street." Jack nodded. "Those streets are close."

"I know the area," Loren said. "CSU's had calls there before. Both streets are off Waco, poorer neighborhoods."

"Looks like some nasty business," Mack said, arriving. "Sorry I'm late."

"Gangs and rivalry," Loren said. "It's a wonder they have time to pro-create."

The scene yielded little—two bodies, blood, and five shell casings. Not a wealth of clues, and very little physical evidence.

It was time to talk to the witnesses inside.

18

PATROL OFFICERS DAVID JUKES and Ollie Richmond gathered the witnesses and held them in the diner. The owner was none too happy.

"Can I reopen? This is killing my business," the owner said as Jack and Lucky entered the diner.

"Are you Joe?"

"No, I'm Ben. I own this joint," the flabby man said.

Lucky made notes in his notebook. "Ben, you own a place called Joe's, but your name's Ben?"

"What of it? Place was named Joe's when I bought it. You got a problem with that?"

"No, I got a problem with your remark."

"What remark is that, huh?" he challenged Lucky.

The diner owner-slash-cook wore a white apron, which emphasized a rather large, protuberant gut. He stood near the counter, next to the cash register, as if protecting it. A server stood nearby, alongside a short woman wearing a server's apron and a young male busboy.

Jack held in a chuckle; his partner was a grumpy camper.

Lucky stepped closer, unfazed by the man's size. "Did you say this is killing your business?"

"Damn right, so what?"

"Two men lay in your parking lot dead—shot and killed right here. And if your place is closed, that's going to 'kill' you... but what about them?" Lucky pointed to the two bodies. The M.E. had already bagged them and placed them on gurneys.

He crossed his arms, grunting. "Punks. Hell, Houston has one die every other day. If not one of them, then decent people get killed. Better them than us, I say." All he cared about was running his restaurant and making a buck.

A frown creased Lucky's face, and his bushy eyebrows did the caterpillar crawl as he stared at the man. Jack watched and waited for Lucky to speak.

"Ben, do you have a brother named Timiteto, and is your last name Kane, with a K?"

Jack had a tough time holding back laughter. Lucky was referring to the "sanitation engineer" from the confrontation at the last crime scene.

"No, I don't have a brother, and my last name is Carter, with a C. Why?" The cranky owner asked.

"Oh, I met a man a few days ago—you could be brothers. Now, Ben, here's what I want you to do: stand beside your cash register and keep your mouth shut until I need to talk to you. When we're done, you can get back to business. That invisible line of people outside your door can get served then—and no sooner."

Lucky walked past him, then turned. "And, Ben Carter, remember that those two boys may have been gang members, but they had families too. A mom and a dad, a grandma, or brothers and sisters. Hell, they might have children of their own. They'll never get the chance to choose a better life because someone cut theirs short. No one deserves to die unless it's in the electric chair. Texas still has the death penalty, and those on death row deserve to be there. Respect the dead, Ben Carter—they no longer have a voice. Now we are their voice."

The man had no comeback. Detective Luck had reprimanded him, and he looked over at his three staff members. He saw it in their eyes—they had lost respect for their potbellied, ill-tempered boss, if they had any to start with.

THERE WERE FOUR PEOPLE sitting in the back area. Jack and Lucky went from person to person, getting the story from each.

"Ma'am, I'm Detective West. What's your name?" Jack asked, notebook in hand.

"Gladys Newcomb."

"Mrs. Newcomb, can you tell me what happened here?"

She shook her head, her graying curls bouncing. "No, I can't. I was in the restroom. I heard the gunshots and the commotion. I was... er, otherwise occupied," she said, flustered, "and I couldn't leave my seat."

"Are you here by yourself?"

"No, my husband Stan is over there."

Jack looked over at the older man sitting at a far booth to his left. Lucky was questioning him.

"What brings you and Stan out here at this hour?"

"Well, me and Stan live in the area. Some nights, if I ain't sleeping, we come here. It's close to our house, and the place is open 24/7. We're both retired, and we're night owls."

Jack handed her his card. "Ma'am, thank you for your time. As soon as we're finished with your husband, we'll let you go."

"Have fun with that, Detective. He was sitting at the very back by the restrooms. His hearing is terrible, his eyesight is worse, and he didn't have his glasses. He left 'em at home."

He walked her to the front table while Lucky finished with Mr. Newcomb, then sent him up front next to his wife.

"Jack, we can let them go. Man said his wife was in the ladies' room, and he was in the back. Said his hearing is for crap and he left his glasses at home. Poor guy can't see a foot in front of him. Said they're night owls and the place is open twenty-four hours and close to their house."

"I know. I heard you repeating your questions louder each time. Go tell them they can go home and lock their doors."

The next witness was Lizzie Tobin—a twenty-year-old Black female.

"Miss Tobin, I'm Detective West. Can you tell me what happened here tonight?"

"Yeah, but I don't want no trouble, and this is gonna be some damn fuckin' trouble."

"How do you mean?"

"This place be a no-kill zone, and those brothers were here to talk, thass all."

"Miss Tobin, do you know the men who got killed tonight?"

"Uh-huh, they be Fiddler and Glib, they Dragons." She shook her head. "This might mean a war, and I ain't down for that."

"Why are you here? Is someone with you?" Jack asked, writing notes.

"Tanika, my homegirl, is. She's the one the other man was talking to. We were at her crib, got hungry, and walked over here."

"What time did you get here?"

"Oh, 'bout midnight, I think. Wasn't looking at a clock."

"So, can you tell me what happened?"

"Fiddler and Glib rolled up. Me and Tanika know 'em, and they came in the diner to chill. We axed them why they were here, and Fiddler said to parlay about territory lines or some shit like that."

"What's Fiddler's real name, Lizzie?" Jack needed to know which man was Glib and which was Fiddler.

"It's Simon, but don't know his last name. He just be called Fiddler."

"What about Glib? You know his real name?"

"Uh-huh, he be Raynon Jones, called RJ or Glib."

"Did you see what happened?"

She nodded, tears in her eyes. "If I tell you, then they come for me. I ain't no snitch, and it ain't safe talking to Five-O, not here."

"Miss Tobin, I need you to sit here and wait for us to finish up, okay?"

"Yes, sir." Scared she'd said too much, she shrunk back into the booth.

Lucky met Jack at the side. Jack gave him Lizzie Tobin's story.

"That's the same story I got from her friend Tanika Washington; however, she told me a bit more. She said she heard on the streets the Cobras didn't want to talk—they want to move in on Dragon territory."

"Did she say why? I mean, there's enough of Houston's ghetto to share." Jack looked over at the girl.

"Nah, all I got out of it was that it's a damn control issue. I do know the Brown Cobras are recruiting more members, and the Spanish population is growing in this area. I guess they feel as if the Dragons need to move further west and let the Cobras have 'Little Mexico.' She won't tell me more. She's scared."

"Well, both she and Miss Tobin are going to get a bit more scared 'cause we're taking them downtown, re-questioning them—see if that opens their mouths a bit more. Who called 9-1-1?"

"The waitress did." Lucky gestured toward the counter. "The busboy was in the back with the owner, and they didn't see what happened. They heard the commotion and came out running. Jukes took their statements when he got here. Ollie said the other female employee was standing near the door to the kitchen when the shots rang out. She hit the floor and all she saw was dirty linoleum."

"I'm going to talk to the waitress. You get someone to take Lizzie and Tanika to the station."

"I'm on it right now."

"All I saw was the car... a gold Chevy with a cobra painted on the side and jacked-up tires. I didn't see who was in it. Don't think I can be much help."

Jack looked around.

"Claudia, does the diner have hidden outside security cameras?"

"Ben's too cheap for that. He says the cops should patrol the area better—they are the 'eyes' on crime. I don't agree with him. Tonight... well, this was the last straw, you know?"

"I understand, ma'am. Thank you for your cooperation."

"Well, Detective West, if you're ever in the area and stop here to eat, don't look for me. It's time to move on to a new job."

Jack didn't say it, but he was positive he and Lucky would never eat at Joe's All Nite Diner again.

"Let's head to the station and see what we can shake out of the trees."

"I'm ready to roll, Jack."

19

LIZZIE TOBIN AND TANIKA Washington waited in separate interview rooms.

Jack pulled up the names Simon Rodgers and Raynon Jones in the criminal database, and it was no surprise they had extensive rap sheets: burglary, evading arrest, drugs, and assault, and each had done time in juvie. It made no difference now, but sometimes you needed to know more about your victim to put things in perspective.

"Lucky, I'm going to talk to Lizzie Tobin. Why don't you see what you can get out of Tanika Washington?"

"I thought you'd never ask." Lucky and Jack did the fist-bump, then headed to the interview rooms.

Jack entered interview room number three. A nervous Lizzie Tobin sat, her hands folded together.

"Lizzie, how are you doing? Would you like a water or a soda?" Jack sat across from her.

"Nuh-uh. Why you got me here? Am I in trouble?"

"No, Lizzie, but it's important that you tell me what you know."

"Dude, I ain't a snitch. If I say, people will say I snitched and that be a helluva lot of trouble for me."

"Who'll give you trouble, Lizzie? Are you one of the gangs' girls?"

"Oh, hell no, they not for me. I don't be part of they gangs. Damn, man, you know how the hood is, and word gets 'round."

"You're already here—might as well cooperate and help us get justice for those two Dragon members. If you don't, do you think people in your neighborhood are gonna like that? Just because they were gang members doesn't mean someone should kill them. People might think you don't care who gets shot down where you live. Is that what you want?"

Lizzie did not respond.

"You knew the dead men, Lizzie. Don't you want them to get justice? What about their families? Don't you care if they get closure? And their moms? Don't you care that they've lost their sons?" He was firing question after question and saw her thinking.

"Uh, I wanna tell you, but if I do, the Cobras be coming to look for me. What I supposed to do then?"

"Remember, they may still hunt you if you cooperate or not. They know you were here. Look, we need to get the shooters, stop a gang war. If you're a smart girl, you'll stay off the streets at night, take yourself out of danger. Where do you live—you have a job?"

"I live with my Auntie and work at the Fiesta Mart."

"I'm glad to hear you have family, and a job. But here's the deal, Lizzie. Don't you want to get your neighborhood cleaned up? Wouldn't you like to feel safer in your neighborhood?"

Lizzie gave a brief nod, and Jack shifted his chair closer.

"We need to get on the same page. You and Tanika can help us. If not, then two killers go free. Free to roam Houston. Lizzie, if you were lying dead in that parking lot, would you want your killer to get away? Then your Auntie would never have closure. And your killer would be free to kill others. You want that to happen?" Jack played on her emotions. He was putting her in the dead boys' shoes. She told him all she knew, and by the time Jack left the room she was crying.

"So, Luck, you get anything from Miss Washington?"

Lucky swiveled his chair back and forth. "One name, and it's not the real damn name. She said the driver was a boy they call Cozy-Man. She's scared to death. She won't talk unless Lizzie does."

"Miss Tobin tell you anything?"

"Lizzie said they walked outside with both the boys. They were cutting up, then Fiddler told them to get back inside and stay inside no matter what. That's when she saw the car with the cobra on the side drive up. She said they didn't get out, but Fiddler and Glib walked up to the car. She couldn't hear them, so she opened the door—heard them shouting.

Lucky leaned back. "About what?"

"Lizzie heard him telling Fiddler he needed to tell his boys to move it back. They ran that area."

"Ran what area?"

"The Brown Cobras want to expand their turf—their drug business is growing. Seems they've tried to work out a deal with territory lines. The Cobras are muscling out the Dragons, and there are more Cobras than there are Dragons. If they wanted a war, they'd be sorry."

Lucky's forehead shot up a titch. "She said that?"

"Well, not as eloquent. I had to clean it up a bit," Jack admitted.

"What did she say triggered the shooting?"

"Fiddler threw out a gang sign, and that's when the guns came out. I think the Cobras had guns at the ready. Makes me wonder if it was a setup." Jack's brows dipped.

"Does Lizzie know the shooters?"

"Just their street names. Let's see if we can find them in the system." Jack input the first street name Lucky's witness gave him.

Dawson read over his shoulder. "Cozy-Man. Jose Velez, nineteen, one charge of burglary. Guess he's adding to his record. What a waste."

Jack typed in the street name, Lil Loco.

"We have a winner. Pedro Perez, thirty-two. Burglary—did a nickel for grand theft auto, assault, fleeing arrest; intention to distribute drugs to an undercover officer. The list goes on. And he's been out on parole for a year."

Lucky swiveled to his desk and typed in the other street name, Gizmo.

"Juan Mercedes, aka Gizmo, thirty-one. Charges of multiple burglaries as a juvenile, a domestic assault charge filed by a girlfriend. A couple of drug charges. Did a stint at Terrell for a bar fight when he beat a guy to a pulp. Sentenced to ten years—served nine. Jack, he made early parole six months ago."

"Get the names of their parole officers. We'll let them both know what the deal is. He sounds like he should have been called Lil Loco, not Gizmo." Jack stated.

"I gotta agree, the punk's loco alright. Maybe he should've been called Muy Loco."

Jack printed out the pictures of Juan Mercedes and Pedro Perez, as well as ten other mug shots, and put a six-pack together to show Lizzie Tobin. Dawson Luck did likewise for Tanika Washington.

Jack set the photos in front of her. "Lizzie, I want you to circle who the shooters are, and sign and date it. Okay?"

Her voice no louder than a mouse fart. "Okay."

Lizzie's hand shook as she picked up the red marker. She looked at the pictures for a long time, and she circled Pedro Perez from one six-pack, and then Juan Mercedes from the other, signed and dated them, then laid the marker down, her hands still shaking.

"You did fine, Lizzie. Wait here, and once my partner finishes talking to Tanika, we'll get an officer to drive you both home."

With a tiny nod, she watched him go, and the silence of the interview room settled around her.

Lucky was at his desk and waiting. "Well?"

"We're in business. She gave me a positive ID."

"I'm gonna tell Miss Washington her friend gave us a positive ID, and now it's her turn."

Back in less than three minutes, Jack looked up. "Well?"

"Miss Washington gave me ID's signed, and she is ready to 'get the fuck outta here,' quote unquote."

"Call downstairs, see if there's an available unit to drive them home."

"On it." Lucky picked up his phone and dialed Dispatch.

Jack prayed the girls would stay in and be cautious until this case closed. He didn't want to work on their murders, too.

20

20

"HEY, I CALLED RICK Tormo. He's going to get his guys to be on the lookout for Jose Velez, AKA Cozy-Man. I want to see if we can get him to roll on the other two, maybe cut a deal. Our two shooters are gonna be lying low for a while. Rick said some of these gang members hang out at a place called Terrell's Arcade and Pool Hall. It's over on Waco Street. He has guys in the area. They'll check it out, see if our boy shows up there, and call us."

Lucky exhaled. "So, now we wait."

"Yep. In the meantime, you keep checking on the silver Nissan or Acura, and I'll keep scrubbing street cams. Let's try to get a lead on the man who was bumping nasties with Jade."

Two days later, Rick Tormo called.

"Hey, Jack. We've got eyes on your boy."

"Where?"

Jack wrote the address down, thanked Rick, and hung up, smiling.

"Rick's guys got eyes on our driver boy. Found him at the pool hall. Let's roll."

"Think we need more backup?" Lucky asked, vesting up before he got into the car.

"Nah, Hogan and Wu from Vice are in the area. Rick's going to call two patrol units for us. That way, they can be close in case it goes sideways."

Jack's cell phone buzzed as he turned onto Waco Street.

"West. Hey, what's up? Where are you and Hoagie? No problem, I understand, but if y'all gotta charge in, we won't mind at all."

"Wu from Vice?"

"Yeah. Him and Hoagie will hang back unless it's necessary to charge in. They've been doing surveillance for a few weeks and don't want to blow their own cover unless we get in a pickle."

"We're covered." Lucky pointed down the street. "One of the black-and-whites is a block down. The other one's not far. Let's go in, pard."

They got out, knowing that these gangs could smell the law ten miles away. Jack parked at the curb less than a block away.

The pool hall—a worn-down building, at the end of a small street-side business strip. Next to it was a tax office, a bicycle repair shop, and a cigarette store.

With a nod, Jack signaled the patrol car moving in to sit tight.

"Five-O," the man said with an upper jerk of his chin. He stood outside the door, loitering, a cigarette hanging from his lips. His gang colors showed he belonged to the Cobras: black shirt and blue jeans, with a black-and-gold bandana hanging from one of his belt loops. A black-and-gold Cobra tattoo adorned his left forearm. A large BC tattooed on his neck.

He also had two teardrops tattooed on his face, at the corner of his eye, signifying one of two things: he'd killed two people or had been in prison twice.

Not a trace of a smile on Jack's face. "Keeping it clean?"

The man jutted his chin up higher, his lips in a downward frown, smirking. "Everything is everything, Five-O."

Dawson Luck kept his mouth shut because if he opened it, they might get an ass whooping—or worse. Even with the two Vice detectives nearby, the two officers in the black-and-white, and one more patrol unit in the vicinity, there was a shitload of wannabe thugs.

Lucky figured positive most of 'em were packing. God, he wanted to take these fuckers to the mattresses for butchering the English language—but held his tongue for safety reasons today.

Jack pushed through the doors; all eyes in the room turned their way.

Five pool tables, two pinball machines, and a short bar to the side of the room. Smoke circled overhead from the smokers. The lighting was dim. Jack focused his eyes, and seeing his target, he pointed and, with a commanding tone, said, "Need to see you now."

A young Hispanic kid walked over with a swagger and an air of *I don't give a shit, I'm gonna take my time*. He was trying to impress the other hoods in the pool hall, acting tough and unafraid of Five-O.

Jack—no nonsense: "Outside with me."

With a hand on the butt of his unsnapped Glock, Lucky kept a watchful eye on the others. The young thug shuffled toward them.

Cops in their pool hall bristled the others and you could feel the unease wafting in the smoky air.

"The rest of you better keep your seats unless you wanna take a ride downtown," Lucky warned his voice loud enough for the entire room to hear.

"Okay, Five-O, no need to unstrap, it's all good, man," the kid slurred as he sauntered toward them.

Jose Velez went out of the front door of Terrell's, Jack holding his arm. Lucky backed out the door, never losing sight that one of them might do something stupid.

The officers in the black-and-white had exited their vehicle, one standing at the front end and one at the back—a second black-and-white pulled up in the opposite direction.

Jack took the young man by the arm. "Come on, Cozy-Man, we're going downtown."

The young gang member tugged his arm out of Jack's hand, took a step to the side, took two more long steps, and then started running.

What a foolish kid, Jack thought, as an officer in the second patrol car jumped out of the passenger door and waylaid him, knocking him flat on his back at the curb.

The man at the door, cigarette still in his lips, took one step forward, but the officers across the street were walking toward the pool hall.

The patrol cop stepped up. "Back up—this isn't your business, Uvaldo—inside. Now!"

The man went in. Both officers were ready to draw their guns if necessary, and the second patrol car was blocking the middle of the street.

Faces pressed up to the glass windows of the pool hall, watching—not cheerful faces. Cops were on their turf, taking one of their own.

Lucky reached down, grabbed the young man by his shirt, and hauled him up.

"Turn around—hands behind your back. You had to make it hard on yourself, now didn't you, Cozy-Man?" He clicked the cuffs shut. "All we wanted you to do was take a ride downtown and talk. You had to act like a big man."

"Thanks for the backup, fellas, glad you were here," Jack waved as Lucky put Cozy-Man in the back seat of the car, shoving his head down in a not-all-too-friendly manner. Jack gave Hoagie and Wu an invisible fist bump. They were nearby—watching.

"Sit tight," Lucky said.

The kid's angry retort was muffled as the door slammed shut.

No one said a word on the drive back to the station. There would be plenty of time for talking downtown.

21

Jack took the key to unlock the handcuffs in the interview room. "Turn around, Jose."

"Va`to. Don't call me Jose, I'm Cozy-Man, don't call me Jose," he spat, while Jack cuffed him to the arm of the metal chair.

"Sure, Jose, will do. Now, sit tight, be back in a minute." Jack left shutting the door and fixing the top lock. Cuffed or not, the kid had no way out.

"Going to let him simmer down and cool off. I'm going for coffee. You want one?" Jack watched the punk, sitting in his best gangster pose—slouched down, acting as if he had no care in the world.

"Yep, coffee sounds great. See if we have some chips in the cabinet by the fridge. I left a bag there a few days ago." Lucky leaned on one elbow, watching their suspect.

Jose Velez sat in the room for forty-five minutes before Jack went back in. Lucky watched the monitor with Xi and Jace.

"Got a show on TV, I see," Jace said, taking a seat next to Lucky, while Xi Chang stood between them both.

"Turn up the volume, Dawson, it's too low. I wanna hear Jack work," Xi laughed.

Jack took a chair, pulled it to the side corner of the table, and got closer to Jose.

"Cozy-Boy—"

His face distorted. "Hijo de puta. It's not Cozy-Boy, it's man, man, Cozy-Man, tu`idiota."

Jack knew a spattering of Spanish and understood his disrespectful remarks.

"First, I'm neither a motherfucker nor an idiot, and you'll watch what you say to me." Jack got in his face. "I think you're in a spot right now. One you don't want to be in, and you little bastard, I'm your only friend right now. Got it? Now, sit back and we're going to talk." Jack scooted his chair on the floor, and it made a loud screeching sound.

In the monitoring room, Xi and Jace sniggered.

"If I was that boy and big ole Jack was in my face like that, I might shit myself." Lucky chuckled, too.

Jack took a relaxed position, slumping a little in his chair.

"Now, Cozy, can I call you Cozy for short? If not, I'm going to call you Jose."

The boy gave an *I don't give a rat's ass* shrug and said nothing.

"Good. Now here's what we have. Two dead men: Fiddler, who was Simon Rodgers, and Raynon Jones, they called him Glib. You know these dead men, Cozy?"

"No."

"Then you weren't driving a souped-up gold Chevy Impala two days ago at one a.m., taking a ride to Joe's All Nite Diner, over off Mesa Road?"

"No, man, I was at home with my moms."

"Speaking of moms, I gotta tell two mothers their sons are dead. How about you go with me?"

His voice calm. "Ain't my job, man, that's your job." He continued to sit in his gangsta slouch.

"No, your job was to drive the car so your buddies could kill rival gang members, right?"

"Hey, ain't no law against driving a car, man. I got a license, and I didn't do shit, man. I was at home with my moms—I told you."

"Do you think your pals won't roll on you to save their own ass? I'm telling you they'd be crying like babies. Dude, if they had to choose between you and the needle, whatdaya think they'd choose, huh?" Jack's voice increased in volume. "They'd roll on you in a second. You might stay out of prison, but hell, if you want to keep protecting men who don't give a damn if you take the fall for this, then your ass can hang. I don't care." Jack slapped the top of the table, and the kid flinched.

"Man, how do I know what they'd say? Like I done told you, I was home, sleeping. My moms can tell you." The boy spat out the words, his voice getting louder.

It didn't rattle Jack, not one iota. He kept his relaxed posture and locked eyes with Jose. Jack was a pro at this. He never had to blink and never lost eye contact.

Jose averted his eyes, letting a minute pass as he stared down at his lap.

"Look, I know for a fact you weren't at home. Here's the deal. I'm going to leave you here to think it over. You're now an accessory to two counts—Murder One. Man, you're gonna be someone's sweet thang. I can see it now. You'll be a sweet thang for life." Jack stood and got down in his face.

"Hope you don't like girls, cuz man, you're not gonna be no girl's sweet thang. Betcha, the biggest one on the cell block gets your ass." Jack stepped back, then opened the door. "And if you don't get life, maybe you'll be lucky enough to get the needle. Then you'll have no worries. You'll never hafta be someone's sweet-thang bitch."

Jack was out the door before Cozy could say a word.

Back in the monitoring room, the other fellas were having a laugh-fest.

"Jack—Jack. Scaring the kid with prison sex. Shame on you." Jace's shoulders bounced with laughter.

"Gonna give him time to think it over, death or anal love. I'll be back, going to get what Becca left for me. Chang, Severson, you gonna be here for a few?"

"Sure, Jack, if you need us to," Chang answered. "Got a fun show going on here, like to see how it plays out." He propped his feet up on the counter and grinned a toothy grin. "We might need to get popcorn."

Lucky and Jace both tried to hold in their snickers, but it didn't work that well.

"Be back in a minute or two."

Jack left them yucking it up.

22

HE OPENED THE MIDDLE drawer of his desk and took the folder out Becca Brenner had left him.

The picture depicted a man—forty-one to forty-two—dark hair intermingled with gray, receding at the forehead. Close-set eyes with crow's feet, thin lips, a weak jawline, and the start of a double chin. Jade Nelson had been a young, pretty girl. Why was she with an old man? He didn't get it. It musta' been love, cause it wasn't his looks.

Gretchen—a beautiful woman inside and out. How did he get that lucky?

Thinking about her, he picked up his cell phone and sent her a text: *Working hard ... have two cases. See you in a few days.* He signed it *Cowboy Jack*, and he could see her smile.

Back in the monitoring room, Jack handed Xi Becca's drawing.

"Who's this?"

"It's the man our victim was having an affair with."

Lucky looked over at Chang, holding out his hand.

"Let me see. This old guy was who Jade was fooling around with? Why?"

"Who the hell knows? Love is a strange thing," said Jack. "Chang, can you get copies made up and distribute them to all the patrol units? Put out a BOLO ... we need to get eyes on this man."

Lucky handed the drawing to Jace. "Jack, you think he's a suspect?"

"Looks like an old fart, or at least the beginnings of an old fart," Jace handed the composite back to Chang.

"Don't know, Xi. I think he was in lust with our victim. Lust or love can drive a person to murder. My gut says he didn't whack her. Why would he have killed the Taylor woman, too? What's his motive? Need to interview him, though because he might be a key to unlock at least one decent lead."

Jack was right. This was all they had going for them to get one step ahead.

"You know, our victim's husband might have an alibi, but that doesn't mean he didn't hire someone. We're still looking into that, since there is a huge life insurance payout," Chang said.

"Problem is, we have tailed the guy and not once has he acted out of the ordinary. I mean, he goes to church, work, and home," Jace said.

Lucky chomped on his potato chips. "Maybe he is the grieving husband, even if she was cheating on him."

"So, how's our boy Jose doing in there?" Jack looked at the monitors. Jose was still sitting in the chair, but he'd scooted up and laid his head down.

Jack stood, put his game face on. "Round two, fellows. Intermission is over."

———ᘒᘒᘒ———

AT THE STATION FOR three hours now, Jack hoped he was breaking the kid down, at least enough to get him to talk. The boy had some important, life-altering decisions to make, and if he were smart, he'd roll on his supposed friends.

"Cozy, have you been thinking how your life after conviction will be, or maybe your death?" Jack sat down in the chair at the end of the table.

"Yeah, dude, I've been thinking 'bout my life if I snitch," he said with a smart-alecky tone. "That could get me killed too, maybe. Either way, I have a death sentence."

"You need a new life, kid. Then maybe you'll live to be an old man."

"What do you know? You don't have my life, Va'to. You crazy if you think you know."

"Plenty of people got out of the gang life, kid. You just gotta make it happen. If you tell me where I can find Lil Loco and Gizmo, and you're willing to testify, then maybe the DA might cut you a deal. If not, we'll find them in time, and you'll be in prison too ... for life. Or all three of you can go one by one and get the needle. I can hear it now—your momma crying, and I betcha you'll be crying, too. It's gonna be nice to tell your buddies who got you in this mess. See you guys on the other side, in hell."

Jack shoved the table over, scooted his chair in front of the boy, and was up in his face.

"What's it gonna be? I ain't dicking around. This is the last time I'm gonna ask you. Take the goddamn deal, be a man for once, and do the right thing."

He pulled his face back and looked at him, not once letting his gaze veer. His eyes locked onto Jose's. Jack never blinked.

"Okay, sweet-thang, get ready to be a victim of gang rape in prison. Man, you're a young, handsome Hispanic dude, and they like that sweet brown meat." Jack slid his chair back, got up, and took a step to the door. "After this, I can't help you even if I wanted to. Cozy-Man, you'll be a victim in jail, and no one will care what happens to you. They'll say you got what you deserved. Or maybe you'll get the needle. I mean, Texans don't like murderers, and Cozy, you're an accessory to the fact on two counts of murder."

Jack turned his hand on the door, twisting the knob, when the boy spoke.

"Man, I'm scared for my moms. I don't want them to hurt her, you know?"

"It's possible to get out, Jose. Plenty of men have cut their gang ties and turned over a new leaf. You do that, and you won't end up a dead statistic. Take this tablet, write what the plan had been and what went down early this morning, then date it and sign it. I'm going to call the DA's office, get them over here to talk to you, see what they will do in exchange for your testimony, okay, Jose?"

"You think I can get outta this life, maybe get my diploma, and help my moms and my two brothers?"

"Hell, Jose, if you want me to, I'll even help you with your homework."

Jose laughed, and at that moment, Jack saw past his punk attitude. He told him that maybe the DA would even cut a deal and drop the charges. He'd seen it happen, but he made no promises.

"Tell me all the places Lil Loco and Gizmo might hang out or hide."

23

THE VCTF (VIOLENT CRIMINAL Task Force) assembled outside the station parking lot. Their destination was an address in the Fifth Ward.

The plan was to roll up on the house, surrounding it from all sides. Everyone knew this would not be a simple knock-on-the-door-you're-under-arrest kind of moment. Both Juan and Pedro had done time for other violent crimes, but murder—well, this was a new ball game.

Panic drove men like that to do crazy things, such as firing at the police—in desperation to escape. To avoid going back to prison, they'd kill or be killed. And they didn't care who they took out along the way.

"The house is the second house on the right corner. It faces west, and there's no back fence," the VCTF commander called out. "We're going to surround it, securing the back area, too. Otherwise, if they're in the house and they run out back, they'll be able to lose us in the neighborhood, and it might put others in danger."

The group said, "Yes, sir," in unison. Everyone vested up, ready to roll.

There were eight task force officers traveling in a van, four vice officers in a separate car, and Jack and Lucky in an unmarked car—all on a mission to take two cold-blooded killers off the street and out of action.

"Team Two, come in," the radio crackled. "What's your twenty?" Lieutenant Louis Foster, the VCTF commander's voice sounded over the air.

"Team Two is turning east on Oats Street, a block out," Jack responded.

"Roger that. Team Three, what's your twenty?"

"Team Three is now on Simpson Street, at the back of the suspect's house," Mark Wong from Vice came back.

"Roger that, Team Three. Team One is headed west on Hershe Street, taking the turn north onto Solo Street, and we have eyes on the house."

"Roger, Team One. Team Two has turned south, and we are at the house on the corner, next door," Jack notified the task commander.

"Roger. Team Three, are you in place?"

"Roger that, Lieutenant. The back area—secured. We're ready to rock and roll."

"Guys, get ready to rumble," Lieutenant Foster said over the radio.

Eight task force members rolled out of the van.

Five headed for the front door, guns in hand, while the other three officers went to the south side of the house.

Jack and Lucky went to the north side of the house, watching for window hoppers, and Vice was holding at the back of the house, eyes on the lookout for back-door runners.

Guns drawn, Officer Bates from the task force stood to the side of the front door and rapped hard with his fist. "Houston Police. Open up."

All hell broke loose when a chair went through the front window, a small table crashed out of the south-side window, and a gunshot rang out.

That was all it took.

Officer Bates kicked in the door and five officers charged the front while Vice rushed the back exit.

Jack and Lucky were coming up the north side of the house when a man dove out an open window headfirst. His entire body weight flew into Dawson Luck's right side, knocking him flat on his back and sending his gun flying out of his hand, landing near Jack. The punk on top of Dawson Luck was trying to roll off to get up and run.

It was as if it were happening in slow motion.

Jack saw Lucky grab the man by his hair and jerk him back, pulling him on top of him. Then Lucky rolled over, taking the man with him to change positions. Dawson Luck knew some wrestling moves. He had the punk pinned down and was struggling with him to get his arms pinned at his sides.

"Give it up, man," Lucky panted.

The man was bucking his lower body with all his might, trying to throw the detective off, but Lucky was a solid mass, holding on tight to his position. His left hand was pushing the man's right shoulder down, and his right hand was trying to keep his left arm pinned.

The punk was strong, and it was like watching a bull rider on the meanest bull in the rodeo, with Lucky trying to make that eight-second ride last.

When Lucky brought up his left knee to put more pressure on the suspect's upper torso, Jack saw the gun in his right hand.

"Lucky. Gun! Right hand" Jack rushed to assist.

Lucky moved his left hand down a notch and grabbed the man's right forearm to get a grip, then slammed it as hard as he could to the ground. Jack stepped on the thug's hand, putting all his weight down, crushing the suspect's fingers and wrist, causing him to lose his grip on the gun — Jack kicked it away.

"You muthafucker, you broke my goddamn fingers. You gonna pay, dog."

"Why don't you tell someone who gives a fuck?" Jack picked up the Beretta .45. "I'm betting the bullets in this gun match the slugs we found in Raynon Jones. You know who he is, right? Now get facedown, hands behind your back." Jack pointed his gun at the man. "Now, or I swear I'll put a cap in your ass."

"Fuck you. I don't know no dude named Raynon. What the fuck kinda name is that?" he spouted in anger. "You don't got nuttin', man. You come bustin' in here. I gonna sue you for breaking my fingers. You wait, you muthafucker—you'll see what'll go down." He kept talking big, but he rolled over facedown.

Lucky grabbed his arms, twisted them up, and cuffed him, then yanked him to his feet. "Raynon's street name is Glib, and Juan Mercedes—you're under arrest for murder. You have the right to remain silent—and I damn well wish you'd use that right. You have a right to an attorney," Lucky cited his Miranda rights.

Jack reached down and grabbed his partner's gun off the ground. "Here. Shoot him in the mouth. That'll shut him up."

Jack's radio crackled, "Team Two?".

"Go ahead, Team One."

"We have Pedro Perez secured. You have Juan Mercedes?"

"Roger that. Lucky's reading his rights as we speak. We heard a gun-shot—came from the back of the house. Anyone hit?"

"Nah. The gangsta badass is an effing crappy shot, and when he saw the four of us holding assault rifles, he dropped his gun in a hurry," the Vice detective said, laughing. "I think he pissed himself."

Jack said, "Yeah, I bet he did. Read him his rights, then haul the ignora-mus to the station ... we can get him clean shorts later."

24

BOOKED, PRINTED, THE GUNS—A .45 Beretta as well as a nine-millimeter semiautomatic—found in possession of Pedro Perez, both sent to Ballistics to confirm what they already knew was a fact.

Cuffed and in separate interrogation rooms, one man pissed as hell, his hand throbbing. Jack called for medical care.

"A doctor will look at you as soon as we get one over here."

"Ptooey." Juan Mercedes spat toward Jack, missing him by inches.

"Maybe I won't get you a doctor, and it hurts and throbs and you cry like a big titty-baby." Jack slammed the door shut and slid the top lock over with force.

At the monitor desk, Jace, Lucky, and two of the detectives from Vice watched.

"Hey, you got some food in your break room?" Smithers asked. "Take-downs make me hungry."

Lucky reached in a desk drawer and pulled out the large bag of chips he'd been working on. "Here, Smitty, knock your socks off."

By the time the doctor arrived an hour later, Juan was like a dog with rabies.

"Son," the doctor said, "if you don't calm down, I'll leave. I'm not fucking with you. Now hold still. Let me look at your hand."

Juan complied, but his jet-black eyes squeezed, and his tough-guy face twisted in a sneer. The doctor took each finger and wiggled them up, down, and side to side. Juan winced, but didn't make a sound. The doctor took his wrist and manipulated it; Juan flinched, pulling it back. The doctor set his hand down on top of the table.

"No, it's not broken, but it's gonna throb like hell for a while. It's a simple sprain. Your fingers are fine. Two Tylenol is all you're getting, and I'll get you a wrist splint once you get to lockup. For now, try to keep from moving your wrist."

With that, the doctor scooted out the door, leaving the angry man in Jack's most expert care.

"I know my partner read you your rights. You do understand them, dontcha?"

Juan stared at Jack, not batting an eye. "Yeah, I ain't stupid. I know what they mean, man."

"Then you're willing to talk to me?"

"Got nuttin' to say."

"Fine, then I'm gonna talk and you listen. If you want to jump in ..." Jack gave a sweep of his hand. "... by all means, be my guest."

Juan frowned. "Whatever, Va'to."

Jack gave him a look; he planned to scare the kid.

"First off, we have witnesses—three of them—willing to testify to what they saw. Eyewitnesses, Juan. We also found your guns. We both know the guns are gonna match up with the slugs we took out of Glib and Fiddler. You have an impressive rap sheet, and now you can add Murder One. You're looking at getting the needle. Texas still has the death penalty."

Juan's head shot up at the mention of the death penalty. Jack had his attention. Juan hadn't considered that consequence. Life in prison was bad, but death ... that was a different story altogether.

"What we have here is more than that. You made parole six months ago, and having a firearm in your possession? That kinda fucks your parole. We called your parole officer, and he's not a happy camper. Now you have that to face on top of Murder One. What a damn shame, man. You did nine out of ten, paroled a year early, and here we sit, discussing what your future is and if you're going to live or die. We both know jail is your next future, for eternity, but man, you don't have to die. Here's the deal, and I'm not gonna offer it but one time."

Jack stopped, waiting to see if the young man would start talking. Dead silence.

"Why don't you sit on what I've told you? When I think I've given you enough time to make a choice—life or death," Jack lifted his hands as if weighing the odds, "then I'll be back to tell you what my offer is."

Juan glared, his face set in stone. Jack left the room, wondering if the man had a conscience.

Back at the monitoring station, Jack found Lucky sitting with a cup of coffee in his hands, working on the chips that Smitty hadn't finished.

"Vice leave?" Jack pulled out a chair to sit.

Lucky nodded, swallowing his mouthful of chips. "Yep, they went back to four, had some reports to finish for Bucky. I've been out here for fifteen minutes, listening to your speech to Juan. You're not as mean as usual. What gives?"

"Well, round two is yet to come. I'm working my way to it. What'd ya get from Pedro?"

"Zilch, and I haven't mentioned the needle yet. He's gonna get an earful once I get back in there." Lucky looked at his watch. "In an hour, I'm going to let him stew a while longer."

"We can watch them on 'TV' stewing for a while, letting it sink into their dumb brains that they have zero futures in the free world. You wanna get a head start on the freaking paperwork?"

"You, Jack West, are going to help with reports? Well, damn, now I'm honored," Lucky said, then stuffed a handful of potato chips in his mouth.

Juan and Pedro both stewed and simmered for over an hour, and Jack was ready for round two.

"Juan, can I get you a soda or some water?"

"No, cerdo, don't want nothing."

Well, at least he'd opened his mouth, and he'd called him "pig" in Spanish ... as if it made a difference saying it in Spanish. What a moron.

"Like I told you, I'd tell you what my offer is." Jack scooted his chair closer, pushing the table down enough to make Juan move his hand. He winced.

"Sorry, bud, forgot about your injury." Jack feigned concern.

Juan jerked his head and sneered. "Whatever."

"Here's the deal, a onetime offer. You confess to Murder Two because, from what I'm told, you didn't plan to kill either Glib or Fiddler. You went to talk, but one of them hauled off and threw up a gang sign, pissed you and Pedro off. They were dissing you, and you opened fire in anger. If you don't confess, then once the ballistics get back—and they will match—we won't need your confession. Then you can kiss your ass goodbye, because you're gonna get charged with Premeditated Murder, and you and your gangster pal Pedro planned a hit. You go to court, and the jury thinks the death penalty is the deserved punishment. Juan, your mom will be heartbroken. If you have any bambinos and you die, they grow up without you, not getting to visit you in prison. At least getting life, you still get to see 'em."

He stopped talking, waiting for Juan to respond. He didn't.

He stood and shoved the chair back in place, knocking it against the table.

"Hell, kid, if you wanna die, fine by me. I was trying to save your life, even if it was to live it out in prison, but hey, you're what, thirty-one, I guess you've lived long enough. As a matter of fact, I don't know how you got this old. You have ten seconds, and when I walk out that door, the offer walks out with me. No second chance. Ten, nine, eight, seven ..."

Just as he said two, Juan spoke.

"I'll take the deal, cerdo. I don't wanna die on your nickel. If I gotta die, it'll be on my terms, not the lawyer's or a judge's, man. Shit, I shot Fiddler and Pedro shot Glib. Dude, we didn't plan to do it. We were there to parlay, you know, man. Fuck it. Fiddler threw up the gang sign, pissed me off and, well, I had the gun, I shot at him, then Pedro got all caught up in it and he shot too, man ... boom-boom-boom ... and they both went down. Then we booked the hell out, Va'to, you know, we got scared, and it was too late, man, to undo it."

Jack's lips pressed together. "Alright, Juan, you wait here. I'm gonna get a tape recorder and you can tell us in your own words, since I know you can't write with your bum hand."

A sullen nod. Juan knew his life was in the crapper. His punk attitude was still there, though; he might need to keep the tough-guy act for prison. Jack knew that all too well.

Jack West and Dawson Luck were sitting in Captain Brooks' office, going over the Mercedes/Perez case.

"Ballistics got clean matches to both guns, huh?" Brooks asked as he shuffled papers on his desk.

"It couldn't have been any closer if the slugs in the two dead men were still in the guns. We have solid cases, Captain, with two eyewitnesses at the scene and the testimony of Jose Velez, who was driving the car."

"So, this Velez kid, he gonna be a credible enough witness?"

"Young man, no rap sheet reading like a novel. He told me he's going to break away from the Brown Cobras. I told him I'd have eyes on him, and if he fucked up, I'd know. The Brown Cobras are not like some of the older, more violent gangs, like the Bloods, Crips, or MS-13 gangs. Maybe the kid has a fighting chance. The DA's office is considering his willingness to testify. He might get a year or two. They haven't decided if they want to dismiss the charges yet," Jack advised Brooks.

"Yeah," Lucky said, "the DA's office doesn't want to send out the wrong message that if you roll on someone, you get off scot-free for a major crime you've been involved in, even if you weren't the trigger man."

Captain Brody Brooks nodded, not at all interested—or it looked like that to Jack.

"Huh. Now, update me on the cases you and 7-11 are working together."

Jack's gut said Captain Brooks had no real interest in what was going on in Homicide. His tone was flat and monotone, and he was asking because they expected it of him. He could be mistaken; maybe Brooks was just that way. Jack hoped that was the case.

The update was pretty short and sweet ... the forensic art, the BOLO ... that was all the news they had, but they'd get back on it, assuring him they, him, Lucky, and 7-11 were doing all that was possible.

"Results, boys. We want results," he said to their backs as they left to go to the squad room. Both detectives frowned.

25

THEY DISTRIBUTED THE PICTURE of the unknown man to all patrol officers, and the BOLO had gone out a week ago. No results had yet been forthcoming. 7-11's case was nearing the four-month mark. Jack and Lucky's case just over a month. No leads. Not a damn one between the first forty-eight hours and now ... this was not good, not good at all. The longer they went without leads, the lower the chances they'd solve the case.

That was until the killer struck again. Someone else might die. The team was racing against time. They needed a lead.

"We're getting nowhere, damn it." Jack paced the two or three steps between his desk and the wall.

"Think we need to grill the husband, Lincoln Taylor, one more time?" Chang asked.

"Waste of time, guys. I don't see his reasoning, except for the two hundred grand to collect. He would've had to kill our victim too, and why? Why did he do that? What reason would he have to kill twice? Not to mention he has a solid alibi. You said so yourself."

"I have to agree with Lucky." Jack stopped pacing and looked at the others. "The murders are similar, and if he had been the perp, I don't think he would've taken all the extra steps in the second murder. Why would he need to do that? Not to mention we know his alibi rules him out for his wife. We need to look at what we do have," Jack said, pulling a whiteboard from where it stood next to the wall.

At the top, he wrote each victim's name and filled in the information they had on each case. As he wrote, the other three spouted info to populate each column.

Stepping back, they all studied the accumulated information.

"So, murder locations: an empty house and a dumpster area ... over fifteen miles apart, no commonality ... the places were convenient. The method of killing is the same, the makeup is the same, the broken finger is the same. We have wig hair on both victims that match, and the killer positioned the bodies as a mortician would for a wake. That's ..." Jack counted "... five commonalities."

"First victim: no Bible, no note, and no highlighted Bible verse," Chang added.

"No dildo shoved up her ... either. Plus, your victim didn't have a head injury," Lucky chimed in.

Jace Severson skimmed the autopsy report in front of him. "Well, that's correct. Our victim had no head injury, but she did have duct tape over her mouth."

"That means she wasn't clobbered but tied up—mouth-taped. Just how'd the killer get her to cooperate?" The gears in Jack's head were turning.

"That house was empty, but hell, the neighborhood's not a ghost town." Chang's forehead crinkled.

"When we canvassed, it shocked me that no one pays attention to what goes on in the neighborhood. The neighbor on the corner next to the empty house saw our victim dropped off in front of the house, which is normal since they showed it at least twelve times a day." Jace stayed on track with Chang's thought pattern.

"She didn't drive herself either. The neighbor said the car left and she saw a Black woman in the front yard. She figured the lady would Uber home—people do that more often these days," Chang took over the story. "She figured the woman was there to look at the house since it's for sale."

"So, no one saw who came up to the house pretending to be the realtor? Did the lady next door notice a second vehicle drive up to meet the woman?" Jack asked. "Neighbors get curious when new people show up."

"No. She said she looked out the window, saw our victim, and then had to cook dinner. Her kitchen is at the back of the house," Chang supplied.

"We checked with Uber. A driver dropped her off, but she didn't get Ubered back—she got 'coronered' back. The neighbor said she thought she heard a car drive up but didn't look out the window. An hour later, she heard another car pull up, only she thought Uber came to get her," Jace finished.

"No one else on that street saw a damn thing. Hell, whatever happened to the nosy neighbors of yesteryear?" Chang got pissy.

"When we questioned Al Mathers, the realtor, there'd been no showing set up for that night either. We know he was having an affair with our victim, and that they met in some of the empty houses he had listed, but he told us they hadn't planned a rendezvous for that night. He does have an ironclad alibi," Jace added.

"Alright, then no one saw anyone or a damn thing. Looking at our victim, same flipping story. The older woman next door gave us a bit more info—at least a car we friggin' can't find. Our dead girl didn't appear to have many friends, at least none she confided in. Her neighborhood ... well, crap, fellas, her unknown killer could live there," Lucky said. He pulled his chair to Jack's side of the desk and dropped into the seat with a thud.

"The locations were miles apart. From what profilers say, a killer kills within their own geographical area—closer to where they live or work. Guess that's no help. Your lady went in without a fuss—maybe she knew her killer. Y'all said nobody tampered with the lockboxes and found zero prints."

"Shit, Jack, there were prints on top of prints. A crapload of agents touched that lockbox. All we know is they went through the back door. Mathers said the back door wasn't deadbolted—it has to be done from the inside. He also said every agent checks to make sure houses get locked, lights off, thermostats regulated—the whole nine yards when they leave," Chang said. "We got one damn print. On the back door. Someone pulled it shut, then wiped the knob. A finger and half a thumb. Not a match to any realtors, and Lord knows it could be a prospective homebuyer's print, too."

"Lockboxes open with an app on your phone, now—you need to be a realtor to get that app. It wasn't a realtor—or at least that's our conclusion since they all alibied out," Jace said.

Lucky bobbed his head. "Then it might be possible she knew the perp. If not, how did he lure her into the house?"

How her killer lured her into an empty house was a mystery they might never solve.

"What do you think, Jack? Your gut talking to you?" Jace asked.

Jack knew Jace wasn't kidding, and he knew most of the time his gut "talked" to him. The other detectives made jokes, but this time they needed Jack's gut to guide them ... somewhere ... anywhere to help catch this killer.

"The locations were convenient, and I don't think a sexual deviant committed these murders either, but I can't tell you why I think that. What keeps gnawing at me is the broken finger. And our victims' cases ... the Bible, the note, and the Bible verse ..." Jack trailed off in thought.

Lucky reminded them, "If we don't get a clue to work with, then what? We can sit here all day chewing the fat on both cases, but while we do that, hell, the killer could be planning number three."

"I discussed getting a profiler in with Chief Yao. He told me to talk to Brooks, which I did."

"What's the scoop, Jack? What did our beloved Captain Brooks say?" Chang said with sarcasm.

"He said we aren't there yet, and we need to work our asses off. Between the four of us, we have too many years on the job and should be able to do it better. It's like he thinks we all have magical powers and a crystal-fuck-ing-ball." Jack raked his hands through his hair.

"Do you guys know the captain either hates Jack or is scared of him?" Lucky questioned 7-11.

"I vote for scared. Jack, go in there and whip his ass. Give him a reason to be scared of you." Jace hooted.

"Well, Jack, word is he doesn't play by the rules. He didn't in Rob-bery, and he ain't fucking gonna in Homicide either. The man's a ladder climber, and if you're on a rung and in his way as he goes up, he'll toss your ass off. He won't care if your fool neck gets broken, either."

Jace and Lucky knew Chang was right.

"I don't know why he has his compass pointed at me. I've heard the gossip through the departments over the years, but most of the time I ignore that shit and just do my job."

"Jack, you took down a judge, and that's not easy. Not only did the judge get conspiracy to cover a murder and disbarment, they also slapped the jerk with moral turpitude. Man, you show up and the judge gets fucked nine ways to Sunday."

"Lucky, we—you and I—we did that together, man. We're a team. It wasn't all me, and that was two years ago." Jack didn't like to dwell on that crap.

"Hey, I know, Jack, but you have a rep with the HPD that I don't. I mean, I have a rep, but not a good one." He leered with his caterpillar eyebrows wiggling up and down, like Groucho Marx.

Jace and Chang both hee-hawed, and Jack laughed too, because Lucky did have what he thought was his "I got game" rep. It didn't work out for him, because it took very little effort to aggravate the females. To Dawson Luck, it was all fun, though he lacked the diplomacy to pull it off.

"Look, Jack, it's a compliment. Just say thank you. I would love for Captain Brody Brooks to fear me ... I'd ask for a raise." Jace boomed.

With that, it was time to stop for the day. It was late, and they had zilch for leads; they'd start fresh tomorrow.

26

PATROL OFFICER CASSANDRA SPARROW and her partner Amy Cordova pulled their second night shift for the month.

"Hope it's a halfway slow night tonight. Got a splitting headache," Amy said, shifting in her seat.

"Baby, this is Houston. It's never slow in Houston," Cass snorted.

"Well, I can hope." Amy frowned, knowing her partner was right. Houston was not suburban—it was urban, with a capital U ... bustling, and full of people, 24/7.

"One Adam-27," the dispatcher's voice came through the radio.

"This is One Adam-27. Go ahead," Amy responded.

"We have a 10-56 over at the Eight-Ball Pool Hall in the 5900 block of Westheimer Road," Dispatch called out.

"Roger that. We're 10-17. One Adam-27 out." Amy clicked off the radio.

"A drunk pedestrian. Not too exciting, but if we have to take him in, I hope he doesn't puke in our car." Cass wheeled back and headed to the pool hall.

Four men were outside the Eight Ball when they rolled up. Two of them were arguing, while the other two were monitoring the situation.

"Geez, they could've told us there was more than one drunk," Amy grunted. She opened her door and reached under the seat for her baton.

"I know, but we got this, girl." Cass mirrored her, grabbing her baton. They approached the men.

"Fellas," Cass raised her voice, "what seems to be the problem here?"

"Ain't no pro'lem, ofisher. Juss tryin' to get my money from thish man," the rather short, stocky man slurred, drunker than Cooter Brown.

"Okay, which one of you is he trying to get money from?" Amy stepped in, baton at the ready. The other drunk held up his hand and belched.

"S'cuze me, I'm the man."

"Look, Officer ..." The first man looked at Amy's badge. "Cordova. Me and my buddy here"—he jabbed his thumb at the man next to him—"walked out and stumbled on these two arguing. They're both drunk. I called 9-1-1 don't want 'em to drive and kill someone or kill each other."

"Come on, fellas, let's take a seat, right over there." Cass guided the two drunks to a small bench next to the doorway of the pool hall.

Both men wobbled and stumbled over to the bench. One of them hit the bench; the other wasn't as fortunate and slid down, hitting the concrete sidewalk. It did not faze him—too drunk to feel a thing.

Cass took charge of the drunks while Amy got the 9-1-1 caller's ID and the story.

"Thanks for calling it in." Amy nodded to them.

Cass and Amy faced the inebriated men, pondering their next move.

"Don't relish the idea of taking them to the drunk tank," Amy muttered, staring down at the two drunks, one of whom was nodding off.

"Sit on these derelicts. I'm going inside. Have the manager call two cabs. I'll be damned, Amy, it's just now twelve-thirty ... ain't near closing time."

Their addresses were verified by their driver's licenses. Cass and Amy asked several times if those were their current addresses. By the third time, Cass' drunk yelled and cursed.

"Fuck, woman, you got cotton ballsh in your earsh ... I done tole ya four timish," he slurred.

Two cabs arrived. They poured the two drunks in, and the cabbies drove off.

"One Adam-27 is 10-23 (assignment completed)," Amy radioed in. "Hey, Cass, you mind stopping at the convenience store up on the corner? I need some coffee or a soda. You want a drink, my treat?"

"Thanks, but no thanks. I'll just wait."

Cass could see through the front window. There was a short line checking out. Why in the hell were people out this late shopping at a convenience store? Three men and one woman were ahead of Amy.

The first two men walked out, and Cass watched them. But when the third man came out, she did a double take. Looking on the dash at the composite drawing for the BOLO, she knew he was the one. Watching in her rearview mirror, she saw him get in a silver Acura, confirming it. The BOLO had said he would be driving a silver Nissan or Acura.

Giving Amy a hand signal that they needed to roll, Amy set her soda down and sprinted to the squad car.

"We get an urgent callout?" she asked, buckling up.

"No, do me a favor. Get the plate number off that Acura. I'm going to follow him. This guy's our BOLO."

"You gotta be kidding me." Amy wrote the plate number down: MJH-4368. Well, they'd had the M and the 68 ... now it was a complete plate number.

"The BOLO said don't apprehend, but if seen, follow or get plate number. We're going to do both."

Cass followed at a distance—not wanting to scare the man. Most people got twitchy when a cop cruiser was nearby.

"Look," Amy said, "he's turning right on Briargrove Drive. You gonna follow?"

"I see him, but I'm gonna slow way down at the corner. Don't want him to suspect we're following him."

Cass had skills. The man did not notice a cop was following him. Either he was oblivious or had a real clean conscience. She saw him turn right on Willers Way and she went straight, then did a turnabout and went back toward Willers Way. She slowed down and looked to see if his car was still on the street. No car. She pulled onto Willers Way, driving five miles an hour.

"There," Amy said, pointing, "that garage door is still closing."

Cass beamed.

They had his address; they had his plate number ... they had him.

27

At the station for less than an hour, Jack's phone rang.

"Homicide, West. Uh, wow, that's fantastic. Who got it, where? Yep, let me write this down."

Jack looked over at Chang. "11, we got a positive ID on our BOLO last night."

"For real? That's awesome."

"What's awesome?" Lucky asked as he opened the door to the squad room, one hand holding a cup of coffee and the other a box with the words, *"Sherry's Donuts and Cakes."*

"Jack just got a call," Chang said, taking the box out of Lucky's hand and peeking in.

"What, no jelly donuts?"

"Chang, don't bitch," Lucky started ...

"We got a hit on our BOLO," Jack spurted out. "Who cares if it's jelly or not?"

Chang grabbed a donut. "He's like a giddy kid in a candy store." Then he took a big bite of a chocolate-glazed donut.

"Perfect. Now we need to go see him," Lucky said, grabbing two donuts and setting them on a napkin. "Hey, where's Jace?"

"He'll be here in a couple of minutes, he texted me," Chang said as he took another bite.

Jack sat down and began keying in the license plate number.

"You guys look like typical cops—donuts in one hand and sugar crumbs on your upper lips." He glanced up to see Chang and Lucky both wipe their mouths with the backs of their hands. He snickered.

"Who caught our BOLO, Jack?" asked Lucky.

"Sparrow and Cordova did."

"They're on the nights? When did that happen?" Lucky garbled, with a mouth full of glazed donut.

"I saw Cass last week. She said they had to take a night shift twice a month for the next six months."

Hitting enter, Jack drummed his fingers until the info popped up. "Here it is … Rafe Preston, age forty-two, lives on Willers Way."

"Where'd they see him?" Lucky took the last bite of his donut.

"They went to Eight Balls on Westheimer, had a couple of drunks to take care of, stopped at a convenience store, and Cass saw our boy walking out. I hope this is the break we need. Now maybe we have a lead. This is terrific." Jack was like a boy at Christmas.

"A lead. All I heard was maybe we have a lead. What lead?" Severson came through the door.

"Maybe you should get to work on time. Then you'd know what's going on."

"Bite me, 11." Jace grinned.

"Bite this." Chang handed Jace a plain glazed donut.

"What the hell, no jelly?" He peeked in the box. Jack, Lucky, and Chang cracked up.

"Let's see his driver's license picture, compare it to the BOLO. Man, that Becca Brenner, wow, she is amazing. Her composite is a mirror image of the dude. She is freaking awesome."

Lucky was still in awe of her talent. Arizona had some decent forensic artists, but Becca Brenner, he said, was one in a million—and he was right.

"She left a note with the drawing that said Shelly Cooper was vague on some of his features. It was all she could remember. Man, we owe BB," Jack said.

"Jack, you gonna call this guy up, or do a 'surprise' drop by?" Chang inquired.

"Yeah, we'll drop by his house tonight. He has no idea we're looking for him. I'd like to catch him off guard."

Rafe Preston didn't need a heads-up; the element of surprise was on their side.

Mid-morning, Captain Brooks came looking for 7-11.

He stuck his head in the door. "Severson, Chang, come to my office." He didn't linger, and his ruddy face disappeared.

"Sure, Captain, we're on our way," Chang called out.

"What the hell, Xi, why does he want to see us?" Jace frowned. "Did we fuck up?"

"Not that I know of," Chang responded. "Let's not keep the man waiting. See you guys later. Come on, Jace, let's take it like men," he said with a short laugh.

"Hmm, wonder what in the hell is going on," Lucky said as he stared at the closed squad room door.

"Don't care what he's up to as long as he stays out of my way, and ..." Jack's cell phone rang, cutting him off mid-sentence. "Homicide, West. Hey, Rick, how goes it on four? Sure, Lucky and I can come down to four if ... sure, Rodeo Goat? Yeah, I'll ask them too, no problem." Jack hung up.

"What does Rick want?"

"Not sure, but he wants you, me, and 7-11 to meet him at two, but not here at the station. Sounds mysterious, Mwuhahahaha." Jack tried to make a creepy sound, but he wasn't very good at it, making Lucky snort out a laugh.

———ell———

It was 2:00 pm, and the lunch crowd at Rodeo Goat had thinned out. Jack, Lucky, and 7-11 were waiting on Rick Tormo, but he was running late.

"Did he say why he wanted to meet?" Chang looked over at Jack.

"No, he didn't say. Hey, why did Brooks wanna see y'all?" Jack asked. "Is it hush-hush, or can you discuss it?"

Jace hesitated. "Uh, no big deal. He wanted to discuss our closure rate, said we needed to step it up, and he gave us a mini-review."

"What the fuck, Jace, you and Xi close at least eighty percent, and that's damn good." Jack looked at them both.

"Jack, we know that, but that wasn't all he brought us in there for. Well hell, Jack, he wanted to ask questions about you," Jace came clean.

"Me ... what did he ask?" It pissed him off Brooks was asking his fellow detectives. If he had questions, he could be a man and ask him to his face.

Xi Chang was not gonna lie to Jack. "Stuff concerning your capabilities, your 'detective' abilities, and the counseling you've undergone with anger management. He's been reading everyone's personnel jacket. Brooks said he wanted our peers' opinions—guess he'll ask you to evaluate us."

"Yeah, I doubt that. He's up to something, I think ..." Jack didn't finish his sentence as Rick Tormo walked up to the table along with his partner, Katherine Sparks, better known as Sparky.

"Hey, fellas, long time I no see you guys." Sparks pulled out a chair and took a seat next to Jace.

"Sparky, how's it going? Nice to see you." Jace shook her hand. Everyone said hello, reaching across the table to shake hands with her and Rick.

"Hey, Sparky, still loving it in Vice, or do you wish you were back in Robbery since Brooks is gone?" Chang looked at her with mirth in his eyes.

"Yeah, right, fun-fucking-times back then. Vice might have some gross aspects and some very sick people we deal with, but at least I'm working with guys who are honest, loyal, and more than accountable." Not a trace of humor laced her voice.

They all chatted, reminiscing, and replaying some funny anecdotes. Once the laughter subsided, Jack got serious. "Rick, why meet here and not at the station?"

"I know some of this is gossip, but ..."

Everyone was listening.

28

It was 6:15. Jack and Lucky were on their way to see Rafe Preston.

"You think this guy knows Jade's dead?"

"Yeah," Jack said. "He knows. He went back looking for her, knowing she hung out there, thinking she'd blown him off, and he was going to confront her. He might've asked the bartender if he'd seen her. Barry Picco knows she's dead. Rafe Preston knows too."

"Well, that punk-ass bartender could have called us, but hell—all the weed he's smoked has burned up his brain cells. I bet he trashed your card the second we walked away. He wants no part of 'Five-O.'" Lucky did air quotes.

"I'm sure he tossed it. That place is full of wannabe rapper gangsters and loose women. Clubbing ain't what it used to be, pard."

Jack turned off Westheimer Road onto Sage Road. Next stop ... Rafe Preston's house.

The surrounding neighborhoods were very middle- to upper-class—homes with manicured lawns, crape-myrtle trees, flower beds filled with colorful flora ... the all-American look of clean living. There were older kids on bicycles and some playing on the sidewalks. A regular suburban area, housed by normal people.

The word *normal* stuck in his head. What in the hell was normal? His mind flashed on people who had appeared to be normal—the Jeffrey Dahmers and O.J. Simpsons of the world—normal, all-American. Whoever they were dealing with, their unknown suspect had been a normal person, except something had triggered a rage in him, and now he was a monster.

Burdened with one question and one question only, Jack wanted to know what had triggered the beast.

"There it is, Jack—3428." Lucky pointed it out.

Parking on the opposite side of the street, they walked over to the house, up the sidewalk, past a cactus flowerbed and up the walkway, stepping over a boy's bicycle, and up to the front door. Lucky rang the bell. "It's showtime."

A woman opened the door. A nine- or ten-year-old boy stood behind her, peering to see who had come calling. She wiped her hands on a dish towel and cracked the storm door open. Jack assumed she was cooking dinner.

"Yes, may I help you?"

"Yes, ma'am, is Rafe Preston here?"

"He's in the back. May I tell him who's calling?"

"Ma'am, I'm Detective Jack West from the Houston Police Department, and we'd like a word with your husband. Can you please go get him?"

"Uh, is Rafe in trouble? I mean, he's not a criminal, I assure you." She remembered her son was there. "Carl, go to your room."

"But Mom, I wa—"

"I said go to your room." This time, her voice was authoritative.

The boy ducked his head and left, not happy, but he minded his mother.

"Carl, tell Charles to stay in his room until I call you both for dinner. Do you hear me?"

"Yes, ma'am, I will."

As the woman turned back and the boy disappeared down the hallway, Lucky asked, "Mrs. Preston, can you let your husband know we need to speak with him, please?"

"Is Rafe in trouble? I need to know, be—"

Jack cut her off. "Ma'am, we aren't at liberty to say right now. If you would, please tell your husband that we're waiting for him on the front porch."

"Yes, I will, and well ..." She didn't finish. She left the wooden front door open but shut the glass storm door.

Rafe Preston appeared a few minutes later, and he was the spitting image of the composite—grayish hair, receding hairline, a weak jawline, and the early stages of a double chin.

"Mr. Preston, may we speak with you out here?"

"Yes, Detective … uh—" He stumbled, not knowing which detective was which.

"I'm Detective West. This is Detective Luck."

"Sure, out here is fine. Sybil, shut the door."

With a worried look on her face, his wife shut the door and wrung her hands, afraid her husband was in trouble. She didn't want to lose him; she had just gotten him back.

"Now," Rafe Preston said, putting both hands in his pants pockets, "how can I help you?"

"Were you acquainted with a Jade Nelson?" Jack jumped right in.

"Jade Nelson—no, I don't think so. Why?" His face was a blank page, no telltale emotions whatsoever.

"That's odd, Mr. Preston. You see, we've questioned several people at a club called The Razz. Two different people gave us your description." Jack pulled out a copy of the composite. "Here's the picture our forensic artist drew from the descriptions given to her by one of our witnesses."

Jack turned to his partner. "Detective Luck, don't you agree this is a near-perfect likeness of Mr. Preston?"

Lucky looked at the composite and then at the man, nodding. "I'd say it's like someone took a picture of Mr. Preston—with a camera."

"We've got information on the vehicle you drive from a neighbor of Miss Nelson's. It's a silver Honda, and she remembered some of the license plate numbers. The first letter is M, and the last two digits are 68. If we were to ask to see the car in your garage, what do you think we'd find?" Jack frowned at him.

Rafe Preston's face paled, and he lowered his voice. "Yes, I did know her, but I don't want my wife to find out because … because I was having an affair with her."

"Are you aware they found Miss Nelson murdered?"

"I found out a few days later. I went looking for her at the club, and the bartender told me."

"We've had a helluva time finding you. Unless you have something to hide, why didn't you come forward? We know you knew Miss Nelson." Jack would not play games with this man.

"You wanna know why I didn't come forward? Are you cracked? I was having a damn affair with a woman who is now dead. God, man, why in the hell do you think I didn't come forward? What—You think I killed her?" His whisper sounded like a hiss.

"Mr. Preston, we can either step inside and talk, or you can come downtown to talk—your choice. And yes, you're a person of interest in this case. If I were you, I wouldn't cop an attitude right now. Your position with me is shaky." Jack's annoyance grew with the weak-jawed, double-chinned man.

"Not here—my wife might overhear us, and you know ..." He trailed off.

"We can meet you at the station. You can follow us," Lucky said.

"First, I need to ... uh ... think of an excuse to tell the wife. I mean, hell, what do I say?"

"Since you've become a person of interest in our investigation, my advice is to tell her the truth. Then you don't have to compound lie on top of lie."

Rafe Preston did not like the sound of that. *Person of interest*. Damn, he'd messed up in a huge way.

"I'll tell her, but not right now. Can you give me some time to get there?"

"I'll give you one hour. We'll see you down at the station no later than an hour from now. Know this, Mr. Preston—if you don't show up, we'll come back with a warrant, and it'll get unpleasant for you. Got that?"

A sullen-faced Rafe nodded, knowing his sins were coming back to haunt him.

29

True to his words, and heeding Jack's warning, Rafe Preston was at the station an hour later and placed in an interview room.

"Another freaking late night, Jack, my wife thinks I've moved out."

"As long as she knows you're still married to her, you got it made. You ready to do this, partner?"

"Yep, Jack, let's do this thing."

In the interview room, Rafe Preston was sweating. The police thought he was involved in Jade's murder, and he needed to get this straightened out, and fast. He had no fear of them arresting him because he was innocent, but it stopped there. However, he feared he'd screwed up his marriage. The little head in his trousers had overridden the head on his shoulders, causing him to act foolish.

"Mr. Preston, would you like water or coffee?" Jack offered.

"No, I want to get through your questions, then get home."

"Fine. How did you and Miss Nelson meet?"

"She works ... worked," he corrected, "at an ad agency where my company was looking at doing radio spots. She came to the office one day, and I became infatuated with her."

"Where do you work, Mr. Preston?"

"Uh, Smith and Thompson Architectural Designs. I'm an architect. Jade came to the office several times, and one day I asked her if she wanted to have coffee with me, and that's how it started."

"Did you tell her you were married?" Jack noted Rafe Preston wore no wedding ring.

"Not at first. Since I couldn't call her every day nor see her that often, I had to come clean," he admitted.

"Were your plans to leave your wife and marry Miss Nelson, then?"

"No ... well, yes, maybe. Shit, I don't know." He raked his hands through his hair. "Hell, I don't know what I was planning. To tell you the truth, I just liked the way she made me feel. When I was with her, I felt alive."

"Did you know what her expectations were?" Lucky asked a question.

Rafe looked at him. "How in the hell would I know that? She never said, I never asked. Jade liked things the way they were, I guess—no real commitments to deal with. And if you're asking me if she asked me to divorce my wife, no, she didn't."

"Do you realize that you're one of the last people who saw her alive? Is that true? Were you the last person to see her alive?" Jack pressed him.

"I know damn well she was alive the last time I saw her," Rafe said with force.

"Oh, I don't know, Mr. Preston. It looks like you've been hiding in the shadows. You knew Jade Nelson and found out what happened to her. Innocent people don't hide, and we've been trying to find you for weeks now," Jack replied in an accusing manner.

"I'm telling you, I'm not the one you're looking for. I didn't do it." His voice got louder with every word.

"When was the last time you saw her?" Jack knew from what the bartender Barry Picco had told them it'd been Wednesday night prior to her murder.

"I saw her on Wednesday, and I was supposed to meet her the next night, and she never showed, and I got mad. I thought she was blowing me off."

Well, that corroborated the story Pothead Picco told them.

"I texted and called her, but she never responded. Believe me, I had no idea she was dead. The next day I called and got her voicemail."

"You have your phone on you?"

"Not that phone. I bought a pay-by-the-minute cheap phone to call Jade on. Crap, I didn't want my wife to see her number on our bill. That woman checks everything. I tossed it in the trash once I was told that Jade was dead.

If you want it, you'll have to go to the city landfill. That's where it ended up, and I can't change that fact." He wasn't trying to hide information; he was trying to cooperate. It was his mission to save his ass.

"What was the phone number for that burner phone?" Lucky was ready to write it down.

Rafe Preston supplied them with the number. "But it won't do you any good to call it. I crushed the damn thing."

"No, but we can match that number up to the numbers on Jade's telephone records, to see what time it was when you texted and called her the night of her murder," Lucky informed him, hoping it scared the shit right outta him.

"So, for several months, you had trysts with Miss Nelson. Where did you go?" Jack ignored the landfill remark. With the number Rafe gave them, they'd be able to get all the information on where that burner phone was at any hour of the day or night with cell tower records—no need to have the physical phone. Jack knew this never crossed Rafe Preston's mind.

"I'd meet her at the club she hung out at, The Razz. We'd have a few drinks and sit at the end of the bar, you know, chatting and stuff. We'd leave the club at ten-thirty or eleven, and we'd go to her place too. You know, I'm positive you do know." He searched their faces, knowing damn well they knew what he and Jade were doing at her place.

"Afterward I'd take her back to the club, she'd get her car, and then I went home. I swear when I left her on Wednesday night, she was very much alive."

No one spoke. Jack watched the man, trying to read him, and Lucky scowled.

Rafe pinched the bridge of his nose; the stress was building up in his head. "I can't believe this is happening."

"Well, it did happen, and this is the consequence for a man who cheats. If I were you, I'd think long and hard before you decide to cheat for a second time," Lucky retorted, his voice laced with loathing. The man's wife was nice-looking, and he had two boys. Why the hell would he want to throw that all away? Lucky didn't understand it at all.

Jack's eyes focused on the man's face, looking for any telltale sign. "Did you ever go anywhere else?"

"A few times we went across town to places that neither my wife nor her parents would ever go. We'd eat dinner and take a walk."

"Did you meet her friends? Did you ever give her money?"

"Look, Detective West, first off, no, I never gave her money. She wasn't selling me sex, and she never asked me for anything. She wanted me, for me. I know you find that hard to believe, but it's the honest-to-God truth. As far as her friends, she told me she had very few, and no, I never met them. It astonished me that friends didn't surround a beautiful, sexy woman like her. She was vibrant with a sweet personality, and people liked her. She was a loner, and I didn't understand it."

"Mr. Preston, you got to the club at nine-fifteen that Thursday night. Where were you before then?"

"Are you asking me for my alibi, Detective West?"

"Jade got killed sometime between eight and nine o'clock Thursday night, and you said you got to the club at nine-fifteen. You had plenty of time to go to her place, kill her, and get to the club by nine-fifteen—where were you, Mr. Preston?" Jack was getting irate.

"I worked until eight that night. You can check with my boss. We were working on a deadline. His name is Gary Thompson. You can call him."

"Once you left your office, where did you go?"

"Hell, I met a couple of buddies for a drink at the Oasis Bar. You want their names and phone numbers?" he asked with a contemptuous attitude.

"Yes, Mr. Preston," Lucky said as he took his pen in hand. "As a matter of fact, we're gonna need their names and phone numbers tonight. Can someone from the Oasis Bar support your alibi? Did you pay with a credit card?"

"Yes, damn it, someone from the bar—the dickhead bartender—can tell you I was there. And no, I didn't pay for my drinks; one of my buddies did. You want his credit card information, then you'll have to ask him. Jesus H. Christ, you'd think I was on trial here." Rafe Preston's face got red.

Jack West slapped the table, leaning in with a black look. "You know, Mr. Preston, there were two gray pubic hairs found on her body, and I'm betting if we did a DNA test they would match your DNA."

The man turned gray, green, then white. He felt sick. "I didn't kill her. I mean, we had sex Wednesday night and that's how they got there, but I'm telling you I didn't kill her. This is a nightmare." Rafe Preston was sweating, and his hands were shaking as he brought them up to his temples. He had the onset of the worst headache he might ever have in his life.

30

"ARE YOU WILLING TO undergo a DNA check and a polygraph? Until we can check out everything you've told us, you're our prime suspect," Jack said. "And knowing you had sex with her the night before her murder, and probable matching DNA, doesn't look too good for you."

"I didn't kill her," he screamed and hit his fists on top of the table.

Matching DNA, his admission to the affair—Christ, he was going to jail ... or he could end up on death row waiting for the needle. He'd seen all the movies, and he knew how this played out.

"If you want my DNA, you can get a warrant. Jade might have been seeing other men. I mean, I wasn't with her 24/7. Christ, she was sexy and beautiful. It might not be my pubic hairs, but you do what you have to do. Only I'm not going to just submit." He sat up ramrod straight and crossed his arms. This body language, Jack knew—Rafe Preston was getting defensive.

Jack rose. "That's fine, Mr. Preston. When we get the warrant to get your DNA, we'll serve it at your house in front of your wife. If you're trying to test me, that won't work. And if you do, Mr. Preston, I guarantee you will not come out on top." Jack bent closer. He and Rafe were an inch from touching nose to nose.

Rafe shoved his chair back with his feet and held his hands up. "Wait, wait, that won't be necessary. If you do need my DNA, I'll submit it without a warrant. I don't want you coming to my house that way." He calmed down, knowing they had outgunned him, and Jack West would follow through on his threat.

"That's better, Mr. Preston. Willingness to assist us is your single option right now."

Dawson Luck scooted his chair toward the table. "Do you think your wife knew, Mr. Preston? Do you think she found out and retaliated?"

"Sybil, are you kidding? The woman might be a part-time nag, but she's a terrific mother and an okay wife. I could never see her hurting a soul, much less killing a person."

"Why cheat?" Lucky wanted to know his lame excuse.

"Excitement, new sex, the thrill of an affair with a younger woman, I guess. Hell, Jade stirred a passion in me I thought was dead. My wife and I have sex, but what Jade and I had was, the only way to put it, animalistic. The woman took my breath away."

"I hate to tell you this, Mr. Preston, but wives have incredible intuition when their man is cheating. The three main reasons crimes get committed are love, money, or revenge. There are two reasons in this mix for your wife ... love and revenge. Mr. Preston, we'll need to question your wife. You need to come clean with her and see what you can do to salvage your marriage. That's on you. We don't care. You've got to answer for that. What we do care about is getting justice for Jade Nelson and her family."

"My wife ... she doesn't know. She would have confronted me. I know that, and I know her. Leave her out of this, please."

"No can do. This is a murder, Mr. Preston. We investigate every angle, and we leave no rock unturned. Now here's what you have to decide. You need to decide if you're going to come clean to your wife and tell her everything. Or will we have to break the news to her when we pick her up for questioning? What's it going to be?"

Defeated, Rafe Preston needed to be the one who told his wife, not these detectives. He was sure Sybil loved him. He never doubted it, but would she still want him? Would she banish him from their home? Would he lose the privilege of being a full-time dad to Charles and Carl? Could he go to jail? He had no idea until that very moment how his animal lust and infidelity had cast him into an endless pit, one he might never escape.

"I'll explain it all to my wife. Would you give me a few days?"

"Mr. Preston, time is not a luxury homicide detectives have. We can give you two days, and once you and your wife have spoken, you call me. But ..." Jack held up his finger. "If we don't hear from you in two days, we'll come knocking at your door. Do you understand?"

"Yes, and I do have two questions." Rafe was passive now. He knew he was the underdog, and he had no fight left in him.

"Sure, Mr. Preston, ask away."

"First, am I a suspect in Jade's murder?"

"Maybe, and until we check your alibi, I'm warning you, don't leave town." Jack narrowed his eyes.

"Is my wife Sybil a suspect as well?"

"Mr. Preston, I can't give you a definite answer. She very well could be. Your wife Sybil is a person of interest, and she better not leave town, either."

———— ✺ ————

SEVEN A.M. THE NEXT morning at the station, Jack was knee-deep looking at phone records. He had taken the cell tower records over to the tech office to do a graph of where Jade's phone had been before, during, and after her murder, as well as Rafe Preston's burner.

Lucky walked in bearing gifts of two coffees and two Egg McMuffins from Mickey-D's.

"Thanks, Lucky. I didn't stop for breakfast this morning." He unwrapped his breakfast sandwich and took a bite.

"I can't believe you gave him a few days to get back to us. Don't you think that was generous?" Lucky took a bite of his Egg McMuffin.

"Yeah, but we need to have the time to verify his alibi, which I think will check out. The guy is sweating bullets or shitting himself, since now he has to confess to the wifey-poo. This'll give him some time in case she throws him out on his ear. But I'm not messing with this guy. I'll get his DNA, and then he'll sweat even more."

"Yeah, and I have to say what a douchebag. He let his little head do his thinking, dumb-ass." Lucky chomped on his sandwich.

"Here. You call his boss, Gary Thompson. See if he alibis up to eight p.m., and I'll call these two guys, Stan Beekman and, uh ..." Jack looked at his notes. "Willard Jones. See if they both say the same thing and Preston was with them at the Oasis Bar."

"I looked up the Oasis Bar last night. It's a bar and an eatery that opens at eleven for lunch. It's off Capitol Street, close to Preston's office. Let's kill two birds with one stone. We eat lunch and talk to the bartender."

"Excellent idea." Jack punched in the cell number for Stan Beekman. "Hope he's awake."

"Everything checked out with his boss. He was with him until eight." It discouraged Lucky.

"Both men said he was with them, but we'll confirm with the bartender, too. I have the copy of Jade's phone records here. That burner phone number he had was 'burning up' her phone. Calls and texts ... man, this guy was obsessive." Jack sifted through the last days that Jade had used her phone; then his own phone rang.

"Homicide, West. Hi, Art, got news for me?" Jack listened. "Yeah, sure, thanks, Art."

"Walsworth from Tech?" Lucky looked up.

"Yeah, he was calling with the cell tower report."

"Did he have any news?"

"No, her phone triangulated from her work and her apartment, which is right at two miles apart on the Thursday she was murdered. Wednesday, her phone pinged near the Club Razz area. The cheater's burner number was near his work, the Oasis Bar, and Club Razz, then his house. It never pinged near her apartment. This solidifies his alibi." Jack figured Preston wasn't the man they were looking for; however, something was niggling at him.

"You know, I don't think his wife is a suspect either, but I don't know, Lucky. You know, I feel Rafe Preston is a door, and his wife is a key. It's an odd feeling I get."

"You think maybe she did know? Maybe she hired someone to off Jade. Your gut-talking?"

"You remember what that bartender Barry Picco told us?"

"I can go look in my notes. What do you want to know?" Lucky was oblivious to where Jack was leading.

"No, I mean, do you remember he said an older woman was sitting at the bar? She was sad, and she was an okay-looking older woman. She'd zeroed in on Jade and the older man, wishing she had a man like that. Makes me wonder if Sybil Preston did know and she followed him one night. Know what I mean?"

Lucky looked down in deep thought. "You know, if she did, and she saw them, she might have had a rage, maybe strong enough to carry out a murder. Jack, women have killed other women for less."

"There's a problem here, though. Jade was the second woman killed. We still have 7-11's victim, that Taylor woman. Is she responsible for that? Did she know the Taylor woman? For that matter, did she know Bunny and Al Mathers? And if she did, would Sybil Preston have killed the Taylor woman for being the other woman cheating with Bunny Mathers' husband?" Jack was tired from just saying all of that aloud.

"That sounds pretty far-fetched, if you want my opinion. How well do you know a person, though? There have been women married to men who've been killers and never knew it. Maybe this is in reverse, and Rafe married an unsuspected murderess." Lucky was sure that wasn't the case in this situation.

"I remember the Green River Serial Killer was married, so was the BTK killer, and the wives claimed to be clueless. The Green River Serial Killer was married to a man. That's not your normal situation either. So, what's going to happen next? To hide her other crimes, Sybil kills a man who's an acclaimed homosexual? I don't see that happening at all." Jack closed his eyes and massaged his temples; this was giving him a pounding headache.

"Vengeful women, or men; love and murder, don't get it. Better to get a divorce and stay out of prison," Lucky stated.

"Love has hurt me, but I never became a crazy man. I don't get the 'obsession' that leads to this peculiar psychopathic emotion." Jack opened his eyes and looked over at Lucky.

"Me neither," was all Lucky could say.

—⁓—

THE OASIS BAR'S FOOD tasty—They ate and then approached the bartender. Jack introduced himself and Lucky, then showed the bartender the composite drawing of Rafe Preston.

"What's your name, sir?" Dawson Luck made notes.

"Elias Maxwell."

"Can you tell us if you remember this man? He would've been in here a month ago with some buddies." Jack gave him the date and time.

"No, never seen him, but then I don't work the night shifts—I go to school at night," the bartender said with frankness.

"I see you have cameras—how far back you keep your recordings?" Jack crossed his mental fingers. Cameras in establishments had been zero friggin' help to the case.

"Uh-huh, the owner has us keep them for a year. You wanna see 'em?"

Jack had been holding his breath. Maybe he was living right. "Lead the way."

Elias knocked on the end of the counter. "Hey, Bernie, hold down the fort."

"Sure, Max," the man at the other end of the bar called back.

Elias Maxwell led them to the back offices, found the tape, popped it in the video player, and then searched for the day and time Jack gave him.

"Crud, there he is, Jack, and the timestamp puts him here until eight-forty-five. There's no way he killed her, did all the 'aftermath' work, and made it to the club by nine-fifteen."

Elias Maxwell's jaw dropped.

"You guys are looking for a killer? Damn!"

31

THEY SAT IN A semicircle ... three groups of seven; twenty-one souls sharing their heartaches with the group. Sessions were held every week in the old Sunday school-room annex building at the nondenominational church, The Gates of Heaven.

"Dealing with Spousal Infidelity" ... it was for all who wished to attend: female, male, heterosexual, homosexual, or lesbian. It didn't matter.

The volunteer counselors were members of the church. A few selected a group and sat with them. They listened and interjected advice or words of comfort, while the others went from group to group.

The man cried. Tears ran down his cheeks. "I know most of you think same-sex marriage is not right, but please don't judge me."

"No one's here to judge you," a woman at the end spoke up.

The male counselor smiled. "Why don't you tell us your story?"

"My partner and I have been together for eight years. I've never had a love like this. I can't breathe when I think of losing him." He bawled and then composed himself.

"Brent and I wanted to expand our family, so we adopted a baby. Her name's Nelle; she's two now. I quit my job to stay home to care for her. Brent was supportive of me as the stay-at-home househusband. Four months ago, he said being at home all the time with the baby and no longer having the nightlife we had when we were childless was getting to him. At first, I understood how he felt. I mean, he works hard. There are days Nelle is cranky and I'm a bit of a nag. He has demanding clients and needs to relax, not come home to more irritations. Brent is a stockbroker. I want him happy—I didn't mind that he went out to unwind. Then he was going out to unwind three times a week, every week, and things seemed strained between us. He became distant, so I hired a private investigator to follow him. Brent's cheating on me with a younger man; a very handsome Hispanic man who's only thirty, with no baggage ... and I can't win that battle," he wailed with his face in his hands.

No one spoke; they waited for him to continue. Jason sniffed and wiped tears from his face. "I have the pictures the PI gave me, and I wanted to confront him, but I'm afraid he might leave us."

"Confronting him might work. Remind him of what he'll lose if he doesn't stop," the male counselor advised.

"No, I don't want to give him an ultimatum. I need him here," Jason pointed at his heart. "The baby and I need his support. I'm a hairdresser by trade, but the hours can be long. I don't want Nelle to suffer either. He's hurting both of us." He wept, then wiped his face and looked up.

"I considered giving Nelle back to the adoption agency, then concocting a story to explain why. I'd follow Brent to catch him and his lover together and kill them both, then myself, cuz I don't want to live without him." He turned to the woman sitting next to him, and she let him weep on her shoulder.

For the rest of the session, other women spilled their sad stories. A counselor who prayed for each by name led the group, drained of emotions, in prayer.

Jason Fryer-Mercer stepped up to the refreshment table and picked up a glass of cola and a cookie when a throaty voice spoke.

"Your story was one of the saddest ones today. Would you like to sit and talk some more?" the throaty, raspy voice asked.

It surprised Jason to get this special attention, especially since he was gay. A single tear slipped out, and Jason told the counselor everything.

—ell—

THE PLAN WAS A clever plan, and it was time. This bar was flashy, and for men only. All the energy in the room charged. The air, filled with a different ambiance than a regular bar, felt euphoric. Men danced with men, men sat with men, drinking, kissing, and holding hands. The belief and lifestyle was not a shared belief, but there was a job to do.

There he was. Yes, he was handsome, just as Jason had said. He was no longer working the bar ... smiling and serving drinks. His shift had ended. Now he was the customer.

The handsome man sat on the barstool, leaning in, whispering in the older man's ear. Then he nuzzled the older man's neck and ran his hand up and down his back. The distinguished older man struck a match and lit the cigarette for his young and attractive companion. The young man inhaled, then blew out smoke, moved the lit cigarette to his other hand, turned his head at an angle to face his companion, and the two kissed like lovers. But the man with him wasn't Brent. It was a different man. Jason had shared pictures. The cheater was cheating on the cheater; it figured.

Monogamy, did it still exist? It seemed not. Heterosexuals, homosexuals, bisexuals, and lesbians ... even men of the cloth strayed. There was no longer sanctity in any union.

The small table in the back would do. A darkened corner to hide your sins. This had to be done. This rage had begun years ago, but it got buried deep within. Something had happened and had awakened the monster. Now you were a "fixer" for those who cried out in pain.

The Lord forgives everything ... even what you're doing ... keep believing; keep believing; keep believing.

He took out his wallet, dropped cash on the bar, and waved off his change. Leaning in, he put his arm across the pouting young man's shoulder, pulling him closer. When the old man gave him a very seductive kiss goodbye, he whispered in his ear. His whispered words made the young man smile, and he placed his hand on his arm to keep him there. The older man stood, stroked the young man's cheek with the back of his hand, and then walked away.

At a small corner table, eyes followed the old man until he cleared the front doors. Fifteen minutes passed. Good, he wasn't returning. If a smile could light up a room, there would have been illumination over the small table in the far corner. The young man sat by himself. His friend was gone ... it was time.

The chair scraped the floor as it moved to release its occupant, and feet walked with purpose to the bar.

A tap on the shoulder and the young man turned and smiled.

"May I join you?" the deep voice said as seductively as possible.

"Oh yes, by all means, take a seat," the young man said, his eyes glossy. He'd had quite a bit to drink and the night was still very young. He was ripe for the picking, languid with alcohol, and worked up by the man who'd just left him.

There was that smile.

32

JACK GOT THE CALL at 5:10 am. He dressed, grabbed his gun and badge, and then flew out the door.

The address was Montrose Boulevard and Allen Parkway, more precisely, under the bridge near Buffalo Bayou. He arrived on scene at 5:40.

Lights on black-and-whites led him to the exact place, and Jack parked his truck off the service road and walked down to the bridge area. Taking his Maglite, he lit the trail he was walking. The terrain was no longer flat but wet and muddy, and it stank of dirty bayou water. Shit, he hoped he didn't see a snake. He was heart-attack-afraid of snakes or a stick, big or small, that might even resemble a snake.

"Jack, we're over here." Chief Yao waved him over with his flashlight.

Slipping, Jack caught himself from sliding downward, grabbing a small tree to keep from landing on his rump in the mud.

"Chief, what'd we get? Where's Captain Brooks?"

"Brooks is unavailable. I got the callout," Davis Yao said, a clear look of displeasure crossed his face.

Davis Yao had misgivings. Brody Brooks leading his homicide team was, in his opinion, not a suitable call. A few detectives still considered him their captain, including Jack. They did what they had to do with Brooks and no more.

"Call came in at four-forty. Caller said a homeless man who lives under the bridge went bonkers and ran up on the main road, and a motorist stopped when she swerved to keep from hitting him. The man was going on and on, saying there was a dead body in his squat under the bridge.

Dispatch sent patrol and an ambulance. The officers called Central Command, and Central Command called me."

"What's the deal, Chief? Is this a high-level issue?"

Yao looked at Jack for a second, panic in his eyes.

"Young Hispanic male, knifed under the right arm, laid out and positioned as if he were in a casket, face made-up ... sound familiar?"

"Jesus, number three? It's been five weeks since we started our last investigation. Who got the call?"

"Lancaster and Estrada. I instructed watch commanders to call me if unusual homicide calls came in. Once I got it, I called your team. Bennie and Mack are on their way. CSU is down there combing the area. It's concrete, muddy, and sludge-filled. Be near impossible to tell one footprint from the next. Too many homeless people in the area, and we're having trouble rounding them up. These guys know the bayou like the backs of their hands. We have more area to cover, Jack. Buffalo Bayou, for Christ's sake, and heaven knows what we're facing here."

"Chief, Jack," Bennie said, as he and Mack both walked up. "Dawson and Jace are on their way down. Xi's not far. He should be rolling up soon."

"Jack, you been down there yet?" Mack asked.

"No, just got here. CSU is down. We'll go down when they're done."

"Where's the body?" Mack looked in the general direction of all the activity.

Yao pointed. "Under the actual bridge, between two concrete pylons. The old man that squats there tagged the area as 'his place.' He told Lancaster he hunts for empty cans. He gets an early start—leaves his spot at midnight to hunt for cans he can sell. Underaged beer drinkers leave cans in the bayou area. He goes to Spotts Park, comes back through the dog park, then back to his place. When he got back at 4:30, he found the body in his place. It scared the bejesus outta him."

"How come he knew the exact time? He checked his watch?" Lucky asked.

The chief chuckled. "No, he carries an old-fashioned wind-up alarm clock in his coat pocket. He sets it to get back to his place by 4:30 every day. He showed me the clock."

"Mack spoke up. "Heard it was a young man this time. Doesn't fit the MO, does it?"

"No, it doesn't. Let's wait until we see the active crime scene. Got a feeling it ain't gonna be too good. Chief, where's Lancaster or Estrada? They still here?"

"Up there." Yao nodded toward the main road. "They have the old man in their car. He's pretty shaken, and Estrada went to get him some coffee."

"Can you call Lancaster on the radio and get him down here, Chief?"

"Sure, Jack. Louie, can I borrow your radio?"

Louie, one of the CSU assistants, handed Chief Yao a radio. In less than three minutes, Lancaster was standing in the muddy earth which ebbed toward the bayou with Jack, the chief, and the rest of the crew.

"Yes, sir," Lancaster asked, "you needed me?"

"Jack does, John," the chief said.

"How's the old man holding up?"

"He's shaken. As a matter of fact, I am too. It was gruesome looking."

Jack knew some patrol cops could work a decade and never see a dead body. In Houston, it could happen in the first year. Lancaster had been first responding officer on several cases he'd caught.

"John, you and Chips take him back to the station." Jack took out his wallet. "Here's a twenty. Stop and get him some food. Give him the change. I want you to get him comfy, 'cause when we get done here, I wanna talk to him."

"Sure thing, Jack, I'll take care of it," Officer Lancaster said with a smile.

Lancaster left and passed Xi Chang on his way back.

"All of 'em are down below, 11. Watch your step," Lancaster warned.

Mack looked at Jack and smiled.

"What, Mack?"

"You, Jack, that's what. That was nice of you to do for the old man. There's still some goodness left in this sick and violent world we see every day."

Chief Yao, Lucky, and Jace nodded in approval.

"Chief ... " Cheech walked up the short incline from under the bridge. "We found little, no footprints we can use."

"Well, hell," Jack swore. "Are y'all done? Can we go get a look now?"

"Yeah, Loren, and the others are on the way back with the photographer and videographer. They're gathering equipment."

"Any fingerprints, Cheech?" Jace asked. "Maybe on the concrete pillars ... can you get prints off concrete?"

"Several homeless people have been down here, and I wouldn't know who touched what, Jace. Loren and I tried, but it's like that empty house where you found your victim. Too many people have been here. We could've spent years trying to sort it out. We were lucky to get half a thumbprint and a forefinger off the back door, even though we can't match it yet."

"Jack, you ready to go down and get a look?" Mack was dreading it; her insides warned her this was worse than most.

Jack led the way, and the rest followed like a human convoy.

33

THE YOUNG HISPANIC MAN lay out, his body straight, arms folded over his chest. Someone had closed his eyes. They'd made his face up, and since he was a man, the makeup made him look like a cross-dresser.

Under his hands was a white New Testament Bible. Mack stooped and lifted his right hand off his left, just enough to see his ring finger.

"They broke his finger, like the others." She grimaced.

Jack and Jace crouched near the body.

"Looks like he was a muscular guy. The killer must have been big enough to subdue him, you think?" Jace asked.

"Plain to see how he died. See the blood pooling under his right arm?" Bennie got next to where the body lay, in between two concrete pillars. Stooped, he lifted the victim's arm, revealing a clear stab through his shirt.

"Time of death?" Yao asked.

"Rigor's just begun in his upper torso —I'd say between one, one-thirty. He's not been dead long. It's cool here under the bridge—this is as close as I can give you," Bennie replied.

"We must've just missed the killer." Jace stood.

"Jack, see if he has a wallet," Yao said.

Jack reached under the dead man's right side.

"No, but there's something," he said as he pulled out two items. "I've got his driver's license and his bank debit card. Driver's license is a match: Sergio Loza, age thirty, address on West Sam Houston Parkway South."

"I know the area," Jace said. "Lots of townhomes and condos. Pretty nice."

Chang inclined his head at the body. "He has an apron on—wonder if he worked in a restaurant or a bar. Check the apron pocket."

Mack hunkered down next to the body and, with her gloved hand, pulled out an empty matchbook and a full matchbook, minus one match.

"Two matchbooks from the Crossover Bar. Y'all know that bar; I'm still new to the area."

"Yeah," Chang said, "it's a gay bar over on Montrose Boulevard, not too far from here either. Maybe he worked there bartending."

Mack turned the matchbook over and laughed.

"You're laughing at a time like this, Mack?" Jack looked down at her.

"I'm sorry. This situation isn't funny, but what's on the back of the matchbook is... humorous."

Cheech squinted. "What's on it?"

" 'Just do it—come out—and see us.' And the words 'come out' are larger and bold—a hidden message in plain sight." Her laugh tinkled.

"Well, you can't say gay men or gay bar owners don't have a sense of humor," Jace remarked.

Mack handed the matchbook to Cheech and, still on her haunches, looked at the dead man and got back to her serious work. She saw a tiny spot on the pocket where the cloth was thicker.

"Something isn't right," she said. She lifted the thick, double-layered apron with her gloved hand, revealing the front of the dead man's trousers—his pants still on, and unzipped. Blood saturated his trousers.

"What the fuck." Jace screeched as he and the others took a step backward.

Mack took her gloved hand and felt in the deceased man's groin area, shaking her head. "If you're all thinking or wondering if they cut his organ off, you'd be right."

All seven men were silent. This was more than each of them could handle as men, and knowing that, well, they all covered their privates.

Mack looked at the dead man's face, scrutinizing his features. On her knees, she inched up toward his face and ran her clean-gloved fingers over his mouth.

"Your killer used superglue on his lips because the mouth would gape open, and I..." Mack pushed alongside the cheek line, feeling a slight hard lump next to the softer part of the cheek.

"He has an object in his mouth." She looked up at all the men. "I think it's... well, y'all know what I think it is, don't you?"

None of the men standing there uttered a word; all they could do was nod.

Mack snapped on a clean pair of gloves, slipped the white New Testament Bible from under the victim's hands, and, standing, opened it.

Jack watched as she pulled out a small piece of folded paper. "Well?"

"Ye are wicked, and what you have done is wicked... no longer will you hurt the innocent... they have suffered—so shall you. I pray God will forgive you and that he will forgive me, too."

"Not the same message left with our victim," Lucky said, "but close enough."

Jack gave her a look. "Mack, thumb through it. See if they highlighted a verse like the Bible found with our victim."

It took several tries at fanning through the pages to catch a highlighted area. On the fourth fan-out, she spotted yellow highlighter. It was faint, but it was there.

"Found it."

The chief frowned. "What's highlighted?"

"Leviticus 18:22: 'Don't have sexual relations with a man as one does with a woman; that is detestable.'"

"Does this mean he got killed because he was homosexual? Are these hate crimes?" Bennie asked.

"Our victim was a Black woman. Jack and Luck's a Hispanic woman, and a known party girl, and this guy is homosexual. Is that it? Because if it is, a helluva lot more people are in danger." A worried look crossed Chang's face.

"I'm certain it isn't hate crimes, but I can't quite figure out what it is."

"Well, don't beat yourself up, Jack. You can't have all the answers. Hell, this is sickening, and it keeps getting worse." Yao pulled a face, looking down at the dead man.

Mack closed the white Bible and bagged it for CSU.

"I'll let them know to bring the gurney, but with all the mud, they might have to put the body in a bag and carry it."

Bennie headed back to get the ball rolling.

"I'll call you from the morgue, Jack," Mack said, "once I have the autopsy completed."

"Sure, Mack. Be careful on your way back up. It's very slippery."

Everyone said sayonara and adios, and then it was just the four detectives and Chief Yao.

"Jack," Yao said, "I'm going to leave this in your hands. The four of you are on this until we catch the sick bastard. I'll handle any new incoming cases which could get plunked on your desks. And I'll handle Brooks."

All four were relieved not to have to deal with Brooks.

"I expect updates on this... daily. You need to get in front of this with Tessa Coy. We need to keep an even tighter lid on this situation, Jack."

"Yep, Chief. I understand."

"Get on it." Yao headed back to his vehicle, leaving the four of them standing there.

Jack looked at his watch.

"Let's head to the station. It's eight. We need to look up our victim in the system, find his next of kin, make the death notification, and I need to talk to the homeless man. Meet ya there."

Each one of them knew what a grim task they had on their professional plate. The hours would be long, and the work painstaking. They knew it was their job to find this killer. Houston wasn't safe with the regular crime it dealt with. This was out of the ordinary realm of crime; the danger was increasing, and others could die.

34

PATROL OFFICER JOHN LANCASTER was on the sixth floor in the break room when Jack walked in.

"John, you're not off duty yet?" Jack poured a cup of strong coffee.

"I've signed out but wanted to see if you needed me or Chips for anything. Oh, and the homeless man is in interview room three."

"Thanks, John. Did he get some food to eat?"

"Yeah, he wanted McDonald's. Was smiling the entire way back to the station because you let him keep the change."

"I need to help my fellow Houstonians more often. I'd appreciate it if you and Chips could be on the lookout for the homeless who might have been in the area last night. Maybe one of 'em saw something."

"Sure, Jack, can do. Too many homeless people. They deserve to be safe, too." He took a drink of his 'sludge.'

Jack took a sip, too. "You ever wanna be a detective, John?"

"Not no, but hell no, not on the Homicide Division. Can't take all the dead bodies daily. Considered Vice, maybe Robbery, but you know, I like my job as a patrol cop. I get a variety of issues to deal with. Think I'll keep at it until retirement, or until I change my mind." He stood and yawned. "I need to be heading home, gotta kiss the wife and see the kid, then get some shut-eye. See ya, Jack."

"Yeah, see ya, John." Jack followed him out—and headed to interview room number three.

When Jack opened the door, the old man looked up.

"Hey, you the one who gave me the twenty spot?"

"Yes, sir. Detective Jack West."

"I wanna thank ya. Nicest thing anybody done for me in a long time." His smile revealed broken and missing teeth. "And the burger and fries were tasty." His face beamed.

"You're welcome, Mr. ..." Jack waited for him to supply his name.

"Clifford Honeywell—but call me Cliff." He stuck his hand out.

Jack didn't hesitate for one second as he reached over and took the homeless man's hand and shook it, not afraid of disease, germs, or dirt.

"Most people don't cotton to shaking my hand. Thank ya."

"I hope I'm not most people, Cliff. Tell me, what's your story? How did you end up living on Buffalo Bayou?" Jack wanted to make the man feel more at ease.

Cliff told Jack a condensed story of a man who had a normal middle-class life: a wife, no children, but three dogs. He'd invested and lost all their money in a Ponzi scheme, and they struggled for a few years, and then he started drinking.

His drinking got him fired, he lost the luster for life, and his wife left him and took the three dogs. He went downhill from there, and he ended up under a bridge on Buffalo Bayou eight years ago.

"I don't mind much. You know, I get shelter when it rains. No one tells me what to do. A few friends like me, and they understand how it is. To top it off, I ain't got nary one bill to pay." His laugh boomed.

"If it works for you, Cliff, and if you're happy, not much I can say, is there?"

The old man shook his head. Then, sudden darkness filled the room.

"Ain't safe if a killer's loose, and that's when I wish I had four real walls, ya know, Detective?" A worried look crossed his face.

"Cliff, did you notice anything out of the ordinary last night? Have there been new people on your block of the bridge?"

"Nope, no new people. Been normal..." He stopped to think.

"My route for bottles and cans is from my place to Spotts Park. I cross over a low spot on the bayou. You know, I know the place pretty good—been there eight years now."

"And—" Jack prompted, "did you change your route last night?"

"Well, 'course. With the rain the last few days, my low spots aren't as low, and I didn't cotton to taking a swim. I went up on the freeway side, you know, the side where the walking path is?"

"Yeah, I know the walking path."

"It was dark, but I saw two fellars a-walking toward me. It was too early for the clubs to be shutting down. It wasn't but twelve-forty, and it was odd them fellas were out here. Anyway, since they could be mean fellars, I hid in some bushes until I knew they were gone."

"Did you get a look at their faces, Cliff?"

"Nah, it was too dark right there. Some lights on the path are out. The city ain't replaced 'em yet. I did hear 'em, though, and one of 'em was giggling, like he might have been drunk, and they were kinda holding onto each other."

His eyes squinted, and he scrunched his nose up a titch. "Don't understand it—men with men—but t'ain't none of my business. I can't be peoples' judge. Got my own worries. Anyhows, I heard the one who didn't sound real drunk had a kinda deep-sounding voice."

"Did you hear what they were saying?"

For a moment, Cliff closed his eyes.

Jack sat patient not rushing him—waiting for him to remember.

"The not-drunk sorta feller said, *I know you'll like it, and ain't nobody gonna see, and no one would catch 'em together.* At leastwise, it's what I kinda remember."

"Did the other man reply? Cliff, did they use names?"

"No, sir, neither of 'em said a name, but the drunker feller sorta giggled and said he was a nasty boy and shouldn't be doing this, or sumthin like that. They weren't whispering, since they didn't know I was hiding in the bushes nearby, but they weren't talking loud. They walked down the path, and once I was clear of 'em, I hauled it outta there. I didn't want to know what they were gonna do, and I didn't want to see either."

"Did you glance back and see where they went?"

"Nope, didn't look back. And if I had thought they would go to my squat, I'da been there in a flat second—ain't nobody touching my stuff.

Asides, I keep my best stuff hidden. Don't want no one stealing it. Most of the people I do know and trust, well, we kinda watch out for each other. You know we're all we got."

Jack understood, and he was unhappy people had to live like this, but Cliff Honeywell felt satisfied with his circumstances, living day-by-day, not bitter at anyone or the world.

"Cliff, I wanna thank you for telling me what you could, and if you remember anything—even if you think it might not be important—here's my card. If you need to, go to a pay phone and call me collect anytime, day or night."

He took the card and placed it in his front shirt pocket.

"Sure, I can do that."

"And, Cliff, if your friends have information, please give them my number. You can be my eyes and ears on the Buffalo Bayou."

"Uh-uh, you bet, and if I don't call ya, means I ain't got no news for ya, deal?" Cliff stuck out his hand.

Jack took his hand, and a thought occurred to him.

"I don't want you to take offense," he said as he reached for his wallet. "It's not much, but it'll come in handy."

Jack handed the man four twenty-dollar bills, and Cliff's eyes lit up.

"For me? Really?"

"It's what I can do today to help a fellow Houstonian. I see too much ugly on the job—feels right to do something good."

Cliff took the money, folded it, and stuck it in the front pocket of his shirt with Jack's business card.

"That's awful nice of ya, and I promise I don't drink no more. Got me in trouble back then. I learnt my lesson." The old man's face glowed.

"Sit tight. I'll go get you a proper escort back to your place. And Cliff, be careful at night. We don't know what we're dealing with."

"I'll be extra careful, and uh, well, I'm much obliged, Detective West, for the cash and the ride. Thank you, sir. You're a nice man."

Jack left Cliff Honeywell waiting, called a patrol unit to come and take him to Buffalo Bayou, sending him back to a life he wasn't unhappy living.

Jack picked up the phone and dialed the *Chronicle*.

"I need to speak with Tessa Coy. This is Detective Jack West."

Tessa came on the line five seconds later.

"Jack, what's up?"

"Tessa, we need to talk here at the station, and it needs to be in the next fifteen minutes."

"Sure, Jack. I left five minutes ago."

Jack paced in the lobby waiting for Tessa, looking at his watch and tapping his foot. She needed to hurry.

"Jack," she called out as her heels clicked on the tile floor.

He ushered her into the elevators, closemouthed, and Tessa saw the grim lines on his face.

"Jack, what's...?"

"Not yet. Wait until we are out of earshot then no one will overhear us."

On the sixth floor, in Captain Davis Yao's old office, Jack shut the door.

"Tessa, a third murder. Same MO. And I need to keep the info hushed. I need your help with this. I'd like to give you details but can't, and I want you to keep it hushed in the paper."

"Oh my God, Jack, are you telling me this is number three and you want me to keep a fucking lid on it?" She narrowed her eyes as she looked at him. "Jack, the people in Houston need to be warned. I mean it. First, a woman of color, then a young Hispanic woman, now a Hispanic male who is an alleged homosexual... this is big. These could be hate crimes, Jack, and people need to be warned. I—"

He cut her off. "No, Tessa. Like I told you last time, do whatever you have to do, but keep the truth out of the paper for now. I mean it. I swear, give us some time. I don't want a panic on our hands. We need to keep a lid on all the details. Hell, as it is, too many people in the department know. One leak—even a tiny one—can keep us from catching the sick bastard, whoever he is." Jack gave her a beseeching stare.

"Okay, Jack, but if there's a fourth, I won't—I repeat, won't—keep shoving this story under the rug. Do you understand? You know, the press can be your friend. I know you and the HPD don't believe that, but we can."

"Look, you're right. The HPD has gotten shitty-rotten press, and yeah, we can be gun-shy, but you know me, Tessa. You know who I am and how I am. The real fact here is I do trust you—I'm warning you, don't screw me over."

"Fuck, now I am worried, Jack."

"I don't think that you're a targ—"

She cut him off. "Not that, Jack. What in the hell is my editor going to do to me when he finds out I kept a lid on this story? That's what worries me."

"Have him call the chief of police. You know he's friends with the mayor."

"Hope his friendship helps me keep my goddamn job, Jack, or you might be supporting me."

"Tessa, don't worry. You'll have your job—and most importantly—the exclusive."

"Shit, Jack, it better win me a Pulitzer."

35

JACK TOOK A SEAT at his desk.

"Okay, fellas, what do we have?"

Lucky flipped open his notebook.

"Sergio Loza lived over on West Sam Houston Parkway South. No priors, and he worked at the Crossover Bar as a bartender—did male modeling on the side."

"I called the number listed as his home and got a machine. The message said, 'Hey, it's Sergio and Smith. We can't take your call, and we can't tell you why, either. Leave us a message.' Then you hear—no joke, fellas—giggling as the buzzer beeps."

"Who's Smith? Is that his last name?" Jack looked at Chang. "Remember, ours is not to judge. Our job is to solve crimes, guys."

"Yeah, yeah, I know. And no, it's not the last name. The man's name is Smith Russell. I think his mom was drunk when she named him. First name is the last name, and the last name is a first—or last—name. You think when they did his birth certificate they goofed and it was supposed to be Russell Smith?"

"It could happen. I've heard the name Smith as a first name," Jace said.

"Well, guys, here's the sad thing. Whether it's Smith Russell or Russell Smith, we hafta give the poor man a death notification," Jack reminded them. Once again, gloom overshadowed the squad room.

"Jack, Jace and I can go. You and Chang can stay here, work on what you can come up with," Lucky volunteered.

"Good of you to offer, partner, but Jace and I are gonna go see Mr. Russell and give him the terrible news about Sergio. I want you and Chang to get a list of the employees at the Crossover Bar and their phone numbers. I need you to dig—see what you can find on Sergio Loza's life—phone records, financials, the works. Check to see if Crossover has inside and outside cameras, and if they do, I want those tapes." Jack was spitting out orders left and right.

"What did Tessa Coy say, Jack? She gonna work with us?" Lucky asked.

If she doesn't work with us, she knows I'll call Chen over at The Daily Sun for all other scoops. She's going to keep this on the down-low through the Chronicle. I'm going to ask Chief Yao to issue a memo that no one—and I mean no one—discusses the cases or the crime scenes. I worry one asswipe will talk to the press and skim right by Tessa. We need to keep this contained. Chang, call the unit who took the homeless man, Cliff Honeywell, back to the bridge. Tell 'em to put a bug in his ear. Mums the word. Don't talk about it. Just keep his ear to the ground. Tell him it's a favor for me, got it?

He was sure he could trust Cliff not to blab if he asked.

Jack and Jace headed out to deliver the sad news, while Lucky and Chang went to work on their assigned tasks.

The neighborhood was nice, well kept, and not too ritzy or too plain.

"I looked to buy over here when I was married to wife number two. I'm glad I didn't, 'cause wife number two didn't hang around long and I would have been stuck with the mortgage. There, Jack, ten-fifty-one... there's a car in the driveway, maybe he's home."

They geared up. This was the hardest part of the job. Even the toughest, gruffest, bad-assed cop wanted to break down and cry with the people to whom they had to deliver this kind of news. Jack rapped on the door.

A voice sang out, "Gimme a minute, be there in a second, I'm getting decent." Such a jovial voice—and the man who singsong'd it out—was fixin' to have his entire world turned upside down.

"Hi, can I help you?" The man was five-foot-ten, slight build, sandy-blond hair, and green eyes, dressed in a light-blue terrycloth robe and fuzzy lion-head house shoes.

"Are you Smith Russell?"

"Why, yes, sir, I am. What can I do for you?" He flashed a smile. It unnerved Jace a bit, but Jack didn't flinch. The man was flirting with them.

"Mr. Russell, I'm Detective Jack West, this is Detective Jace Severson. Can we come in for a moment?" Jack unclipped his badge to show the man.

It was all it took. Huge tears sprung up in the man's eyes, and his face contorted in anguish as he unlatched the storm door and allowed them inside. Smith Russell shut the door and led them to a very stylish front room, gestured for them to sit, then he sat on the small loveseat across from them. The poor man fell to pieces.

"Som-m-m-thing hap-p-pend to Sergio, didn't it?" His hands covered his face.

"Yes, I'm sorry to have to tell you this, but he's been a victim of a homicide, and we are very sorry for your loss," Jack voice compassionate.

Jace didn't speak.

He was never good at this. It tore him up inside every time.

The man cried, hiccupped, and sniffed, wiping his face and nose with the sleeve of his robe.

"What... what happened? Where's his body? I need to see him." Smith's voice cracked as he tried to hold it together.

"Mr. Russell, right now we can't let you see him. He's at the morgue, and sir," Jack was saying, but Smith jerked his head up.

"No?" He jumped up. "Please don't cut him up. I can't stand the thought of people cutting him up. It's not right, it's not humane." He wept, collapsing into the loveseat.

"Sir," Jace said, getting up to sit next to the distraught man. "We've got to learn everything to find out who did this. Don't you think Sergio would want the same if it had been you?"

If it shocked Jack at how Jace was handling this, but he kept his face a blank. Jace let Chang handle the death notifications. It was an unspoken law between the two of them.

"Yes, he would." He became silent, his eyes not focused, just glazed, not seeing.

Jace sat on the edge of the loveseat and angled—he had eye-to-eye contact with Smith. He was used to a woman sobbing. That was hard enough, but this poor soul seemed more fragile than any woman he had encountered over the years.

"Mr. Russell, can we ask you a few questions?" Jace's voice a soft, even-keel.

Smith Russell squared his shoulders, sat up straighter, and pulled the terrycloth belt tighter. He crossed his legs, and looking down at his fuzzy lion-head house shoes, he pumped his foot up and down.

"Yes, I'll tell you what I can. I don't think I..." He stopped mid-sentence and frowned.

"Mr. Russell,? Jace frowned. "What are you not telling us?"

"He was cheating on me," Smith said, his tone even.

36

JACK AND JACE EXCHANGED a glance. Smith continued talking, neither detective needing to prompt him to get rolling.

"I know right now our marriage isn't legal, but we had a mock ceremony with a few of our friends present. We were making it official when his mom got back from overseas, next month." He paused, closing his eyes. "I guess now she'll have to come home earlier than she expected for a different reason altogether." A fresh stream of tears slid down his face.

Jack jotted notes. "Do you know the man he was cheating with?"

"Yes, but he wouldn't have killed Sergio. I'm positive. This was a fleeting liaison for Sergio, you know ... sow his last wild oats before we tied the knot, in the official manner."

Jace tilted his head. Smith caught the look and laughed.

"I know what you're thinking. I just wanted to believe it was him sowing his wild oats one last time. It wasn't the first time—there've been others, but well ... " He held his hands up and shrugged. "What can I say? I loved him and looked the other way, and it was better than losing him."

Jack leaned forward. "You think he would've stopped once your marriage was legal?"

"I'd hoped—but now—well, now I'll never know, will I?"

It was time to ask some of the tough questions, but Jack had to do it. Jace remained the comforter.

"Mr. Russell ..."

"Please, call me Smith. I mean, this is personal. Don't you think first names are in order?"

Jack lifted his pen. "Smith, can you tell me where you were between midnight and two a.m. this morning?" He doubted Smith was their man, but he had to cross all the t's and dot every damn i.

"Here, at home. You can check my phone and see where I've been. I might be gay, but I do watch some cop shows. I was talking to my sister who lives in Wisconsin at eleven-thirty, and we were on the phone for at least an hour."

"Of course we'll be checking on this," Jack warned.

Smith's face contorted with anguish. "Where was he found? How was he ... he, uh, you know?"

Jack shook his head. "We aren't at liberty to say. There are things the killer would know no one else would, and we don't want this to get out, do you understand?"

"Did he have on his engagement ring? I'd like to get that back. It was expensive. It looks like mine, but his was copper and silver." Smith held out his hand. "It's valued at over nine thousand dollars. The diamond is two carats. And of course, Detective, it's the same for us as it is for you heterosexuals. Left-hand rings mean engaged and married. It's not like we add a finger or wear them on a unique part of our body." He winked at Jace.

Jack bit his lip to hide a smile. "I'll have to ask. I don't recall seeing it." He lied. He knew the ring wasn't there; he'd seen the broken finger — another trophy for the bastard.

Jace opened his notebook, ignoring the wink. "Where did Sergio work?"

"At the Crossover Bar on Montrose Boulevard—you know it?"

Jace nodded, and Smith's eyebrows shot up.

"You do? Do you go there often?" The man tried not to smile, but the corners of his mouth twitched. He sensed Jace was uncomfortable. Smith Russell was very used to that.

Jack pressed his lips together to keep from laughing when he saw Jace's face. He knew Smith Russell was having a bit of fun. He couldn't fault the man for not having a sense of humor at this unhappy time. It impressed Jack that he could find a momentary tunnel of comedy.

"Uh, no, I, uh, well, I know the area, that's all," Jace stuttered, lost for words.

Smith leaned back. "Detective, get a grip. I know you're both straight, could tell a mile away. I'm just having a little fun with you."

His face dropped as he cast his eyes downward, looking at his hands folded in his lap.

"Sergio would have loved this ... this teasing. We did it with straight men all the time, made them a tad uncomfortable, just like you, but it was funny, at least to us, and it sort of broke the ice when we were in mixed company." A soft, close-mouthed chuckle sounded, and a melancholy look emitted from Smith's green eyes.

Jack leaned in. "Was the Crossover Bar his primary job?"

"Yes, but he was modeling on the side, trying to make it to the big time. You know, there were several gay photographers, and a few times he felt he had to do the 'casting couch' route, as it's called, but it didn't work out for him."

"Why do you say that?" Jace asked.

"Well, he wasn't a household name in the modeling profession. He didn't sleep with the right photographer, I imagine."

Jack scribbled notes. "Do you know who would have wanted him dead?"

"No, everyone liked him. He was sweet and most of the time the life of the party."

Jack set his pen down. "This man he was cheating with, Smith. Do you know his name?"

Smith pressed his lips together, holding back a sob. "Yes."

"Who is this man?"

"Which name do you want, bachelor number one, or married bachelor number two?"

Jace's eyes widened.

"Two men? He was seeing two other men?"

"One of them was a new guy. I saw them together one night at the Crossover." He exhaled. "This affair never worried me."

Jack leaned forward. "Can I ask you, why not?"

"I know, gentlemen, because I've had an affair with the same man a few years back. The man only does short dalliance. He gets bored and moves on to the next pretty face. I'd wondered when Sergio would get his turn, and I didn't care. The man was very generous."

Jack and Jace collected two more names to check out, along with Smith Russell's phone records to confirm his alibi, which Jack knew would check out.

They thanked Smith Russell and assured him they'd keep in touch.

"Don't think he did it, Jack, do you?"

"No, I don't, but you know, people can surprise the hell right outta ya."

Jace nodded, thinking that he had surprised himself today.

Back in the squad room, Chang looked up. "How'd it go?"

Jack sat down and shook his head. "As expected, but Jace here surprised the shit right outta me."

He gave Lucky and Chang the story, and Chang glanced over at his partner.

"Well, I didn't even know you had a real heart, buddy," he said.

"Yeah, well, it surprised the hell outta me too," Jace confessed.

Lucky spoke up. "We've been running down the employees at the Crossover Bar, got ahold of the owner, and he got someone to fax us a list of phone numbers, too."

Jack checked his watch. "Bar open this time of day?"

"No, bar's closed, doesn't open until nine tonight, but there was a number to call, and I left a message. I'll be damned—got a call back in less than twenty minutes. The manager was cooperative and upset. He said Sergio was a fabulous bartender and a nice kid."

Jack leaned back. "Run down many of the staff?"

"I took half the list—Lucky had the other half. We got ahold of most of them and did phone interviews. The bartender who worked that night said Sergio was with an older man most of the early evening."

"That must be the fleeting relationship Smith referred to. Man's name is Gordon Lott, right?" Jace affirmed.

"Yeah," Chang confirmed.

"Gordon Lott, the same Gordon Lott as in Lott's Limos and Limo Service?" Lucky asked.

"Maybe, I don't know. I couldn't reach him."

Jack turned to Lucky.

"You know this Lott guy?"

"I know his name and that he has money to burn. I had no idea his door swung that way, though. There have been photographs of him running with some hot babes. He was in an article I saw a few years ago — a list of the top 'players' in Houston. Funny, it said women flocked to him, that's women, not men."

"What magazine was this?" Jace asked.

"The Houstonian. My wife used to subscribe. Read it years ago and the name Lott's Limos stuck in my head."

Jack nodded. "Got an address? Maybe we need to take a ride, huh, Lucky?"

"Sure, Jack. First, you wanna know what else we found out?"

"Yeah, I just want to catch a freaking killer ... sorry I'm rushing ya," he said. "What else ya got?"

Chang took over. "No inside cameras. People want privacy. No one at the club discloses who's been there or with whom. The barkeeper I called sang like a blue jay when I explained what would happen if he didn't talk."

Jack cocked his head. "They have outside cameras?"

"For insurance, three outside cameras. Problem is, they angled lenses to show patrons as shadowy figures. Decent bead on the main parking lot, enough to see if someone tampers with cars, but not who."

"What the hell does that do?" Jace asked.

Lucky looked at Jack. "Most likely won't help much, but we can get a look-see. Close to the time of death, we might see someone staggering out, holding onto their companion. Cliff said one was drunk, but not stumbling drunk."

"Cameras won't help if we can't see clear," Chang added. "Tech might enhance it, though. Worth a shot."

Jack nodded. "Call the club manager. Tell him we need those tapes as soon as possible. Pick them up, check what you can see. If nothing, take them to Tech. While you do that, Jace, pull phone records on Smith Russell to verify his alibi."

"The club owner left me his cell number. I'll call and let him know I'm headed over. On the way back, I'll grab us a bite. You want me to pick up lunch?"

Jack shook his head. Lucky raised an eyebrow.

"Well, hell, Jack, I might be hungry."

"Fine, we can grab a bite on the way out. Then we need to see a man about a limo and check in with Brent Mercer, our other married cheater."

37

JACK AND JACE EXCHANGED a glance. Smith continued talking, neither detective needing to prompt him to get rolling.

"I know right now our marriage isn't legal, but we had a mock ceremony with a few of our friends present. We were making it official when his mom got back from overseas, next month." He paused, closing his eyes. "I guess now she'll have to come home earlier than she expected for a different reason altogether." A fresh stream of tears slid down his face.

Jack jotted notes. "Do you know the man he was cheating with?"

"Yes, but he wouldn't have killed Sergio. I'm positive. This was a fleeting liaison for Sergio, you know ... sow his last wild oats before we tied the knot, in the official manner."

Jace tilted his head. Smith caught the look and laughed.

"I know what you're thinking. I just wanted to believe it was him sowing his wild oats one last time. It wasn't the first time—there've been others, but well ... " He held his hands up and shrugged. "What can I say? I loved him and looked the other way, and it was better than losing him."

Jack leaned forward. "You think he would've stopped once your marriage was legal?"

"I'd hoped—but now—well, now I'll never know, will I?"

It was time to ask some of the tough questions, but Jack had to do it. Jace remained the comforter.

"Mr. Russell ..."

"Please, call me Smith. I mean, this is personal. Don't you think first names are in order?"

Jack lifted his pen. "Smith, can you tell me where you were between midnight and two a.m. this morning?" He doubted Smith was their man, but he had to cross all the t's and dot every damn i.

"Here, at home. You can check my phone and see where I've been. I might be gay, but I do watch some cop shows. I was talking to my sister who lives in Wisconsin at eleven-thirty, and we were on the phone for at least an hour."

"Of course we'll be checking on this," Jack warned.

Smith's face contorted with anguish. "Where was he found? How was he ... he, uh, you know?"

Jack shook his head. "We aren't at liberty to say. There are things the killer would know no one else would, and we don't want this to get out, do you understand?"

"Did he have on his engagement ring? I'd like to get that back. It was expensive. It looks like mine, but his was copper and silver." Smith held out his hand. "It's valued at over nine thousand dollars. The diamond is two carats. And of course, Detective, it's the same for us as it is for you heterosexuals. Left-hand rings mean engaged and married. It's not like we add a finger or wear them on a unique part of our body." He winked at Jace.

Jack bit his lip to hide a smile. "I'll have to ask. I don't recall seeing it." He lied. He knew the ring wasn't there; he'd seen the broken finger — another trophy for the bastard.

Jace opened his notebook, ignoring the wink. "Where did Sergio work?"

"At the Crossover Bar on Montrose Boulevard—you know it?"

Jace nodded, and Smith's eyebrows shot up.

"You do? Do you go there often?" The man tried not to smile, but the corners of his mouth twitched. He sensed Jace was uncomfortable. Smith Russell was very used to that.

Jack pressed his lips together to keep from laughing when he saw Jace's face. He knew Smith Russell was having a bit of fun. He couldn't fault the man for not having a sense of humor at this unhappy time. It impressed Jack that he could find a momentary tunnel of comedy.

"Uh, no, I, uh, well, I know the area, that's all," Jace stuttered, lost for words.

Smith leaned back. "Detective, get a grip. I know you're both straight, could tell a mile away. I'm just having a little fun with you."

His face dropped as he cast his eyes downward, looking at his hands folded in his lap.

"Sergio would have loved this ... this teasing. We did it with straight men all the time, made them a tad uncomfortable, just like you, but it was funny, at least to us, and it sort of broke the ice when we were in mixed company." A soft, close-mouthed chuckle sounded, and a melancholy look emitted from Smith's green eyes.

Jack leaned in. "Was the Crossover Bar his primary job?"

"Yes, but he was modeling on the side, trying to make it to the big time. You know, there were several gay photographers, and a few times he felt he had to do the 'casting couch' route, as it's called, but it didn't work out for him."

"Why do you say that?" Jace asked.

"Well, he wasn't a household name in the modeling profession. He didn't sleep with the right photographer, I imagine."

Jack scribbled notes. "Do you know who would have wanted him dead?"

"No, everyone liked him. He was sweet and most of the time the life of the party."

Jack set his pen down. "This man he was cheating with, Smith. Do you know his name?"

Smith pressed his lips together, holding back a sob. "Yes."

"Who is this man?"

"Which name do you want, bachelor number one, or married bachelor number two?"

Jace's eyes widened.

"Two men? He was seeing two other men?"

"One of them was a new guy. I saw them together one night at the Crossover." He exhaled. "This affair never worried me."

Jack leaned forward. "Can I ask you, why not?"

"I know, gentlemen, because I've had an affair with the same man a few years back. The man only does short dalliance. He gets bored and moves on to the next pretty face. I'd wondered when Sergio would get his turn, and I didn't care. The man was very generous."

Jack and Jace collected two more names to check out, along with Smith Russell's phone records to confirm his alibi, which Jack knew would check out.

They thanked Smith Russell and assured him they'd keep in touch.

"Don't think he did it, Jack, do you?"

"No, I don't, but you know, people can surprise the hell right outta ya."

Jace nodded, thinking that he had surprised himself today.

Back in the squad room, Chang looked up. "How'd it go?"

Jack sat down and shook his head. "As expected, but Jace here surprised the shit right outta me."

He gave Lucky and Chang the story, and Chang glanced over at his partner.

"Well, I didn't even know you had a real heart, buddy," he said.

"Yeah, well, it surprised the hell outta me too," Jace confessed.

Lucky spoke up. "We've been running down the employees at the Crossover Bar, got ahold of the owner, and he got someone to fax us a list of phone numbers, too."

Jack checked his watch. "Bar open this time of day?"

"No, bar's closed, doesn't open until nine tonight, but there was a number to call, and I left a message. I'll be damned—got a call back in less than twenty minutes. The manager was cooperative and upset. He said Sergio was a fabulous bartender and a nice kid."

Jack leaned back. "Run down many of the staff?"

"I took half the list—Lucky had the other half. We got ahold of most of them and did phone interviews. The bartender who worked that night said Sergio was with an older man most of the early evening."

"That must be the fleeting relationship Smith referred to. Man's name is Gordon Lott, right?" Jace affirmed.

"Yeah," Chang confirmed.

"Gordon Lott, the same Gordon Lott as in Lott's Limos and Limo Service?" Lucky asked.

"Maybe, I don't know. I couldn't reach him."

Jack turned to Lucky.

"You know this Lott guy?"

"I know his name and that he has money to burn. I had no idea his door swung that way, though. There have been photographs of him running with some hot babes. He was in an article I saw a few years ago — a list of the top 'players' in Houston. Funny, it said women flocked to him, that's women, not men."

"What magazine was this?" Jace asked.

"The Houstonian. My wife used to subscribe. Read it years ago and the name Lott's Limos stuck in my head."

Jack nodded. "Got an address? Maybe we need to take a ride, huh, Lucky?"

"Sure, Jack. First, you wanna know what else we found out?"

"Yeah, I just want to catch a freaking killer ... sorry I'm rushing ya," he said. "What else ya got?"

Chang took over. "No inside cameras. People want privacy. No one at the club discloses who's been there or with whom. The barkeeper I called sang like a blue jay when I explained what would happen if he didn't talk."

Jack cocked his head. "They have outside cameras?"

"For insurance, three outside cameras. Problem is, they angled lenses to show patrons as shadowy figures. Decent bead on the main parking lot, enough to see if someone tampers with cars, but not who."

"What the hell does that do?" Jace asked.

Lucky looked at Jack. "Most likely won't help much, but we can get a look-see. Close to the time of death, we might see someone staggering out, holding onto their companion. Cliff said one was drunk, but not stumbling drunk."

"Cameras won't help if we can't see clear," Chang added. "Tech might enhance it, though. Worth a shot."

Jack nodded. "Call the club manager. Tell him we need those tapes as soon as possible. Pick them up, check what you can see. If nothing, take to Tech. While you do that, Jace, pull phone records on Smith Russell to verify his alibi."

"The club owner left me his cell number. I'll call and let him know I'm headed over. On the way back, I'll grab us a bite. You want me to pick up lunch?"

Jack shook his head. Lucky raised an eyebrow.

"Well, hell, Jack, I might be hungry."

"Fine, we can grab a bite on the way out. Then we need to see a man about a limo and check in with Brent Mercer, our other married cheater."

38

BRENT MERCER LIVED IN a high-dollar neighborhood.

Not a blade of grass was out of place, or a crack on a single driveway. Homes ran $1.2 million on the low end—upward of $3.2 million.

Jack pulled into the driveway, backed out, and parked at the curb. "This guy, Brent Mercer, does well for himself."

"Yeah, reminds me of how poor I am," Dawson Luck said, eyeing the lawns.

The house was enormous, with simple lines, and well designed. The ambience of success hung in the air. There were no pretentious high brick walls or tall iron gates protecting the homes. Having money had no bearing on what kind of person you were. Brent Mercer might be wealthier than most, but he was still a piece of crap in Jack's book.

He rang the bell at the overly large double doors and then took a step back to wait.

"You know, we still need to talk to that Rafe guy's wife, Sybil Preston," Lucky restated.

"Yeah, it's on my list, including a call to Mack. See what came up during Sergio's autopsy."

A man answered, holding a small child, and a yappy dog was at his feet.

"May I help you?"

"Mr. Mercer?" Jack asked.

"Yes." Then he looked down at the noisy dog. "Hush, Twinkle-toes. Sorry, she's a big yapper. She's a Chihuahua out of control."

"Brent Mercer?"

The man bounced the child on his hip. "Oh, no, I'm Jason Fryer-Mercer, Brent's my husband."

"Is he home?" Lucky asked. He looked down at the slip of a dog, who was giving out a low growl, and as tiny as it was, it sounded a bit menacing.

"No, he's at work, and Daddy gets home at seven, right, Miss Nelle?" he asked the child who, from what they could understand, said, "Daddy home."

"Can I help you?" The man's smile didn't reach his eyes.

"No, sir, we'll try to reach him later."

Jack found it strange that he didn't ask who they were or why they were looking for his husband.

"Okay, say bye-bye, Nelle," the man said, looking at the little girl and holding her chubby little hand up to wave.

"Uh, sir, your husband—what he does for a living? I don't mean to pry, but this is a beautiful neighborhood—I think I'm in the wrong business." Lucky was fishing for information.

Jack thought he might be stepping over the line asking since the man didn't know them from Adam.

Jason Fryer-Mercer laughed as he hugged the baby girl.

"Tell them, Nelle, your daddy is a stockbroker. Yes, he is, isn't he?" Jason Fryer-Mercer said in baby talk. "He works at Morgan Stanley, one of the biggest firms in Houston. We're proud of him, aren't we, Nelle?"

Jack had enough of the baby talk and the growling dog.

"Thank you, sir. Come on, we need to get back to the office." He gave Lucky a look.

"Yeah, we do. Now I wish I'd become a stockbroker," Lucky lied.

In the car. Jack cranked it and pulled away from the curb. "You know, Lucky, he didn't even ask who we were."

"Yep, the yapping dog and a two-year-old on his hip. He seemed distracted all right. Sort of weird I thought. There was something else I saw."

"What's that, Jack? We didn't get past the front door."

"There was something in his eyes, like he wasn't happy being a stay-at-home dad. Smith Russell gave us two men. Gordon Lott—bachelor number one. Brent Mercer is bachelor number two, but not a bachelor, since he's married. Out of curiosity, is the proper term 'husband and husband' or what?"

"You're asking me, that question? Shit, man, as gorgeous as my wife is, and some of my stupid comments I make pissing off women personnel in the department, you think I know?"

"Well, crap, Lucky, I thought you knew everything. You knew about the black market sex toys. That was a crapload more than me."

"West, you're a dickhead, you know that. Now, back to what we need to be discussing. What was it you saw?" Lucky crossed his arms and gave Jack a side-glance, his caterpillar brow dipping.

"Okay, I am serious here. Jason Fryer-Mercer is unhappy ... you know, the way you can tell when a woman is unhappy in a relationship, know what I mean?"

"You think he knows his husband, this Brent fellow, has been cheating on him?"

"Maybe, and it's made me think."

Jack turned his blinker on, looked over his left shoulder, and took the on-ramp to West Loop South, heading to the Morgan Stanley investment offices.

"Are you going to let me in on what you're thinking?"

"Nah, it's a pretty stupid thought anyway."

Dawson Luck huffed. "Huh. Fine by me. I think you've said enough stupid shit for the day."

He enjoyed getting under Lucky's skin and irritating him like a sand chigger. Dawson was like a kid in a sandbox. He knew the chiggers were there, but he jumped into the sandbox, anyway.

39

THE MORGAN STANLEY OFFICE was in the ten-story Tenaris building on the first floor. They walked through double glass doors into a plush office and up to the front desk.

"Afternoon, gentlemen. Welcome to Morgan Stanley. How can I help you today? Do you have an appointment?" Poised, professional, and attractive, the receptionist addressed them.

Jack lay his badge on her desk without taking his eyes off her—she looked down. "Well, no, ma'am, we don't, but we need to speak with Mr. Mercer, and here's my card."

Standing, she was five foot ten, trim and filled out in all the 'good' places. Her red dress, on a shorter woman, would have been below the knee, but on her, it was above the knees, showing quite shapely legs. Her shoulder-length, thick auburn hair swung, to-and-fro, as she walked down a carpeted hallway to the back offices. Jack and Lucky couldn't help but watch her walking as her backside and hips swayed in a hypnotic rhythm.

The woman did make his heart speed up a notch or two ... but not as much as Gretchen. His girl was the down-to-earth type he needed, not the socialite, snobbish Ms. Red Dress seemed to be. Jack didn't know her from Agnes to Zelda, but he knew her type, or thought he did.

She returned in three minutes, same sway, same everything, a smile on her glossy red lips revealing even white teeth.

"Mr. Mercer will be with you gentlemen in a few minutes. He's finishing up a call."

"Thank you," Jack said, taking a few steps backward, putting space between him and her desk.

The door opened down the hallway, but the carpet muffled the sound of steps. Brent Mercer appeared at the end of the hall—a well-dressed man, dark hair, rugged features. He had a definite GQ look, and his house fit him as well as the suit he wore.

"Gentlemen, do you mind if we speak in my office?"

"We'll follow you," Jack said, turning to the receptionist. "Thank you, ma'am."

"Of course, Detective West, anytime." Her words slipped off her lips in a sultry, silky manner, and there was a certain sparkle in her eyes when she looked at Jack. He hoped he wasn't blushing; all he could do was nod.

Lucky jabbed Jack in the arm with his elbow as they followed Brent Mercer down the hallway, giving him the eyebrow-wiggle look.

Jack shot him a *fuck-you* look, rolled his eyes, and shook his head.

"Please, take a seat," Mercer said. He settled into his plush leather executive chair, placing his arms on the desk, crossing his hands, and staring at them. He acted calm and collected, as if police visits were part of his daily routine.

"May I get either of you some Evian?"

"No, Mr. Mercer, but thank you. I'm Detective Jack West, and this is Detective Dawson Luck. We're with the Homicide Division and need to talk to you regarding a Mr. Sergio Loza."

At the name Sergio Loza, all the color drained from Mercer's face. The GQ look disappeared; shock froze his features into a not-so-pleasant mask.

"Is he... is Sergio dead?"

"I'm afraid so, Mr. Mercer. That's why we need to discuss your relationship with the deceased."

His balled-up fist came to his mouth, and he stifled a small cry. Tears welled up, and he swiped them away.

"Wha... wha... what happened?"

"Mr. Mercer, can you tell us about your relationship with Sergio Loza?" Jack's gaze bored into him; he wasn't releasing details on a need-to-know basis, though his gut told him Mercer wasn't their man.

"I, uh... well, we were seeing each other." He sniffed and grabbed a tissue from the box on his desk.

"So, you were a couple then, I take it?" Jack wanted to see if he lied and to gauge his character.

"No, we weren't. I'm married. Sergio and I were having an affair."

"Mr. Mercer, when was the last time you saw Mr. Loza?"

"Look, I want to explain something first."

"No need to explain. Just answer the question." Jack didn't care about the reasons for cheating.

Brent blew out a long breath. "The last time I saw Sergio was last week, on Friday at a bar we met up at."

"What bar was that?"

"It's a new gay bar called The Man's Closet."

"Where's the bar located?"

"It's off West Dallas Street and Interstate 45. New place—we met there—didn't want anyone we knew to see us. He's in... or rather was... in a relationship, too. I didn't want my husband to find out. I needed a break, you see."

Jack cut him off. "Mr. Mercer, we're neither your judge nor your jury. I hope you don't need either."

He was silent; his face screwed up a bit.

"Mr. Mercer, we need..."

"Please, call me Brent," he cut in. "Am I a suspect?"

"Right now, you're a person of interest, Brent."

"I know how it is. You'll go to the bar, ask if anyone saw me or him together, and you'll want to know which motel we went to, the same scenario." He frowned.

"Is there something you need to tell us?"

"We had a slight argument at the club. I know the bartender saw us and heard us."

"Why did you argue?"

"I told him we had to end the affair. It was only infatuation, that's all. Sergio wasn't ready to end it yet. And I do love my husband."

"Then why cheat, Mr. Mercer?" Lucky asked bluntly.

"Detective, it happens in same-sex marriages. We're no different from heterosexuals. Jason, my husband, and I adopted a baby a year ago. Nelle's two now. Between work, a baby, and Jason, I went cuckoo. I met Sergio when he was bartending at the Crossover. He was fun, very sexy—I needed some of that in my life. I knew how it was."

"Just how was it, Mr. Mercer?" Lucky pressed.

"Sergio was a fling, a fun fling, but a fling. He was getting married, and I wasn't the only one he was seeing on the side. I knew that. Sergio was a big flirt. He was all over the place, and the older man he was sleeping with, and his live-in... we weren't the only ones."

"Do you have names of these other men?"

"No, Detective, I damn well don't. It wasn't like I asked for a list. I knew the score."

"Do you think Jason knew you were stepping out on him?"

Brent raked his hands through his hair. "I don't know, maybe... Oh my God, Jason's not a killer. He's the kindest, most sensitive man I've ever met. He could never, I mean never."

"There have been unsuspecting people who've committed monstrous acts of violence. We can't say what might drive someone to this atrociousness." Jack didn't want to remind him of prior killers.

"Not him, never him," Brent insisted.

"You know we'll talk to him, just warning you upfront." Jack's voice was firm, all traces of compassion gone.

Brent sunk in his expensive chair, lowering his head in what Jack hoped was shame.

"I do need to tell him. I want to break this to him myself—if that's acceptable."

"Mr. Mercer, sooner is better. Homicide detectives don't have time to waste chasing a killer."

"Yes, sir. I'll tell him tonight. I hope he forgives me. I don't want to lose him—or Nelle. I hope he forgives me."

"You should think on that next time you stray outside the bonds of marriage, Mr. Mercer." Lucky's bluntness hit. Jack shook his head, but agreed wordlessly.

"I will need Jason down at the station tomorrow. If you haven't come clean, we'll do it for you, understand?"

"He'll know tonight, I swear."

Jack handed him his card. "Mr. Mercer, I hope it ends well for you."

Brent reciprocated. There was no reason to be mad at the detectives. He'd put himself in hot water and hoped he could salvage what he might have destroyed. For such a successful man, he'd been a moronic idiot.

40

"I'M GLAD I WON'T be a fly on their wall tonight, and I don't feel sorry for the guy. If he ends up losing his husband and daughter, it's his own fault." Lucky was still ranting.

"Yeah, me neither. I just want to catch the sick bastard who's doing this crap."

"Are we headed to talk to Sybil Preston?"

"Uh-huh, and I hope something comes of it. You know, Lucky, if we don't hurry, a fourth person could die."

Jack knocked and geared up. Mrs. Preston opened the door, none too happy to see them.

"Detectives, don't know if I should say nice to see you or not... your, uh, Detective... which one are you?"

"Jack West. Ma'am, do you have a moment to speak with us?"

"Detective West, I'd rather not discuss this here—not in front of my boys."

"When can you come down to the station?"

"Can I meet you there in an hour? I need to finish up dinner, and Rafe will be home by then. He can watch the boys." Her eyes shimmered with happiness.

"Fine. Ask for me. We'll see you in an hour."

Sybil Preston shut the door, and the detectives returned to the car.

"Lucky, was it my imagination, or did that woman seem blissful?"

"For a woman whose husband came clean about his affair with a woman half her age, I'd say she was in better spirits. Yeah, that's odd."

Back at headquarters, Xi Chang swiveled his chair at the sound of Dawson Luck's voice.

"What's stuck in your craw, Lucky?"

"We're out of damn coffee filters. How do they expect us to work without the java juice?"

"Yeah, Jace went to five to steal some from Robbery. Steal from Robbery—ain't that funny?"

"Yeah, Xi, a laugh a minute. He needs to hurry; Lucky's coffee-deprived and cranky." Jack sat down, closed his eyes, and relaxed.

"So, what's up?"

"We spun our wheels on the church membership leads and got nada. I called Al Mathers' wife, Bunny Mathers. Jace and I are going to talk to her. I want her to tell me one more time how her husband would never cheat."

Dawson Luck propped his elbow on the desk, resting his chin in his hand. "Yeah, I'd like to understand all this cheating crap. I don't get it."

"Since you guys are taking another run at the Mathers woman, did her husband ever come clean with her?"

"I don't know, Jack. That's his problem, not ours. Al Mathers is a big boy. He just might have to take his medicine. Ain't mine and Jace's problem."

"You hens still squawking?" Jace came in, bearing the nectar of the gods—hot, steaming cups of black coffee.

"God bless you, Jace. We all needed a caffeinated pick-me-up." Lucky grabbed a cup.

"We've been discussing Mathers and whether he's told the wife yet," Xi said, sipping his coffee.

"Guess he'll have to suffer her wrath if he hasn't. We've kept the DNA bit from her." Jace handed Jack his coffee.

"She doesn't know, Xi?" Jack sat up, stretched, and slumped back, stretching his long legs.

"Nah, we told him he needed to tell her, just in case this came up. We're all out of leads. Time for no-holds-barred action."

Jack was all for it. If the cheaters started confessing—even just to cheating—who knew what else might come out, even by accident.

It was 4:50. Jack picked up the phone and called the morgue.

"Crime lab, Marlo Makos."

"Mack, are you still working?"

"Hiya, Jack. Funny, I was just going to call you."

"By any chance, did you find a ring in Sergio's pockets?"

"No, he didn't have jewelry on him at all. Why?"

"Doesn't matter. Just asking."

That wasn't her worry; it was his. Another potential link to the killer was gone.

"So, you were fixin' to call... whatcha got? Wait, let me put you on speakerphone—the gang's all here. Tell everyone."

"Sure, Jack."

"Go ahead, Mack. We can all hear you."

"Hiya, fellas, let me jump right in. First, Sergio's fatal injury is the same as the Taylor woman and the Nelson girl. Same size gashes, same knife, same makeup, same broken finger. No duct tape residue. No ligature marks. He was never bound. Toxicology screen won't be back for days, maybe weeks. Cheech called me two hours ago; he lifted two partial thumbprints on an empty matchbook. The near-full matchbook has what looks like a thumbprint on the front cover and a partial print on the back... light print, but possibly matchable if we knew who to compare it to, since it's not in AFIS." Mack sighed. "Now, to the not-so-fun stuff. What was in his mouth was what everyone thought. First time for me, hope it's the last. If he hadn't bled out, he would've choked ...I can say he was well endowed."

"Jesus, Mack! You can leave some of this info out. We can read the report, it's embarrassing." Jace turned from pink to deep red.

"Jace, get a grip," Jack chortled. "Forgive him. He's been dealing with men all day—men who smile and wink."

"No, Jack, that's not it."

"Uh, Jace, that's it... a dick."

Xi and Lucky lost it, laughing.

"Hell, Jack, just stop," Jace frowned.

A deafening *ahem* sounded over the phone.

"Are you finished? I've got more but need to get home..." she paused. "My wife and I are going out tonight."

"Yeah, Mack, what else you got?" Jack glanced at Xi and Jace. Lucky stared at the speaker, shaking his head. Jack winked—7-11 were in on the joke that Mack had a wife.

"Got synthetic wig hair. Same color as the others. Found three this time. Sergio had one on his thumbnail; the nail had a jagged ridge. Some other unknown debris under his thumb and ring finger. Can you find out if he was left-handed?"

"Why?" Jack watched the phone as if the speaker were in front of him.

"Whoever killed him got scratched on the right side—cheek or forearm. A fair swipe. Might be deeper than a plain scratch. One last thing."

"Let's have it, Mack."

She exhaled. Jack could envision her dark bangs lifting. "When I undressed the victim—trousers and boxer shorts—uh, his... you know..."

"Don't say it, Mack," Jace shuddered.

"Sorry, Jace, I gotta. His penis was outside his pants. Sadly, it was lopped off prior to death, hence the blood. Once he was dead, someone put the apron on him."

Jace groaned first, then Lucky, Jack, and Xi, all at once.

Silence followed. Every man receded into his own thoughts. This brutality was every man's nightmare. Mack waited, letting the deafening silence stretch.

Jack broke it. "Mack, I hope that's it, shit, we..."

She cut him off. "Yes, Jack. That's it. And that's plenty. I hope you catch this son of a bitch soon. Each murder's gotten worse. Lopping off his uh... while still alive shows deep-seated rage."

"He's getting angrier."

"Exactly. I'll have a copy of the report in a few days."

"Okay, Mack. Hope not to see you soon. No offense."

"None taken. See you when I see ya."

"Hey, tell your wife the guys said hello; we can't wait to meet her," Lucky sputtered.

Mack bit her bottom lip, hiding a laugh. "Sure thing, Detective Luck. I'll tell her you said hey." She hung up.

The four sat in staid silence, digesting Mack's report and knowing Sergio Loza had suffered unimaginable pain.

"Detective West," a female voice called. Her head appeared in the squad room doorway.

"Juanita, come in. What's up?" Jack rose.

"No, thanks, I'm on my way home. A lady downstairs says she's here to see you."

"Mrs. Preston?"

"Yes, sir."

"Tell her I'll be down in five minutes."

She giggled. "Yes, sir. I will." Hunky Detective West made her nervous.

Xi checked the time. "Bunny Mathers should be here too. Hope she shows."

Dawson Luck's cell phone rang, playing *Baby I'm a Want You* by Bread.

"Hello, babe. Slow down, take a deep breath." His caterpillar brows dipped into a deep V. "It'll be alright, Viv. See you as soon as I get there."

"Trouble in paradise, partner?"

"Shit. Upstairs water heater busted. Ceiling in living room caved in. Colossal mess. She got home and found it. I need to get home."

"Go. Check the mess. You have homeowner's insurance?"

"Hell, yeah. Never buy a home without it."

"I thought that was American Express—'never leave home without it,'" Jace quipped.

Lucky twisted his face. "I hate a water mess. Reminds me of heavy rains here."

"Don't jinx us," Xi warned as his phone rang. "Homicide, Chang. Good. Jack can bring her up when he gets down there. Thanks."

"Who am I bringing up, Xi?"

"Bunny Mathers. She's downstairs with Sybil Preston."

41

41

SYBIL PRESTON WAITED IN interview room three. Bunny Mathers waited in six.

The door to room three opened. A cool, very calm Sybil Preston sat at the table.

"Sorry, didn't mean to keep you waiting."

"No problem."

"Has your husband told you—?"

She cut him off. "Sorry to interrupt you, but I want to get this over with."

Jack wondered if a confession was about to take place. "Of course. The floor is yours."

She drew in a cleansing breath and let it out. Then: "Yes, Rafe confessed he had an affair. This, uh, incident—well, it scared the you-know-what outta him. He promises this will never be a problem in our marriage again. Ever. Rafe had nothing to do with the murder, either."

She stood. "So, that's it."

"Sit down, Mrs. Preston."

The look on her face was incredulous.

"I don't understand. Isn't that all you needed to hear from me?"

"May I call you Sybil?"

She nodded, clearly confused about why she was still here.

"Coming clean about cheating on your wife is one thing," Jack said evenly, "but murder, Sybil, is a much more serious matter. Wouldn't you agree?"

"Well, yes, but—"

Jack cut her off. "There are a few questions I need to ask, if you're willing to talk to me."

"I've nothing to hide, but you seem to think I'm a suspect. And I've got to tell you, I'm a victim. Not a dead victim—but I'm still a victim. Your dead woman was a home-wrecker. I'll just say this... you reap what you sow. And those are God's words, not mine."

She sounded pleased that Jade was dead and out of her way. Her reference to God made the hairs on Jack's neck twitch.

"Did you know your husband was cheating on you?"

"Of course I did." Then she backtracked. "Well, not at first. But signs started building up. Detective West, if your husband suddenly doesn't want sex anymore, that's a red flag."

"You never confronted him?"

"Heavens no. I cried every day and prayed—at first."

"At first? What does that mean?"

Sybil Preston avoided eye contact.

"What does that mean, Sybil?" His compassion evaporated, his tone turning sharp.

"I'd rather not say." She narrowed her eyes, her lips flattening into a thin line.

"Fine. I suppose you'd rather be a suspect. Last month, Thursday the fifth—where were you at eight p.m.?"

She turned snooty. "Let me look at my calendar."

Pulling her cell from her sweater pocket, she clicked and scrolled.

"I was at a PTA meeting from seven-thirty to nine. Do you need the PTA president and the other members' numbers?"

She crossed her arms and met his stare without wavering.

"Just the PTA president's name and her number."

"*Her name* is Pete Waters, and here's *her* number."

She slid the phone across the table. Jack wrote it down.

Smart-ass bitch. Not the demure homemaker, he'd assumed. That woman had left the room.

"Let's go back to what you said earlier. What did you mean by 'at first'? What happened later?"

Sybil adjusted herself in the chair and crossed her arms. Rolling her eyes toward the ceiling, she huffed before answering.

"I followed Rafe one night. I had to know what he was doing."

"What happened?"

He suspected she was the older woman Barry Picco had described—the one sitting at the end of the bar in tears. The same woman Barry said he'd run from.

"He went to a club. A hip-hop club. Can you believe that? He's no spring chicken—and God, he can't even dance."

Jack said nothing, waiting.

She blew out a hefty sigh. The stereotypical annoyed wife.

"He didn't see me in the crowd, but I saw them together. I guess I looked sad, because that pothead bartender came over, trying to cheer me up. Told me I should be rocking out. How stupid is that?"

Jack's voice stayed flat. "What did you do?"

"Nothing. I left after watching them for a while."

Her eyes sharpened. "They sat there, and I'm sure his hands were—you know—probably feeling her up while he kissed her. I know he had more than his hands in her once she had her panties off."

She wiped spittle from her lip. "As the old saying goes, a picture is worth a thousand words."

Her face twisted with rage, eyes pinched tight. The evil bitch inside her fought to get out.

Jack kept his face neutral. He hadn't expected this Susie Homemaker to speak this way.

Wow. Bipolar. Scorned. Raging. The anger in the room was palpable. Yeah—she could kill. He saw it in her eyes.

"So, you didn't confront your husband that night?"

"No. I looked for death because I can't compete. She's sexy and young—and I'm not."

She stopped, pulled a tissue from her pocket, blew her nose, wiped her tears.

Now the pitiful, *oh woe is me* martyr appeared.

Fourth or fifth personality, at least.

"What did you do?" Jack pressed. "Hire someone to kill her—or did you do it yourself?"

"No, I did not." She scooted her chair back as he leaned closer. "I called for help. I needed someone to talk me out of what I wanted to do."

"Which was what, exactly?"

"Kill myself. Or kill her and me. Or kill all three of us. Hell, I don't know. But I didn't do it. I'm alive—and Rafe is, too."

"Jade Nelson's dead. Did you forget that part of your story?"

She clenched her teeth. "I didn't kill her. I called a suicide hotline. We prayed, and I left it in God's hands. And damned if my prayers weren't answered. I got my husband back. That's all I have to say. I wanna go home."

"I wanna go home" came out as a hiss.

"Fine. One last thing—don't leave town."

She smirked. "Wouldn't even take a trip without your permission."

Jack escorted her to the elevators. He said nothing—no thank-you, no goodbye—unsure which personality might surface next. He bit his lip to keep from laughing.

Sybil. What an appropriate moniker.

He remembered a movie he'd watched with his mom—Sally Field playing a woman with multiple personalities. Terrifying.

But Jack had a gun.

And if he wanted to, he could shoot all of Mrs. Preston's personalities with a single bullet.

42

"JACE." JACK SAT DOWN. "Do you believe that woman?"

"Wow, what an emotional roller coaster... did the ride make you sick, Jack?"

"Have you ever seen that seventies movie, *Sybil*, the one with Sally Field?"

"Yeah, matter-of-fact, my second wife read the book, then she rented the movie."

A light flicked in his head.

"Oh, my Lord, Jack, her name's Sybil." Jace Severson almost fell out of his chair.

Chang opened the door. "Jack, Bunny Math... what's so funny, Jace?"

"Bunny Mathers is gonna have to wait a minute, 11. You gotta see this tape of Jack's interview, then he can explain."

Xi Chang was holding his sides laughing by the time Jace spilled out his part. It wasn't a laugh-out-loud funny, more like a tired, giddy kind of amusement. They were all sapped and slap-happy.

"Jack, you have a run at the Mathers woman. She's sticking to her guns on this, and no matter what I toss at her, she hits it outta the park. I explained the DNA discussion Al and I had. She said I was trying to pressure her, and Al would never submit DNA."

"Did he submit?"

"Nah. We got the M.E. report. There were two sets of DNA mixed—two different men—and I suggested he submit. That's when he gave up the truth. He confessed to at least sleeping with the woman."

"You taped his interview, right?" Jack looked from Xi to Jace.

"Al Mathers' interview? Yeah. Why?"

"Did he sign a waiver?" Jack looked from Jace to Chang.

"Yeah, and we... well, damn, Jack, that never crossed my mind," Chang admitted.

"Get it set up. She can see her husband's interview. He confessed he'd been sleeping with your victim. He can confess to the wife, too."

7-11 felt stupid for not thinking of that themselves.

"Hey, it's been a long few days. You'd have thought of it in the end."

"I'll put this one on you, 11. You are way smarter than me."

"Thanks for stepping up, Jace," Chang said with a chuckle. "I'll get the disc, Jack. You go grab a laptop."

The door to six opened and Jack stepped in, laptop in hand, and he set it on the table.

"Uh, where's Detective Chang?"

"He's still here. I'm Detective West, ma'am. We're working this case together."

"If that's so, then you know everything I've told Detective Chang, twice now." Her tone was bitter, her face expressing total annoyance.

"Yes, ma'am, that's true, but sometimes a fresh outlook on a case like this can help. I'm that fresh outlook."

"Suit yourself, but from the time he left and you walked in, nothing's changed." She got up, straightened her skirt, sat down, crossed her legs and arms, and gave Jack a look that said: go ahead, I ain't budging on my story.

He scooted his chair to the end of the table, took the laptop, and opened it.

"Mrs. Mathers, can I call you Bunny?"

"If you must," she said, her tone abrasive.

"Did you know Corrine Taylor?"

"Yes." The single word oozed disgust.

"Can you tell me how you knew her, ma'am?"

"We went to the same church. Al and I were in the Sunday school class with her and her husband, Lincoln." Her monotone explanation grated on his frayed nerves.

"Had you known her long?"

"They joined the church a year ago—that's when we met. Listen, I only saw them on Sunday at church. I wasn't friends outside of that with her, or her husband."

"Did you ever think your husband was cheating on you, with...?"

Anger sparked in her eyes as she cut him off. "Al Mathers is a moral man. He would never cheat, has no reason to cheat. Do you understand what I'm telling you?"

"Yes, ma'am, I do, but..."

She cut in again. "What do I have to do or say to make you people understand?" Her right hand came down on the table with a heavy thwack.

Jack's brows shot up, but he didn't flinch.

"Nothing. You don't have to say a word, ma'am. You don't have to convince me at all. The burden is on me—to convince you."

He hit the power button, booting the computer.

She shifted in her seat, angling to look at him, watching him push buttons on the laptop. He took a plastic disc case out, popped the DVD in, and looked at her.

"A lady is dead. Someone killed her, and we don't know why. We're trying to figure that out." He omitted telling her about the other murders connected to this case. "We have to look at everything that may or may not be involved in this case, even the smallest detail. Do you understand?"

She shrugged. "I suppose so, yes."

"Now, Bunny, they found this woman in an empty home your husband's realty company listed, and we don't know why she was there. She owned a home with her husband, and they had no intentions of buying, selling, or moving."

Bunny Mathers smirked. "I get that, Detective. Maybe the killer knew the house was empty and he broke in to do his deed."

"Nope. There was no break-in... someone had a key, and someone lured Mrs. Taylor there to kill her."

"That has nothing to do with Al. I've told the other detective repeatedly where Al was that night. There are witnesses to verify my statement. What's your point?"

He hit play, turning the screen toward her. Her husband's face appeared, and she heard his voice. The interview concluded with her dabbing her tears. He turned off the recording.

"I'm sorry, Bunny. Now, did you know he was cheating on you? This time there's no reason to defend him. I need to know the truth."

Bunny Mathers wiped her nose with a tissue and nodded. "Yes, I suspected, but didn't know for sure." She sniffed, then wiped her eyes again.

Jack watched her face. Something was amiss, and he couldn't put his finger on it. He sat silent. He'd let her do the talking, or they'd just sit there. Silence: his weapon of choice right now.

"That woman... that whore. And it wasn't just Al, either. It was all the men. It disgusted me at Sunday school watching her flirt. I mean, we're at the house of God, and she's flirting. Everyone watched her. Other wives made comments, too. Al ignored her, never letting on he liked the flirting—I didn't worry. A year after the Taylors joined, several couples transferred their memberships to other churches. Her brazen hussy actions were why they left. Al and I've been members for over five years. That's our church home. She was an interloper."

"What church?"

"A nondenominational church called The Gates of Heaven."

Well, at least that was the truth.

"Did you ever confront your husband?"

"No, because I figured he'd confess. I could see it eating at him. I know he loves me, but I guess he needed something exciting, and he picked her." She looked down at her folded hands. "He's cheated before."

Bunny knew he'd cheated before. Why was she adamantly denying it—and just confessed what she knew?

"I know what you're thinking. Why did I deny I knew? Thinking he wouldn't cheat on me for the third time... if I don't believe it, then it isn't true, do you understand?"

He wanted to, but he couldn't, so he gave her no reply.

"Did you discuss this with a close girlfriend, or have anyone's shoulder to cry on?"

"No, I kept it to myself," she blurted.

His gut tightened, and he saw it in her eyes. Another lie from her lips.

"You didn't confide in anyone at all?"

"I just told you I didn't. Are you going to continue to badger me? This has been humiliating enough, and I don't want my dirty laundry aired out. And worse, it gets back to my Sunday school class, don't you understand?"

"Bunny, did you murder Corrine Taylor or hire someone to kill her?" He watched her face.

Bunny Mathers sat up and looked him right in the eye. "No, I didn't kill Corrine Taylor, or hire a killer to do the job, either."

He stared at her, trying to read her face. She had nothing there to read.

"That's it for now, Bunny."

The woman stooped and grabbed her purse from the floor.

"Fine, I'd like to go home now."

Jack walked her out, then made his way back to the monitoring room.

"Excellent job, Jack. At least she admits she knew," Jace congratulated him as he punched in some buttons and shut off the monitors.

"Not that it helped. It didn't get us a damn inch closer to the killer." He plopped down into a chair.

"Well," Chang said, yawning, "now we can cross her off our list."

Tired, and with nothing new, they called it a day.

Jack said goodbye and headed to the Lone Star Saloon to unwind with a few beers—and some Gretchen time.

43

"WELL, WHAT KIND OF mess did you walk into yesterday?"

"Awful. We're gonna need to replace the ceiling, the carpet, and some furniture—and repair the wall—Viv cried."

"Be thankful for homeowners insurance—she would've cried even harder."

Lucky agreed with a frowning nod.

"What's the plan today, Jack, after Mr. Jason Fryer-Mercer's interview?"

"Well, I—"

The door to the squad room opened and 7-11 came storming in.

"Morning," Chang greeted them.

"Hey, Lucky, everything good on the home front? Did you have to get out your rubber raft when you got home?"

Jace kidded—but not really. His house had flooded during the heavy rains of Hurricane Ike, devastating him. Jack remembered how the entire department had helped him recoup. Then his third wife left him, and they'd been there again, helping him pick up the pieces of another part of his life, keeping him sane.

They were laughing at Lucky's smart-ass remark when Captain Brooks stuck his head into the squad room, sucking all the cheerfulness out of the air.

"Good, you're all here." He pushed the door open and stepped inside. Looking from Chang to Severson, then to Lucky, Captain Brooks' gaze landed on Jack—and stayed there as he spoke.

"No one's updated me in three days. Is there a reason for this?"

His voice was filled with irritation as he stared at Jack.

Jack didn't flinch, nor did he smile. He knew Brooks dumped everything he could onto his shoulders, and he didn't understand the captain's clear hostility toward him.

"Nothing new to report. We've been re-interviewing some people to be thorough, but it hasn't led to anything. We're interviewing the husband of the Taylor woman today. That's the most updated update I can give you." He paused for several beats, then added, "Sir."

Brooks cleared his throat, his eyes never leaving Jack's face. "Get the report on my desk as soon as you have it, understood?"

A clear emphasis landed on the word *my*, and Jack knew exactly what he was inferring—*his* desk, not Chief Yao's. Don't overstep.

"Understood." Jack read his face loud and clear—but he never blinked or looked away. He excelled at this. He had all day, and if Captain Brooks wanted to play, Jack would give him a run for his money.

The other three detectives were stone statues.

The only things moving were their eyes—Jack to Brooks, Brooks to Jack.

An onlooker might've gotten the funny picture of one of those old black-and-white Kit-Cat Klocks: a wall clock with a black cat, big white eyes shifting back and forth. The only difference—no one had a tail.

Brooks dropped his gaze first, but Jack didn't. No way was he averting his stare.

A coughy, throaty, choky sound came from Brooks.

Jack didn't know whether their ruddy captain was clearing his throat or fixing to spit. He watched the captain's face as he leaned back, settling into a very comfortable posture—arms resting on the chair arms, long legs stretched out, ankles crossed.

The fat captain better think again if he believed he scared him. Brooks was a bully, and Jack had done nothing to deserve it. It wasn't the first time Jack had met a man like Brody Brooks.

Brooks took a step back, then looked at the other three.

"Right. Well, keep at it, boys. We have a maniac killer on the loose. HPD needs to wrap it up—get him locked up."

With that, he turned and walked out, his potbellied front side leading the way by at least five inches as the rest of him followed.

Silence... stale silence hung in the air.

"I'm gonna go get a fresh cup of joe. Anyone want one?"

Everyone understood Chang's question. It gave him an excuse to see whether Brooks went back to his office. Best to know the man was out of earshot.

When Chang returned with coffee, he reported, "He went back into his office, shut the door, and pulled the blinds closed. What a dickhead. Wow, Jack, the man can't stand you."

"Did you pee in his Post Toasties or what?" Jace looked from Chang to Jack.

"You guys know as much as I do. I've never had cross words with the man. I don't have a damn clue what put the burr under his saddle."

"You ever think it was because of Judge Wolff's takedown, Jack?" Lucky offered.

"Don't know. Never had a reason to ask Brooks if he was close to the judge or not—never cared. You know, if we didn't already call Becca Brenner BB, I'd take to calling Brooks that."

Chang puckered his brow. "For Brody Brooks, since that's his initials?"

Jack smirked. "Nah—for 'Big Belly.'—fits him."

They cracked up and the doomsday feeling Brooks brought into the room evaporated.

It was a long, boring day. No new cases cropped up—no pop-and-drop, no gang shootings, no lover's quarrels ending with bullets flying. What were the criminals doing, taking a holiday? This kind of lull was unusual for Homicide. They knew Robbery and Vice weren't as fortunate. Those guys had something not just daily, but hourly.

"It's five-fifteen. Jason Fryer should be wheeling in soon, Jack."

"Hope he's in a decent mood, but finding out your husband was cheating—who knows. He struck me as a very sensitive type. Did you get that vibe too?"

"Yup, and I hope he doesn't fall to pieces in here. Don't know if I can take that." Dawson Luck had enough crying with his water mess the night before.

"Lucky, you should be glad you weren't with us at Smith Russell's house then, huh?"

Jack agreed with Jace. Lucky wouldn't have done well in that situation, and to his surprise, Jace had handled it better than expected.

Juanita stuck her head in the door. "Detective West, there's a man in the lobby—Jason Fryer-Mercer—asking for you."

"Okay, Juanita, tell him I'll be down in five."

"Yes, sir, I will. Have a nice night."

"Oh—and Juanita," he called.

She poked her head back in. "Yes, sir?"

"We've got to stop meeting this way. The boys will talk." Jack flashed a playful smile.

Juanita's cheeks reddened and she gave a nervous giggle, saying nothing as she shut the door.

"Jack, you're a turd, you know that. Maybe worse than me," Lucky admonished.

"Why is that, may I ask?"

"The girl has a crush on you, and you're egging it on." Lucky wagged a finger, tsk-ing.

Jace rocked back in his chair laughing.

Jack rolled his eyes. "Yeah, and she's what—twenty-three? I'm old enough to be her... uh, older brother."

Jason Fryer-Mercer sat in interview room four. Jack, Lucky, and 7-11 watched him on the monitor.

"He's no killer, Jack. Look at him," Chang said.

"I know he's not, but maybe he knows something—crap, anything—that points us somewhere."

"He's nervous—scared nervous. See his hands? He keeps rubbing them on his pants, like he's wiping off sweat," Jace noted.

"He's not killer material, that's for sure. But I've seen killers who didn't look like killers since I've been with HPD," Lucky said.

"Lucky's right. Killers can look like anybody. It's the inside person who's the true killer."

Jack had a point. Sometimes murderers were spontaneous, not intending to kill, but passion or rage triggered them. One time was all it took. One time could land you in prison for life—or thirty years or more. Even that wasn't guaranteed. Sometimes the perp got less, and Jack didn't see eye--to-eye with the system. A life for a life. If you took one, losing yours—or at least, your freedom—was a fair price.

"Alrighty, dudes, I'm going in." Jack grabbed the recorder, the file, and his notebook.

"You wanna team up, or go solo?"

"This guy's fragile. I want to make friends first. Two of us will intimidate him if needed."

"Yep, your call, Jack. You're senior man on the totem pole. We'll be here, eating popcorn, watching the sensitive drama play out."

Dawson Luck opened a file drawer and pulled out a family-size bag of Fritos.

"Hey, pass me some," Jace held out his hand.

44

THE DOOR SWUNG OPEN, and Jason jumped up.

"Sorry, didn't mean to keep you waiting," Jack said, extending his hand.

Jason wiped his hand on his pant leg. "I'm sorry, I'm quite nervous. This is my first time in a police station, and it scares me a bit," he confessed as he sat back down.

"Jason, can I call you Jason?"

"Of course. Mr. Fryer-Mercer is a mouthful." He snickered but didn't go into the inside joke he and Brent shared.

"You hyphenated. Can I ask why?" Jack took the chair across from him. Keeping the conversation light sometimes drew a person in, easing their nerves. Jason relaxed a little.

"Well..." he drew the word out, "for a long time I figured I'd be wearing the pants in the family, if you know what I mean." He smirked, his brow lifted, eyes sparkling.

"Sure, I understand."

"Then one day, I understood who I truly was. To tell the truth, it was an enormous weight lifted off my shoulders. I wasn't pretending anymore. One thing, though—I was the only son and grandson—no one would carry on the family name. When Brent and I married, I told him I had to keep my last name. He didn't care, but after we adopted Nelle, we hyphenated. You know..." His eyes filled with tears, and his voice cracked.

"Jason, is something wrong?" Jack asked, surprised at the tears before even beginning the real questioning.

"I... I'm sorry, Detective West. I get very emotional and cry at the drop of a hat."

"That's alright, but why are you crying?"

"Before all this—the cheating stuff—we were discussing a second adoption. We wanted a boy. That way families' names would go on."

"Okay, let's talk about the cheating you learned about last night."

Jason wiped his eyes with his sleeve—snuffling.

"Before Brent talked to you last night, did you suspect anything?"

"Not at first. I never dreamed he'd do that. He'd had some rough workdays, and I felt like I pushed him into cheating."

"Pushed him?"

"I nagged, Nelle cried, he was tired and frustrated. I suggested he get out of the house one night, have a drink or two, relax. I never imagined he'd meet a man and go down that path. I just wanted him to be happy. After adopting Nelle, we became domesticated—a real family, no longer party animals."

"Was that what you both wanted?"

"Of course. The first year was a tremendous change, but we worked at it together. I quit my job to be a househusband—it suits me. I'm the nurturing type; Brent is the man-of-the-family type." He smiled, asking a silent question. Did Jack understand?

"I get it. You're the wife, and Brent's the husband—even though you're both husbands." Jack's dimples appeared.

"For a straight man, Detective West, you're perceptive about the gay world," Jason said with a laugh.

"What makes you think I'm straight? Maybe I just haven't come out yet?"

Jason chuckled. "You're dripping with masculinity. If I weren't married, I'd try to swing you to my side of the... closet."

Jack blushed. He could imagine the others in the monitoring room cracking up at his expense.

Once the pink faded, he found his voice. "Jason..."

"I'm sorry, Detective. I wasn't trying to embarrass you. My playful personality, my eyes and smile, that's what Brent said attracted him." Jason shot him a look, but Jack shook it off. He secretly smiled; the man was purposely testing him.

"Jason, I have a favor to ask. While we're interviewing, please refrain from flirting. You don't want to cheat on your husband, do you?" Jack's piercing stare made Jason blush.

"You're right, I apologize. Just having a little fun. But why am I here?"

Jack asked the questions, didn't answer them.

"Did you ever think of confronting Brent, telling him what you suspected?"

"No, never. Brent has an alpha personality. I felt he'd see it as an ultimatum. I wanted him to make the right choice himself."

"Did you know Sergio Loza?"

"No, but I knew of him."

"How?"

Jason's expression pained. "When Brent became distant, stopping paying attention to Nelle, I realized he wasn't himself. Two, then three nights a week, he'd 'get away.' I hired a PI, who followed him and got pictures—at the club, at a motel."

"You had proof. Why didn't you make him come clean?"

"Have you ever been in love—truly in love? I needed Brent, not just for stability for Nelle—I need him, too." Jason tapped his chest. "I would do anything for Brent."

"Would you kill for him, Jason?"

45

JACK'S QUESTION TOOK JASON Fryer-Mercer by surprise.

"No, never," he sputtered. "I'd only, well, it doesn't matter. I wouldn't, that's all."

"Let me make this clear to you. A young man got killed. Murdered. He'll never get his chance to grow old with the man who loved him, and he'll never have the chance to be a father like Brent, or the nurturing househusband you are. I'm going to ask what you meant by 'you'd only' ... you'd only what?"

Jason's leg jiggled back and forth, and his eyes filled with tears. He sniffed and then looked up at Jack.

"I contemplated giving Nelle back to the agency, and then I would kill his lover, then myself. I wanted him to know I loved him that much, but I didn't want to kill or be dead. The crack in my heart was growing."

"Did you talk to your friends, a best friend, a close family member, and ask for advice?"

Jason put his hands to his chest, and his eyes grew wide. "Oh, good gracious, no, I'd never do that."

"No close friend to confide in?"

His was a bitter laugh. "No. All our friends were 'our' friends, and if I'd discussed this with them and Brent found out, it would mortify him."

"Jason, weren't you feeling humiliated? I mean, your husband was sleeping with another man. You think your friends might not have seen them in the bar together?"

Jason let out a fun laugh. "Detective, there are several gay bars in Houston. You think there's just one bar we all go to, and everyone knows everyone?"

"No, but if he had a favorite spot, he might have gone there."

"The PI followed him to a new place; I think the name of the bar is The Man's Closet. Cool name, huh? I've never been there, but last night Brent told me we were going to get a babysitter for Nelle, and he was going to take me out. He suggested that new club, but I said no."

"Why?"

"Brent went there with Sergio, and that needs to die down."

"Where were you last week, on Friday night, between twelve-thirty in the morning to one?"

"At home, of course," Jason said.

"Who can corroborate that?"

"Brent can."

Convenient—you can alibi each other out. Don't you find that coincidental?"

"Well, I never ... " This upset Jason. "I'd never hurt or kill a person, ever. Neither would Brent."

"Jason, do you want me to rewind the tape to the part where you said you would kill his lover, then yourself, to prove to Brent how much you loved him?"

Jason's eyes were wide, his pupils dilated to twice the size, and his expression, had it not been a very serious moment, would have made a funny caricature.

"I made an idle threat. I'd never be able to actually do it. I'm ... I'm ... " His willowy body quivered.

"If Sergio loved him and wanted him to leave you and threatened to expose their affair, would Brent be able to kill him to keep his dirty little secret?"

Jason Fryer-Mercer jumped up, and his fist hit the table. "No. No. Brent would never, he couldn't."

"Sit down, Jason. Now." Jack didn't flinch. "Since your daughter can't talk, she can't tell me if both her daddies were home, how can I ... "

Jason inhaled when a revelation hit him, and he cut Jack off. "Wait, I've got proof we were home that night."

Jack gave Jason a wide-eyed, brow-arching look as he waited for him to explain.

"Nelle got sick, some baby stomach flu. Poor baby woke us up at midnight, feverish, with a poopie diaper, and she'd thrown up in her bed. Sweet baby, crying and pulling at her ears. I called the pediatrician and left a message. He called back at twelve-thirty, said the stomach flu was going around, and she most likely had an ear infection. She'd been at a playdate, and ... "

"Jason, get to the point."

He didn't want to hear the story of puke, poop, earaches, and playdates; he needed to find a damn killer.

"The doctor called in a prescription, and I had Brent go pick it up. He got up and dressed and left at ten till one to go to the pharmacy."

Jason sat back, crossed his arms, and glared. "There's your fucking alibi, Detective West, and I'll not apologize for my language, either."

"I'll need the doctor and pharmacy phone numbers."

Jason took out his phone. Jack wrote the info.

"This is easy enough to check. Now, was there anyone, and I mean anyone at all you talked to ... a neighbor, even a pastor?" Did gay men go to church? Jack had no idea. He would not discuss religion with Jason Fryer-Mercer.

Jason's eyes bugged out a bit, and a look of realization hit him.

"I did go to group counseling, and infidelity group."

Jack shook his head, his forehead squished up. "There's cheaters anonymous group?"

"No, it's a group counseling session called Dealing with Spousal Infidelity. I saw it on a grocery store corkboard—I took a picture. It stayed on my mind for several days before I went."

"Why, didn't you want to go?"

He assumed Jason might want to confide in someone, even a stranger. Jason struck him as the 'I need to cry on someone's shoulder' type.

"Because." Jason said. "It was at a church. Even though the flyer said all were welcome ... gay, lesbian, straight ... it scared me. What if they turned me away? That would make things worse. But I went and was glad I did. There are tons of people with cheating spouses, and I got to cry my heart out, and it felt good."

"What church was this, Jason?"

He eyed the detective, trying to figure him out. Why was this even important?

"Jason?"

"Is the name of a church relevant to this matter?"

"With murder, Jason, everything is relevant."

"Fine, but I don't want Brent to know I went. Can you not tell him?"

"There's no reason for me to share this with your partner."

"It's a nondenominational church called The Gates of Heaven."

Jack West almost dropped his pen.

"WHAT'S GOING ON? I mean, this case just got weirder." Jace Severson rolled up the half-empty Frito bag and dropped it into a drawer.

"Yeah? I mean, what's up with this church?" asked Lucky.

Chang took a chair. "I don't see it connecting anything to anything. Jade Nelson ... Jack, how does she fit?"

"She didn't go to church, or at least not that one. It could be one of those weird coincidences, but y'all know what I say about coincidences."

"No such thing in homicide," Lucky responded to a non-question.

"Not much we can do tonight, Jack. We might as well pack it in, pick up in the morning. Whatdaya say?" Chang got up and stretched. "Jack?"

"Sounds like a plan. Hey, Luck, tomorrow I want you to watch the Preston woman's interview and the Mathers chick. We've all seen them, twice."

"You want to start Lucky's day off with a laugh, Jack?" Jace grinned.

"Yeah, he'll get one, won't he?"

"Why? What's on the DVD? Did she slap Jack ... hey, that's another one, Slap Jack, you know, the kid's card game."

"Stow it, partner," Jack said with a half laugh. "No, she didn't slap me. You maybe, yeah, I could see that happening since you don't have a filter when talking to women."

"Now you're just being a dick, Jack."

"Nope, Lucky, that's not one ... there's no such game as a dick-jack," Jace smarted off.

"Right. Okay, tomorrow, Jace you bring the popcorn, Xi you bring the fudge, I'll bring the soda," Lucky ticked off his list.

"What in the hell ... food ... you're making a snack list?" Jack looked at him as if he'd gone barmy.

"Hey, we need movie food. I never watch TV without something to eat."

This was a fact. Lucky ate and ate, and no one could figure out why the short man with a unibrow, enormous feet, and an enormous nose did not weigh at least three hundred pounds.

Jack waved and headed to the back stairwell. This group was wacky, cracked, and sometimes unbalanced, but he loved them like brothers. They were all brothers, in blue and in Kevlar; brothers who carried guns and had your back in the spray of bullets, and brothers who were there when the chips were down. He was a lucky son of a bitch; he had a better family than some blood-related families.

46

"MORNING, LUCKY. WE GET to play cops and robbers again today."

Lucky grabbed his neck and rubbed it, turning it every which way.

"Stress land in your neck or are you getting old, Dawson?"

Lucky's unibrow took a dive toward his nose. "No, if you have to know, I slept on the couch last night," he grumped.

Jack opened the bottom drawer of his desk and propped his feet up. "Trouble in marital paradise, my friend?"

It's my fault. I should've known the wife wasn't in a humorous frame of mind with this water damage shit going on."

"What'd ya do to piss her off?"

Dawson Luck stretched his arms out and arched his back. "Vivian shopped online and bought some new clothes and modeled them for me. She had on a pair of new jeans and asked me if the jeans made her look fat."

"Oh God, you didn't tell her they did, did you?"

"No, worse. I said, honey, I don't think it's the jeans. Man, she got pissed. Mad enough to make her face go red—I've never seen her that mad. Told her I was kidding. She started crying and yelling, threw a pillow at me, told me to go get my own fucking blanket and park it on the sofa."

Jack laughed so hard he thought he'd fall out of his chair. It took him three minutes to stop.

"I... I'm sorry, partner," he said, trying to get his breath back. "Serves you right. You just had a water disaster and Viv's not gonna be in a jovial mood, you moron. Even I know women are sensitive when there's a home catastrophe."

"She's not mad anymore. We made up early this morning. Said she was sorry she acted so sensitive."

"Dawson Luck, you let her apologize to you? You're an ass—a big fat ass."

"I apologized first, just so you know, you jerk."

Jack snorted. He could always get under his partner's skin.

"What's all the commotion in here? We can hear y'all laughing down the hall."

Jace walked in, Chang on his heels, carrying a large cup emblazoned with—Sherry's Donuts.

Chang glanced between Jack and Lucky. "Yeah, guys, what's going on?"

They found Jack's story hilarious. Then Jack held up a disc case. "Is it too early for a movie with popcorn and candy?"

They sat in the monitoring room as Jack played Lucky the Sybil Preston interview.

Lucky snickered. "Lord, that woman is bipolar, or close to it. She turned into a possessed she-devil."

"Have you ever seen the movie *Sybil*, you know, the old one with Sally Field?"

Jace watched Lucky's face and saw the clicking of gears in his head. The proverbial light bulb flicked on, and Dawson Luck cracked up.

"Oh, hell. Her name's Sybil, too. Now that's damn funny."

Jack switched the disc. "Now, partner, look at Chang's interview with Bunny Mathers. Then you can watch my interview with her."

Lucky watched the interview, then looked at Chang. "Man, Xi, she's a tough cookie and holding to her story. I think you're right—she's trying to convince herself the ol' hubby wouldn't ever cheat."

"Yeah, and I hate to admit it, but Jack was more on the ball than Jace and I were."

Lucky looked back at Jack. "Whatcha do, partner—get in her face like you did Juan Mercedes?"

"No," Jace said. "He let her husband get in her face."

"Shit. Lucky, he thought to get her husband's interview to let her watch." Chang sulked for a second.

Jack stopped the recording once Bunny Mathers had seen her husband's interview and his admission to sleeping with Corrine Taylor.

Lucky sneered at the frozen frame of Bunny Mathers' face. "Guess she can't deny it now. I can't imagine why she'd be that adamant. The man cheated on her before. She knew the Taylor woman, too—and that's odd. If she suspected, she could've confronted the woman. This Mathers woman seems headstrong, and I'm not profiling here, but Black women don't take kindly to another woman messing with their man. She'd be getting in her face."

"Yeah, she might. My second ex-wife had a very close girlfriend—a Black chick—with a boyfriend who was messing around. The 'other woman'"—Jace used air quotes—"got the snuff smacked out of her."

Lucky looked from Xi to Jace, then to Jack. "I don't understand why she denied he was cheating. What the hell purpose did it serve her?"

"That has me stumped," Jack said, "other than she just didn't want to deal with it—turn-a-blind-eye kind of attitude."

He hit play and let Lucky watch the rest of the interview.

"Stop. Rewind it. Back to where she gets up and walks out. Pause it—there."

Lucky scrutinized the screen for a minute.

"What are you looking at, partner?"

Jack and Team 7-11 stared at the screen.

"Chang, get your murder book."

"Sure, Lucky." Chang returned seconds later and handed it over.

"Okay, my man, what are you looking for?"

Flipping through the book, Lucky found it. "Now, I know I'm a guy, but is it my imagination, or does the purse Bunny Mathers is carrying look like this one?"

Three sets of eyes looked from the screen to the photograph in the Corrine Taylor murder book—the same purse Lincoln Taylor said he wanted returned to give it to his daughter—a purse that cost over two-thousand dollars.

"Yeah, but there had to be more than one made. Maybe it's a strange coincidence. Maybe one of 'em saw it and wanted one just like it."

"I have a feeling if Corrine Taylor had hers first, Bunny Mathers would never get one. She couldn't stand the woman. Xi, get Mr. Taylor on the phone—ask him when his wife bought the purse and if she paid by credit card."

Jack looked from the screen to the picture, examining both purses.

Xi took out his phone. Taylor answered on the fourth ring. Xi asked, listened, and disconnected.

"It'll take him a few minutes, but she did use a credit card. He's going to look it up and call back."

The room stayed hushed.

Chang's phone rang three minutes later. "She bought the purse three years ago. Used her American Express."

"So what do we do—ask Bunny Mathers when she bought hers and how she paid?" Lucky rolled his neck.

Xi grinned and shook his head. "Nope. We need to get a look at Bunny Mathers' purse."

Jack's brows crinkled. "What on earth for, Xi?"

"Oh, I forgot to mention—his deceased wife tagged her purse in case it was ever stolen."

"She did? How?"

"She paid an alteration shop to cut the bottom seam and sew in a leather tag with her full name, DOB, and the last four digits of her SS number under the lining."

"Well, bloody hell, mates—women do love their expensive handbags, now don't they?"

"Yeah, they do. And Jace, when did you become British?"

"So now what?" Lucky asked. "We get a warrant to see a purse?"

"Yeppers."

"A warrant for a purse?"

"A woman will understand," Jack said. "Judge Nora Yorke-Carlson."

Lucky shook his head. "All right."

"Lucky, start the warrant. Jace, find out where Bunny Mathers works. Xi, call the courthouse and get Judge Carlson's schedule."

"What are you going to do, Jack?"

"Go see Jade Nelson's mother and get a better picture of her missing ring, then Smith Russell for Sergio's engagement ring. If these are trophies—and if that purse is Corrine Taylor's—I want them all."

The team scattered as Jack headed to fleet.

47

ON JACK'S TRUCK SEAT were photos: Jade in a glamor shot with her wearing the ring, and Sergio Loza and Smith Russell showing off their engagement rings. He pondered all that they knew. Al Mathers met Corrine Taylor at church, The Gates of Heaven. Jason Fryer-Mercer had gone to a church for a workshop on how to deal with spousal infidelity, held at The Gates of Heaven. Where did Jade Nelson fit in? Did she tie in with the church? The Prestons' weren't members, or at least they weren't on the membership roster. He set his jaw. What connection was he missing?

Jack pushed the squad room door open. "Where are we with everything, fellas?"

"Judge Yorke-Carlson won't be back in the courthouse until tomorrow. You want someone else, Jack?" Chang—ready to dial whomever Jack wanted.

"No, I want her. We can wait. Get her tomorrow. Jace, you find out if Bunny Mathers works?"

Jace read from his notes. "Not a paying gig. She helps at the church from time to time, does some clerical work for the pastor, and odds and ends."

"Huh, well, guess her husband does well in real estate cuz one-income families are sort of rare these days. Lucky, roll that whiteboard back over here, would ya?" Jack requested.

The whiteboard sat between Jack and Jace's desks.

Chang leaned back in his chair. "Jack, what rabbit you have up your sleeve now?"

"By the way, who erased our frigging whiteboard?" Jace sneered.

"I think Potter and Reed used it last week. We can recreate."

Jack got a dry erase marker. In no time, he had all three victims listed and all the known facts on each. He placed a star beside all the known connections, then stepped back to study the list. "This looks like all the same info we had last time."

"What do we add that's new, like what other dots to connect to see a motive?" Jace asked.

Jack looked at the whiteboard, scratching his chin then said, "You know, at first, we said this could be hate crimes. Corrine Taylor, African-American woman, no other things pop on her. She's a regular middle-class citizen. Jade Nelson was a Hispanic party girl. The two women could be a race crime. Now with Sergio Loza, we have two things... he's a Hispanic gay person. Taylor and Nelson both women."

He stopped and tapped at the board. "Why would our killer jump from women to men?"

"Excellent question—wish we had an answer," Jace intoned.

Jack continued as he frowned at the notes. "Besides the fact that they live miles away from each other, all three have very distinct lifestyles."

"Jack, what's the connection here ya think?"

"Lucky, what else did the victims have in common besides how they were murdered?"

Dawson Luck thought for a minuscule second. "Well, they were all sleeping around."

Jack tapped the whiteboard with his marker. "Exactly, and ... "

Lucky had an epiphany and interrupted Jack. "The broken finger, like Mack said."

Chang turned his chair. "What'd Mack tell you? Bennie did our victim's autopsy."

"I couldn't figure out the meaning of Jade Nelson's broken finger during her autopsy," Lucky explained. "Mack said it was the wedding ring finger."

A light bulb went on over Jace's head.

"Well, dip me in ink. Hell, boys, I've been married three times and that never occurred to me. Crap, I'm a dummy," he berated himself.

Jack's attention returned to the whiteboard, and he said, "Nope, you're not. We're all clueless about the killer's motive. All we have is conjecture."

Dawson Luck nodded. Then: "Jack, the first murder differs from the others."

"My guess would be that with the first murder he wasn't as angry. After that, it festered. Who can say what triggered more rage?"

"Okay," Jace spoke up, "all three victims were sleeping around: a married woman, a single woman, and an engaged man. Their relationship status isn't the connection—just the cheating. But ... "

As usual, Xi Chang stepped in. "So, the question is: why them? Why not the people they were sleeping with? What made them the targets? Why weren't Al Mathers, Rafe Preston, or Brent Mercer targeted—they were cheaters too."

Jace gave his partner the thumbs-up. "That's what I was gonna say, Xi."

"Maybe we should be doing a list of the ones they were sleeping with, you think?" Lucky piped up.

He drew lines connecting Al Mathers to Corrine Taylor, Rafe Preston to Jade Nelson, and Brent Mercer to Sergio Loza, then stepped back.

"All three cheaters have solid alibis, as do their real significant others—this leaves us with freaking squat."

"Wait a minute, one of them doesn't," Chang said. "Bunny Mathers doesn't have a solid alibi."

Jack looked from Jace to Chang. "What's her shaky alibi?"

"She told us she was at the church. Until today, we had no idea she volunteered her time doing clerical work for free; she told us she'd been in the office talking to the pastor in confidence about some personal issues." Chang paused for a second, and then Jace took over—as usual.

"Yeah, we asked the pastor if she was there. He confirmed she was there after he'd left."

"Jace, what time was this? Can it fit in your murder window?" Jack sat and looked at Jace, then at Chang. He never knew who would speak next.

Jace spoke first. "Her murder happened somewhere between nine and ten-thirty p.m., Bennie's report said. The house was cold enough to slow decomp ... "

"Yeah, and they didn't find her until late the next morning when someone went to view the house," Chang finished for him.

"The pastor said he left her at the church at nine, where she was still typing a few letters and filing papers for him. He didn't mention she did this often; we thought it was her way of paying for his counseling time," Jace clarified.

Jack drummed his fingers on his desk. "So, he left her at nine; how close was the vacant house to the church?"

Chang grabbed the file and flipped through some pages. "Maybe a little more than a fifteen-minute drive. That fits within our murder window."

"Well," Lucky spoke up. "She had a way to get the key to the house since her husband's the realtor—without breaking in."

Jack looked at them. "That all makes sense, at least for your victim. But the other two, what reasons would she have to kill them?"

No one had a reasonable answer.

"Did anyone else see her at the church?" Jack asked.

Chang flipped through his notes on Bunny Mathers. "The pastor said his wife was still at the church when he left; she had to lock up, but we never questioned her."

Jack sat down and frowned. "Why not?"

"She went out of town, her mother got sick, or something, and we never got back to her." Jace ducked his head.

"To be honest, Jack, once your case came up and we had two similar murders, we crossed her off our list. We were all thinking it might be a serial, just didn't say it aloud. Then the homeless dude found the Loza guy on the bayou, which confirmed a serial." Chang took up for his partner.

"You've got a point, Xi," Jack said, swiveling his chair and staring at the whiteboard in silence.

"The church." That's all Jack said.

"What's on your mind, Jack Frost?" Lucky asked, his focus also on the whiteboard.

"Jason Fryer-Mercer went to some workshop for spousal infidelity, and Mathers met his lover—your victim—at the same church." He paused, thinking.

"Jack, Jade Nelson has no association with the church. It doesn't fit," Lucky said.

"Sybil Preston," Jack said to no one in particular.

"Jack, her alibi is rock-solid, you said so yourself," Chang retold him.

"Yeah, I know. She said she called a suicide hotline and was ready to end it all. The person on the other end talked her out of it and told her they would pray and wait to see if God would answer her prayers. Remember, that was on her interview tape."

Jack picked up the phone and dialed the number for Sybil Preston, while the other three sat and waited.

"Mrs. Preston, this is Detective Jack West," he said, hoping she projected the nice Suzie homemaker personality today.

"Yes, please don't tell me you need me to come to the station." Her voice hinged on the 'I can turn into the she-devil if you say yes' side.

"I just have a question, and I need you to cooperate."

"Yes, Detective, what is it?"

"I need the number of the suicide hotline," Jack said, waiting as the silence stretched.

"I don't want this to come back to my husband... I was foolish when I called. I think they keep everything confidential. I doubt it would help you."

"Ma'am, I have no intention of airing this out unless it's a breaking factor in our murder investigation. You understand I could get a warrant for your phone records and review every call you or Rafe have made. Your husband was seeing our victim, and we have witnesses to corroborate that, as well as his taped interview. I also have probable cause to investigate your phone records."

She was silent, and Jack could hear other personalities pressing to get out in her breathing, imagining her face contorting in anger.

He heard a loud exhalation escape from one of her many personalities. "Fine. Give me a minute to find the number."

"I'll be happy to wait … "

Sybil slammed her phone down with an over-exaggerated eye roll. In less than six seconds, she was back on the line.

"The number is," she said, and he wrote it down.

"Thank you, I apprec … "

She cut him off. "Whatever. Now, if you would leave me alone." She ended the call without a by-your-leave, a kiss-my-butt, or any pleasant goodbye.

Jack set his phone down with a "whoa" look, pulling his lips into a slight eek-face. "Got two personalities today, but I could hear the rest of 'em scratching to get out."

He looked at the other three while punching in the number she gave him, and a soft, compassionate voice came on the phone: "Your life is important to me. How can I help you?"

Jack stated his identity and the reason for calling. The woman told him to hold while she got her supervisor.

"Hello, this is Dorothy Cushman. How can I help you?"

"Mrs. Cushman," Jack began, "I need to talk to the person who sponsors your hotline—the owner or someone in charge…"

"Detective West, we're a call center run by volunteers. All I do is open the doors, keep the log schedule, and handle real case emergencies with the local Police Watch Center in our neighborhood and with the fire and ambulance services." She sounded frazzled.

"Who pays the bills, then, or who made you supervisor? I need to get to the top."

"I guess I can give you a number if you really need it. Hold on."

He heard paper rustling and waited until she said, "Here's the number, Detective."

Looking at the others, Jack dialed the number. He said the first thing that came to mind: "Ma'am, do you need an appointment to see the pastor?"

Once he'd said pastor, Lucky, Jace, and Chang knew what it meant.

The phone number Sybil Preston gave him led straight to The Gates of Heaven Church.

Now they had their connection.

48

Looking at the others, Jack said, "The number is 19," said the first ds
and called to hands. As much he had an appointment "...

JACK HUNG UP, TELLING her he would have to look at his schedule and call back.

Jace scratched his head. "This church holds the key, but how?"

Chang checked off a mental list: "I'd never think of the pastor, but he's the connection to the church—the church connects with the suicide hotline, the infidelity support group, and the members."

On his feet, Lucky grabbed his coffee cup. "No one got his alibi. He left the church and the Mathers woman was still there—he had time. Just cuz he's a preacher. We shouldn't let him off the hook, ya know?" Lucky pointed to his cup then to each of them. He was coming back with three extra coffees and one extra-large for himself. *Crud.* If you didn't want to be a waiter, he thought, then don't take orders.

Jace squared his chair to face Jack. "Jack, whatdaya think? We get him in here, see what he has to say?"

The door opened, and everyone expected Lucky with the coffees—but to their dismay, Captain Brooks walked in.

"West," he said, walking toward Dawson Luck's desk. Grabbing the chair, he plopped his weighty body down. "What's the update on this serial?"

Jack sat up and locked eyes with the captain. "I put the report on your desk last night; didn't you see it?" He was tired of Brooks' shit—and his poisonous attitude toward him.

"I did, and I want a further update." He looked at his watch. "It's now nearly noon. What've you got?" Crossing his arms over his big gut, he leaned back in Lucky's chair.

Jack wished the chair would break and dump Brooks on the floor, but he gave a half smile and filled him in on the little that had happened since last night's report.

Lucky walked in mid-update, and the look on his face when he saw Brooks' fat butt in his chair was comical. Jack, Xi, and Jace struggled to keep a lid on their laughter.

Captain Brooks cleared his throat, his saggy jowls wiggling.

"We need to get this case buttoned up. I'm counting on you to get this maniac soon." His eyes never left Jack, and he acted as if Jack were working the case alone.

"We are all doing our best, and we want this guy as badly as you want us to get him... Captain," Jack said with an edge to his voice. If Brooks was too stupid to hear it, Jace, Lucky, and Xi could; they knew Jack, and they knew he was holding in smoldering anger.

Without a word to Xi, Jace, or Lucky, Brooks rose, shoved his chair back, and left. No one spoke for at least two minutes until Chang got up, went to the door, and cracked it open.

"He's gone," he said, making his way back to his desk.

"Jack, when this investigation ends—and I hope it's soon—we need to dig into why Brooks hates your guts," Jace said, with Xi seconding.

"I'm thinking we all need to head out, hit someplace for lunch." Jack headed for the door, needing distance from the station—more accurately, distance from Brooks.

With food ordered, they settled in a back corner to discuss the case.

"We need to get Pastor Davenport into the station, Jack, dontcha think?"

"Yeah, Luck, I do. We'll set it up for tomorrow."

"Why wait?" Jace asked.

"I want the warrant for the purse; we need a look at it. When we get back to the station, I'm gonna drop you guys off. Jace, call the church and set up the meeting with Pastor Davenport in the morning at the station. Lucky, track Judge Carlson down, call Mava, and get her to tell you how to reach her. If Mava hem-haws, tell her it's a favor for me."

"Yeah, you guys know Mava has a crush on Jack, dontcha?" Lucky chuckled.

"Well, she's two-timing ya, Jack—she has a crush on Jace, too," Xi sounded off.

Jack and Jace looked at each other and shrugged. "She has excellent taste, I'd say. Wouldn't you, Jack?" Jace winked.

"What do you want me to do, Jack?" Xi Chang asked, looking across the table.

"You and I are going to make two visits: one to Sybil Preston and one to Jason Fryer-Mercer."

Chang didn't ask why. Whatever Jack planned, he was onboard.

When Brooks questioned him and Severson regarding Jack West and his capabilities, he ought to have informed the captain that Jack possessed the highest case closure rate among all detectives in the department. Jack was a natural, listening to his gut—far more capable than several veteran detectives marking time until retirement.

West was a man dedicated to the job, his personal mantra: to get justice for the dead, no matter who they were or their lifestyles. Even if a criminal got whacked, Jack sought justice because everyone mattered.

If a jury or judge said they had to die, then so be it. He wasn't the judge or the jury; he was the deliveryman. His job was to round 'em up and take evil off the streets that threatened his beloved Houston. Brooks was an asshole ladder-climber, but if someone murdered him, Jack would work just as hard to get justice for him as he would the lowlife scumbag.

"Chang, did you hear me?" Jace punched his arm.

"Uh, no—sorry, must be in La-La Land."

His mind was on Brooks and Jack, and he knew he'd keep his ear to the ground. Jack was far more important than that butt-munch, Captain Brooks.

"I said," Jace gave him a sideways glance, "you need to protect Jack from the demon personalities of Sybil Preston. If she's not the reincarnation of the original Sybil, she might be the gal who spewed green pea soup vomit in *The Exorcist.*"

Chang, expressing amusement, shook his head. "What? Face her back in case her head swivels around?"

Lucky snickered, adding, "Sounds about right."

Everyone tackled the tasks Jack assigned, and he and Chang headed for Sybil Preston's house.

49

To say it shocked her to see them at her door was more than an obligatory understatement.

Jack noticed the bitchy hellcat pop out of her eyes.

"I'll be damned. You—again. Do I need to get a lawyer and file police harassment charges against you, Detective West?"

Sybil folded her arms. Her hip jutted. Her head tilted—her face hard with hate.

"Give it your best, but you already know how this plays out. Either way, it's your call. I thought you'd appreciate our visit while the kids are at school. I'll get a warrant for your arrest if necessary, Mrs. Preston." Jack's voice stayed flat and dangerous.

"Ha! I'd like to know what the hell you could arrest me for."

"Obstruction of a homicide investigation, I think that's plenty."

She flung the door open, forcing Jack to move back to keep from getting his nose broken.

"We can talk here. I see no need to offer you a seat. This will be short, won't it?"

"As long as you cooperate." Jack kept his cool.

"This is Detective Chang."

She shot him a slanted glance—but did not acknowledge him.

Chang remained silent. She wasn't worth the wasted breath.

"We need to discuss your call to the suicide hotline."

"How is that related to your case? My unhappiness has nothing to do with it."

"We can do it here or down at the station. And" Jack glared. "Once we've caught the sick bastard, maybe the prosecuting attorney will subpoena you. You get to tell the jury about the hotline call. This is newsworthy—it gets printed in the paper. Do your boys read?" Jack threatened. He didn't know if it would happen, but it might scare her silly. He was fed up with this woman's personalities.

"I called the hotline the day after seeing that harlot and Rafe at the club. I wanted to die. When I told you I'd been foolish, it wasn't for making the call." She snorted. "It was telling the person my damn name, first and last. Then I let it slip and said Rafe's name, too. I begged the volunteer to keep that confidential."

She stopped talking, her vile demeanor dropped, replaced by humiliation, and all the fight in her evil persona diminished.

That solved one puzzle. Whoever was on the phone knew her and her husband's name. He wondered if the suicide hotline had a way to trace the number to the caller—in case of emergencies.

"Mrs. Preston," he said, taking a lighter tone with her. "Do you know if the volunteer was a woman or man? Did they tell you anything personal, you know, to comfort you or empathize with you?"

Without a word, Sybil turned and walked to the formal living area and sat on the light gray cloth couch. Jack and Chang took their cue and followed.

She was composed. "Please sit."

Jack struggled to keep up with the woman's changing moods.

A demure Sybil sat, hands folded. "We didn't exchange personal info, only my drama. To be frank, the voice was both raspy and low. I have no idea if it was male or female. I mean, the voice wasn't soothing, but the words were. Does that make sense?"

"Yes, it does, ma'am. If you heard the voice, would you recognize it?"

"Yes. It was very distinctive. Funny. Until you asked me this question, I hadn't thought about the voice at all. You know how a smoker's voice sounds, or maybe a deep voice that has laryngitis. Well, it sounded a little like that."

Chang asked his first question. "Could it have been someone disguising their voice?"

She gave him a look of confusion. "Why would they need to disguise their voice? I mean, it should be the caller, or that's what I think."

"You have a point, ma'am," was all Chang said.

Chang figured it was a valid point, but she didn't know all the details. Should a church member call while the pastor is dealing with a suicide call, he'd want to keep it on the down-low.

Jack's voice softened. "I hate to ask you this, but what else can you tell me? It may or may not be important, ma'am."

Sybil hesitated. Worry and regret wrinkled her face.

"I know you have no mercy for the other woman, but no one deserves to be murdered. Everyone matters in this world. Jade had a family and friends. If you were the person murdered and someone else was sitting here, I'd ask no less of them. Do you understand?" Jack's eyes never left her face.

Her posture relaxed, her eyes were brimming with tears. Wiping her cheeks, hanging her head, she blew her nose and then spoke, her eyes glued to the light-beige carpet.

"I told the volunteer counselor I'd followed Rafe to the bar and replayed my conversation with the bartender ... the pothead bartender knew the girl's name and where she worked. I drove to where she works and followed her to her apartment—those ratty apartments."

She looked up. "Detective, I wanted to kill her and myself, but in truth maybe Rafe should've died. He was destroying our lives. The counselor said death meant forever and asked me if I wanted to do that to my boys ... you know ... scar them for life. I knew I couldn't kill her, or myself. Then the counselor said God had a plan and I should trust, and we prayed. That's the truth, and even though I hate that dead girl, you're right, she didn't deserve to die. No one does until it's their time."

Tears rolled down her face. "I have to say though, murder can't be God's plan. That's a sin, isn't it?"

"Sybil," he said, closing his notebook. "You've been a tremendous help, and I want to say thank you. I know this has been hard on you, and yes, no one deserves to die, not like that. I'm sorry for you, too."

"Me? Why?"

She looked up into his eyes, her own face now at peace. She had done what she needed to do and should have done long before ... told him everything.

"I have a feeling you didn't deserve to be cheated on, either."

"Thank you. It's nice of you to think that. If you need me for anything else, I promise I won't be such an uncooperative, hateful bitch."

This time, she smiled as she walked them to the door. She grabbed Jack's hand and didn't let go right away.

Jack furrowed his brow a smidgen as he looked her in the eye.

"If, God forbid, something unnatural ever happens to me, I hope you're the man that finds justice for me. You're a nice man, Detective West. Don't take offense to this either, but I hope we don't meet again, ever."

She let go of his hand.

"None taken, ma'am. I hope things work out for you."

With that, Sybil Preston shut the door, and they headed to the car and to Jason Fryer-Mercer's house.

Jack had a new outlook on the woman. With her messed up life, he might have developed different personas to help him cope, too.

50

JACK RAPPED ON THE door frame. He didn't want to ring the bell and upset the dog or wake the girl. He needed Jason to focus—no distractions.

"Detective West, to what do I owe the pleasure?"

"Jason, this is Detective Chang. We need a few minutes of your time."

Jason invited them in. "Nelle's napping, and Twinkle Toes is at the vet."

"Hope the dog's not sick." Jack was grateful the little yappy ankle biter wasn't there.

"She's fine. She's getting spayed."

Jason took a chair across from them.

"Now, how can I help you? Nothing's changed since the last time we spoke. Well, one thing has...Brent and I are much better. We've planned a getaway, a kind of second honeymoon." He blushed.

"Nice to hear things are better on the home front, Jason." Then Jack dove in. He had no time to waste. "Jason, I want you to explain to me everything you can recall on the day you went to this infidelity support group."

Jason leaned back, crossed his legs, and gave a shrug. "I was the only gay man there, that's for sure. There were only a few guys, mostly it was women. They split us into groups of seven. Twenty-one people."

"Are the church counselors certified or volunteers?"

"I didn't ask for credentials, and no one was wearing a name tag. There were ten — I thought they were church member volunteers."

"Was there one-on-one counseling?"

"No, and why are you asking me these questions? I mean, how does this tie in with your case?"

"Jason, we're trying to get every fact we can. We're just covering all our bases."

"I can tell you they were kind and didn't judge me, even though most of the people there didn't approve of my lifestyle choice. I appreciated that. God-fearing people don't want to look at me, much less talk with me. I make them uncomfortable, but I'm human, too."

"Yes, you are, and we aren't here to judge you. We need to catch a killer, that's our purpose. Is there anything else you can tell me, anything at all?"

"They had refreshments when it was over and," he paused, "yes, there is one other thing. While I was getting refreshments, a counselor approached me and asked if I wanted to sit and talk."

Chang jumped in with a question. "Can you describe this person and their voice?"

"A smoker's voice, raspy and sort of deep, with sad, compassionate eyes," he paused in thought.

Jack glanced at Chang. A raspy deep voice, same way Sybil described it, and same analogy ... a smoker's voice.

"I was comfortable, so I spilled my story, showed off pictures of Nelle and Brent. Funny, I even talked about the clubs we went to and the one where Brent was meeting Sergio when he was stepping out on me, but if you want a name, I never asked for one."

"Jason, if we put you with a sketch artist, do you think you could give a description of him?" Jack's insides were bubbling with anticipation that this might be the key.

"No, Detective West, I couldn't give you a description of him."

"You saw him face-to-face, why not?" Jack's ire rose. Was Jason Fryer-Mercer playing games with him?

"Detective, for your information it wasn't a man, it was a woman."

Chang's forehead and brows shot up, and Jack's jaw dropped.

"Does this help you?" Jason asked.

Once the initial shock passed, Jack found his voice.

"Could you give us a description of this woman?"

"White, tall, five foot ten, larger-boned, stocky woman in her late forties to early fifties. I don't mean to be cruel, but she was a bit of a she-man type. It's funny, when I heard the voice, I expected a man, and, well, she sort of was in a way... but don't get me wrong, she was very nice."

Jack's heart skipped a hundred beats faster.

"What else can you tell us?"

"Not much. I was crying and I wasn't memorizing her, you know? She had short black hair, and her makeup was a little heavy. I think she was trying to be more 'girlish.'"

"If we got you with our forensic artist, could you give her a description?"

Jason Fryer-Mercer let out a deep-throated chuckle.

"Detective, do you think a woman, one as compassionate as she was, would be involved in this nasty business? I can't see that at all. If you think it might help, I'll try. I was a mess that day, and my head wasn't on straight."

"We can't leave anything to chance, Jason. Even the tiniest of pebbles need to be looked under."

———ele———

"A WOMAN, NOW I wasn't expecting that. Whatdaya think, Chang?"

"It puts a new perspective on Bunny Mathers seeing that she's Black. A woman? Then what's the damn motive?"

"Xi, this doesn't mean she's who we're looking for. The infidelity group and the volunteer suicide hotline are connected. It could be this woman, whoever she is, works at both places. You know I don't believe in coincidences though, at least not in a murder investigation. Let's think for a minute here. Sybil tells this person everything ... names, addresses and the entire backstory ... and Jason, he said he told this woman everything, too. He showed her pictures of Brent, told her the clubs he went to, and mentioned Sergio by name. So, this person, this woman, had all the places and names that would have led to the victims."

"I see your point, Jack, but we still have Corrine Taylor. I know she went to that church, but Taylor didn't call the suicide hotline, nor go to the infidelity support. How do we explain her murder?"

"Didn't you say the night of the murder Bunny Mathers stayed at the church talking to the pastor?"

"Yeah, she was, but she was talking to the pastor, not a woman. Unless Pastor Davenport is the J. Edgar Hoover type and dresses in drag. He's a big fella too, with black hair. Jace and I met him. A preacher who dresses in drag, then goes undercover in his own church activities incognito, as a woman, sounds unbelievable."

"Hell, it does sound stupid. What's he doing? Eradicating the world of evildoers? If that were the case, why didn't he murder Rafe Preston, Al Mathers, and Brent Mercer? They were just as guilty because they cheated, too."

"Great question, Jack, and I have no answer." Xi drummed his fingers on the armrest. "All I've got to say is these victims were all involved in some type of off-the-book relationships and they died. Did it have something to do with the cheating?"

"Yeah, death and cheating ... guess you could say they are all involved in lethal liaisons..." Jack said as he turned into the parking garage at the police station.

51

THEY WALKED INTO THE squad room, and Lucky was gone.

"Where's Lucky, getting coffee?"

"He found Judge Carlson and went to get her to sign off on the warrant."

"You get the preacher set up, Jace?"

"He'll be here at noon tomorrow. He has a funeral to officiate at ten—said he'd come once the funeral was over."

"Good deal." Jack picked up the phone to call Becca Brenner, the forensic artist.

"Jack. I'll be ... two calls to me in a month. Now that's not normal, ya know." Becca twittered on the other end.

Jack told her what he needed. "Here's the address. I'll call and tell him you're coming later. BB, I'm going to stay at the station until you get here, no matter how long it takes."

The door opened, and as of late, since Captain Brooks kept popping his fat head in, no one said a word until they saw the whites of the eyes of whoever was walking into the squad room.

It was Dawson Luck, waving a warrant in the air.

"Judge Carlson signed the warrant, and you're right, women understand about purses. I filled her in on all three murders. You shoulda seen her face when I told her how Sergio's death went down. She said she felt like puking."

"Chang, call the Mathers' house, see if she's home," Jack said. "I am sick of spinning our wheels."

"Damn, no answer, and I'm not leaving a voice mail."

"Call her husband's cell, he'll answer, he won't want to take a chance and lose a prospective home-buyer or seller," Jack proposed.

Al Mathers picked up on the third ring. Chang asked for his wife, listened, frowned, and then hung up.

"Well, damn it," he swore, "she's out of town and won't be back until late tomorrow morning." Chang's agitation level soared. "I wonder if she took her purse with her."

"If that purse is the Taylor woman's purse, then Bunny Mathers has it glued to her side. Even if it isn't, other women see that purse and become envious."

"Jace, what do you know about purses?"

"Been married three times, Jack, and having two wives with champagne tastes on my beer budget. They could spot the real thing right off. A knockoff Louis Vuitton, they'd see and smirk, but the real thing, their eyes lit up and they drooled. I was never gonna let them spend two grand on a purse."

Jack put his forefingers up, one on either side of his nose, and raked his hands down his face. He felt frustrated. "Shit, fellas, roadblocks, stupid damn roadblocks."

"Look at it this way, Little Jack Horner. We have things to look forward to," said Jace.

"Hey, Jack?" Lucky called out.

Jack looked across the desk at Lucky smiling like an idiot. "What?"

"I feel we should find you a new woman."

"What for? Don't you like Gretchen?" Jack's face sunk into a frustrated frown.

"We need to get you a gal named Jill. I think Jack-n-Jill would be cool." Lucky said with enthusiasm.

Jace laughed, Chang snorted a short laugh, and Jack, well, he told Lucky to fuck off and get off his name and all the things that went with the first name Jack.

That was the opening Lucky was looking for. "So, you want me to get off Jack or Jack off?" Then he busted up laughing, as did Chang and Jace, and Jack couldn't help it. He laughed too ... he had walked right into that.

—⚬⚬—

JACE, CHANG, AND LUCKY left for the night, leaving a somewhat discouraged Jack at the station waiting for Becca Brenner. He had given Gretchen a quick call, and thumbed through three murder books, flipping page to page, thinking one simple thing might pop up and slap him in the face. If this woman, this she-man Jason described were involved, why, what would her motive be? How did the Taylor woman fit in? Bunny Mathers claims she never talked to another person about her hubby cheating. This had him stymied.

Jason's description of this woman had Jack profiling her. If she was more masculine than feminine, that raised a few questions ... was she single or married? Was she straight? Was she racist? And were these hate crimes?

Jack was locking up the murder books when the squad room door creaked open and he gritted his teeth, hoping not to turn and see Captain Brooks.

Chief Yao walked in. "Jack, are you burning the midnight oil?"

Jack released his breath, pleased to find that it was not Brooks.

"Yeah, waiting on Becca."

Davis Yao sat. "Why don'tcha fill me in on what the progress is?"

Jack updated him.

"Sounds like you guys have done your legwork."

"Yeah, but according to Brooks, our legs aren't moving fast enough and our freaking crystal ball isn't working. At least mine's not working."

"Whatdaya mean yours isn't working?"

"He called Jace and Chang to his office to question them about my performance and work. God, Davis, it's like his mission it to single me out—like my work is shoddy or I don't do my job well enough."

"Jack, Brooks is an ass. I've got your back, and I'm his superior. Let me say this ... Brooks is on my radar for certain reasons. Keep a cool head and don't let him rattle you. Just curious, when are you taking the sergeants' exam? You know you'll ace it."

"I haven't had time, Davis. I know I should. Maybe when we get this case wrapped up and we put the bastard away."

"It'll bump your pay up and piss Brooks off—at least do it to piss him off."

Jack was laughing when the squad room door opened and Becca Brenner stuck her head in.

"Jack."

Yao turned to look at her.

"Becca, it's been a while," Yao said, rising to his feet.

"Sorry to interrupt."

"Nah, we're just jawing, not important. You have a composite for me?"

Becca handed Jack the folder.

"Thanks for doing this on short notice, Becca."

"Anytime, Jack, you know that. I gotta run, though." Becca bid them goodbye and left.

They stood together, studying the composite.

Yao's face wrinkled. "That's a woman? Are you sure?"

"Jason called her a she-man, and I know how talented Becca is. Her drawing of Rafe Preston was a dead ringer."

"Huh. Well, I hope this is a decent lead, Jack. I'm not pressuring you at all. I'm not Brooks. I know you're doing everything possible, and your team is working hard."

"Thanks, Chief, maybe tomorrow will be the day, huh?" Jack slipped the picture of a very manly, unattractive woman back into the folder.

"I pray each night we catch this bastard. I'm outta here. You go home too, Jack."

"Be leaving in a few. Have a nice night," Jack said as Davis Yao opened the door and left.

He slipped the composite drawing out, staring hard at it.

His voice lowered. "Are you who I'm looking for? Are you my killer?"

A woman ... hell, he had his doubts, but in homicide, there were no boundaries.

52

CHANG PULLED A FACE. "That's one ugly woman, Jack."

"Yeah, Chang," Jack said. "And what you said about the J. Edgar Hoover remark might not be too far-fetched. Picture resembles him—I looked it up on the internet. What a damned ugly woman he made, back in the day."

Chang laughed and handed Jace the composite. "What do you think, Jace? Does it look like Pastor Davenport?"

"Huh, well, there's a remote possibility... put some makeup on him and a wig, that would be the key—then show it to Jason."

"By the way, where's Lucky? Hope he's late 'cause he's buying jelly donuts."

"He's on his way. Text him to stop and get some."

Jace got on it, texting: *Buy donuts, get jelly.*

Jelly and chocolate-glazed donut crumbs on Jace, Chang, and Lucky's upper lips cracked Jack up. He had one glazed, but he wasn't shoving 'em in like the others. He rolled his eyes at the typical cop-donut-coffee status and grinned.

"Chang, can you call the Mathers woman, see if she's back in town?"

He did, then hung up.

"Well, is she home?" Jace asked.

"Husband said she's expected back by one today."

An hour and a half later, Jack's desk phone rang.

"Detective West. Hey, what's up, Sarge? Thanks, I'll be down in a minute." Jack disconnected. "Wickers said Davenport is in the main lobby."

"Jack, I'll go get the preacher. You get the files you need, be back in a flash."

"Jace, put him in room four for me."

Jace Severson popped out of his chair and headed to the main lobby, while Jack gathered files and the folder with the composite drawing. He looked at Chang and Lucky.

"Y'all go pick up Bunny Mathers. Make sure she brings her purse with her."

"You got it, Jack. She'll be here," Chang said.

Jack walked into interview room four. "Pastor Davenport, thank you for coming in."

"I'm glad to help the HPD. Now, if you would, can you explain to me why I am here? I'm concerned."

Jack ignored him—he'd be asking the questions, not answering them.

"Tell me about the service you officiated over this morning."

"Ah, yes. The deceased was a member of my church, an elderly lady, and now she's home with the Lord. She'd lived a long life—would've been ninety-six next month."

"Nice to know some people get to live to a ripe old age, isn't it?"

The pastor sat back, taking on an air of self-righteousness, raised his head higher, and crossed his arms. "God rewards those who live a pure and good life, and sometimes your reward might be living a long life. God decides."

Pure and good lives—his remark stuck to Jack like glue. Whoever killed the three victims thought them wicked, not pure or good. He let the pastor's words float in the air without comment.

Pastor Davenport cleared his throat. "Ahem... in your expertise as a homicide detective you've seen more death at younger ages. I mean, gang members, prostitutes, drug lords—all pure evil. Debauchery runs amuck in your world. In my world, there's more peace. I work on souls, helping them stay pure."

Not many people use the term *debauchery*—most say wicked or sinful. That word had been in a verse at Jade's murder scene, and Jack's radar went up.

"How long have you been a minister?"

"In my heart, forever, but I got the calling over twenty-five years ago. Fifteen years ago, the Lord told me to open a church, and I did."

"That would be The Gates of Heaven, correct?"

"That's right. We rented a small space to use when we first opened the church. However, my congregation grew, and we've been in the same building now for almost twelve years."

"Your suicide hotline—how does that work?" Jack sat back, trying to make Davenport comfortable. He wanted the man relaxed. Maybe he'd slip up and say something incriminating.

"Our church couldn't accommodate more phone lines or volunteers. We leased a small building ten blocks down the road. I'd like to think we're doing superb work there—saving lives and helping desperate people. We don't always succeed, as we've lost a few tormented souls."

"How can you know this?"

"Detective West, I don't just read the Bible—I read the newspaper, too. And those who take their own lives, I pray God shows them mercy at the pearly gates."

"Aren't your callers anonymous?"

"For safety, we have a caller ID where the name doesn't appear, but the number does. The volunteer will log the number, and for potential urgent matters, they signal a supervisor who calls out to the closest police or fire station. It's sad when a human cannot be saved. However, time runs out for all of us."

"Real streamlined, huh?" Jack didn't care how it worked; he just wanted to catch a killer.

"Look, Detective West, I have a full schedule and I'd like to know why you have me here." He sat up straighter, pulling at the knot in his tie and adjusting his jacket.

"You have volunteer counselors for your infidelity support group?"

A heavy, exasperated sigh blew out of the haughty, holier-than-thou preacher.

"Yes, we do. Besides that, we have a drug and alcohol support group, a small daycare service for part-time moms, prayer meetings, and sometimes Sunday socials. What do you want from me?"

"Are you married?"

"Now listen here—"

"I asked you a simple question, Pastor. Answer it."

"Yes. One wife, no children, and one cat. What else do you need to know? Perhaps my damn blood type?"

The pastor cursed. Jack saw his aggravation—pleased to know he had gotten under his skin. They held each other's gaze for a moment, then Jack got to his feet.

"You'll need to excuse me for a minute. Sit tight, I'll be back."

Jack gave him zero opportunity to speak. He grabbed his files, left the interview room, and locked it.

"Whoa, Jack, you're rubbing the pastor the wrong way," Jace laughed as Jack walked into the monitor room.

"Yeah, he's a self-righteous, pompous, 'I-am-so-holy' horse's ass. I'm going to let him stew a bit."

"Chang texted. They're on the way back with Bunny Mathers and the purse."

Jack stared at the monitor.

The pious preacher sat ramrod straight, hands folded on top of the table, eyes closed as if praying—or maybe cussing Jack out for having him here.

Jack didn't like the man. His gut intuition told him Davenport was pond scum, no matter how he professed to be saving souls.

Davenport took all the credit and gave little to God. Something niggled at Jack—the man revolted him, and he wasn't sure why.

He'd never called a minister pond scum before. Davenport left Jack feeling less connected to a moral lifestyle. He'd met his share of sleazebags, and now he could add Harold Davenport to his list.

Jack's intuition suggested Davenport was a deceptive creep—not at all who he claimed to be, a man of God.

53

"BUNNY MATHERS IS IN five, Jack," Lucky said, when he and Chang walked in. "She's jumpy, too."

"Maybe she has a reason to be jumpy. Chang, you're going in with me as the silent partner. Lucky, stick your head in room four in fifteen minutes. Ask Pastor Davenport if he wants a drink. Tell him I got tied up and should be back soon."

"Got it. We'll be out here watching the show if ya need us."

"Come on, Xi, let's go—and grab that empty box, would ya?"

The door opened, and Jack went in, followed by Xi Chang.

"Mrs. Mathers," Jack said as he took the seat at the end of the table closest to her, "you remember Detective Chang?"

"Yes, I remember you both, and the last time I saw you, I hoped it was the last time."

Jack placed the empty box on the floor and set a folder on top of the table. His eyes met hers.

"Look, nothing—not a thing—has changed since the last time I was here, so why am I here?" Her tone was snappy.

Jack looked down at his feet, cutting his eyes to the other side of her chair, and he saw the purse. Good.

"We've got some new information, and I needed to talk to you."

"Can you make it quick? I have a hair appointment in two hours, and I can't miss it. My hair's a mess."

"Mrs. Mathers, may I see your purse?"

"Detective, are you joking? You want to look at my purse? I mean, this is absurd. What does my purse have to do with your investigation? You either have real questions for me or not. I will not sit here and—"

"Mrs. Mathers, put your purse on the table now." Jack's voice was forceful, and her face registered shock at his tone.

Bunny leaned forward, picked up her purse, and set it on the table, clutching it. "It's a purse, no cosmic mystery, and I'm not carrying a weapon, if that's what you think."

Jack picked up the empty box and set it on top of the table. "Please take out the contents and place them in the box."

"I... well, I..."

"Do it now!"

She opened the purse, took out the contents, and placed them in the box. When she finished, she closed the purse, put it in her lap, crossed her arms, and glared at Jack with unadulterated rancor.

"Hand me your purse—"

"You are not taking my purse. You have no right—"

Jack held his hand up. "Stop talking." He slipped the warrant out of the folder and placed it in front of her. "Here's my warrant for your purse—I'm taking it." He jabbed his finger on top of the warrant. "Read right here, Mrs. Mathers. This is my authorization. Now hand it over."

She pulled her face, eyes smoldering, clutching her purse in a death grip.

"Don't make me ask twice." Jack rose to his feet, looming over the woman.

Detective Xi Chang sat with an apathetic stare, watching in silence.

Her expression twisted; she jerked the purse from her lap and shoved it at Jack with unnecessary force.

"Fine, but I want it back when you're done, and you need to speed it up. I'm not gonna miss my hair appointment. Do you understand me, Detective?"

"Sit tight, Mrs. Mathers. We'll be back."

"Holy kamoly, Jack, she's pissed off. She did not want you to take her purse. You notice she didn't even tell you it's a real Louis Vuitton either,"

Chang remarked as they walked back to the monitoring room, finding Lucky and Jace munching on Cheetos.

"Hey there, badass purse snatcher. Oh-m-gee. What a bitchy woman." Jace widened his eyes.

Jack sat the purse on the counter, opened it, then took the utility knife Lucky was holding and cut along the bottom seam, trying not to damage the purse. He opened the flashlight app on his phone.

"Here, Xi, hold this over the purse—I need a look inside."

Chang held the light while Jack pulled the lining from the bottom to get a look.

"Is there a tag in there or not?" Lucky asked.

"Boys, we've hit pay dirt." Jack raised his head and looked at the three of them, who all looked one by one at the tag: Corrine Diane Taylor, her DOB, and last four digits of her SS number.

"I'll be a monkey's uncle. I'da never suspected her, would y'all?" Lucky was stunned, but not convinced. "Okay, here's a question for you. Why Jade and Sergio? Why would she kill them?"

"Her motive for the Taylor woman is clear—the woman was sleeping with her husband. I don't see the motive for the other two." Jace stroked his chin and wiped off the Cheetos dust he knew he'd just deposited on his face.

Chang stood. "Time to see a lady about a purse, huh, Jack?"

"Without a doubt. Let's go."

"Give me back my purse." There was no asking please, no politeness, no manners—just the attitude of a bitchy, snapping turtle.

"I'm afraid we can't—" Jack said, but Bunny jumped up, her face contorted in fury.

"What do you mean you're afraid you can't?" she cut him off. "I've told you I have to leave. Do your ears not work, Detective?" She pushed away from the table and walked toward the door. "Your superior is going to hear abo—"

"Sit your butt down, or I'll set it down for you." Jack slammed his fist on the table. Bunny's eyes bugged out, and her hostility was palpable.

She puffed up, moved the chair with her foot, and plopped down at his demand.

Jack set the empty purse on the table. "Tell me one more time how well you knew the decedent, Corrine Taylor."

"I detested the woman, and was not her friend, because of her floozy ways and how she acted like a slut in our Sunday school class. I told you this before."

"Did you despise her enough to kill her?"

"Are you out of your mind? Do I look like a killer?"

"So, Mrs. Mathers, what does a killer look like? Have you met any? Are you friends with any?"

"No, I'm not. I see things on television, and I am not one of those people." She tightened her lips.

Jack took the purse and shoved it over in front of her. "Open it."

Bunny Mathers took the purse, snatching it off the table, then she opened it and screamed. "What in the hell have you done to my purse? You've ruined the lining. This is an original Louis Vuitton. Do you know how much this purse cost?"

Jack looked her square in the eye, his face held a certain stony abhorrence. "I'd say the price was very high. It cost one woman her life."

"What does that mean?" She folded her arms, giving him the evil eye. "Are you accusing me of something?"

He took the purse from her, pulled out his phone, and clicked on the flashlight app. "Stand up."

She rose, and with abrupt force, she knocked the chair against the back wall.

"Pull the lining open—look under the larger pocket, Mrs. Mathers."

She did. Inside was the tag that had the name, DOB, and last four digits of Corrine Taylor's SS number. Jack watched her face, thinking of those commercials that had the tagline, *"and the looks on their faces—priceless."*

This woman of color paled. Speechless, she sat down with a thud that sounded like a two-ton whale landing on a wooden boat deck. He removed the purse from her hands, handing it to Xi Chang. "Detective Chang, will you bag and tag this evidence while Mrs. Mathers and I discuss how she came into the possession of our murder victim's purse?"

With a nod, Xi Chang left the room.

Jack sat like a ghost, making the atmosphere uncomfortable with his staid silence. He stared at her, waiting for her to speak—hell, he had all day and all night and the next day too.

Bunny trembled, distraught and scared to death. "I—I didn't know it was hers, or I would've never bought it."

"You bought it? Where?"

"At the church bazaar over a month ago. I knew it was an original Louis Vuitton—for thirty dollars, I snatched it right up. I swear, I didn't know it was hers. How could I have known that?" She looked at him, expecting him to believe her.

"You went to the same church. You must have seen her carrying it, or—"

She cut him off. "No, I never saw it. She never had a purse with her at church. I swear." It scared her to death. She had the purse of a murdered woman, a woman she'd admitted she hated.

"It's very convenient that you have bought her purse. She was sleeping with your husband, and now she's dead."

"Are you saying I'm a suspect?" Tears filled her eyes. "I—I think I need a lawyer, and I want to call my husband." She swiped the tears and gave Jack a hard look.

With that one word—*lawyer*—he knew the talking was over. Damn it.

He left her in the interview room and headed back to the monitor room.

"Jack, you think she's our perp?" Chang asked.

"I could believe it if Mrs. Taylor was a single victim, but what's her motive for Jade and Sergio?" Jack plopped down into a chair.

No one could come up with a plausible reason.

"Jack, Brooks came by while you were interviewing Mathers," Jace said, watching both monitors.

"What did he want? My resignation?" His attitude was flippant.

"He wants to know when we're gonna have this. Let me quote: 'fucking case tied up, you're needed for other cases and you should know that,' end quote." Jace scowled.

Jack rolled his eyes. Who did Brooks think they were? Magicians? He would have responded to Brooks' damn comment if he'd said it to his face. What a moron.

Jack watched Bunny Mathers cry into her hands. Did she sob because her life was over? His intuition told him it scared the hell out of her, but she wasn't culpable. He'd need to check out her church bazaar story, which might prove tough.

"Chang, get Mathers' prints, then let her go. We can't hold her on the purse issue—tell her she damn well better not leave town. Jace, get a search warrant started for her house. We need to search for a wig, a knife, and two other rings."

Jack would roll with this and see what panned out when he finished with Pastor Davenport.

54

THE INSTANT JACK WALKED into the room, Harold Davenport stood up, pushing his chair away from the table with such force that it rattled. Deep furrows formed between his hairy eyebrows.

"I am not a criminal. How dare you lock me in here then leave me—for what..." he yanked his arm up, shoving his jacket sleeve back looking at his watch, "over an hour. I'm leaving. I have things to do and no more time for you."

His large body came around the table aiming for the doorway.

"You can leave, Pastor, as soon as I'm done, and I'm not done yet—sit down."

It was a stare down for a few minutes, as they glared, eye to eye, neither man wavering. His eyes glued on the pastor's face, he gave his head a tiny jerk, a sign for him to take a seat.

Harold Davenport grabbed his chair, yanking it out with a screech and plopping down with such force that it slammed against the wall.

"Let's start over. I apologize that you've had to wait—but let me make myself clear. We're investigating not one, but three murders. Each case has a common connection, which is the Gates of Heaven Church."

"My church? How's that possible?" His temper toned down, and the rage melted from his face, replaced with disbelief. "I mean, Mrs. Taylor, a member of my church, got murdered; however, I don't understand the connection to the other victims. None of them are church members or I would have heard about it."

"We're keeping details of the other murders confidential for the time being." He would not clarify or go into details, because as far as he knew, the pastor could be his suspect. His connection to the suicide hotline and the infidelity support group tossed him into the pool as a person of interest.

"Tell me, Pastor, how does your church bazaar work?"

"What's to tell? Our church members donate unwanted items, such as clothing and housewares, books, and the likes, and we have a sale to raise money for certain events or church building repairs."

"Are all donations strictly from church members?"

The pastor laughed. "Well, of course. We don't go around soliciting donations from house to house. We announce our plans at a church service and ask the members to donate as well as volunteer their time. What does this have to do with your investigation?"

"Do you keep a list of members who donate?" He avoided Davenport's questions.

"No, we don't, and we don't inventory items. We price them reasonably, and then whatever we don't sell we donate to the local homeless shelters. Are you going to tell me why you need to know this or not?"

"Pastor, thank you for coming in. If I need you, I know where to find you." Jack rose. "I'll walk you out."

Once at the elevators, he spoke.

"I'm sorry I couldn't give you any information, but I hope you catch the man who's doing this."

"Pray that we do, pastor, pray hard that we do."

"Nothing. No wig, no knife, and no rings. Now what's the plan, Jack-sprat?" Chang asked.

"Other than her having the purse, we have nada, except for her motive to kill Corrine Taylor, but she has no motive for the other two killings, not a one," Jace said.

"Shit, Jack, we're no further than Jace and I were four months ago."

"Did either of you call to see if the prints found at the Taylor murder matched Mathers' prints?"

"Yeah, I called while we were searching her house, and no, we didn't get a match—Jace is right. We're still at ground zero." This discouraged Chang.

"No, we aren't, fellas, we have the purse and we know it came from a church member who donated unwanted items for their bazaar."

"Man, Jack, that's a shitload of suspects, you know?"

"Yep, Jace, it is. Why don't we quit for the day and get a fresh start in the morning?"

No one argued. Going home was a perfect idea since they had bupkus.

While the other three headed home for the night, Jack headed back to the station. He needed to think. If he went home, he'd grab a beer and park in front of the TV, and that's not what he needed to do. He needed to focus.

With the murder books spread out in the task force room, Jack went through the reports, studying the pictures, and when the door opened he looked up, expecting one of his compadres, but his night got worse. It was Brooks.

"West, what are you doing here?"

"I'm working on the cases." He felt like coming back with: "what the fuck do you think I'm doing here, you moron," but held his tongue.

"You close to getting someone nailed or not?" Brooks acted like he had put them on a project, and their deadline was nearing.

"No, we aren't." Jack got out of his chair, his reply curt. He was not up for a long discussion. Brooks wanted this wrapped up in a nice neat bow so he could say he led the team, and this was horseshit. He stared at Brooks. He had replied to the question and the proverbial ball was in the captain's court. Locked in a gaze, they held their positions. Brooks averted his eyes first, and Jack smiled.

"Well then, keep at it. We need to nail this guy before he kills again. Who knows what sets him off." He coughed, clearing his throat, and then left Jack by himself in the task force room.

Jack stared at the door as it closed, then glanced up at the military wall clock. What in the hell was Brooks still doing here? The realization hit; Brooks spent more time at the station late at night, way past his normal quitting time. That was a puzzle he did not have time to piece together.

Maybe he could investigate the whys and wherefores later. Brooks was a fat pain in his ass, but right now, he had bigger fish to fry.

Jack sat, staring at the wall.

There were HR posters, HPD rules, and regulations, the FBI's Most Wanted List, and a plethora of other things you might find on the wall of a task force room, but it was all a big blur.

His mind was clicking. Something Brooks said gave him an idea.

After closing all three books, he carted them back to the squad room, locked them up, sat down, pulled his phone out of his pocket, scrolled for the number he needed, then propped his feet up on his desk.

"Hey, it's West. You got a minute? I need a huge favor. How good an actor are you?" Jack made a second call.

"Hiya. Listen, I've got a sting I need your help with. Are you game? Thanks—I'll be contacting you in a day or two."

One last call—and then he was out of there. He punched in the number and turned off his computer as the phone jangled in his ear.

"Fleet, Carl."

"Hey, man. It's West in Homicide. You have a car I can use?"

"Ain't it kind of late, West?"

"Carl-Carl, my man, it's never too late. You know all homicide detectives are vampires."

"Come on, bloodsucker. I'll fix you up with a used hearse."

Jack grabbed his coat from the back of his chair and took the back stairs to the garage.

He jumped into his truck and headed to fleet—on a mission.

55

JACK PARKED THE UNMARKED car in the lot across the street from the church.

A rundown area and uninhabited at this hour.

From his spot, he could see the front and side doors. Small frame houses scattered the area, and everyone was locked in for the night.

The strip mall he parked in was devoid of cars; stores closed for the night. Windows and doors—barricaded by bars, and the area lit with dim lighting.

Parked just outside the boundaries of the Fifth Ward, he knew he sat on the cusp of gang territory. Davenport picked a very piss-poor area to move his church congregation.

After unhooking his seat belt, he got comfortable and trained his eyes on the church. He had no clue why he was staking out the church. All he knew was gut intuition. His intuitions didn't always work out.

Hell, he had no wife, kids, or a dog at home. He could sit here and observe. He was fine with that. Even if all he did was to lose a little sleep, it wouldn't be the first time.

Happy he'd gotten a few bottles of water, two bags of chips, and a candy bar, at least he wasn't gonna starve. He sent Gretchen a text, told her he'd try to call her tomorrow if he had time, and maybe they could have dinner together.

Then he silenced his phone, took a bag of chips, opened them, and ate while he stared at the empty church. It was 9:30 pm.

Jack stretched his back, yawned, and looked at the time on his phone: 10:25, and all was hushed on the home front.

He knew people were active, and as the night grew later, more activity would come alive—not the fun kind, but the scary kind: gang members and punks.

If they chose to be vandals, it made no difference to them if the building was a church, a house, or a place of business. If they could get away with it, they would vandalize and graffiti the hell out of the police station.

Crap, he thought, he had been here long enough. This was a stupid hunch, but hey, he had lost little time.

Just as he was ready to call it a lost cause, he saw a car drive into the church parking lot. The car parked next to the side door.

The driver killed the motor, turned off the lights, and got out. Jack hadn't been surprised to see Pastor Davenport step up to the side door, unlock it, and enter the building.

It was odd, though. Why was the preacher at the church—or even out at this hour—alone, in a neighborhood that was at most iffy with crime?

Jack waited and watched the side door. For fifteen minutes, nothing happened.

Maybe he was preparing his sermon for the up-and-coming Sunday—but that was four days away. Today was Wednesday, and the Wednesday night services were over.

Jack glanced at the church schedule and realized they had something going on almost every day: Sunday, morning and night services; Monday, the neighborhood outreach program; Tuesday, night visitation; Wednesday, prayer meeting; Thursday, mid-morning alcohol support group and early-evening infidelity support group; Friday, children and adult choir practices. Saturday was the only day without an event.

Oh, and four days a week, the suicide hotline ran from 8:00 am to midnight. Jack wondered why those hours were set. In his opinion, suicidal threats didn't follow a schedule—this seemed ludicrous. A call center for potential suicides should be a 24/7 hotline. Was this just a system the pastor set up to make himself look good?

He was ready to leave.

Whatever the pastor was doing, he was alone, and this was lunacy on his part. Maybe he was just reaching—that's when a second car parked beside Davenport's.

Jack spoke under his breath. "Well, now, what have we got here?"

A well-dressed woman got out of the car. Jack watched as she smoothed down her skirt, then looked into her side mirror and put on lipstick. She patted her hair, rearranged her boobs, and then walked up to the door. She took a key out of her purse, unlocked the door, and entered.

Jack wished to be a fly on the wall, and then he decided, on second thought, he didn't. Two and two equaled four, and in this case, two and two equaled something else altogether. He was more than positive it wasn't Mrs. Preacher—so he waited.

An hour passed. It was close to midnight.

He heard no screams, no gunshots—knives made no sound. He contemplated storming the gates. His hand was on the car door handle when the side door opened.

The woman walked out first, her hair disheveled, blouse no longer tucked into her skirt, and she was carrying her heels. Harold Davenport walked out next, pulling the door shut. Jack watched as Davenport came up to the woman, pushing his front side to her backside and wrapped his arms around her, placing his hands on both of her breasts, nuzzling her neck.

He thought he might vomit at the sight. He could feel the bile rise, and his temper flare. This was sickening. He was a minister and he was whoring around—under God's roof, of all places. He watched as they parted ways, each leaving in opposite directions, and he sat there with a frown on his face.

Davenport was having an affair.

That didn't mean he was a killer.

It did mean he was a filthy dirtbag, one of the worst—he was a minister, but that was it.

He cranked the engine and semi-chuckled. If you could arrest people for cheating in Texas, then you'd have to buy the State of Oklahoma and turn it into a large prison.

As he drove home, he was still chuckling.

Sixteen states he knew of had laws against adultery, and five of them considered it a felony. Sometimes, cheaters' fines could surpass ten thousand smack-a-roos, and sentencing might be a three- to five-year stint in jail.

Damn, you'd hear an echo in Texas if the state passed a law making adultery illegal and a felony, and they upheld the law. The prison for cheaters would be full, and Texas would be empty.

As he pulled into his driveway, his thoughts went to people and their moral compasses. He figured thirty percent of the population had broken moral compasses; hell, it might even be a bigger percentage than he figured.

56

AT SIX IN THE morning, the squad room was a ghost town. Jack set down the box of Kolaches, Klobásník, and jelly donuts he'd bought on the way in, along with the extra-tall coffee mug he'd brought from home. He went to the break room and set two pots to brewing for the fellas.

Taking the plate number from the unknown woman's car, he punched it into the DMV program. Marsha Frost—so she was the "other woman."

Jack took the membership list and cross-referenced her name. Yep, there she was: Mrs. Marsha Frost, married to Clyde Frost. Jack wondered if Clyde suspected. He pulled up Clyde Frost next. Huh, Clyde was much older than his wife by eleven years. Jack didn't see him as a person of interest.

"Hey, man, do you sleep here or what?" Lucky walked in, bearing his own box of donuts from Sherry's Donuts and Cakes. It was straight-up eight o'clock.

"You get jelly?"

"Hell, yeah. I don't want Team 7-11 bitching 'cause there's no jelly."

"Jelly... did I hear someone say jelly?" Jace barreled into the room, sliding over to Lucky's desk and grabbing the box.

"Oh yeah, man, I love the raspberry ones." He bit into a raspberry jelly donut and, with a mouthful, muffled, "Thank you, Lucky, you're an okay guy." Then he swallowed the first bite and crammed the rest in his mouth as raspberry jelly dripped down the side of his lip. Two bites was all it took Jace Severson to eat a donut, a bear claw, or even a cinnamon roll. It didn't matter what it was.

"Jace, if that's how you eat in front of a woman, no wonder you've been married three times." Jack shook his head and then grabbed a Klobásník.

"So, Jack O' Lantern, what's on the schedule today?" Glazed donut in one hand, coffee in the other, Lucky looked every bit the old-timer detective. All he needed was a gray fedora.

"Got some news and a plan, and as soon as Xi gets here, I'll fill you in. Don't want to repeat it twice," Jack said.

They were fine with that. They were busy with breakfast anyway, and Eleven would be wise to hurry, or they'd wolf down the entire two boxes of donuts before he could say "jelly."

Xi Chang walked in fifteen minutes later, grateful Jack had bought Kolaches and a few jelly donuts. What was left of the crushed and trashed box from Sherry's Donuts and Cakes was sugar dust.

"Thanks, Jack," he garbled, his mouth full of a creme-filled donut, "for saving me a few."

"I got your back, Chang—even if it's your stomach." Jack gave him the box, which contained another jelly and two kolaches, arching his eyebrows with humor.

Chang frowned at his partner, then at Lucky, as he took the box and pretended to guard it.

Lucky and Jace made the yikes faces and grinned.

"Guys, if we're all done with breakfast and fartin' around, I wanna tell ya what I did last night."

"You came back here?" Jace propped his large motorcycle boot–clad feet on the corner of his desk.

"Yup, didn't want to go home—stayed and went over the murder books. Sad to say, though, Brooks came in the task force room while I was here."

"Why was he here at that hour? He should be getting out of here by at least six." Chang frowned.

"I'd like to know why he's at the station all the time late at night, but that has to be on the back burner for now. Worrying about Brooks is not high on my list of priorities. But he said something last night that gave me an idea."

"Look, Jack, once we close this case and you have time, I believe you need to find out why Brooks has it in for you. Don't you think so, too?"

"Maybe, Xi. Only I don't intend to be caught up in stupid shit or politics, ya know?"

"Yep, I get it. Just be on your toes—that's all."

"Xi, you know I am." Jack knew Chang worried more than the other two did. The ambiance in the room went from DEFCON 5 to DEFCON 3 whenever Brooks was the topic.

"Okay, Jack-of-All-Trades," Lucky intoned, "what did you do last night?"

"Are you shitting us? The pastor is having an affair—and he's doing it at the church?" Jace couldn't believe his ears.

"What a slimy dude, preaching the Ten Commandments but not following the rules." This disgusted Dawson Luck and was the coup de grâce.

"Did you get her plate number?" Xi got back to business.

"Yeah, I ran it. She's a church member. I cross-referenced the list you had: Marsha Frost, married to Clyde Frost. I don't think Clyde or the creepo pastor is involved in our case, although Clyde's a casualty of infidelity, and the pastor is an adulterous dirtbag."

Lucky leaned in. "Okay, what else ya got brewing in that head of yours?"

"Strange as it is, I got an idea from something our fat, miscreant captain said last night." Jack described the plan.

"Listen, this may or may not work, but we'll give it a shot. We'll have to stay on Penny until something happens—if it does."

Yep, they would need to keep eyes on Penny once Katherine Sparks did her thing at the Gates of Heaven Church.

57

KATHERINE SPARKS AKA SPARKY, sat at the end of the semicircle. Her thick red hair pulled up in a ponytail and her face devoid of makeup, looking as unattractive as possible. She had dabbed peppermint oil on her fingertips to generate tears when the time was right. Her job as a vice detective required her to role-play with conviction, sometimes even feigning tears.

There were fifteen distraught individuals and six counselors—a mix of men and women. Split into teams of five, three counselors remained stationary while the other three rotated among the groups. Sparky told her story last.

"Hi," she said, using her mousiest voice, "my name's Joy."

Everyone said, "Hello, Joy," and waited for her to spill her story.

"Well, Joy might be my name, but I have no joy left in my heart."

As she spilled out her tale of woe, she closed her eyes, placed her forefingers on either side of the upper part of her nose, and wiped under her eyes. The peppermint oil now under each eye, the tears flowed as she unburdened her bogus heartache to the group.

Sparky finished her story, and three other women were crying; she'd laid it on thick. Her face was red and blotchy, and she'd had to blow her nose at least half a dozen times. Her stellar performance would've amazed the fellas.

"Joy, we are heartbroken, and we pray God will bring you through this," the counselor said in a soft, compassionate voice, then glanced at the group and gave a gentle smile.

"Shall we bow and I'll lead us all in prayer?"

Sparky had no idea a prayer could last that long, but the woman prayed for each person in her group, listing all the wrongs that needed to be righted in each person's life.

"Please help yourselves to a drink of juice, water, or cola, and there are cookies on the back table. Talk to each other, make a new friend, and look for some happiness within our group." She dismissed them.

Sparky gravitated toward the refreshments, staying alone, avoiding eye contact and not approaching the others. She needed to continue to look sad and beat down.

"Joy," the deep, coarse voice said, causing her to turn.

"Yes," Sparky said, turning to see a rather large woman—unattractive, with very short black hair and manly features. At five foot five, Katherine Sparks had to look up at the woman who stood over five foot eleven.

"Your story was one of the saddest I've heard in a while. Would you like to sit and talk? I feel there is more you need to unburden, isn't there?"

Sparky wiped a peppermint-doused finger under one eye to start a fresh set of tears, keeping the act going, and nodded. "Yes, there is more. How did you know?"

"I empathize with you; similar hurts have left me nearly broken. Shall we go sit and talk?"

Sparky wiped her eyes. "Yes, please. What's your name?" She blew her nose as they walked to an empty corner to sit.

The large she-man patted her hand, causing Sparky to look down. The woman had oversized hands—manly hands—that went with the rest of her masculine look.

"We don't share our names. We stay as impersonal as possible. This is all about you and your needs, Joy. I am only here to hear your problems." Her voice was deep and rather throaty for a woman. Her eyes expressed definite compassion and something else akin to sadness.

Katherine Sparks studied the woman's face as she looked her in the eye. Her skin was rough, her features rather husky, and her eyes, although compassionate, lacked a luster for life. Even if the woman wore makeup, she'd need a magician to make her look attractive, and that was sad. Sparky looked down at her hands and saw that this big she-man wore a wide gold wedding band.

Was she married, or was that false advertising?

"I am here for you, Joy. I want to help, and I know I can. Tell me everything," the throaty she-man said, keeping her hand on top of Katherine's smaller hand.

Sparky went on with her sad tale of woe in the make-believe life of Joy, the wife of an adulterer. She shared pictures of her hubby as she wiped her peppermint-laced fingertips under her eyes once more, conjuring more tears and a very runny nose.

Once finished with the new woes of Joy, Sparky heard the she-man sniff and saw her wipe a tear from her eye. Wow, Katherine Sparks was one helluva actor.

———*ele*———

THE NEXT DAY, SPARKY walked up the back stairs to Homicide and headed to the squad room in search of Jack and his team.

"Hey guys, howzit going?"

"Let's have it, Sparks. How'd it go last night?"

"I laid it on thick, Jack—tears and all. It was an Academy Award performance—if I say so myself.

I pulled out the wallet with Gilly's photos—wanted them to see what he looked like. Shit, I passed it around, and I'll never tell Craig this, but they all thought he was a damn hunk."

Jace rolled his eyes. "Yeah, keep that a secret. Craig's already got a big enough head. Don't want it to get bigger."

"Did you get a one-on-one with a volunteer counselor once the groups broke up?"

"Yup, I did. That composite you showed me is spot on. Only I have to say she is a bit more, uh, homely and manly than even Becca's composite reveals. Crap, her hands are huge—bet she could palm a basketball better than an NBA player. The woman listens and is compassionate, just like that Jason fella said."

Katherine looked at Jack. "You know how your gut does that thing?"

Jace popped off, "Yeah, it growls when it's hungry."

"I can attest to that," Lucky concurred, his face beaming.

"No, I'm serious, fellas."

"Sparky, are you telling us you now have a Jack gut?" Xi grinned.

"Okay, you assholes, mock me."

"It's all good, Match-Head," Jack said, referencing her red hair. "I can't be the only detective with that special power since these lug heads haven't got a clue." He winked at the others. "What did your newfound gut say?"

"Something isn't right with the woman. She was nice and concerned, but under that compassionate look, a few times while I spun my tale of woe, I saw her teeth clench, and there was underlying anger in her. I could just feel it, ya know?"

Jack stroked his chin in thought. "Like she's been through this before, or what?"

"Yes, and no. The anger increased when I told her I had been pregnant and, because of the stress of my so-called husband cheating, I lost the baby."

Xi Chang clapped in applause. "Way to work it, Sparky."

"Don't tell Gilly he's gonna be a daddy—that'll scare the shit outta him," Jace Severson haw-hawed.

———❧———

EVERYONE KNEW CRAIG "GILLY" Gillespie's story: first a firefighter—his longtime girlfriend could not handle the pressure of him fighting fires and the danger—he quit and got a civilian's job. All it accomplished was ending his longtime relationship and leaving him alone and unhappy with his new profession—selling damn cars.

Craig started watching cop shows, got the itch, and applied to the police academy, and his happiness returned. After fighting crime in Houston for twelve years, he'd never regretted his choice and never looked back.

———ꞔꞔ———

LUCKY LAUGHED. "YEAH, GILLY changing diapers. Now that would make for a hilarious YouTube moment."

That comment had them rolling.

Jack was back to business first, while the others simmered their laughter down.

"You tell them in the group the days and the place you suspected he was meeting his lover?"

"Oh yeah, just like we discussed. I told them I followed him several nights to see what he was up to, and that the affair had been going on for over three months, and I was losing the desire to live."

"Perfect. Oh, I gotta ask—how did you conjure tears? I mean, isn't that tough to do?"

"Excellent question, Jack. Are you that talented?" Xi asked, curious how she pulled it off.

"Jesus, guys, don't you ever Google crap at all? A dab of peppermint oil on my fingertips, then get them close to my eyes, and the waterworks are almost immediate—as well as a damn runny nose."

"Well, huh, live and learn," said Xi.

"By the way, Sparky, did you mention you knew who your fake hubby was cheating with?"

"Of course I did, Lucky. I mentioned the bar and the motel, and One-Cent better gussy the fuck up. I told them she was gorgeous."

"One-Cent—she's sort of like that *Miss Congeniality* movie. I bet she cleans up real nice," Jace Severson said, and the way he voiced it, he had everyone staring at him.

58

TWO WEEKS—TWO DAMN WEEKS—AND nothing. No new developments on the cases Jack's team was working. He was glad no one else had died, but a killer was still on the loose, and who knew when he'd strike again.

Nobody had to take lead on another case. Houston had plenty of crime, and Jack and his team had their share of the work. Gang killings or drug-related murders were enough to keep the Homicide Division busy. Even domestic violence led to murder; perhaps not planned, but murder was murder.

Jace worked with Robbery on a string of convenience store burglaries near the outer area of the Second Ward. Lucky and Xi were helping in a drive-by shooting case—three killed and one injured—in the Fifth Ward.

Lead Detective Cooper Norris and his partner Tate Minton had their hands full and welcomed the help. Jack's assignment was working with Detectives Potter and Reed on a domestic violence case that had turned into a murder in a wealthy neighborhood.

Just because you were fortunate and had money to burn, a vast house with expensive décor, and fewer worries than the poor, did not mean life was grand.

Delilah Nilson found that out when her husband of fifteen years bludgeoned her to death with a three iron and dumped her body in an empty, undeveloped wooded area less than two miles from their $1.9 million home.

Framers working construction on a new home near a large, wooded lot found the body two days later when the stench wafted in the wind.

No one had reported her missing, and it took four days to identify her. Once their Jane Doe was identified, the dominoes started falling, pointing them to her killer. It was a damn shame—a rich, affluent man who had been a pillar of the community was now in hiding and, once caught, would face a probable life sentence, maybe even the death penalty.

<hr />

THE CASES OF CORRINE Taylor, Jade Nelson, and Sergio Loza sat boiling on a back burner—far from forgotten. The setup to catch the killer was still ongoing.

Detective Craig "Gilly" Gillespie from Robbery and his partner Penny 'One-Cent' Salato had been hooking up at the small bar for drinks for two weeks—three times a week, even throwing in a Saturday night. They even faked their rendezvous at the motel. The one Joy (Detective Katherine Sparks) had spilled to the infidelity support group—the one her fake husband and his harlot used for their nastiness, as she had put it.

Jace and Lucky ribbed the crapola out of Craig and Penny about the entire undercover assignment.

"Under the covers last night?" Jace snickered when Gilly dropped by with a report.

"Crap, man—fake drinking and fake romance. What a shitty deal. One-Cent and I ham it up, but man, it's a drag when you are with your all-day partner and you are trying to make it look convincing."

"I gotta know. When you go to the motel room, what do you do?" Lucky's unibrow wiggled up and down, laughter in his voice. Hell, they were both single and attractive. He'd wondered if they had ever—well, everyone knew what he wondered; they all wondered the same thing.

"I lose money to her—that's what we do," Gilly spurted a laugh.

"Huh?" Jace didn't get it.

Gilly barked out his laughter.

"One-Cent beats my butt at gin rummy. We play two cents a point while we're in the stupid, seedy motel room. We keep the shade drawn tight, turn on some seductive music, and she makes sex sounds. I gotta tell ya—it was unnerving when she first did it. My face turned cherry pie red, and she almost choked herself trying not to laugh."

Jack, Lucky, and 7-11 all cracked up.

"Penny's a goober. Now she makes stupid faces with the sounds. Every so often I'll go to the headboard and bang it, hitting the wall with a tap-tap-tap—you know, in rhythm with—"

"Jesus, Gilly, I don't think ya need to explain it to us," Xi said between snickers.

When the boys calmed down, Jack took the floor.

"It's been two steady weeks of your illicit love affair, and now it's time to set the rest of the plan in motion. Sparky's going to call the suicide hotline, and if the voice is the voice we're looking for, she'll spill her tales of woe. She's gonna ham it up and tell the 'voice' she's pregnant again and can't go on living—that she and the baby will die together—and it's the best thing for them both."

"Excellent spin, Jack," Lucky said.

"What if it's not the voice she's expecting?" Xi Chang wanted to know.

"She hangs up—simple as that—and then calls back in a few minutes until she gets the voice."

"I thought you said they have a caller ID for emergency reasons. What if they trace it here? Then what?"

"She's going to block her ID, Jace. That's why she's going to wait a couple of minutes between calls—keeps it less suspicious."

Would this plan work? Would whoever they were looking for take the bait and target the fake lover, Penny Salato—or were they barking up the wrong tree?

Jack had worked like a dog with his team to check on the purse and the church bazaar, but that had yielded a big fat zero. No one kept records of items—just the money collected. That had been a brick wall.

There was no evidence Bunny Mathers did a single thing, and she stuck with her story that she had not confided in anyone, including the pastor.

Jack knew this was a lie, but he had no proof and could not arrest her for lying or for having the purse. Her punishment came down on her in an unusual form—she no longer had an original Louis Vuitton.

———ℓℓℓ———

SPARKY PICKED UP THE phone in Davis Yao's old office, now occupied by the COD, much to the dismay of one Captain Brooks. Katherine could not stand that piece of shit Brooks and hoped her path did not cross his today—or ever. Jack set her up to call the suicide hotline from this office for privacy, knowing she could block the station's number.

She punched in the number, hoping the deep, throaty voice would be on the other end. Jack sat in the chair across from her, watching as the phone rang in her ear. In a matter of two minutes, Katherine Sparks hung up and frowned.

"Fart-knockers—it's not the voice," she said, looking at Jack and shrugging. "I'll try in a couple of minutes."

"No worries, Spark. I'm a bit at your mercy."

Sparky furrowed her brow, bit her bottom lip in deep thought, eyes cast down, then looked up at Jack.

"Remember the lunch we had at Rodeo Goat a few months back?"

Jack nodded but didn't speak. She had the floor.

"Once we sew these cases up, I'd like to talk to you one-on-one."

"Sure," he said, a bit of concern etched on his face. "Sparks?"

"I'm fine, Jack—don't go all worrywart over me. When the cases are closed, then we'll talk. Don't make a mountain out of a molehill, Jack." Her tone snappy—on edge.

"You got it, Match-Head." He winked and then gestured to the phone.

She dialed the Suicide Hotline, and this time luck was on her side when a volunteer with a deep, throaty voice answered: "Your life is important to me. How can I help you?"

The persona of Joy—the very unjoyful, woe-is-me, pathetic cheated-on wife—came to life, and Jack had to admit Katherine Sparks could vie for an Academy Award for her telephone acting scene. She had talent.

Jack rubbed his hands together when she hung up.

"If that didn't set something into action, Sparky, nothing will, and we're at a standstill with our wheels spinning, doing nothing but digging a huge rut."

"Jack, you guys keep eyes on Penny—closer now."

"Yeah, I'll let her know you made the call and for her to watch her back."

Jack prayed the new cases the four of them were assisting with didn't throw a wrench in their plans.

He would let 7-11 and Lucky know he made the call, and now it was just a matter of time.

Everyone involved needed to be on high alert.

59

"JUMPING JEHOSHAPHAT—A DAMN WEEK and a half and nothing new, nothing's happened. Y'all think the killer got all his rage out with the last victim, Sergio?" Jace scooted his chair back, propping his giant feet on his desk.

"I'll have to say," Lucky said, "all they did to that poor man—you'd think whoever it was, his rage was definitely unleashed."

"Has Penny said anything unusual in the past week? Odd stuff she's noticed?"

"No, Xi, or at least that's what she told me early last week. We've all gotten tied up, even her, and she hasn't reported back." Jack picked up his phone. "I'll see if she's around. Maybe she can drop by and give us all an update."

Twenty minutes later, Penny sat with the four men in the homicide squad room.

"Well, gentlemen, nothing out of the ordinary. No lurking evil."

"It's hard to see lurking evil when you're tied up with other evil," Jace said.

"Yeah, the evildoers hitting the convenience stores are still at large," Penny commented.

"Are you even close to a perp?" Jack leaned back and closed his eyes. His frustration grew. The possibility of never finding the perpetrator of the three murders was wearing on him.

"We suspect members of the Bloods," Penny said, "but the problem is, no one's talking—not the store clerks, no one—they're scared."

Jack didn't open his eyes. "Cameras?"

"You'd think, wouldn't ya," Jace scowled, "but the stores either aren't set up with video surveillance, or it's malfunctioned, or just plain broken."

"We've got Vice squad working undercover to see what they can find out. We need to nail these bastards before they kill someone," Penny added.

Jack's eyes opened. "With Robbery and Vice working together, I'm sure you'll get your perps. Let's hope Homicide gets to take a pass."

Three days later, a witness emerged, and the string of convenience store burglaries moved forward with a positive lead. The drive-by killing Xi assisted Detectives Cooper and Minton with yielded zilch. The three were frustrated. It would be a long haul to find out who the shooters were.

Arrested and charged with his wife's murder, Tyrell Nilson made head-lines. The press had dubbed him the "Golf Club Killer." Every joke regard-ing that famous golfer had already made the rounds—no pun intended. Detectives Potter and Reed started gathering all the evidence to support the case for the DA's office.

"Jack, we've got it from here," Jesse Potter told him. "Man, thanks for all your help."

"No problem, guys. I'm happy to assist."

Austin Reed laughed. "Brooks thinks he set this assist up, Jack. He's such a moron."

"Yup," Potter chimed in, "he has no interest in finding out if our case is progressing, which I find disturbing."

"You do? Why's that, Pots?"

"Jack, he might be the captain over Homicide, but that's just a title. He never wants updates, and he's never been on the scene for our callouts."

"That's true, Jack. He's nowhere near the captain Davis Yao was, and I don't trust him—not a speck." Austin Reed no longer smiled.

"Yep, I've heard that from the guys," Jack said, shrugging. "Doesn't bother me if he doesn't show up. I'm all for him staying out of my way."

He had a point. Captain Brooks not getting in their way—perfect.

Jack left them to take care of the paperwork, reports, witness statements, and all the rigamarole for the DA's office and headed back to his own part of the world on the Homicide floor—his desk.

Preoccupied, the three unsolved cases weighed on him as he tried to come up with the next step. The perp had not taken the bait, or perhaps the voice, as they called it, was not the perp.

Shit.

He sat back, closed his eyes, and wondered if maybe the voice was an unsuspecting source for the real killer.

Maybe this she-man-looking, raspy-voiced woman had a big mouth and was relaying information to a crazy man. Scenario after scenario played through Jack's head, and he was getting a freaking headache.

He was unsure of the timeline for Taylor's murder. Bunny Mathers claimed she hadn't spoken to a soul, so there was no way to know when the perp discovered that Al Mathers and Corrine Taylor were having an affair. He speculated on the timelines for Jade Nelson and Sergio Loza's murders. He knew when Sybil Preston had called the suicide hotline, and he knew the date when Jason Fryer-Mercer had gone to the infidelity support meeting. The last two murders occurred two weeks later.

Damn. Sparky had gone to the infidelity support group over three weeks ago and had called the suicide hotline at the end of the two-week fake affair.

He rose and took a deep breath.

What next? What next? he thought.

He had one idea: to try one more time, have Gilly and Penny meet up for one last fake rendezvous, and pray that whoever this sick killer was took the bait.

60

"Jack, sorry, man, we can't go until late. We're tied up right now," Gilly explained.

"Sure, Gill, I understand. And hey, tell Captain Thompson we're grateful he loaned y'all to us."

Jack wanted to make sure the new captain of Robbery, Walt Thompson, got the thanks he deserved. Enough that the man had to deal with Brooks—because Walt Thompson seemed like a decent person. Brooks was a rotten seed, and Jack hoped he did not pollute Walt Thompson.

"We'll let you know when we get to the bar, okay, Jack?"

"Sure. Text me. I'm gonna hang here at the station with Jace. Luck's headed home, and Xi's headed to a late dinner date."

"Huh. Xi's got him a girl now, does he? Wish I had time to chew the fat over that, but I gotta get going. Penny's giving me the evil eye—I gotta run."

"Sure." That was all Jack said as he hung up the phone.

Jack and Jace sat and went over every detail of all three cases, one by one.

"I swear, Jack, there's nothing—not a thing that we've missed." Jace yawned and looked at the time on his computer screen. "Crap, it's almost ten-thirty. You think Gilly and One-Cent are still busy with whatever?"

Jack shrugged, then got up and stretched. "He didn't say what the deal was."

"I say we give them a little more time—maybe an hour and a half—and then we just chuck the idea until tomorrow night. What do you say, Jack?"

Jack yawned. "Yup, sounds good to me."

Time crept by, and Jack's eyes were tired from rereading the murder books. He was an odd Joe, passing time with murder books or Googling old crimes for entertainment. Jace, however, leaned back in his chair, feet propped on his desk, eyes closed, and three minutes later, he was snoring.

Jack's cell phone rang, and Jace almost toppled over, jerking awake at the noise.

"West. Cool, we're still here. That works for us. Sure, we'll wait to hear from you."

"They headed out to the bar?"

Jack nodded.

"Maybe they should have a real drink this time—not just a beer."

"Jace," Jack said with a chuckle, "they have to keep their heads on straight, you goober."

"Yeah, I know. Hey, when these cases are closed, the four of us—Gilly, Penny, Sparky, Rick—how about we all go out one night and get shit-faced?"

"We need a designated driver, you blockhead. We can't all get shit-faced."

"Bring Vivian and Gretchen, and we'll take Vivian's minivan. It seats eight. Gretchen can sit on your lap."

Jack let out a bark of laughter, but deep down he thought it was a damn fine idea. Maybe they would plan a celebration—but not one where that many detectives got shit-faced in the same bar. That would be a clusterfuck waiting to happen.

DARKNESS SHROUDED THE SMALLER vehicle. In the lot across the street, eyes watched the door of the hole-in-the-wall bar. Why would self-respecting people even come to this place?

These people were wicked. They had no respect for themselves and needed a place to hide their sins. That's why they were here. The other patrons were just scum—dirt-poor, spending their last dollar on booze.

Disgusting. They didn't even try to get themselves out of the gutter. But that was a different crusade, not the one being worked tonight.

Tonight, the mission was to save a baby and a mother—to rid the evil that caused her pain. Accomplishing this mission, all would be right, until the next time.

Hands clenched the steering wheel, fury gurgling. It was time to release this rage until it boiled again.

They exited the bar. She was hanging on him, touching his face, rubbing against him. The puke and bile inched up, then was swallowed back down. No time to be sick. It was time to collect payment from the wicked.

Gilly led Penny to her car, then embraced her in a hug. He nuzzled her neck.

"Damn, Pens, I'll be fucking happy when we can just be partners and stop this romance shit. And, uh, you smell good."

"Gilly, you asshole," her voice hissed. "Stop tickling my ear with your sweet nothings. And it's hamburger you smell; you freak."

She ran her hand up his back, grabbed the hair at the nape of his neck, twisted it, pulled his face closer, and laid one on him.

If you were watching, it would incline you to believe this was a fervent, sexy kiss—and two lovers were parting, a sad goodbye.

The driver in the darkness watched them, thinking that very thing.

——ele——

GILLY CALLED JACK ON his way home.

"Yeah, we're still here. Let me put you on speaker. Alrighty, Gilly—Jace can hear you too."

"We didn't see a damn odd thing tonight. Pens and I know all the regulars since we've been here so many times. Hell, she even knows all the cars in the lot—not who goes with what car, but she's got better than decent recall. There was nothing—no people, no nothing out of the ordinary tonight."

"Penny headed home?"

"Nah. Said she's stopping at a 24/7—needed a few things, then she's heading home. I told her I'd call in twenty minutes to check on her."

"You headed home, Gilly?" Jace wished he was in bed right now, sawing logs.

"No, I'm headed up there. Left some stuff in my locker I need to take home — I'll come up to six when I get there."

"It doesn't look too promising tonight, Jack. I'd say give it time, but hell—the night's nearly over. Maybe tonight ain't the night, maybe no other night, for that matter. Maybe he's done killing." Jace voted no more deaths. However, he thought if the bastard would just fuck up, they could catch him.

"Someone who kills like this, more than twice, is gonna repeat the process. We just don't know when. He just needs to fuck up once—that's all we need, and then we got him."

Funny, Jace thought. He had just thought the same thing—he just hadn't said it aloud. Sometimes, Jace thought Jack was scary, but not in a bad way.

61

GILLY TOOK THE STAIRS on the back stairwell two at a time as he hoofed it to the homicide squad room.

"Gilly, man, did—"

He cut Jack off. "Look, Jack, I tried calling Penny's cell twice now. It's been over twenty minutes, and she hasn't picked up."

Jack straightened. "You call the burner phone she's using for this setup?"

Craig nodded. "Yeah. She has them both, and there's no reason she shouldn't be answering at least one of them. She knows I was gonna call her." He paced between Lucky's and Xi's desks.

Jack said nothing as he picked up his phone and punched in a number while the other men watched in silence.

"Art, this is Jack. No, man, no time. Where are you?"

"Just leaving the Lone Star—"

Jack cut him off. "Art, listen to me. I need you to get to your office—and hurry. It's urgent. Call me when you get there. I'm at my desk."

"Yeah, Jack, I'm on my way."

"Art is down the street," Jack said as he hung up. "As soon as he gets to his office, I want him to ping Penny's phones. Damn it. You know what store, Gilly?"

Craig Gillespie shook his head, worry etched across his face.

"No. She didn't even say it was a grocery store—just a 24/7. Hell, Jack, she could've gone to a gas station or an all-night pharmacy for all I know." He ran his hands through his hair.

"Try her phone once more and give me the burner number. I'll call it," Jace told him.

Both men let the phones ring multiple times—still no answer.

Jack's phone rang, and he snatched it up.

"Jack, what's going on?"

"Art, write these two numbers down." Jack reeled them off and waited for confirmation.

"The first number is Penny Salato's personal cell. The other is a burner she's using in a murder setup. We need to know where both phones are—and we need to know yesterday. Got it?"

"On it. I'll call you back as soon as I have it."

Art's heart rate sped up. He could hear the panic in Jack's voice.

"Jace, call Xi and tell him what's up—he lives closer to the station. Then call Lucky. Gilly, you call the night watch commander. Explain the situation and tell him when we have locations, we want units rolling immediately. I'll call Chief Yao and update him."

"You gonna call Brooks?" Jace asked as he punched in Xi's number.

"You kidding? He doesn't care about the citizens of Houston unless they're wealthy—and even if he used to be Penny's captain, you think he gives a damn?"

"Jace, Jack's right," Gilly said. "He hated the women in his department. There was stuff—let's just leave it at that."

"Okay—fuck Brooks then. Hey, Xi, it's Jace—listen—"

—ele—

TWENTY MINUTES EARLIER.

The small mom-and-pop store was a ghost town, and Penny liked it that way—no one in her way as she milled around, looking for whatever caught her eye.

She needed toothpaste, shampoo, lettuce, and bread, but every time the list was short, she never stuck to it. Her buggy already held chips, salsa, and cookies, and she'd migrated to the cereal aisle.

She squatted to reach the last box of granola shoved to the back of the shelf. When she pulled it free, something jabbed the small of her back.

She started to turn.

"Be still, or I will shove this knife right through your kidneys," a raspy voice ordered.

Penny froze, closing her eyes—angry with herself for letting her guard down.

"What do you want? If it's money, look in my back pocket. There's—"

"Shut up. I don't want your money," the deep voice whispered, standing close. "Don't talk. Just nod if you understand me. Do you?"

Penny nodded.

"Now do as I say, or I swear you're a dead woman. Understand?"

She nodded again, her heart pounding.

"We are walking out together. You keep your eyes forward. Don't look at me. Don't make eye contact with anyone, or I'll shove this knife in so deep it'll never come out. Do you understand, slut?"

Penny exhaled and nodded once. Her mind raced. She had to get the upper hand—she *needed* to get the upper hand.

Shit. Shit. Shit.

She spotted her car less than fifty yards away. Her service weapon sat locked in the console.

Motherfucker.

Her cell phone was with the weapon—but the burner was in her front pocket, on silent. Thank God for that. If Gilly thought of it, he could at least ping her general location.

The trunk of a small compact car popped open. Penny's heart thudded.

The car was parked in a dark area, backed up against the wall of an empty building next to the store.

"Get in—face-first—and roll toward the back, eyes closed."

Penny didn't move. If she did, she'd be dead before Jack or Gilly could find her.

The knife pressed harder. She could feel the blade through her blouse.

"I said get in or die. Your choice, bitch."

She forced herself to comply. Hands on the trunk lip, she climbed in face-first, pulled her knees up, and rolled into a half-fetal position, facing the trunk wall.

The burner phone in her front pocket was her only hope.

"Keep your eyes closed," the unknown voice rasped.

A hand reached around her. A cloth covered her mouth and nose.

The smell—sweet. Instantaneously recognizable.

Chloroform.

Panic seized her as the world began to dim.

—ele—

JACK, ALREADY READY TO drive to Tech and put a fire under Art Walsworth, jumped when his phone jangled. He almost dropped it grabbing for the call.

"Art—is that you? What've you got?"

"Yeah. Thanks, Art. We've got it from here."

He hung up and looked at Jace. "Call units to roll to the store. Mom-and-Pop 24/7 on Westcott Street. Art says her personal cell pinged there."

"Jack, that's close to where she lives—Minola Street," Gilly said, voice tight. "Send someone to her house, too."

"I'm on it," Jace said, calling the watch commander.

"Where did her burner ping?" Gilly asked.

Jack answered without hesitation. "Memorial Park—somewhere off East Memorial Park Drive."

"Holy fuck, Jack. That park's over fourteen hundred acres."

"Exactly. Jace, let's move. Gilly, call the watch commander back. Have him radio all units in the area. Priority—Code One. Officer-involved kidnapping. No lights. No sirens."

"Jack, I'm going with you."

"No, you're not. You're too close. She's your partner. I need you here. Go to Central Command and help coordinate."

Gilly's face fell. "But—"

"I said no. I'm leading this investigation. Jace—let's hook it."

They left Craig Gillespie standing there, hands shaking, heart lodged in his throat as he made the call.

If anything happened to Penny, he'd never forgive himself—or Jack.

62

JACK'S CELL RANG AS they pulled out of the station. Jace, at the wheel with his game face on, headed to the location Art had given them on East Memorial Drive.

"West."

"Jack, it's John Lancaster. Chips and I are out here with Xi at the Mom-and-Pop 24/7, and we've located Penny's car. Her purse is in the front seat. Xi called her cell and we could hear it ringing inside. Here—Xi wants to talk to you," John said, handing over the phone.

"Jack, her car is locked. We're going inside the store. They have surveillance cameras, and I'm taking the initiative without a warrant to see the footage. You okay with that?" Xi's voice was tense.

"Yeah, Xi. Tell the store owner it's a matter of life or death. If there's a problem, get Chief Yao on the horn ASAP."

"You got it, Jack. Lancaster and Estrada searched the parking lot but found nothing. If—no, not if—when you locate her, call me. Is Gilly with you?"

"No, I made him stay with the night watch commander. He's too close to this."

Jack was right. Gilly would be too emotional. Better if he stayed out of the way.

Jack hung up, updated Jace, and prayed Penny was okay.

—⁓—

PENNY, NOT ALERT YET, felt fuzzy. The initial stages of a massive chloroform headache crept in. She opened her eyes a slit and tried to speak—but couldn't. Then the realization hit: someone had duct-taped her mouth. Her hands were bound as well.

"So, you're waking up, are you? I was afraid I might have used too much chloroform this time."

Penny's eyes opened, but she could not focus. Whoever had abducted her held a flashlight, shining it at her face.

The voice was gruff.

The face fuzzy.

She could make out a dark suit and light-colored hair beneath an old hat. Her eyes shut, trying to stay awake.

"Good. Keep your eyes closed or I'll poke your eye out with this mascara brush."

Penny felt the brush against her lashes, then across the top of her eyelids and several times on her cheeks.

"In a few minutes, you'll look like the harlot you are, you shameful woman. God punishes those who are evil, and you've been immoral. I have a Bible for you—you can hold it—maybe God will forgive you if you have his word in your hands as you die."

Penny's muffled words were unintelligible, but her abductor understood.

"Why am I doing this? God told me to. He leads me to the vile and wicked. I know there are more, but He gives me the chosen ones."

Done caking the makeup on, her abductor stretched out Penny's legs, crossing one ankle over the other. She heard the rip of duct tape as her ankles were bound.

"I'm going to take the tape off your mouth, but don't dare scream, or I'll put it back. I am not quite ready to kill you. Do you understand me? Nod if you do."

Penny managed a nod despite her head's heaviness. Fighting to stay awake, she focused on both her captor and her surroundings.

Once the tape was ripped off, Penny inhaled, feeling less suffocated and hoping she could breathe enough to snap out of her chloroform funk.

Her voice was soft. "I can change my ways if you give me a chance. I know I've done wrong. Can you please give me a second chance?" She added, "Doesn't God give second chances?"

She was buying time, hoping to appeal to her kidnapper's sense of divine mercy.

"You've had plenty of chances to stop, but you didn't. No, you must be punished."

With her eyesight sharpening, Penny made out the captor's face.

A large, unattractive woman wearing a wig. Her face bore pits from out-of-control adolescent acne, and her features were rather manly. Her dark, bushy brows reminded Penny of Detective Dawson Luck.

Large hands reached for Penny's ponytail, fanning her hair out as a photographer would.

"Pucker your lips," the she-man ordered.

Penny complied, glancing side to side to assess her surroundings. Her heartbeat quickened.

They were in a park—or woods—she wasn't sure which. Jesus, she thought, how would Gilly or anyone find her? She could be the next homicide case for Jack West—and she was not ready to die.

"Yes. Red lipstick—whore-red, as I call it—suits you. Now, hold your face still. Don't smile," the burly woman said, pulling out a digital camera to photograph Penny.

Penny wanted to scream. Don't smile? In a situation like this?

After taking the photos, the repulsive butch-woman sat back on her haunches, satisfied.

Penny prayed: *Cheap burner phone, someone ping it, please—oh God, please, Gilly, please find me.*

63

THERE WERE UNITS ALL over the area where Art Walsworth told Jack Penny's burner phone pinged. It was within three-quarters of a mile, but Art had no exact location. Tall trees and dense woods could interfere with cell signals, he explained.

Jack radioed the night watch commander, who dispatched units up and down East Memorial Drive to cover the area Art had approximated.

"Jace, stop here. Park and block the road."

Jace obeyed. Jack sprang out, grabbed his Maglite, and instructed, "Fan out to your left."

"Should we call out?"

"No," Jack said. He shined his flashlight downward, cutting a narrow path through the trees. "We don't want to spook our perp."

Jack's radio crackled. "West, over."

"West, this is Jukes. We're with two other units at the backside of the area on the unnamed road. You're on the other side—we'll head toward you. There are two other units on either end—we should meet roughly in the middle. Over."

"10-4," Jack replied, and he and Jace moved in.

The area was dense, with no obvious trails. Recent rain had turned it into a bog, leaving only small, trampled paths.

Jack pushed branches aside, sweat forming on his upper lip. Houston humidity was nothing compared to the adrenaline pumping through him. His fear of not reaching Penny in time matched the intensity of a full workout.

Jace was at least two hundred feet to his left, lost in the brush, but Jack could see the faint glow of his Maglite.

Jack's instincts pulled him northeast. Something—fear or intuition—told him to go that way. The snapping twigs and the sound of men plodding nearby unnerved him. Was the perp still there? He hoped so. Otherwise, imagining what he might find sickened him.

"Please, please, can't we talk? Can't you pray with me first?"

Jack froze. Someone was speaking, but he couldn't make out the words. He turned off his light and radio, letting his eyes adjust to the darkness, and silenced his cell phone. Inch by inch, he crawled toward the voice, hoping it would guide him.

"You're just delaying the inevitable, but if you must, I can pray with you—not that it'll change your fate."

The voice was deep and raspy. Jack felt certain this was Penny's abductor, who had no idea HPD had surrounded Memorial Park.

"Please, I'd like for you to pray with me. I'm a terrible person, but I wasn't always this way, I swear. And if you could pray with me so I can have forgiveness—I'll die at peace," Penny's voice cracked.

Jack's feet itched to run, but his brain told him to stay low. He crawled closer on hands and knees, rationalizing—illogically—that he might seem like an animal or stray if he made minimal noise.

Within five feet, he peeked around the end of a bush. Shadows moved—one person on the ground, Penny, and another, a large figure kneeling with their back to him. White-blonde hair peeked from under a hat, tied in a ponytail.

Unsure if the assailant still held the knife, Jack avoided sudden movements. Penny's life depended on his patience.

He rolled onto his back, drew his gun, and moved into thicker undergrowth, making two more rolls to position himself. The killer's light shone on Penny, revealing just enough to see their hands.

The left hand was raised, palm up, as if worshiping. The right clenched a large knife; the blade aimed at Penny. Too close. Jack knew a jump could mean she'd be stabbed before he could fire.

Penny's eyes were closed as if praying. When she finished, the knife would target her axillary artery. It was now or never.

Jack lunged from the brush, gun aimed at the perp's back. "Police! Freeze!"

Penny's eyes widened in slow motion. The man—or what Jack thought was a man—raised the knife. Jack pulled the trigger. The shot struck the upper left quadrant of the attacker's back. The body collapsed face-first onto Penny, the knife falling into the dirt.

The shot echoed, alerting everyone in the manhunt. Jace, Jukes, and Richmond crashed through the brush as Jack moved to free Penny.

"He's dead, Penny," Jack said, rolling the body to untie her.

Jace helped her up. "Shit, One-Cent, I'm glad to see you. You look a bit like a clown, though."

"I've never been so glad to see you, fellas, but don't get used to me saying that," Penny said, her voice still shaky.

Jack instructed Officer Jukes and Richmond. "Dave, call in an officer-involved shooting. Jace, notify the night watch commander, get CSU and the M.E. here, and tell Gilly Penny's safe."

Jack turned to the body. "Ollie, glove up. Check for ID."

Penny interrupted. "It's not a man."

All four men turned to her.

"Once you roll the body over, you'll see our perp has very large breasts."

Eyebrows arched across the group. Ollie Richmond retrieved a wallet from the body's jacket—a light blue woman's wallet—and handed it to Jack.

"Jack," Officer Jukes said, pointing to a bag.

Jack looked over Jace's shoulder. "Yeah, Dave?"

"A small white New Testament Bible, and a sack of makeup."

Jack opened the wallet, then looked at Jace. "Jace, meet our alleged killer: Doris Davenport."

Penny had no reaction; she hadn't heard the name. Jace's jaw dropped.

"Jack," Penny said, "she has a digital camera in her pocket. She took my picture. Might be others on there too."

Jace pulled the camera out. "I wonder if she photographed the other three?"

"Odds are she did, and we'll have all the proof we need," Jack said.

64

It was close to 4:00 am and CSU got the evidence bagged and tagged, and Bennie had shown up to assess the body.

Once they were free to turn the body over, Jack knew the face. He looked down on the person from the composite drawing Jason Fryer-Mercer had described. Davenport ... Doris Davenport.

Jack was positive this woman was married to one Pastor Harold Davenport, the scumbag adulterous preacher. She was dead, and now they had no chance to ask her the one question that ran through all of their minds ... why?

Jack watched them bag, then strap the body to a gurney.

He didn't have to wonder the why; he knew why. She knew her husband was cheating, without a doubt it hadn't been the first time, and something inside her broke. The pent-up fury was unleashed with devastating consequences.

He saw the pieces fall together after Penny relayed her ordeal. The Bibles and the Bible verses, the broken wedding ring finger, and even the wording stating she hoped God forgave her.

She took the entire story with her when she died, and now she'd never tell it. Jack knew she had to be the voice that had been on the other end of the phone at the suicide hotline.

The fact was, both Jason Fryer-Mercer and Robbery Detective Katherine Sparks could identify her face and her voice—there was your positive ID.

She wasn't attractive; however, there must have been an attraction between her and Harold in the past. Her husband, Pastor Drop-His-Pants, might have believed that divorce would not be good for his ministerial position.

It might have ruined his undemanding job, and Jack half smiled. This story would be breaking news to his congregation.

He would tell Tessa Coy at the Chronicle, that Pastor Drop-His-Pants was purportedly stepping out on his now dead wife as an anonymous tip. He would not give Tessa names, but he *would* put a bug in her ear. She was waiting for him so she could write a Pulitzer, and this might be the one. He smiled. Or at least get her a book deal.

Jack knew now how their killer knew Corrine Taylor and Al Mathers were sleeping together. Bunny Mathers must have confided in her. Bunny worked volunteering in the church office—their paths crossed. That had to be the how. He wondered if Doris Davenport had confided in Bunny that her own husband was cheating. Well, he thought, it's a moot point now.

"Jack."

He turned to face Detective Austin Reed, Homicide—handling the OIS investigation.

"Hey, Reed, I wondered who'd get the callout." Jack stuck his hand out and Reed reciprocated.

"Yeah, I got lucky. I need to get your statement, but off the record, I'd say it's a clean shoot since I have Penny's statement ... you know, a matter of life or death for a fellow officer. I'd close it right now but we gotta follow protocol."

"No worries, not the first OIS I've been involved in. It won't be the last either." Jack's smile was not heartfelt.

"Yeah, I'm sure you know the drill ... me, then Forensics, then, oh boy, Internal Affairs. Since this ain't your first rodeo, you know the civil rights attorney by first name, huh?"

"Yep, I seem to know everybody these days." Jack shrugged. He didn't worry anymore, not after the first two OIS cases he'd experienced.

"Jack, I'll never admit to saying this, but off the record, watch out for Brooks. He'll take something like this and try to twist it up." Austin Reed's face grew serious, and his brows dipped.

"Thanks, Reed, appreciate the warning. I've heard tell he has it out for me, but have no idea why."

Austin Reed took Jack's statement and just as he had finished, Chief Davis Yao walked up.

"Chief," Reed said, nodding.

"You done with Jack, Austin?"

"He's all yours, Chief. See ya, Jack, and hey, don't worry, man."

"Thanks, Reed. See ya when I see ya."

Silence followed Reed's departure before Chief Yao spoke. "Penny told me the story, Jack. I wouldn't worry."

"Not worried at all, Davis." Jack grinned as he unholstered his service weapon and unclipped his badge from his belt. "Here, take these with you, save me a trip to the station to bring 'em in. It's better this way. I don't have to field a ton of questions and I don't want the fellas all giving me the sad-eye either."

Chief Yao nodded understanding. He had been in Jack's shoes, rather boots, one time himself.

"I understand, Jack. It'll get smoothed out before ya know it and I'll give you your gun and badge back. You headed home?"

"Yep, need to get some shut-eye. Been a damn long day that's lasted over five months. Know what I mean?"

"Uh-huh, I do. I'll be calling you in a few days."

"Yep, Chief, I'll be waiting."

Jack saluted and walked over to Jace. "Get Jukes to give you a ride back to the station," he said. "I'm heading home."

There would be many ends to tie up, but 7-11 and Dawson Luck could handle all of it. Finding Jade's and Sergio's rings were one thing, and Jack hoped they could locate the articles for the victims' loved ones.

Explaining the killer's motive to Jade's mother would be more difficult. How do you tell a mother her daughter died because she was seeing a married man?

Unluckily, Smith Russell would understand since he knew Sergio was cheating. Lincoln Taylor, 7-11, had figured he knew his wife was cheating—maybe he'd understand.

Hell, who really would understand why someone killed a person, so, no, they shouldn't have to understand, but they were getting what they needed ... closure.

Jack's mind ran over everything as he walked to the car that blocked the middle of the street, opened the door, and got in. He turned the key and started the car, but sat staring into the darkness, thinking, and then he smiled.

No, he was not going home to his empty house in Deer Park, with an empty pantry and unwanted solitude.

At this very minute, he knew his exact destination.

He headed to Gretchen's.

The End

Author's Note

Word-of-mouth is crucial for any author to succeed. If you enjoyed Lethal Liaisons, please leave a review online—anywhere you are able. Even if it's just a sentence or two; it would make all the difference and would be very much appreciated.

Thanks,

Deanna

Scan ME!
Deannakingwriting.com

Acknowledgements
Thank you to my Beta readers, Thomas Faught and Sharon Jaeger, your candid opinions have been a blessing to me.
To my husband, Travis, thank you for your continued support and encouragement.

Lethal Liaisons is the second book in Deanna King's *Jack West Mystery Series*.

Deanna lives in Texas with her husband.

www.ingramcontent.com/pod-product-compliance
Lightning Source LLC
Chambersburg PA
CBHW012113020726
47493CB00018B/2904

* 9 7 9 8 9 8 5 6 9 8 2 1 3 *